get your mojo workin'!

Johnny

Dead on the Internet
The MIT Murders

by

Johnny Barnes

authorHOUSE®

AuthorHouse™
1663 Liberty Drive, Suite 200
Bloomington, IN 47403
www.authorhouse.com
Phone: 1-800-839-8640

First published by AuthorHouse 6/3/2008

ISBN: 978-1-4343-7806-4 (sc)

Printed in the United States of America
Bloomington, Indiana

This book is printed on acid-free paper.

Table of Contents

All our deeds follow us from afar,
And what we have been makes us what we are.

The stars above were still faintly visible as white clouds rolled across the early morning sky. The tall gray skyscrapers stood proudly alongside the city's old red brick buildings. And as the dark sky lightened from black to blue and the streets filled with morning light, crime time slowed to a crawl, the night people took their rest, and the rats returned to their nests.

At daybreak another bold Boston skyline was created. On this day the early morning November sun was hiding behind the buildings as a lone student rowed her thin wooden shell across the dark river water. A gray-haired man wearing a long brown barn coat walked his dog along the Cambridge side of the Charles River near MIT.

As the man and his dog walked along the riverbank the powerful black and brown German shepherd saw something up ahead and took off, tearing open the fingers of his master's fist, breaking the hold his owner had on the end of the dog's leash.

"Hold on, Sam!" the bespectacled owner shouted and then he muttered, "Goddamn fleabag," quietly, as if the dog would be offended if he heard his beloved owner disrespect him.

The retired gentleman began to pick up his pace, chasing his dog, walking faster and faster, breaking into a jog and then finally a run. The dog growled up ahead then flattened out on a dead run with the leash waving out behind him. The retired gentleman chased his dog along the muddy riverbank dodging beer bottles, Styrofoam cups, and the assorted flotsam and jetsam that washed ashore from upriver. The man was tiring fast and contemplated giving up the chase when Sam pulled up abruptly and growled at something in the brush along the Charles. The hair along the dog's shoulders and back stood on end.

The sudden stop caused the dog owner to stumble and fall forward, rolling down the riverbank.

"Goddamn it, Sam Shepherd!" the man shouted as he rolled. Just before tumbling into the dirty water of the Charles, the man stuck out his right arm and his right hand submerged in the riverbank muck. It stopped his rolling just short of the water.

The dog owner lay there in the thickets and weeds quietly, his eyes closed for a moment as he ran an internal check to feel for any bumps or bruises. He silently cursed his dog, who was still growling on the riverbank.

The man opened his eyes to realize that he was face-to-face with a partially decomposing corpse. As it lay on the riverbank, the ghastly and surrealistic-looking body resembled a department store mannequin. The skin was wrinkled and the flesh looked yellow and rubbery. The dead man's hair looked matted and artificial. The one cloudy eyeball remaining in the corpse's head was open and staring. On the other side of the dead man's face was an empty eye socket.

The small wake from a passing rowboat splashed against the riverbank just enough to rock the bloated body. As the corpse rolled slightly, it groaned, expelling some of the nauseating and repulsive gases built up inside it.

A small brown multi-legged water bug crawled out of the empty right eye socket of the swollen face as the elderly dog walker recoiled in horror then struggled to his feet. He felt light-headed as the blood drained from his brain. His eyes darted around alarmingly as he grew increasingly unsteady and gasped for air.

The big German shepherd growled then sniffed the air and looked to his master for guidance.

Chapter 1

The 100 Steps

Jack Kelly wore a cheap dark blue suit as he sat at the half-empty bar in the Black Rose Tavern near Boston's Faneuil Hall Marketplace. He was watching the bartender pour overpriced drinks to the businessmen and women that stopped by the popular watering hole after work. Jack made forty-five dollars an hour plus expenses for reading the *Boston Herald* while bar spotting for the bar's owner. All he had to do was watch every move the bartender made to figure out if he's pocketing money and to ascertain if the business was being ripped off.

Jack put down his newspaper, pushed his dark reddish brown hair back with his hand, and ordered his second Remy Martin cognac and his third bottle of beer.

"I suppose I can't light up this Dominican cigar at the bar?" Jack asked the young Irish lad working the bar.

"Yes, sir, you cannot," he replied, adding, "nowhere in the whole building."

"I suppose soon they'll ban smoking within the city limits."

"Yes, sir."

"I'll have to jump on the Red Line, head out to the Dorchester Yacht Club, take a rowboat out to George's Island, and hide behind a goddamned tree to light up."

"Yes, sir," the bartender agreed.

"Or maybe I'll have to row out past the three-mile limit, as long as I'm not in the shipping lanes or under the flight path to Logan. The Homeland Security Coasties will be putting a .50-caliber round across my bow, and I'll have to explain that I just wanted a smoke, while they're running my name and number through Interpol."

"Yes, sir," the bartender said.

"You'll agree to everything I say, won't you?"

"Yes, sir," was the reply.

"I'm going outside for that smoke," Jack said, sliding a $20 bill under his Sam Adams. Jack went outside into the cool gray November night, walking down the cobblestone walkway in the middle of the marketplace. He had just lit the expensive cigar with a cheap plastic lighter when his cell phone vibrated in his pocket and he answered it. It was the client who owned the bar where he was spotting, asking about the surveillance.

"No, he's not, Peter. No. No. He pours a good drink that will keep your clients coming back to get their money's worth, but I haven't seen him do anything you need to be concerned about. I've been in the bar watching him for three hours and he hasn't cost you a dime. I don't think he's skimming. He pours a good stiff drink but he's not over pouring, he's not shortchanging, or giving anything away. Now let me go back to work. I've got two more hours. I'll e-mail you a report and a bill in the morning," Jack said, disconnecting.

There are only two seasons in New England: winter and July. On this cold rainy day the tourists were all bundled up and driving down the street in an amphibious duck boat. Two loud, boisterous families from New York riding in the duck boat's open cockpit drove past the Durgin Park restaurant headed for the harbor as Jack walked back towards the bar. A group of young men walking towards the bar spied the New York Yankee baseball hats and jackets worn by two of the kids and they yelled, "Yankees suck!"

Jack watched as the youngest kid turned his Yankee hat around backwards and gave the group of young men the finger. Kelly jumped as the cell phone in his pocket vibrated, again.

The deep and sensual female voice said, "Mr. Kelly? I've got a case I'd like you to work on."

"Well, I'm working on a case...several cases....What is it, Ms....?"

"It's kind of...private," her voice trailing off to just above a whisper. "Ah...sort of a private, personal affair."

"Do you feel uncomfortable talking about it over the phone, young lady? Could we do this face-to-face?"

"Ooh! I like face-to-face. But I guess I should explain... Well, I guess I should try, if you'll bear with me, Mr. Kelly."

"Call me Jack," Kelly said as lightning flashed somewhere east of the city and a light rain began to hit the street. "And you have my full attention," Jack said, puffing on the cigar and stepping into a doorway next to the bar.

"You see, Jack, I had just arrived at my apartment here in the Back Bay, I was changing out of my tight black leather skirt and spiked heels, I slipped out of my thin white satin blouse... and I thought I'd take a bubble bath..."

Jack loosened his tie and his jaw dropped as the woman continued.

"I lit a candle and settled down in the warm water under the soapy bubbles. I poured a glass of chilled Dom Perignon champagne and took a long drink as I was soooo thirsty," the lady giggled.

"Ms….? Ah… where are we going with this?"

"I'm getting to that now, Mr. Kelly… Mr. Jack Kelly."

"Just Jack."

"Well, Just Jack… I was trying to think of someone who makes me hot, but I couldn't think of anybody. But then I found your name in the Yellow Pages. I put my finger on your name. And I wanted to know a few things about you."

Jessica waited but Jack said nothing. She knew he recognized her voice as she continued.

"Do you carry a gun? Are you packing heat? Where do you carry your heat? Would you like to guard my body? …Are you still there?"

After a brief silence Jack said firmly, "Where are you going with this, young lady?"

"Straight down; you wanna come?" she said playfully.

Jack saw a flash of lightning and heard the crack of thunder reverberate through the downtown buildings. The Nor'easter was moving into the city from the Atlantic Ocean. The rain got heavier as Jack swallowed hard and asked, "And then what?"

"That's it! I needed someone. Then I saw you… your name."

"You saw what? Where?"

"You. In the Yellow Pages. On the table by my bubble bath," she giggled. "I threw open the book, it opened to

4

'Detectives,' and I put my finger on a name. It said Jack Kelly's American Detective Agency. You are now the object of my sexual fantasies. I'm your fatal attraction. You are my object of affection. My obsession."

"Is that it, Jessica? Are you done?" Jack said.

There was a long pause.

"You're no fun, Jack. Why don't you try talking dirty to me once in a while?"

"How come when a man talks dirty to a woman it's sexual harassment and when a woman talks dirty to a man it's $4.99-a-minute?"

"What time are you coming over for dinner?"

"I'll be there by eight, Jesse," Jack said and disconnected.

Kelly couldn't wait to get to Jesse's apartment. He couldn't stop thinking about her after her little sham. Her little fantasy scenario. She was fun, and it had gotten him more than a little excited. He couldn't wait to see her.

He was glad the last two hours of his bar surveillance were uneventful. Jack left the bartender a large tip. Why not? The owner would have to pay Jack back. The rain had all but stopped as Jack walked the eight blocks to his little fourth-floor Chinatown apartment office. He hiked up the 100 steps to his office, typed a report and a bill, and e-mailed them to his client, the bar owner. Then he washed up and changed into more comfortable blue jeans, a black turtleneck, and slipped an old faded blue Barracuda jacket, over his thin five foot eleven frame. He headed out for the fifteen-minute walk to his girlfriend Jessica Paris's apartment across town. She lived on Beacon Street in the Back Bay and Jack was headed for the dinner at eight. Jack loved Jessica.

Kelly walked through the thin, greasy Chinatown streets that were covered with the shredded paper of thousands of exploded firecrackers and hundreds of used scratch cards. There were tiny rows of shops with hanging herbs and cheap clothing. Jack could smell the heavy aroma coming from the many tiny restaurants. Kelly made eye contact with a small and frail Chinese man that looked to be nearly a hundred years old. The man was expressionless as he looked into Jack's eyes and smoked the tiny end piece of his hand-rolled cigarette. Kelly walked past storefronts with plucked and cooked ducks and chickens hanging in their windows.

From Chinatown Jack walked along Washington Street through what used to be the Red Light District. Only in Boston it was called "The Combat Zone." It was more like the Demilitarized Zone now. The DMZ wasn't as wild as it used to be. The Zone had harbored the First Amendment Book Store, the Two O'clock Lounge, the Caribe, the Naked i, the Erotic Entertainment Center, the Pussy Cat Lounge, the Liberty Bookstore, along with some other strip clubs. But the Chinese community had been instrumental in buying up property, petitioning against the seedy strip clubs, and forming progressive citizen crime watch groups that in conjunction with city licensing boards drove the hard-core sex industry, junkies, prostitutes, and thieves outward. Only Centerfolds and The Glass Slipper still survived on LaGrange Street.

It had long turned dark and cold on this November evening as Jack walked along. He could hear a jukebox playing "Rip It Up," an old Little Richard song, from the open door of a street-level bar on Tremont Street. He could smell the aroma of the cooking pretzels coming from the cart on the corner of Park Street in front of where Jack's Joke Shop used to be. He stopped and bought a giant hot pretzel and put mustard on it.

Kelly ate the pretzel as he walked. His cell phone vibrated and startled him. It was Sergeant Donavan of the Boston Police.

"Jack Kelly, you scallywag! The last time I saw you, ya were chasin' dat fat diamond thief white wigger kid wid the goddamn unbelievably baggy-ass pants out of da Jewelers Building on Washington! The chubby bahstard couldn't run holdin' up his trousers wid one hand and the bahstard fell right down on the fahkin' Freedom Trail at dah end ah Washington. Jesus, Mary, and Joseph, may your sainted mother smile down on you from heaven," Sergeant Donavan said in his affected Irish brogue.

Sergeant Donavan was a lifer married to the Boston Police Department. He worked an ungodly amount of hours and had been a patrol sergeant for thirty-four years. He was born in Boston but seemed to have somehow acquired more than a slight Irish accent.

"What's up, Donavan? Are you calling on behalf of the Boston Police Department, begging me to come back to the Homicide Unit to find Whitey Bulger? Or are all the drugs still disappearing from the Evidence Room? Or let's see… what other scandals have the Boston Police Department endured since I left? Drug protection? After-hours clubs? The Boom Boom Room? No…. I don't remember the Silver Shields club. Never heard of it. Oh yeah, are the bodies still stacking up in the hallways at the morgue?"

"Yeah, Jack. They got some of da stiffs in a gahddamn trailer in da pahkin' lot. But as I recall yah did more than yahr share of contributin' to the stack o' bodies brought to the morgue. Gahddamn it, Kelly, you've got your grandfahder's wise-ass tongue!"

"Where did you get my phone number?"

"Not from your grandfahder, God rest his soul! He was my pahtnah for tharty-two yars before he died. And he thought the world ah you, Jack Kelly! Where da yah tink I got you're fahkin' number? You're in the fahkin' Yella Pages, lad. I am the long ahm of the law, yah know. I can reach out and touch yah whenevah I needs ya. And… I know you're defiling that sweet Lieutenant Detective Jessica Paris ovah at Homicide. That ain't no secret! What she sees in you I cannot undahstand."

"Don't ya be reachin' out and touchin' me at all," Kelly said, enjoying the banter from his old friend.

"Listen, Jack, I gave a guy yahr numbah. He can't find his son. Is that OK? Can yah take the case? He's a nice man, I know him parsonally. He comes to the station wid his son missin, the poor guy is miserable, but it's a low priority wid the PD. His son is an adult, yah know, Kelly? We dahn't go 'round chasing grownup gahddahm cahledge kids. MIT, ya know?"

"Sure, Donavan. Do you think hiring me will help?"

"Well… the odds are slim, fat, and none… and slim and fat just left town. Look, Kelly. You're a PI and his kid's missing. I want you to look for him, OK? It's a simple plan. As simple as Officer Hodge standin' heah next to me. Only *the plan* might actually work."

"So what's your connection to this guy, Donavan?"

"Maybe I went to MIT, Kelly."

"What were you doing? Mowing the lawns or filling the Coke machines?" Jack asked.

"In the sixties I worked undercover and did more smokin' of the grass than cuttin' of the grass, Jack. But I never did the coke. But how about a little respect for my family? We came over on the *Mayflower*."

"Mayflower Movers?"

"Look, seriously, Kelly, the kid probably took off for his spring break a little arly, seein' as it's Novembah and it was Tanksgivin' just last Tuesday. The fahder's got plenty o' money and he dun't think the pleece depahtment is doin' enough. So thar you go, lad."

"Sergeant Donavan, I will clear my schedule for you. You have the father call me right away." Kelly said goodbye and closed his cell phone.

Kelly walked from the Combat Zone, across the Boston Common and the Public Gardens. Jack looked up at the gold dome of the State House as he headed down the six more blocks to 435 Beacon Street. He opened the gate and walked down the black wrought iron stairs from the street to the courtyard below street level. Jack knocked on Jesse's basement apartment door. It was a small one-bedroom apartment with a fireplace and a red bricked courtyard with a basketball rim that Kelly had bolted to the apartment's brick wall a few months back. The installation of the rim was the most commitment Jack had made to a relationship in a long while.

Jessica referred to Jack as being "immature and short-sighted," but he knew his vision was fine.

"Dinner at eight, I believe you said," Kelly shouted, walking into the apartment.

"Be right out," Jesse yelled from the shower.

Jessica, Jack's girlfriend for a couple of years now, is also a detective lieutenant in the Boston Police Department, presently assigned to the Homicide Unit. Domestic homicides and homicides in the workplace are the fastest-growing violent crime in the United States today, so murder was her business and business was good. Prior to that Jessica had been in Vice for seven years. Jack had been her field training officer and mentor. She had only spent a few years in the Patrol Division when she signed on to the BPD. Jack had known Jesse's father and was a dozen years older than Jessica, yet there had been a very strong mutual attraction. Jack remembered the moment he fell in love with Jesse Paris. One night on patrol while he was still training Jesse, he asked her what she would do if she had to arrest her own mother. She said, "I'd call for backup."

She had been a sharp Northeastern University CJ major and she had been through the FBI Academy, in Quantico, Virginia. Jack had never graduated from college; he was too busy as a senior patrolman, then a Burglary and Homicide detective. He was involved in what seemed like every high-profile case in the city of Boston. Back then they both knew of the attraction between them but were involved with other people at the time.

When Jesse left the bedroom and entered the apartment's living room she looked great to Jack. She wore jeans with a plain white blouse and white sneakers. Her shimmering black hair was still wet. Jack could smell the scent of her shampoo in the air as she walked past him combing out her shoulder-length hair. She looked up with her big piercing blue eyes and smiled warmly at him. He tried not to let her see him melt.

She said, "You look nice," as Jack just stood there in his clean but faded jeans and blue Barracuda jacket.

"I base my sense of fashion on what doesn't itch," he said.

Jack wanted to take her in his arms and kiss her but at times he was afraid to show his emotions and instead shoved his hands deep into his pockets.

Tonight, Jesse grilled some marinated beef strips out in the courtyard, prepared a salad, boiled some small red potatoes, and served Jack several Corona Lights with wedges of lime in the bottles. Jack had selected some Miles Davis, Muddy Waters, Milt Jackson, Charles Mingus, Charlie "Bird" Parker, and Thelonious Monk CDs and fed them into Jesse's CD player and hit the Random button.

After dinner, while watching the Leisure Log burning in the fireplace, Jesse said, "Why don't you stay over tonight, Jack?"

"I wouldn't want to impose," Jack said, knowing the routine.

"You can't keep a straight face, can you, Jack?"

"I thought I was doing a pretty good job."

"I would love you to stay over. You could watch 'The Game.'"

Jack scratched his chin and his eyes squinted.

"I don't think 'The Game' is on tonight, honey."

"Oh, please? You know I want you to stay here tonight."

Jesse brought Jack another Corona and they moved to the couch. Jack leaned in to kiss Jesse, but the cell phone in Jack's pocket was still on the vibrate setting and when a call came in, he was startled and jumped.

"Jesus Christ!" Jack yelled. He stood up and pulled the phone from his pocket.

It was just another night in Wonderland.

Jack spoke on the phone for about half an hour. He walked out into the courtyard with the phone. He walked back in, still talking. Then he went in and out of the bathroom. He looked in the refrigerator with the cell phone to his ear. He occasionally said, "Yes" or "No." Jack walked out the door of the apartment, took two steps, and ducked back in. Then he walked into the bedroom where Jack came face-to-face with Jesse and he turned around 180 degrees and walked back out into the living room. Then with a few "OKs" and a "9:15," he disconnected. Kelly blew air across the top of the cell phone and spun the phone back into his side pocket like he was the Lone Ranger spinning his .45 revolver with pearl handles back into its holster.

"So… you owe the wise guys money?" Jesse asked, entering the living room.

"No. That's about a case referred from Sergeant Donavan. A guy's son has been missing… for about a week. The father is concerned the police aren't doing enough about it. Imagine that," Jack said with a deadpan stare at Jesse.

Jesse had no comment.

"I'll probably take the case," Kelly said.

"Of course you will. You are the White Knight. And you are a do-gooder."

"Not really. I just make you think I'm a do-gooder."

"How do you do that?" Jessica asked.

"It's just one of my little tricks."

"I thought I was one of your little tricks."

"Listen, I'm not the White Knight. I'm the *Blue* Knight. And don't ruin my reputation with that do-gooder stuff. I'm wild. I'm dangerous. Sometimes, when I go to the supermarket, I check out in the line that says, "10

Items or Less" when I have 12 items in my basket… I'm uncontrollable. I'm so irresponsible… You know, I used to use a bar of soap in the shower right down until it practically disappeared. But one time, I got below one-half of the soap's original size and I just threw it away… I just don't care. I'm wild and unruly. I am irrepressibly disobedient. And I am so not 'green' that I may be personally responsible for a large part of the Earth's global warming. I'm telling you, I wreak havoc."

"You reek?"

"And I have also committed seemingly senseless, random acts of kindness. I create chaos. I am throwing the Earth off its axis."

Jessica Paris was staring at Jack Kelly.

Jack regained his composure and continued. "His son is an MIT student. A grad student. He's supposedly a great kid. He allegedly never takes off anywhere without calling Mom or Dad. You know the story. I'll meet the dad tomorrow morning at the office, get the rest of the details, and start the investigation *after* I get a check. Then I'll try and check the hospitals, hotels, morgue, cell phone records, credit cards, airlines, e-mail, computer, friends, and neighbors. I'll do all the legwork that cops are too important to check."

Jessica took a mock swing at Jack's head but he blocked it, held her arm, and pulled her towards him until they fell onto the couch.

"Now, where was I?" Jack said as he again leaned in to kiss Jesse.

It wasn't long before they moved to the bedroom. Jack asked her to put on the tight black leather skirt she had talked about on the phone earlier but she said she didn't really own one.

Jessica turned out the lights in the bedroom and they made love.

After… when sleep was coming… and Jack began to drift, he was hoping to dream about the jazz club he would own someday, but his mind began its inevitable progression and he was already on the case. As Kelly began to drift, he heard a voice whisper, "I'm out there, just beyond your peripheral vision… I'm in the back of your mind… just out of reach… and on the tip of your tongue. You can almost hear me in the distance." Jack had played it down in front of Jesse, but something the missing student's father had asked Jack reverberated through his sleepy consciousness. The father's simple questions played over and over in Jack Kelly's mind.

"Can you find my son? Mr. Kelly, is my son dead?"

Chapter 2

The Floater

An unshaven, unwashed, alcohol-challenged homeless man stumbled his way along the river by Back Street. He looked sixty but was only thirty-five. He was going to take a pull from the bottle of Hennessey inside the brown paper bag in his long, dirty coat's pocket but he noticed a Boston Police cruiser parked further up the street near Mass. Ave. Instead, he shuffled his way through a hole in the fence and went down the embankment. By the water's edge he took a long drink from the pint bottle. As he relieved himself against the cement retaining wall he heard a loud splash coming from under the garages. The torn and tattered urban camper put his business away and took another pull from the bagged bottle, draining its contents. He was about to throw the bottle into the river, then thought better of it.

The wino belched and stood looking out over the river as the body of a young Asian male floated by, about six feet from the shore. As the outstretched and duct-taped hands of the corpse momentarily got snagged on a piling, he could see the young man's face turn upward; the eyes seemed to be staring out at the homeless man. The wino's knees began to buckle. He felt like he was going to fall into the water with the dead body. The bottle dropped from the wino's hand. As the floating body rolled over and then sank, the drunk screamed, turned, and scrambled up the embankment.

As the ragged man got up to the street, he turned to hurry away but instead bumped into a uniformed police officer. It was Sergeant Donavan who had been on routine foot patrol with Patrolman Hodge in the area and heard the bum's shriek.

"Heah, heah! What's going on heah? What's gotten inta ya? What are ya up ta?" Sergeant Donavan said as he backed the bum up, pushing him against the fence.

"Hodge! Go down ta dat riverbank where dis ah… gentleman cum from and see what made him screech like a wild banshee."

Hodge obediently twisted and turned his way down the embankment.

Donavan shoved the scared-sober homeless man and said, "Now tell me what ya was up ta or I'll cuff ya aside the head!"

"Nothin,' honest. I didn't do nothing,'" the man said, shifting his eyes from side-to-side and then down to the ground.

"You look like ya did sumpin,'" Donavan said, mixing up his affected Irish accent with a Southern dialect.

Hodge came scrambling back up to the street.

"I didn't see anything, Sarge, just some piss on a wall, is all."

"Don't ya be pissin' on ma walls, in ma paht of town. Now I know where ya stay when yahr sobah… at the Pine

Street Inn. Now get over there and wait outside 'til ya sobah up. And if I find anyting else askew 'round heah I will find ya." Donavan gave him one more shove to send him on his way.

The two cops went on their way walking down the Esplanade by the river. They didn't see the lifeless body of the promising young Asian MIT graduate student very slowly rising to near the surface and then slowly tumbling and twisting, falling silently back to the river's bottom. Seng Li slowly rolled on downriver, turning and hanging as in a suspended animation. The dead body continued along the river bottom parallel to them as they slowly walked.

"You see, Hodge? We're doing God's work out here."

Chapter 3

It's Alive!

Jack walked up the 100 wooden stairs to his fourth-floor office carrying a giant Styrofoam cup of Dunkin Donuts coffee with milk, no sugar and the *Boston Herald* under his arm. The ring of keys clipped to his belt loop jingled and jangled. He thought himself like a janitor as he pulled out his ring of keys at the top of the stairs. It was a good feeling. He inserted the key and opened the outer office doors. He hung up his navy blue jacket and pushed open the unlocked inner office doors.

Kelly flipped on the lights and walked across the office, placing the coffee and newspaper on his big oak desk. He took a push broom and swept the floor. He emptied the waste baskets and ashtray, and straightened the desk. Jack took the giant coffee and walked past the bathroom into the kitchenette area in the rear of the 1,800-square-foot loft. He washed some dishes and coffee cups in the sink. There was a room in the back that had a bed Jack slept in, a dresser, and a closet. Jack got a clean black shirt from the closet and stared into the full-length mirror while he put it on. He pulled on his plain black leather cowboy boots. His five-foot, eleven-inch frame was square shouldered with a thin waist. He was clean-shaven and probably needed a haircut. One long, straight shock of reddish brown hair fell across one side of his forehead, over his eye.

He had just finished tying his light blue tie when the door buzzer buzzed.

Jack pressed a button by the office door, moved a wooden chair to a position across from his desk, and straightened the leather couch on the other side of the room. Jack opened the office door just as Rich arrived by the modest self-operated elevator at the top of the stairs.

"Please come in, sir. I had hoped I would get a phone message from you stating that your son had called and was well and that you would not need my services," Jack said as he took the father's London Fog raincoat and hung it on a peg in the entryway.

"But you'd be out of a job, Mr. Kelly."

"I'd take a day off anytime for that kind of happy ending, Mr. Rich. I was just going to make some coffee; can I get you some?"

Rich nodded his head and said, "Cream and a little sugar if you've got it."

Jack went out to the kitchen and poured the coffee from the Dunkin Donuts cup into two just-washed cups and added some powdered creamer and two sugars in one of them. He started the microwave, hoping Rich didn't hear the loud beeps, and when it was ready returned to the office area, placing one cup on the coffee table in front of the couch, where Rich had chosen to sit.

Mr. Rich was in his late fifties to early sixties. He was graying, balding, and probably thickening, too. He had a bushy gray mustache and he was a little on the shorter side. He was well dressed and well spoken. He told Kelly his son, Michael, had not been heard from or been seen by friends or relatives for the past six days. Thanksgiving was three days earlier and his family had not heard from him. Michael's mother was extremely upset, thinking something must be wrong. There had been no activity on Mr. Rich's credit card that Michael kept and used for everything. Rich had checked his son's apartment at the frat house and there were no signs of his son. Nobody at the Alpha Omega Delta fraternity house had seen him.

"My son Michael wasn't into drugs or gambling, Mr. Kelly. He was working on some experiments with robots and computers to help stroke victims… and the space program."

"Call me 'Jack,' sir, please."

"OK, Jack. I'm not sure how much Sergeant Moses Donavan told you but… just let me give you a little background. As you know, I think Sergeant Donavan may have told you, my name is Cecil Rich, I'm a plumber, and I live in Nahant with my wife, Dorothy. You may address me in any way you seem fit. 'Cecil,' 'Mr. Rich,' or 'hey you.' I don't take on any airs. Now, let me tell you about my son. My son is totally involved with his college life. He loves it. He never misses a day. He's a graduate student. He works in the A.I. Labs… that's the Artificial Intelligence Labs. The Computer Science and A.I. Lab had just merged. It's truly some experimental stuff. It's highly advanced, cutting edge, beyond state-of-the-art, Jack. For one thing, his group was trying to incorporate living microbiological organisms into computers. Robots, actually. Do you know what I'm talking about here?"

From the blank stare on Jack's face it was obvious Rich had lost Jack somewhere along the way. Even though Kelly had never finished enough college to get any degrees, he had been through dozens of college courses and two police academies, and he had accrued an incredible amount of training seminars in his twenty-one years as a police officer.

Kelly envisioned the blending of human organisms and robots and blurted, "Living organisms blended with computers? This would be the creation of the ultimate Frankenstein!"

Rich seemed articulate, level-headed, and intelligent. But Jack was having a hard time wrapping his small brain around the merging of microbiological cells with metal gears and transistor circuitry. Jack read *Time* and *Newsweek*, watched the news regularly, and tuned in occasionally to the Discovery Channel, but he wasn't up to speed on experiments in this particular field of computer research. Jack finally said, "I think my computer's broken. I keep pressing the Escape button, but I'm still here."

"I can see you're struggling with this, Mr. K… Jack. And you're probably thinking this talk about robots has nothing to do with my son's disappearance, and you may be right, but… he was so involved with his work… ah… I don't know. It was so important to him. The way my son described the work to me was that everything is electrical, or conducts electricity. Everything can be broken down to the atomic level, electrons, protons, the nucleus, all vibrating at the atomic level. And at this level they could be merged. The robots they are trying to construct make use of the integration of electricity from certain liquids, chemicals, batteries, metals, and microbiological substances down at the atomic level."

"This is the first step in the robots' world domination!" Kelly said, pointing his finger at Mr. Rich but getting no reaction.

"At least I think that's something along the lines of what Michael told me. I am a plumber who owns my own company and I didn't know what he was talking about most of the time. He told me once that they were trying to program human cells. What does that mean?" Rich asked Jack.

He was asking the wrong person, but Jack ventured, "All I can picture is an old laboratory down a dark cobblestone alley in Cambridge with body parts strewn about and cadavers lying on gurneys with wires and beakers of bubbling multicolored liquids attached. Finally Dr. Frankenstein throws a switch, there's the smell of electricity, and the monster sits up and growls!" Jack was smiling, amusing only himself, as he shouted, "It's alive! It's alive! ARGH!!! I am man! Not beast!"

With this inappropriate outburst finished, Jack finally caught himself and regained his composure.

"Let me put it this way, Jack. There are still experiments going on in Cambridge, mostly involving MIT and Harvard. There are still continuing sociological, behaviorist, and psychological experiments. There is still a spirit of excitement and adventure pushing the envelope into uncharted territory… and some day the artificial intelligence being created may border on the development of self-consciousness with its inherent instinct for self-preservation.

"There are experiments at Harvard that rival and go beyond the B.F. Skinner experiments with conditioned reflex involving not only pigeons, dogs, and lab rats, but his own daughter. Another well-known example of past forays to the edge was the post-CIA psychologically mind-altering chemical experiments of Harvard professor Dr. Timothy Leary in the sixties. And you better believe there are still experiments being conducted in out-of-the-way labs on darkened streets."

Jack got out a pen and small notebook from his pants pocket and asked Mr. Rich for what he called, in police-speak, "the vitals": Michael's full name, DOB, current and family addresses, S.S. number, and scars, tattoos, or other identifiable physical characteristics that Jack could match to all unidentified bodies.

Kelly also got Mr. Rich's contact information and asked Rich to fax some recent photos of Michael to him, head shots and a couple of full body shots.

"Should I tell you where I've looked for Michael, Jack? So you don't waste time going over what I, and the police, for that matter, have already done?"

"No, that's OK. I'll be working this up from the bottom, starting from scratch. Square one. From the top. But… up from the bottom. Yup. From top to bottom. Bottom to top."

Jack thought he could see Rich's confidence in him wane slightly as Mr. Rich looked away. Jack wondered if Rich was having doubts about hiring him, and he said, "What I mean, Mr. Rich, is that we will be very thorough. I promise you. We will find him. We go where the police cannot."

"How many people work for you?"

"About half of them," Jack responded imprecisely.

With confidence seemingly restored, the two men concluded the business at hand and walked to the office doors. Rich and Kelly shook hands.

After Rich left, Jack sat down at his desk and stared alternately at the red brick walls of the old office building and at the notes he had scribbled on his yellow legal pad. Soon the beginnings of a plan of action, a method of investigation, started to take root. He made one call to order Chinese food for lunch and one call to an operative that worked for the detective agency.

"Big M," Jack spoke into the phone.

"Hey, Jack. What's up?" The Musician answered.

"Did you have a nice Thanksgiving? All your kids get fed?"

"Yes, it was good. We stayed home. We had my wife's sister and her five kids over, too. Hey, have you ever noticed how everything sounds dirty at Thanksgiving?"

"Like what?"

"Just spread the legs open and stuff it in, or tie the legs together to keep the inside moist. Don't play with your meat! You still have a little on your chin."

"Jesus Christ, Willie," Jack moaned.

"Use a nice smooth stroke when you whip it. How long do I beat it before it's ready?"

"How long will it take after I stick it in? You'll know it's ready when it pops up," Jack offered.

"That's one terrific spread. Talk about huge breasts. I'm in the mood for a little dark meat."

"All right, already. I've got a case and wanted to know your availability. It's a Missing Person. He's a college student. Six days now. You'd be doing some leg work, if you'll pardon the expression, and maybe a lot of surveillance. You'd fit right in over at MIT."

"The Musician is always ready to go; I've only got a couple of recording studio gigs and a light rehearsal schedule and only a couple of scattered gigs with The Nightcrawlers. I'd love some hours. I've always wanted to go to college, but I was hoping for Boston College, BU, or Emerson. That's where the hottest chicks go," The Musician said. Kelly sighed audibly and shook his head from side to side.

"But I'm sure the geeky chicks need loving, too," The Musician added.

"You're married."

"I'll never understand my wife. She pours hot wax onto her inner thigh and then rips the tender little hairs out by the roots. Yet she screams if she sees a spider or a mouse."

Jack agreed to call him back with more specifics on the case.

The Musician had been working for the detective agency for six years now and was extremely talented and resourceful. He's a part-time construction worker and a struggling thirty-five-year-old musician who lives in a three-decker in Southie, is married with five kids, and has a variety of odd jobs. He does studio work and plays bass guitar with a half a dozen bands on a gun-for-hire basis. His dark, smooth, and youthful street appearance lets him fit in just about anywhere he goes. His name is Willie Crawford but he refers to himself as The Musician and had business cards made out as The Musician with his phone number, website, and e-mail address printed on them. He usually gets mad when anybody other than his wife called him other than The Musician.

Jack picked up the Chinese food from the Golden Palace next door. He went back to his office and spread the food out on one side of the desk and his notes and a notebook on the other side. Jack kept a running log of all case-related calls, conversations, and events with their corresponding times. It helped with billing and the justification for the billing because as Jack said, you never know what's going to come back and bite you on the ass. Jack was usually allowed to use his notebook if he testified in court.

He made a call to the cell phone of Lieutenant Jesse Paris. She didn't answer but he left a message. "Jesse, the missing student is Michael Peter Rich, 12/13/84, blond and blue, five-eleven, 180. Short hair. No facial. Can you check if the City Hospital morgue has any DB fitting that? And he has some kind of a Japanese tribal tattoo around his left bicep. Run his RMV history, vehicles, CORI, and a Triple I, Interstate Identification Index. Michael Rich was doing some advanced, cutting-edge, experimental work at MIT. It may be classified. The NSA may see military implications as is the case with a lot of the research going on at MIT. Can you see if you can get me a copy of the kid's departmental BPD Missing Persons file? I know they just got this case last week, but I'd be so grateful. And I don't mean that as a bribe. Not a sex bribe. Well, I'm not saying no, but I mean, you could still have the sex… I mean. Ah… OK. It's a sex bribe." Jessica's cell phone beeped as the message time ran out.

Jack hung up the phone and flipped on the FM radio receiver in his office. It was already on WGBH 89.7 FM, the National Public Radio station playing classical during the day and jazz all night. Jack loved all kinds of music. After all… music is the refuge of the lonely. The station was playing Wolfgang Amadeus Mozart, the undisputed master of classical music. It was Mozart's 250th birthday. Mo' only lived to age thirty-five. Listening to Mo' is supposed to increase one's I.Q. Jack could use a lot more Mo'.

Kelly debated having a small cognac to celebrate Mozart's birthday but instead promised himself a double after the day was over. The NPR station was playing a symphony Mozart had written when he was six years old. At age six, Jack was wearing a paper bag hat and swim goggles under the back porch playing in the dirt, making exploding bomb noises, lining up little tin soldiers and toy tanks, and knocking them down with a red plastic dinosaur.

Jack Kelly knew he would have to go to Michael Rich's frat house room and start poking around. He put all his notes into a manila file folder, put the file folder into a green backpack, put in a laptop computer, shoved his notebook and pen into his pants pocket, and pulled his Colt double-action-only .45-caliber semiautomatic out of the safe. He got an inside-the-belt holster and stuck the gun in. He pushed the whole rig down the front of his pants just to the right of center.

"Happiness… is a warm gun," Jack sang as he went out the door.

Chapter 4

The Super Geek

Kelly rolled his bicycle along with him as he walked out of his office and took the elevator down to street level. He had shed his "basic black," and dressed in the more common campus attire of cargo pants, sneakers, Red Sox baseball cap, a blue hooded sweatshirt and the requisite backpack. The Chinatown businesses were in full swing on this afternoon as Jack got on his bike, got his balance, and headed towards Boston Common. Kelly zipped across Charles Street, through the Public Gardens onto the center walkway path between Commonwealth Avenue East and Commonwealth Avenue West.

The MIT campus was right across the Charles River from Boston. When Jack got to Mass. Ave. he took the Harvard Bridge across. The bridge was more often referred to as the Mass. Ave. Bridge, and the Mass. Ave. Bridge was jammed up today with cars, half a dozen mass transit buses, bicycles, skateboarders, skaters, and students walking across in both directions. Kelly rode his bike across the bridge on the sidewalk, hugging the rail to the right. Although it had been a mild fall the dark waters of the Charles River looked chilly.

Jack began to enter the world of MIT. As he rode along the bridge he noticed the short, numbered, painted blue lines along the sidewalk every five and half feet or so. They were the markings of the Units of Smoot, measurements made in the late fifties denoting the length of Oliver Smoot, a fraternity pledge. The frat brothers had him lay down, end to end, and they marked it. The frat brothers had decided they needed to measure the distance from their frat house in Boston to their classroom at MIT. Mr. Smoot laid himself down approximately 364 times to measure the distance from the house on Beacon Street in Boston to the MIT campus across the river by Units of Smoot. In great tradition the fraternity of the Lambda Chi Alpha repaints the blue markings every year.

In fact, in the Massachusetts Institute of Technology experience, the students were traditionally responsible for many hacks, as they called pranks, over the years. One bright and clear morning the students and faculty arrived on campus to witness an MIT Police cruiser on the great dome of MIT's massive Building 10. Its emergency lights were flashing and behind the wheel was a dummy dressed as a police officer with a half-eaten box of donuts on the seat. There was a parking ticket on the windshield for *"No Permit for This Location."*

The only route to the domed roof is through a three-by-four-foot hatch. It was a fitting feat for the engineering school. This same great domed fifteen-story building was dressed to look like Star Wars characters, robot R2-D2 at one time and Darth Vader another time. It was also decorated once to appear to be a massive breast during Breast Cancer Self-Examination Month.

These legendary MIT hacks have become a part of the cultural fabric of the MIT experience. Harvard has often been victim to the MIT hack. The letters "MIT" have been burned into the turf at Harvard Stadium. During a football game in 1982 between Harvard and Yale, the play had to be discontinued: At the forty-six-yard line the slow but steady growth of a six-foot weather balloon with "MIT" written across it emerged. The balloon inflated until it exploded, shooting talcum powder into the air.

Upon pulling up in front of the biggest building at the massive MIT campus, Jack locked his bike to the crowded bike rack next to the grand staircase and ran up the stairs and went inside. It was just an old red Mongoose mountain bike Jack had picked up at a police auction for $12 and had fixed up, but he knew it could be stolen in just a few seconds. He grabbed a campus map and directory from the welcome desk.

Jack saw a coffee shop just inside the building and went in. He purchased a cup of hot Green Mountain coffee with milk, sat at a small table, and looked at the map. He noted that he was in the Rogers Building.

Jack took a cue from the Asian girl at the table next to him. He removed his laptop computer from his backpack, got online, punched in WWW.MIT.EDU, and soon found the address for Michael Rich's fraternity, Alpha Omega Delta, at the Edgerton House. Jack looked back and forth from the laptop to the paper map. He checked the Google Earth satellite imaging program on his computer screen and zoomed down on the fraternity about six blocks away, then quickly checked the map again and plotted his course to Michael Rich's fraternity.

As Kelly stared at the MIT campus on the map, it looked like there were forty or fifty campus buildings on the east side of Mass. Ave. Most of them appeared to be connected by miles of internal corridors. The Techs called them the Infinite Corridors. There were another thirty or more buildings across the street and more campus buildings on the next several blocks over to the north. The Charles River bordered the huge MIT campus on the south.

Buildings and departments had names on the MIT campus map, such as Superconducting Generator Test Facility, Brain and Cognitive Sciences Project, Koch Biology Building, Draper Laboratory, Media Labs, Space Research, Visual Arts Center, Computer Science Laboratory, Biotechnology Processing Center, Chemical Engineering, Earth Atmospheric and Planetary Science, Energy Laboratory, Nuclear Engineering, Plasma Science and Fusion Center, and Electronics Research Lab. Jack also located on the map the Artificial Intelligence Laboratory, the place where the missing Michael Rich spent countless hours.

Kelly walked across Mass. Ave. and towards Harvard Square for four blocks. Jack walked up Albany Street for a block and a half, and across the street from the MIT Nuclear Reactor Lab was Edgerton House.

The shabby brown shingled four-story tenement looked to be over a hundred years old and about to fall down. Its brown shingles were faded and in some places missing. It was all the more odd for being nestled in among the huge modernistic concrete MIT buildings that surrounded it. Jack walked up the old stairs to the porch. The white paint was flaking; he wondered if the rotted stairs would support his weight. He looked for any sign of life before knocking on the old wooden front door.

A thin olive-skinned young man with black curly hair and the makings of a beard came to the door. In his shirt pocket, pens and pencils brimmed from the requisite pocket protector. A thin calculator poked its head over the pocket protector. His glasses were held together with tape at the bridge of his nose. If you saw two people talking and one of them looked bored, he'd be the other one. He appeared to be the classic geek stereotype right out of central casting.

"Hi, I'm Jack Kelly, I'm checking on a possible missing person. I was wondering if you could show me to Michael Rich's room."

"You got a warrant?" the young man asked.

"Michael Rich may be missing," Jack told him.

"I know you need one. Do you have a warrant?"

"I don't need a warrant. I'm working for the family of Michael Rich. He's missing, remember? I'm here to help, OK, let's not get off on the wrong foot." It was not entirely by accident that Jack casually pulled back the dark blue sweatshirt he was wearing and put his hand into his pocket. This action revealed the handle on his .45-caliber Colt semiautomatic.

"Come in. Come in. Please, come in," the young man quickly changed his mind and stepped back. "I'm Dexter. I'm doing some graduate work at AI with Michael, but I'm in Cognitive Neuroscience, a postdoctoral researcher at our Institute for Brain Research."

"That's nice, kid." Jack said, not understanding half of it.

"I'm sorry, Mr...."

"Kelly."

"I told his father and the MIT and Cambridge cops he hasn't been around since, well, over a week, now. It isn't like Michael. He's been living here for three years with us, and he's never gone anywhere without telling someone. He's very excited and involved in our work at the labs. He hadn't quacked up, yet."

"Quacked up?"

"Just a word we Techs use to describe a student that works way too hard, and gets wacky, you know, he cracks up, under the pressure."

"The pressure gets that bad, here at college, huh? You should try getting a real job, in the real world, Dexter."

"You mean like poking through people's trash, sneaking around following people, taking surreptitious photos, peeking around corners and into windows wearing disguises. Have you ever dressed up as a woman, Mr. Kelly?"

"OK. Point taken, Poindexter."

"It's Dexter!"

"It's Jack. And to answer your question, what I do on the weekends is my business," Kelly said, smiling and sticking out his hand in an offer to shake. He was feeling a little guilty about strong-arming the super geek into letting him go up to Michael's room.

The two shook hands and Dexter guided Kelly up the narrow stairs to a small apartment on the fourth floor. Dexter said, "The cops looked around for five minutes and left. They were looking for some sign of a struggle, but they didn't find one. I heard one of the MIT cops say that Michael was probably shacking up with a Boston University student and was too ashamed to come home."

The fraternity brother went back downstairs and Kelly began looking around. The top-floor apartment was a converted attic space. He wondered how they got a couch up there. It reminded Jack of the first apartment he had in Southie, while he drove a Checker Cab for a living and went to Berklee School of Music and Harvard Extension School. Southie was a great place. It was within walking distance of downtown Boston and the North End, the Combat Zone, Chinatown, and the Financial and Leather districts. It was an exciting place to be. And it was relatively safe for its inhabitants.

At one time Southie was the home of a loosely organized and ruthless group of old-school gangsters and mobbed-up career criminals. But now the gangsters all did prison time and wrote books.

Michael's loft was one long room and a bedroom with clothes strewn about. There were empty food and drink containers brimming from the waste baskets. Something smelled like rotten bananas. The plants were dying from lack of water. There were small windows at each end of the long attic space.

As Jack began to search he looked through the desk drawers for anything that might provide a lead as to where Michael might have gone. He checked the waste baskets, unfolding and examining trash and then washed his hands. He checked to see if Michael had packed a bag for a trip but the sock and underwear drawers were full to their tops.

Jack sat down at Michael's desk and slid the computer's mouse across its pad. The monitor lit up. The computer was online and was open to an Internet page searching recent articles on developments in microbiological and computer fusion. Maybe these academic worlds of Michael and

Poindexter were way beyond Jack. Jack was in over his head in this advanced academic environment. Jack suddenly felt he was one of the tiny tin soldiers playing army under his back porch and he was about to be attacked by a red plastic dinosaur. Jack felt like a simple child playing an eight-key plastic toy piano in the Land of Mozart.

On the dresser next to Michael's bed Jack found the missing student's wallet with IDs, money and credit cards inside. Michael's cell phone and electronic day planner were there, as well as some keys and another $120 in cash. Jack had been thinking, or hoping, that the student had just hooked up with some friends and gone on a planned or unplanned Thanksgiving vacation to some remote and exotic location, perhaps with some college girls that had gone wild. Maybe they went to the Caribbean, Hawaii, or Las Vegas and were in a hot tub right now, with margaritas all around.

But Rich wouldn't have left without his wallet, identification, cell phone, and credit cards. Kelly feared that perhaps something more sinister was in the works.

Jack copied the phone numbers stored in Michael's cell phone into his notebook. Just in case Michael returned to his apartment, Kelly left a note for him to call Kelly's cell phone number. He locked the door behind him and headed down the stairs. On the way out he thanked Dexter for his cooperation, handing him a business card and asking that he have Michael call him immediately upon returning. Jack walked back to the Rogers Building, retrieved his locked bicycle from the bike rack, and rode back to his office in Chinatown just before dark.

Chapter 5

Death Be Thy Name

Jack had changed his clothes, made his supper of American chop suey, eaten it, lit a cigar, and tuned the stereo receiver onto the evening jazz program on the local NPR station. Kelly turned away from his computer as soon as he had finished writing his log for billing purposes. He spread out everything he had concerning this case on his desk. It wasn't much. He had his notebook with the missing student's vitals, some cell phone numbers, a map of the MIT campus, and… that was it.

Kelly referred to his notebook and located his notes with the last dialed number listed in Michael's cell phone. This would coincide with the day Michael went missing. The last number Michael had called was eleven days ago at 8:15 p.m. Jack looked through his *Cole's Reverse Directory* for a name and address to go with the number but it wasn't listed. So he called the number. A female voice answered and said, "C.E.S."

Jack said, "Is Michael Rich there?" and the female voice said, "Who?" Jack hung up. He was shooting in the dark.

Jack looked at the calendar on the office wall. He looked at the picture of a forty-six-foot catamaran anchored in the shallow green waters of a pristine cove at St. John's U.S. Virgin Islands and wished he was on it. He imagined diving off the boat into the green waters. Then he looked back eleven days to November 15, the day Michael might have gone missing. Jack scribbled "Mike missing" across the square for the fifteenth day of November on his calendar.

He turned to his computer and went online to the *Boston Globe's* website. He maneuvered his way to the edition of November 15th, and combed through the Obituary Page, then scanned the Metro crime section, the headlines, and the Local section. He repeated this for November 16th, 17th, and 18th.

He was getting discouraged, when he saw it. The November 19th headline in the Local section read, *"No ID for Body in River."* The story mentioned a body found by a man walking his dog in the early morning of November 17 along the Cambridge side of the Charles River by the MIT campus. A man walking his dog had found a body washed onto the grassy shoreline and the description was a white male in his twenties, five feet, eleven inches tall, weighing about 195 pounds, with short blond hair, blue eyes, and no beard or mustache. There was a contact number for anybody with any information to call Massachusetts State Police Trooper Archambeault at the CPAC Unit. The trooper's name sounded familiar.

Kelly backtracked online to the *Boston Herald* archives to the days after the body was discovered and he found the article from the *Herald's* November 18th edition, *"Body Found in River."* This article explained how Mr. Will Jones, a retired Cambridge resident, was walking his dog Sam at approximately 6:25 a.m. by the banks of the Charles River on the Cambridge side just downriver from MIT and discovered the "distended and waterlogged body." No wallet or identification was found.

Jack was disheartened. He knew that his first piece of business was to call Trooper Archambeault to see if the John Doe had a tribal tattoo on his left bicep. And if he did, Kelly could tentatively identify the body. That could, and probably would, be the student he was hired to find. The description was too close for comfort. This case might be over.

Jack didn't want to tell the father that his son was dead. That he had washed up, a bloated corpse on the banks of the Charles River. Jack didn't want to tell the father to go to the basement at Boston City Hospital, into that cold steel morgue. And Jack didn't want to have the attendant pull out the body drawer and pull back the sheet, and have that poor father look down on the partially decomposed face of his son.

Jack had made many death notifications as a police officer, but it never got easier. It got harder. Jack knew that this time, he would have a hard time calling Mr. Rich. What would he say? "He is dead, sir. Your son, the beautiful child that you spent your life raising. This kid you loved with all your being, the child that had so much promise. Michael had a career and a future, everything was ahead of him, but now he is dead."

Jack would tell him, if it came to be. That's what he had to do. That's what you do in a civilized world. You honor fellow human beings enough to tell them the truth in a timely manner. That's not asking too much, is it? And after that Jack would be out of a job and he wouldn't even be able to bring himself to send Rich a bill.

Jack picked up the phone to call Archambeault. Then he put the phone down on its receiver and sat there staring at it. When he finally decided on what he wanted to say, he picked it up again and dialed the number listed in the newspaper article for the State Police, asking for Trooper Archambeault.

The extension rang and rang. It was nighttime and Jack had expected to leave a message but when the trooper answered, Jack introduced himself and told him he was a PI working a missing person's case.

"Are you the same Jack Kelly that worked with my father in the BPD Homicide Unit about... ah... twelve years ago?"

"Yes, I was partnered up with your dad for my first year on the squad. You would be Jay, right? He spoke of you all the time. He bragged about his son all the time. Bragged about every little thing you did. How you looked as a baby. How good you were scoring your first goal at soccer. Your first base hit. After striking out fifty times. The rest of us referred to you as the 'Baby Jesus,' because in your dad's eyes, you could do no wrong! You walked on water! Archie was a great man, a good cop, and a hell of a fisherman, too."

"He got to spend the last few years of retirement fishing off the Cape Cod Canal for striped bass six days a week during fishing season. Why is it that after we retire, we die so soon, half the time, Jack? Ah... well... he was very happy those last few years. He used to say, 'A bad day fishing is still better than a good day at work,' Then the Alzheimer's got him. How's your health, Mr. Kelly?"

"I feel like I'm twenty-one, as fit as a rookie," Jack lied.

"Well, the way they're accepting overweight and out-of-shape cadets into the Police Academy these days, you could probably be in *better* shape than a rookie. Not that you're overweight and out-of-shape."

"When me and your dad went through the academy, we had to get up at 5:30 a.m. and run six miles before breakfast. There were twenty-five-minute meals and two-minute showers. And we had P.T. and classes all day. Then it was kitchen duty, study hall in silence, chores, and then bunks at ten. And if you stepped out of line just a little bit, they'd rip you a new cheese cutter. Now the cadets show up at eight, go home at four, they gotta make sure they don't work too hard, and they're hydrated! The cadres and drill instructors can't even touch them… never mind whack them!"

"What can I do for you, Mr. Kelly?"

"You can call me 'Jack.' Basically, Jay, you've got a body without a name and I have a name without a body," Jack said flatly.

Jack's statement was met by silence, so he continued, "I've been hired by the father of a missing MIT student. You have an unidentified body pulled from the Charles, matching his description, with no name as of yet. Is that still the case?"

"Yes. MIT student, huh? That might explain a few things. The stress level is so very high in that educational pressure cooker, we've gotten quite a few floaters in the Charles, usually around grading time."

"Are you talking suicide?" Jack asked the trooper.

Jack was again met by silence until Jay Archambeault said, "My John Doe is between twenty-one and twenty-four years old, white male, five feet, eleven inches, blond and blue. Not quite sure on the weight, he was in the water, all bloated up."

"OK. Let's cut to the chase here, Jay. Does your floater have a tribal type tattoo, around or on his bicep? One of those jobs that looks like thorns on a vine or barbed wire?"

Trooper Archambeault had gotten the case file out of a drawer and was shuffling through some photographs of the deceased from the case file on his desk.

"I'm looking at a photo of that tattoo right now, Jack. It's on the left bicep."

"I was afraid of that."

"Sorry, Jack. Did you know him, personally?"

"No, but I feel for his father. I guess I'll call him and arrange for us to come down and do the ID. Is he at the Boston City Hospital morgue?"

"Yeah, Jack, he's at the Boston Medical Center, Office of the Chief Medical Examiner at 720 Albany. Ah... Can I get the name?"

"Oh, yeah, sorry. His name is Michael Rich," Jack sighed. No matter how many times Jack has looked into the face of death, he could never get over the waste of a life that held so much promise.

"Do you want me to call the father, Jack?" Archambeault asked.

"No, Jay. I'll try to call him as soon as I ring off with you. What was the medical examiner's preliminary? He drank too much water?"

"Huh?"

"Did he drown?" Jack said, but got no laugh. "Do you have the preliminary autopsy report?"

"Ah… I don't know… no… not yet. I think it's in my mailbox. I'll bring it to you and the student's father tomorrow morning at the ID," the state trooper said a little mysteriously.

Kelly gave the trooper all the contact information for Mr. Rich and assured him he would arrange to meet the trooper with Michael Rich's father at the morgue early the next morning.

Chapter 6

Music for the Dead

Jack sat in his big leather chair at his office apartment, kicked off his shoes and sighed. There was no doubt about it. He was officially depressed. He thought of eating the pint of chocolate Haagen-Dazs ice cream that was sitting in his freezer but he instead poured Remy Martin cognac into the bottom half of a snifter. He went through his CD collection and found Wolfgang Amadeus Mozart's "Requiem," turned on the power, and shoved the CD into the player's slot. The swells and crescendos of the Berlin Philharmonic quietly filled the room. Perfect. It was Wolfie's music for the dead.

Even though it was late, Jack knew he had to call the father to tell him that they must go to the morgue the first thing in the morning and identify the body of his son. Jack knew it was Michael. He could feel it. He found the father's phone number in the file folder. He picked up his phone and then put it back down on its cradle. He took a sip of cognac, picked up the phone, and dialed the number.

"Hello, Mr. Rich. This is Jack Kelly. I hope I'm not disturbing you, sir."

"Hello, Mr. Kelly... err... Jack. Have you had any luck? I heard from Sergeant Donavan you were good, but... you've got a lead already, don't you? Or have you found him? Did you find him, Jack? Can he call me? He's all right?"

The silence on the line was brutal and Jack just wanted to say he had another call and hang up the phone. But he knew he could not.

"Jack?" Rich's plaintive voice was calmer now and began to tug at Kelly's heartstrings. Kelly cleared his throat and began slowly retracing his investigative steps.

"Well, sir, I visited..." Jack's voice faltered slightly and he cleared his throat and downed the remainder of the cognac. "I visited Michael's dorm room, ah... I mean, fraternity house room, and poked through his belongings, did a short interview of a roommate, well, not a roommate, a fraternity brother, he would be... ah."

"Is something wrong, Jack? Is he dropping out of MIT? Did he get married? Has he moved to New York City?"

"No... no... just a minute, please, sir... So, Mr. Rich, one of the things I did was to establish the date when your son went missing. Then I went back and checked the newspapers for that approximate date and I checked certain sections of the local papers. Anyway..." Jack just forged ahead, pouring a little more cognac into his glass. "One of the things I look for was any unusual accidents or crimes... maybe I look for something like, say, amnesia victims, or people in the hospital as a result of an accident or a crime. And I...I came across a report of a man who was unidentified."

Jack drained the glass and poured a little more cognac. He let his words seep into the father's inquiring mind a little as he took a deep breath and continued, "So I checked a little further, by reading this report and other related articles that were in the newspapers, and... the description is not unlike... your son's description. So I can't rule him out, you see."

"What are you saying, Jack?"

"Sir, we have to go and look at this unidentified person, to see if it's your son."

"What? He can't talk? He can't say his name? He is in the hospital?"

"No," Jack said forcefully and sipped the cognac loudly.

"He can't write his name?"

"No."

Jack took another sip of cognac as Rich was hit with the realization that the person Kelly wanted him to "look at" was not... fully functional, to say the least.

"So, what is he, dead?" When Jack didn't answer Rich said, "Oh... I see. What happened to... this person?"

"The newspapers said early one morning a man was walking his dog along the banks of the Charles and he found a body, in some thickets, mostly in the water. I called the state police investigator handling the case of the unidentified man and from the descriptions I have gotten we think you should go with us to the morgue at Boston Medical and take a look."

"OK... OK. I don't think Michael... I mean... I don't think it would be him...." the father struggled, and said, "Where along the Charles?"

"Ah… near MIT… and no… it might not be him. But just to rule this body, this John Doe out, though, we should take a look."

Jack was getting sick to his stomach and needed to end the conversation; he said, "So, I'll pick you up in the morning, say eight, and we'll be back by 9:30? How's that sound?"

"I think I know where the city's morgue is, the old Boston City Hospital, now the Medical Center. I can meet you there," Rich said.

"OK, I'll meet you there at eight, sir. Good night." The receiver felt heavy as Kelly hung up.

Going to the morgue to attempt an identification of the unidentified body sounded pretty lousy to Jack. Sometimes he hated his job. He often wondered why he was in this business. This dirty business revolving around crime. This business of deceit, corruption, thievery, betrayal, violence, and death. And that was on a good day.

Jack poured the cognac left in the glass down his throat, turned the stereo to a local jazz program, turned off the lights, and staggered to his bedroom. The stereo blared on from Jack's office, pumping out jazz classics. Jack hoped he could escape from the thoughts of Mr. Rich's missing son, who just may be the pale and swollen corpse lying on a cold steel table at the morgue.

He wanted instead to dream of Johnny's Place, the jazz and blues club he hoped to open after he retired. He began to envision turning a corner on one of Boston's cobblestone streets and following the sounds of the drifting bass, drums, and saxophone coming from the nightclub.

He began to fall into dreamland. And as he walked the cobblestone streets of Beacon Hill, he came to the blue and purple neon sign saying "Johnny's Blues and Jazz Club" in the window. The heavy oak door of the nightclub was propped open. Jack heard the sounds of glasses filling with ice cubes and the cash registers opening and closing with the sweet sounds of success. He could smell the perfume worn by the women, the beer and liquors mingled with a little cigarette and cigar smoke. One of the couples sitting at a table in front of the jazz band waved as Jack walked in and a bar-back greeted Kelly with "Yo, Boss!" It was good to be the owner and Kelly felt relaxed and content for the first time in a while.

He sat at the end of the bar and ordered an Absolut White Russian from his favorite bartender, Jimmy. The bartender put a wrapped Dominican cigar with a book of matches and a clamshell ashtray next to the drink. Jack lit the cigar, picked up a remote control, and flipped the power on for the TV bolted up in the corner of the room. The channel was on CNN Headline News. A pretty brunette woman with ample cleavage was reading the news. She said, "Now the weather," and as she turned to the weatherman standing in front of a map of the United States, she said, "How about it, Bob? Where's that seven inches you promised me last night?" Jack couldn't believe it.

Bob the weatherman came on the TV screen and pointed to the map, when an old man who looked to be about 100 years of age began pushing the weatherman out of the picture frame. The old man moved into the TV's screen. He had long gray hair and a long gray beard. The old man wore a white robe and his face seemed to be changing, almost imperceptibly.

Jack wasn't sure he believed in God anymore. But if there was a God, he wondered if he could ever buy back his soul. Maybe he could buy it all back with one shot. Everything… Every sin he committed, every bridge he burned. Every time he laughed in the face of death. Every time he laughed in the face of God. All the times he pushed it, stretched the envelope to its busting point. Maybe if he begged for mercy or acknowledged The Presence… Maybe if he praised the Lord with a voice so clear and strong… well… maybe he could buy it all back if there was a God.

"And now the news… from God," the old man in the white robe said. He looked straight out at Jack with sympathetic-looking eyes and a stern voice, and said, "There is some unfinished business today in the greater metropolitan district. A well-known Boston private investigator thinks he has found a dead boy and tomorrow will bring his father to him. Experts wonder why he is taking so long," the old man seemed to read from a script.

Jack was shocked and stared wide-eyed at the TV with his mouth hanging open. He pinched his chin in a vain attempt to comprehend whether or not he was, in fact, dreaming, but it was to no avail. He looked at the bartender, waitress, and a table with some men and women dining, but no one else paid any attention to God on the TV.

God continued.

As God spoke his faced changed from benevolent to scolding as he said, "This 'investigator,' this 'detective,'" God spit out the words, his voice getting louder, "this man, who should know better, who was raised by the best and taught by the rest, must have no heart in his chest," God seemed to be rapping and rhyming until he looked at Jack and addressed him directly, saying, "Just what do you think you're doing, letting the father wait to find out if his son is lying on a slab in the morgue? Why are you trying to get a good night's sleep while the poor man struggles for answers in Purgatory?"

Jack looked around incredulously, and God shouted, "Goddamn it, Jack Kelly! Who the hell do you think you are?"

Jack's legs were numb and he almost fell off the barstool as he mumbled, "I… I… I don't… I didn't… ah…" Jack swallowed hard and said, "I tried… I… I'm trying. I didn't want to face… I don't want to face… ah… I'm not sure… What was the question?"

"The dead boy, Jack!" God's voice thundered down from the TV.

"Well, it is not like he's going to go anywhere," Kelly said with a slight smirk and then a wince as he saw the face of God tighten, his penetrating eyes shooting light waves out from the TV and through Jack's chest.

"Jack Kelly, your mother taught you better than that!" God's voice now had a slight Irish accent and God sounded just like Jack's mother but his eyes looked Asian.

Jack hit the Change Channel button on the remote control and the programming switched to a rerun of "The Sopranos," only instead of Tony Soprano driving his sports utility vehicle over the bridge into New Jersey, it was God behind the wheel, smoking a cigar. The Lord looked over and spoke to Jack in his mother's voice, "Treat everyone the way *you* want to be treated, Jackie Boy."

"I miss my mom," Jack said with his lower lip dropping slightly. Jack glanced around to see if anyone was looking at him but the jazz club was in full swing. He hit the Power Off button but the old man was still on the screen. He turned the remote towards the TV and pressed the Channel

Up button. A big multicolored weather map covered the TV screen completely until God stepped into the frame and said to Jack, "You know, the weather is still one of my proudest achievements," he said, pointing to a "backdoor front" over New York. "Of course, you think sex is the best thing I ever created. That's one of my best tricks. God... that's me... split into the two sexes... We're all basically making love to ourselves. So *we* split into the two sexes! I mean, we could take care of ourselves, and many adolescents have... Ah... but we look at the opposite sex and think, hmmm, so different, so sexy, nice pointy tits! And check that ass! Maybe a man has broad shoulders, a swarthy face... But basically we're just doing ourselves."

God continued, "I set up the parameters for music and art. That was a good day. By the way, I love the jazz here in your nightclub. Do you have any Dexter Gordon or Thelonious Monk?"

God's face and voice on the TV screen changed almost imperceptibly through different races, sexes, and ages as he spoke to Jack about life and said, "We are Aliens. Matter can neither be created nor destroyed. We... well, *you*, are made up of carbon-dated molecular cells from the stars. Birth, death, and infinity. Amino acids, the building blocks of life, are spread throughout the universe in the interstellar dust. All that is needed to form life is for these amino acids to settle on a rock, like our third rock, in the orbit of a sun that's not too far away or too close. Like Goldilocks said, 'Not too hot and not too cold.' And life will form. There are life forms less evolved and life forms more evolved. But we are Aliens."

Kelly raised an eyebrow and was unable to refrain from wisecracking, even if he was talking to God. "You know, you need to do more work in the preventive medicine field. People are getting killed by floods, fires, disease, hurricanes, tsunamis…"

"Who are *you* to talk, Mr. Didn't Graduate from Berklee School of Music or Harvard Extension School?" God's voice grew louder until it was a thunderous echo. "Do you think you are Socrates? I know what you're really investigating, Jack Kelly! You want to know who you are and why you're here!"

Kelly squirmed under the penetrating gaze of The Creator as his voice shook Jack's ribcage. "You know I didn't get everything handed to me, like most of you spoiled Americans. You all think you are the Chosen Race. In fact, almost every race that has evolved thinks they are the chosen people."

God's face was changing from African to Arabic to Mediterranean to Asian, with both masculine and feminine features, as his voice altered through different accents. "This is what leads y'all into the problems of the world. Goddamn religious zealots are the problem. What did your mother teach you, Jack? 'Treat people the way you want to be treated!'" God said in Jack's mother's voice and then continued in a powerful male, stern, and commanding voice, "Is that so goddamned hard? Is it hard?"

"It's harder than a priest on a playground!" Jack joked, unable to refrain from criticizing God on the abhorrent behavior of some of *his* priests.

"You've got a warped sense of humor, Kelly! But, really, is that so hard to understand? Treat people the way you want to be treated. Is it so Goddamn alien to you? Hey, and speaking of aliens…" God's face went into the form of a large, domed, pale, big-eyed space creature and then morphed into some kind of mechanical robot. "How'd you like me to send some real spooky-looking space creatures down here to use y'all for food, OK? Speaking of which, I'm having dinner guests tonight, so you better start figuring out what I'm trying to tell you. I've got things to do. You think the Goddamn world revolves around you. Well, let me say it so you can understand it. There ain't no Goddamn Chosen Race. Zippo. Nada. Zilch. I love my mongrels and mixed breeds the best. I love all my peoples. Now don't get me worked up! You're starting me up, Goddamn it, Jack. You don't wanna get me going!"

"Why do you keep saying 'Goddamn'?" Kelly said and again tried to change the channel. Kelly wanted out of this situation and glanced over, out the door, hoping for an opportunity to make a quick exit, but saw God smiling at him, sitting at the wheel of a waiting taxicab in front of the club. Jack clicked the remote. God was back on the TV screen yelling and selling a variety of new coffins, "Why pay more from an expensive funeral home that has you by the short hairs? This expensive-looking mahogany and gold coffin is encrusted with 333, that's right, 333 diamonds, but it's yours for the heavenly price of $555. That's right, $555! How about you, Jack? Tired? You'll sleep when you're dead! Are you ready to give it up yet? Maybe you're already dead. You ready to call it a day, Jackie Boy? All tuckered out? Don't even have the energy to tell the poor father that his son is dead? Is that too much for you?"

"I'll tell him. And please don't call me 'Jackie Boy.' I'll tell him!" Jack shouted.

"Raise your right hand and swear it, Jack. Come on, swear it!" God demanded.

Jack reluctantly raised his right hand and said, "As God is my judge," and bolted upright in his bed, a warm sweat trickling down the back of his neck.

Chapter 7

As God Is My Judge

Jack felt a little nostalgic as he walked past the row of brownstone apartment buildings along Boston's Mass. Ave. in the Roxbury neighborhood. It was there, in a first-floor apartment, Kelly learned to play the guitar, jam, with other musicians as a teenager. He remembered fondly, the hookers dancing on the sidewalk and the old drunk yelling, "You sound like a saxophone, man! You sound just like a saxophone!"

There were more black faces than white on Albany Street as Jack rounded the corner from Mass. Ave. and headed down the street for the entrance to the city morgue at Boston Medical Center. A thirty-year-old homeless man with a week's growth of beard, a dirty raincoat, and torn black sneakers sat on the Albany Street curb playing electronic games on a cell phone. He stood up and took a long pull on a wine bottle in a paper bag and held it up to the sky, proclaiming, "I am the Holy Tube! All water passes through me and turns to wine! I am the vessel, the Holy Tube. I am the pipeline…" the bum shouted as Jack walked by. Then the bum relieved himself on the wall of the hospital and Jack heard him chuckling and murmuring, "and I love to squirt the Holy Water."

It was 7:45 a.m. and Rich was already standing in front of the cement-and-brick entrance to the morgue, even though Jack had gotten there fifteen minutes early.

"Good morning, sir," Jack greeted Mr. Rich with a somber tone. The father seemed fatigued, a little agitated, as he stared at the wino.

"Let's go in," Kelly said, quickly taking Rich's arm.

"Jack, do you think this... really might be Michael?"

"Well... eh, look, Mr. Rich. There is a definite possibility, sir... ah... I don't know. I pray not. But we must take a look. We must exclude this unidentified body. Desperate times call for desperate measures... and you hired me to explore every possibility."

"Yes, yes. Let's carry on here, then, Jack. I have a bit of a chill, though. I don't like this. Let's just forge ahead, then."

The cellar door was locked. Jack looked at his watch. The morgue viewing had been arranged for eight, but Jack saw a figure moving inside and knocked on the door.

The morgue attendant opened the door and silently ushered the two in.

Jack spoke first as the three men walked down the corridor; the neon lights hummed and flickered overhead.

"Hello, I'm Jack Kelly and this is Mr. Cecil Rich. Did Trooper Archambeault contact you about us attempting to identify your John Doe?"

"We've got two John Does and no, I haven't spoken to any troopers yet this week. But I haven't checked my voice mail since Friday at noon. Hello to you, gentleman, I'm the day supervisor, Harry Belmont."

"Two John Does? You've got two?" Jack said, a little excited, the pitch in his voice rising.

"Well, I've got one in Holding. It's a Jane Doe, actually, black female," Harry Belmont said, glancing back at Jack and Rich.

"No. We're here for the white male, twenties, with a tattoo."

"What kind of tattoo, Jack?" Rich said, with heightened interest.

"Well, let's just see," Belmont said as they came to the end of the long corridor. Then the day supervisor opened the door to the so-called "slab room" of the Boston city morgue with an electronic passkey. Jack wondered how many times this guy had witnessed the identification of the dead. And he wondered what a personal toll it might take.

Inside, along the wall to the right, were five gurneys for the transporting of bodies. There were two waist-high stainless steel autopsy tables slightly slanted for drainage and with raised edges and gutters to keep blood and other fluids from flowing onto the floor. Along the back wall, there were three rows of eight stainless steel drawers that opened outward. These held the bodies. Jack felt the cold in the refrigerated room and pulled his brown leather jacket's collar around the back of his neck. His suspicions were strong the dead body Rich would gaze upon would be that of the man's son.

The lights hummed and crackled as the attendant walked over to a chart hanging from the middle row, then he moved to a lower drawer in the second row, and pulled on the handle. The drawer slid out almost silently and stopped when the covered body was completely out. The supervisor looked at Rich and over at Jack and then slowly pulled the sheet back to the dead man's waist and stepped away from the drawer.

The ashen-skinned young man on the slab was clean-shaven except for a day's growth, his blond hair was cut close, one blue and jaundiced eye was staring straight up and the right eye socket was empty. Jack had seen enough dead bodies to know that from the postmortem lividity expressed on the back and hips of the corpse that he had died and then lay on his back for a few hours. Inspection of the arms revealed that he had a deep purple tribal tattoo that looked like thorns around his left bicep.

Mr. Rich stood silently for what seemed like a very long five or six seconds as it seemed like the air was being sucked out of the room. Jack was hoping that the young man was not going to turn out to be the missing MIT student.

Rich's lower lip began to tremble and his knees began to shake and he appeared to wobble slightly. Then his knees buckled and he fell to the cement floor, striking his head on the wheel of a nearby gurney.

Jack and the supervisor, although caught unaware, scrambled to Mr. Rich's side and helped him struggle to his feet.

"Oh, no!" Rich moaned.

The supervisor looked at Jack and Jack said to Rich, knowing the identification process required certainty, "Is this your son, Mr. Rich?"

After a silence lasting an agonizing ten seconds, Rich moaned, "Yes… yes, it is my son."

The poor man stood trembling slightly. He moaned out again and sobbed loudly in the worst moment a parent can feel. Jack could only step back out into the corridor and give his client a few moments alone with the body. Mr. Rich had found his son.

Chapter 8

Cold-Blooded Murder

The state trooper was dressed in a dark business suit this morning and carried the file folder with a slight swing of his arm as he walked through the morgue's Albany Street doors. He was a meticulously clean and polished young trooper with a squared-away look. His short light brown crew-cut was high and tight.

"Hey, who started the party without me?" Jay Archambeault said when he saw Jack standing in the morgue's corridor.

Then the trooper heard a loud sob come from within the slab room and his eyes popped wide open.

"Jesus! You've already been in… and made a positive? Jeez, Jack, I'm so sorry."

"Sorry we went in without you, Archie, I mean, Jay, but we were here… and the attendant let us in… and well, one thing led quickly to another, and yeah, it's a positive," Jack said with a sigh, looking into the room at Mr. Rich. "I don't have a clue as to how hard it is, to face what that man is faced with right now…"

Kelly and Trooper Archambeault entered the slab room and the trooper stood by Mr. Rich as he looked down on his son. Rich had one hand on Michael's arm and was squeezing it as if Michael might arise from his slumber. After several minutes went by, Trooper Archambeault asked the same question Jack had. He pointed up to the tribal tattoo on the deceased's bicep, "Is this your son, Mr. Rich?"

The father answered much quicker and with a stronger voice this time, "Yes, this is my son. Michael Peter Rich."

"I'm so sorry," Archambeault said and introduced himself. He told the grieving father again that he was sorry to meet him under these circumstances and said, "Sir, I have to ask you… are there any reasons that you know of why your son would want to take his own life?"

"Absolutely not," the father said, looking at the state investigator.

"Once again, I'm sorry for your loss."

"If you are sorry for my loss then tell me what you know, Trooper. Tell me what you've got in that file folder you're carrying."

Jack walked back over to the body-viewing drawer as the young trooper was taken aback by the father's response.

Archambeault looked at Jack and then said, "Well, sir, I will be conducting an investigation into this death and I… will be asking a lot of questions, to a lot of people…"

This response was met by silence, and he added, "For starters."

"Trooper Archambeault," Jack said, stepping in to buffer this slightly awkward situation. "Do you have a preliminary report from the Chief Medical Examiner's Office as to the cause of death? We'd like to hear what it says. If there is something to indicate suicide, we want to know what that is. I'm sure Mr. Rich has questions about what happened to his son."

"Well, the ME hasn't *officially* released the cause yet, Jack."

Jack scratched his head in the long silence.

Rich was still staring at his dead son. He had seen something and reached out and grabbed his son by the hair and turned his son's head so that much of the back of the skull was exposed, and asked, "Then what might this be, Trooper?"

The head had been shaved in the back, revealing a round, slightly jagged, and very traumatic-looking gunshot wound. Gray black discoloration from burned gunpowder indicated to Jack that it was the entrance wound.

"Those black speckles around that round entrance wound make it a close-range gunshot wound, and if the bullet was shot from a distance it could tumble and make an irregular-shaped entrance site. I think I can see a muzzle imprint on the skin," Jack said matter-of-factly.

"There's no exit wound, either," Archambeault said. "It could be the bullet's energy was absorbed by the tissue of the brain or a hollow point designed to deform and cause maximum damage..." The trooper realized that the young dead boy's father was standing right there and he said, "Ah, sorry, Mr. Rich."

"I want to know," the grief-stricken father said.

Archambeault sighed and read from the unofficial and preliminary medical examiner's report, "Cause of death, possible close-proximity gunshot wound to the back of the cranium. X-ray reveals the bullet and fragments are still in the skull. Angle of entry from the lower back base of the cranium, severing upper spinal functions and lodging in the jawbone. The pressure force of the high-caliber weapon may have caused right eye socket to expunge right eyeball. Nitrate tests positive on the entry wound, negative on the victim's hands. I repeat: No gunshot residue on either hand. Method of demise, preliminary. Possible trauma. Apparent massive sub-intracranial bleeding. Subject had expired before entry into fresh water... No water in the lungs. Cannot conclusively rule out suicide at this time. Possible homicide."

"And what does 'No gunshot residue on the victim's hands' mean to you, Trooper?" Jack asked.

"Kelly, you know I have to cover all the bases. Look, he probably… ah… all right, I believe he possibly did not fire that weapon. But in this preliminary stage of the investigation, until I get the official Cause of Death from the ME, I'm not ruling out suicide, homicide, fratricide, patricide, or pesticide. OK? But, yeah, it looks like it could be cold-blooded murder, all right."

Chapter 9

The Brass Rat

Kelly felt relieved to be out of the morgue on the sidewalk. He took a deep breath of the morning Boston air and blew it out audibly. He tried to brush the smell of death from his clothes. Trooper Archambeault loosened his tie and pulled at the collar of his shirt with a finger. Rich looked downward, devastated. He shook his head and said, "Oh God. How am I going to tell my wife and my family?" The man was crying now and it was all Jack could do to keep from busting up, himself.

"Refer all questions to me, Mr. Rich," Archambeault said.

"Thank you, Trooper. I've been quite upset with this. Please forgive me if I seemed rude or ungrateful." The dad had class.

Trooper Archambeault handed Rich his card, said good day to Jack, and headed off, perhaps to another case involving the total devastation of another family, just as Mr. Rich had his whole world cave in this morning. Rich seemed deep in thought as they walked back to Mass. Ave. and he said, "Please say you'll stay on, Jack."

"I'm here for you, Mr. Rich. But we did locate Michael… but I will be around… if you want to talk."

"No, Jack!"

"OK. If you don't want to talk, that's OK, too."

"No, Jack! You've got to help, now more than ever. You found my son and now I need you to find out who killed my son!"

"That's a police matter now, sir. I would hope they might solve this in a timely manner,"

"Jack. You've been at least one step ahead of the police all along. And 'they *might*' are the operative words here. You've *got* to help. I'm a man of substantial means and I want to hire you to look into this matter. You once told me you could 'go places the cops can't.' Well Jack, it's time for you to go there. This is the most important thing in my life, right now. I love my son… *loved*… my son…," the man's voice cracked, "and I've got to find out everything, Mr. Kelly. Please! He's been murdered! Someone killed him for some reason. They took a gun and pointed it to the back of his head and pulled the trigger. Did you see Michael's face, Jack? He was missing his eye…," the father's voice quivered.

Jack was inspired by this father's strength even as the guy was ripping out the little bit of heart Jack still had remaining after twenty-five years in police work. It had been ripped out more than a few times. But apparently there was still some left.

"Yes, sir. I will put everything else aside and give this my full attention."

"Thanks, Jack. Now I've got to tell my wife, Michael's aunts and uncles, nieces and nephews, and the rest of my family. But I couldn't sleep if you weren't looking into this for me. Our prayers are with you, now. You found him, Jack!" Rich said and put a hand on Jack's shoulder and squeezed.

"I wish I hadn't."

"Oh, by the way, Jack. It may be nothing, but Michael's Brass Rat was missing."

"What? What rat?"

"The gold MIT beaver ring he always wore on his finger. It was missing. The Techs call them Brass Rats."

"Oh? Interesting. I'll check with Trooper Archambeault about the whereabouts of Michael's personal effects. It may be in an envelope somewhere, with the contents of his pockets. I'll type something up for you to sign, giving me your authority to inquire on your behalf. I'll take care of the legwork for you. You take care of your family."

"I'll sign that authorization, and thank you so much, Jack, for helping me with this. I don't know… if," his voice was faltering again. "You know what I was thinking when I saw Michael's body? I saw his tattoo and I thought to say to him, 'You see, Michael? This might not have happened if you hadn't gotten that tattoo!'"

Chapter 10

Represent the Dead

It was raining hard this cold late November morning as Jack walked back up the 100 steps to his office on the fourth floor of the rickety Chinatown building. He swore as the large and hot Dunkin' Donuts coffee spilled out from under its lid onto his hand as he took the stairs up from the street. There's a self-operated elevator in the tiny lobby, but he liked to walk the stairs. It was cheaper than a health club. He was cheap. He was the cheap detective.

Jack needed more exercise. For years he had played basketball on Mondays and Thursdays, but not lately. He used to windsurf but he hadn't done that in a year. He took Tae Kwon Do karate for three years when he was a patrolman but he broke a rib and quit just before he made his black belt.

Someday he'd get a dog, he always told himself. He would get a dog that needed him. Maybe he'd get a nice big friendly dog from a shelter that would walk him every day. But Kelly knew he spent too much time behind the wheel, flying a desk, researching, or on surveillance. He figured if he walked up and down the stairs to his office, it was like getting the workout without paying the big bucks for a membership at the local high-priced gym. And Jack figured he got exercise jumping to conclusions, running off at the mouth, flying off the handle, dodging responsibility, and pushing his luck. He liked long walks but only when they were taken by other people.

Just before he reached the fourth floor, Kelly swore again as the hot coffee trickled down over his fingers. He unlocked and opened the outer office door, hung his wet leather jacket and Patriots ball cap on a hook, and opened the inner office doors. He put down his coffee, bagel, and the *Boston Herald* on the oversize desk and immediately strode over to the entertainment center. He selected six CDs and put them in the disc changer and hit the Random Play button. The first cut was "Eighty One," from the Miles Davis Quintet. Jack wondered how the rest of the CDs would play out. He had also inserted, along with Miles Davis, a Modern Jazz Quartet CD and a Ravi Shankar CD, and to mix it up, he threw in the Chemical Brothers, Fatboy Slim, and Crystal Method.

Jack Kelly knew he had much work to do. He really had to get moving on the investigation.

Jack also knew he had to slow things down and slow them down now. This murder case was too important to go about investigating it in a slipshod manner. No mistakes. He had to proceed with caution, but proceed. Jack was old school. He sat down with a pen and paper and drew lines and made lists. He wrote down the things he had to do. He circled some, drew lines to others, and then numbered all the circles. He idly wrote at the top of the paper "The Steps of Procedure." He knew the longer he took to develop the best plan of action in the initial planning stages of the investigation, the faster he would be able to carry on the investigation, in the long run. But right now Jack had to slow it all down.

After he washed his face and hands, he checked his e-mail and phone messages, sat at his desk, tossed the *Herald* out to one corner, and pulled over another pad of paper and a pen from the other. He sipped the coffee and within ten minutes he had a list of four things to do.

1. Call Jesse.

2. Print out the Authorization and Release form and bring it to Mr. Rich in Nahant.

3. Call Archie and tell him about the missing MIT beaver ring and ask him to release all property belonging to the dead boy. And ask about any other physical evidence.

4. Go to Michael's room and poke around.

Kelly started with the first.

He located Lieutenant Paris at her desk in the Homicide Unit of the Boston Police Department at Area A on New Sudbury Street, Government Center, downtown Boston. It was nestled in, near the Federal Building, One Center Plaza with the FBI, and a block from Boston City Hall and the State's Public Safety Offices.

He brought her up to speed and filled her in on the day's occurrences. But what he really wanted was for her to run this case by word-of-mouth past as many police personnel as she could, hoping that some tidbit of information, or some correlation, or recollection might occur. Yes it was a shot in the dark but Jack was going to use every way he knew to uncover the truth. This was a case that struck home with Jack whether he wanted to admit it or not.

Next, Jack called Trooper Archambeault, only to be shunted off into his voice mail. Jack thought about the problems of a multijurisdictional case where the law enforcement agencies didn't share information, making it very hard to proceed. Most people felt that all law enforcement officers shared the same brain but in reality the Boston PD doesn't share information with the Cambridge Police, the Cambridge Police don't share with the MIT Police, and the Mass. State Police don't share with anyone.

Less than half an hour had gone by and Jack had already at least attempted to cross two things off the list. He thought about what he might have for lunch and then felt so guilty about it that he scolded himself in a bitter internal dialogue. How could he? What the hell was wrong with him? Thinking of lunch when Rich's son has been brutally murdered. Rich was making arrangements to bury his son and Jack was making arrangements for lunch!

Thoroughly disgusted with himself, Jack started working on altering his Standard Authorization and Release form to fit this case. He punched it up on his computer, then put in the correct names and address and hit Print. After that he called Mr. Rich to make arrangements to get it signed. The Rich family lived in Nahant, an island attached by a manmade causeway, just about ten miles northeast of Boston. Jack drove out from Boston over the Mystic River Bridge and through Revere and through Lynn. He sang the local nursery rhyme as he drove: "Lynn, Lynn, city of sin. You never come out the way you went in. Trot,

trot to Boston, trot, trot to Lynn. You better watch out or you might fall in." Soon Kelly knocked on the door at 96 Wilson Road. Rich met him, escorting him into a beautiful sunroom with a view of Nahant Bay.

The rain had let up but the wind had not as Jack admired the group of twenty or so windsurfers shredding across the bay with their colorful sails, doing twenty-five knots over the waves. Kelly wished he had more time off to pursue this healthy hobby. He hadn't even had time to make the Regular Rotating Monday Night Poker Game Jack and his friends had been running for about fifteen years. He looked further back to the southwest and saw the clouds breaking up and the sun streaming through the skyline of Boston, a sight that never ceased to radiate a warm feeling deep inside his mind and soul.

Jack's blissful musings were cut short by the high-pitched wail of a woman from somewhere in the house.

"I'm sorry, Mr. Kelly. My wife's not taking this well. Mike was our only son," Rich said, looking away.

"Oh, I can understand, sir; my deepest regrets. I won't bother you another moment, just sign this release form and I'll get going… on seeing what I can do." Jack felt quite awkward and wondered why he pushed himself to get that little one-page form signed today. What was the big deal? Jack could get going on the investigation without it. But the little businessman inside told him to get the signed authorization and release. The family's authorization gave someone in the private sector, a civilian, which is what a private detective is, a little more power and authority to conduct an investigation. Kelly would also be a little less liable if anything went wrong as long as Jack acted in a lawful manner and in good faith. Now his actions and his detective agency were somewhat legally protected.

Jack wondered why he had to walk the line on some things and could stretch the boundaries so far in other instances. As a P.I. it seemed like sometimes he had to be very careful to cover his ass. And other times being a private cop allowed him to stretch the boundaries to get the job done. He could use pretext. He could use some little white lies.

Kelly took the signed document from Rich and started towards the door. Rich grabbed his arm and turned him around and put a personal check in his hand. Kelly quickly folded it and stuck it in his jacket pocket as Rich continued.

"Here's your check, Jack. Ah… who is going to be in charge of this investigation? The Cambridge Police? Or even the MIT Police? Is there any way you can run this whole thing?"

"Ah… no, sir. Cambridge and MIT Police, and I, with your authorization, can all look into it, but this is going to be the DA's and the states' case. State Police CPAC Unit, will handle, ah… they are the Crime Prevention and Control Unit assigned to the District Attorney's Office. Young Trooper Jay Archambeault will probably be the lead investigator."

"Oh, my. I'm so out of my league, Mr. Kelly."

"You don't want to play in this league."

"I thank you from the bottom of my heart. If it weren't for you I couldn't stay here with my wife, she's not doing well. She needs me. But I've told her about you and she believes in you, Jack. If I know you are working on this, I can stay here, and take care of her. Please call me and let me know how you're doing."

Chapter 11

The Slab Room

Jack had taken a right at the Tides restaurant and cut through the parking lot. A white, brown, and black cat scampered from behind the Dumpster and Jack turned his car slightly to avoid hitting it.

"Cats; the other white meat," he said out loud.

He pulled out onto the Nahant causeway, heading back to the mainland, and almost hit some seagulls.

"Rats with wings!" he yelled out the window. The cell phone in his pocket buzzed making him tense up involuntarily. The phone always made him jump, though this time it wasn't even set on "vibrate."

"Jack Kelly's American Detective Agency," he answered.

"Hi, Jack. The ME wants us to meet him back at the slab room. When can you make it?" Archambeault was all business.

"I can be there in twenty-five minutes."

"OK. It's 11:35. Meet you there just after twelve?"

"You got it, Jay. Want me to bring lunch? We can eat it right there, on the autopsy table. How about we have Honey-of-a-Ham and cheese sandwiches and some tomato juice, or a nice Bloody Mary?"

"See you there, Jack," Archie said as Jack heard a click and dead air.

By the time Jack got through the detours of the third fixing of the Big Dig, parked his Jeep on Mass. Ave., and went through the basement doors of the morgue at Boston Medical Center, it was 12:35. He entered the morgue slab room.

Seventy-two-year-old Dr. Lee Ryan, the state's medical examiner, was dressed in light blue scrubs with a white lab coat. He had the naked body on the stainless steel examining table. He was standing over it, putting on black latex gloves. The body looked waxy and gray and even less human than it had when Mr. Rich had viewed it. One arm of the corpse seemed to hold out an extended hand. Kelly could see the remnants of fingerprint ink on the fingertips. The medical examiner had removed the dingy clothes the body was brought in with and had put each article in a separate paper bag and marked it.

"Where's my lunch, Jack? I figured you stopped at the market, went to that little office in Chinatown you call home, and put together those ham sandwiches," Archie said from a seat by the back wall.

"No, I decided I don't eat pig, Arch. I'm giving it up. Do you know what they eat? I read an article in *Meat Lovers* magazine. No more swine... unless it's bacon, I love that. But I could run out and get you something. Did you want a BLT?"

"Yeah, sure. Hold the L and the T," Archie said.

"Hi, Doc," Jack said but Dr. Ryan didn't even look up as he brushed his longish gray hair back with his sleeve and put on a surgical cap and mask. He selected a scalpel from an array of tools on the side of the table. Kelly and the ME had known each other since before Jack was a rookie cop. Kelly's other grandfather was the ME before Dr. Ryan. But since Jack's granddad had passed away, Dr. Ryan handled most of the autopsies in the Greater Boston area for the last twenty years.

On a table next to the ME were tools, instruments, a small digital camera, an ultraviolet light, and a tape recorder. The forensic pathologist began his preparation of the body for his second, more detailed postmortem examination of the son of Mr. Rich. Dr. Ryan made a deep "Y" incision from the front of each shoulder to the bottom of the breast bone then straight down from the sternum to the pubic bone, barely deviating around the naval. There was little or no blood and little fluid at all until he began cutting into the cadaver's stomach. When he finally addressed Jack, his voice was dripping with sarcasm.

"Kelly! Haven't seen you since you shot that guy in his forehead at the Charles Circle gas station! Or was it the body in the window seat at the book warehouse in Southie? Is that where I last saw you? Maybe it was that dead lawyer? You were doing the community a service on that one. Or… wait a minute… I think it was the midget folded up in a cardboard box at your little Chinatown office?"

"Dwarf… They prefer to be referred to as dwarfs," Jack said.

"No! I think maybe it was the 725-pound serial killer Thaddeus Reno that you push… I mean… that *fell* from the eighth-floor fire escape at Massachusetts General Hospital and got crushed in the trash compactor. Oh… but maybe it was the poor soul that was thrown out of the third-floor window up on Beacon Hill, then shot twice with a high-powered rifle, and if that weren't enough, run over three times by Reno in a Cadillac Coupe DeVille?" the ME continued sarcastically.

Jack added, "You forgot about the skinny Provost Brother that tried to run me over with that same Cadillac. I shot him in the shoulder and then he drove in front of a moving freight train at the rail depot in Southie."

"Oh, I remember that. There was barely enough left of him to take an x-ray."

"He was on a crash diet."

"I had to dig your slug out of that mess. Do you know there were little pieces of glass, metal, and plastic imbedded in that guy? Flesh. Plastic. Blood. Metal. All meshed together."

"Sounds like what they're trying to build over at MIT. Are you trying to throw a spook on me, Doc?"

"It's just that… I can't help thinking… there is some kind of a theme working here… with you, Kelly." The doctor stopped cutting and looked up at Kelly, saying, "There's a theme, but I just can't figure it, yet. Some pattern with you. The trail of dead you leave behind is particularly evil."

"Jesus, you're morbid, Doc. Stop it, you're scaring me," Jack countered.

"I know you're a born and bred cop, but there's something different about you, Kelly. And I'm going to figure out what it is."

"Don't strain your brain, Dr. Ryan. He's not that deep," Archambeault said from his ringside seat.

"What can you tell me about *this* boy, Doc? Which of the five is he? Accidental, natural causes, homicide, suicide, or undetermined?" Jack knew the answer and wanted to proceed but he didn't expect this demonstration to yield anything that would help him find out *who* put the bullet in Michael's head.

Dr. Ryan pulled up the skin from the dead boy's chest and pulled the top flap over the face. With a small vibrating electric saw, a hand saw, and some shears he cut through the ribs and the cartilage and lifted the sternal plate. He lifted the chest wall out to expose the organs underneath. He examined the heart and lungs by removing them, weighing them, and taking slices and placing them in a solution.

"Nice pink lungs! He must have been a nonsmoker. Are you still smoking those filthy Dominican cigars, Kelly?"

Kelly didn't answer.

"You really shouldn't smoke those nasty things," the forensic doctor said.

"I could use that young man's liver and his lungs," Jack said.

"Well… Are you still smoking cigars?"

"My father lived to be eighty-nine years old," Jack said.

"Did your father smoke cigars?" the ME asked.

"No. But he minded his own fucking business," Jack said, feigning irritation.

The ME lifted the contents of the cadaver's stomach out with his gloved hands and put them in a stainless steel bowl. As he began to sort through the contents he brought an overhead light down closer to the bowl and with tweezers he began removing tiny articles from the bowl and placing them on a small stainless steel plate.

The only sound now was the hum of the fluorescent lights and the metal on metal tapping when Dr. Ryan put another tiny food item from the bowl onto the stainless steel plate with his tweezers. Jack heard a squishing sound as the coroner took a spoon-like implement and dumped some gray liquefied stuff in a separate stainless steel bowl. Jack was thinking the state should budget some piped-in music to this old morgue. Maybe an endless loop of happy and gentle music would be nice. He shook involuntarily.

"Come to think of it, Kelly, I'm testifying at the trial of one of the Provost Brothers, there at Super Court. I'm telling the court about the guy I did an autopsy on... the guy that Provost shot and Reno ran over with the Caddy, and the district attorney says to me, like I'm new at this, 'How many autopsies have you done on dead people?' So I look up at the judge and in a loud voice I say, 'All of my autopsies have been on dead people.'"

"Got big laughs, huh, Doc?" Jack said, deadpanning.

"The DA says, 'How far away was the vehicle at the time of impact?' Can you imagine that? I just stared at the judge. Honest to God, I don't know where these kids are getting their education. I told him the victim was shot in the lumbar region and he thinks the shooting took place in the woods!

"So a week later, in this other case, the same young DA, Jay Thomas I think it was, says, 'As a result of your examination, was she pregnant?' So I tell him, 'The young lady was pregnant, but not as a result of my examination.'"

"You were killing them, huh, Doc?"

"*You*'ve been killing them, Jack. But comedy-wise, yes, I guess I was. Now, come here and I'll let you extract some vitreous fluid from his remaining eyeball with this syringe. Just put the needle in the side of the eye… ah… that's it… now suck out the fluid. Good."

"I'm from a long line of doctors. Cops and doctors," Jack said, as the milky lens of the eye collapsed a little more, like a grape with the juice being sucked out. Jack handed the full syringe to Dr. Ryan.

"I know, I worked with both of your grandfathers for years. This fluid will tell me a lot. You know about dead men, Jack?"

"I know you always say, 'Dead men talk.'"

"That's right. I should write a book and call it *Dead Men Talk*."

"I think someone already did. Cheap pulp fiction, as I recall. Or maybe that was 'Dead Men Wear Plaid,'" Jack countered.

"I love Steve Martin," Dr. Ryan said. "Do you remember in that movie, 'The Man with Two Brains,' do you remember the 'cranial screw top'?"

Neither Kelly nor Archie answered as the ME elevated the cadaver's head and made a cut from behind one ear, over the crown of the head, and ending at a point behind the other ear. With a little effort the scalp was pulled away from the skull in two flaps, with the front flap going over the face and the rear flap over the back of the neck. Dr. Ryan took the electric saw and cut a round "cap" into the skull. Then he proceeded to pull this skull cap off, exposing the brain. With a scalpel he cut through the brain stem, severing the spinal cord. Dr. Ryan put down his tools and pulled the brain out of the skull with his two hands. It made a squishing sound and then a pop from the suction.

He examined it closely in the light, took off several slices, and dropped them into a glass bottle with a solution in it.

Jack wished his sense of smell would stop working altogether and his stomach wasn't so unsettled. The ME put the brain back into the skull and held up a small blue patch of litmus paper. He dipped the paper into the steel bowl with the gray stomach contents in it. Then he said as the paper turned red, "I have good news and bad news. The good news is he's not pregnant."

"You should try working stand-up at the Comedy Connection at Kowloon's on Route 1," Archambeault said.

"The bad news is the stomach content has field-tested positive for methamphetamine. That's just a heads-up between us gentlemen. His blood didn't test positive. The official toxicology results won't be back for five weeks."

"I knew it. Suicide by drug life," Trooper Archambeault pronounced.

"Hey, wait a minute, Archie. That kid didn't put the gun to the back of his own head," Jack said and looked at the pathologist and added, "Did he, Doc?"

Dr. Ryan shook his head from side to side and turned Michael's head so he could see the entrance wound. "There is the presence of black gunshot residue and coagulated necrosis."

"In English, Doc,' Trooper Archambeault said.

"An abrasion ring forms when the gases blow the skin surface back against the gun muzzle. I can almost see the imprint of a gun muzzle. Would you hold the head, Jack, while I take a few more pictures?" the ME asked.

Jack looked around uncomfortably for some rubber gloves as he rubbed his hands on the sides of his pants.

He finally took a pencil out of Archambeault's sports coat pocket and pushed the cadaver's head on the temple holding the head to the side as the ME snapped four or five pictures.

"Besides," Jack continued, looking at Archie, "meth is shot, snorted, or smoked. I don't think there would be a batch in his stomach."

"Toxicology will tell us to what extent and for how long it was circulating through his system, in a few weeks," Dr. Ryan added.

"The father says his Brass Rat is missing," Jack told Archie.

"What rat?" the trooper asked.

"That's the gold MIT school ring," the doctor interjected, holding up the dead boy's left hand and pointing to a white band of skin around the ring finger.

"Yes," Kelly continued, "Michael's gold MIT school ring is missing. It has an engraving of a beaver on it."

"I found traces of an adhesive on his wrists. I believe his hands were taped together. There were minimal traces of gunshot residue on the deceased's hands. Probably defensive," the ME said.

"So… you're saying that the killer shot him in the back of the head, stole his ring, and then poured crystallized meth down his throat?" Archie inquired.

"I'm not sure," Ryan said.

"What about you, Jack?" the trooper asked.

"I don't know what I'm saying," Jack sighed. "But where is his ring? Is it with his personal items?"

"There were no personal items, Jack. Not a thing on him. Not a nickel, or keys, or ID. Nothing, not even a pocket protector filled with pens and pencils, like most of those MIT geeks have sticking out of their shirts."

The medical examiner stared at Trooper Archambeault, who apparently hadn't noticed the pocket protector filled with utensils brimming over the top pocket in the ME's lab coat. The forensic pathologist spoke into his tape recorder for a minute and then the doctor replaced the flaps of skin and sewed up the scalp. He returned all of the internal organs and placed them back in the body and used a baseball stitch to close everything back up.

With Kelly's reluctant and completely unenthusiastic help, Dr. Ryan turned the body over and took more pictures. After turning the corpse right-side up again he inserted an eight-inch hemostat into the wound channel in Michael's head and pushed it all the way to the back of Michael's face. He leaned over the body and pulled furiously inside the skull with the tool, which resembled thin needle-nose pliers. With a bit more effort and some squishing sounds the ME pulled the tool out from Michael's skull.

"Oh good," the medical examiner said, looking up. He smiled and held up a bloody and slime-covered bullet fragment within the teeth of the pliers. He was obviously delighted and said, "Yippee! Now I won't have to use the Sawzall to saw off his lower jawbone!"

Jack looked down at the corpse. He felt a little woozy and almost fell off the stool he was sitting on and said, "You're killing me, Doc."

Chapter 12

Blues, Wine, and a Short Skirt

Jack loved Jesse.

They had experienced a platonic relationship when Jesse was a young police officer. But this time it was different. He had been falling hard for her since they'd gotten reacquainted about three years ago. He loved the way she looked. Her short dark hair was cut straight across in the front. She was not much prettier than the average college girl. But when Jack looked at her it was as if the wind was blowing back her dark auburn hair and sunshine seemed to stream from her cobalt blue eyes. Jack was smitten all right. Big time. And it was about time. Jack hadn't given his heart to anyone for a long, long time.

Everything was right about her, this time. She knew him, who he was. She knew about his past. She knew about his work and how the job affected him. She knew his viewpoint would be jaded. And he would always be suspicious. She knew about the weird idiosyncrasies and the mental and physical manifestations of sleep depravation accented by the adrenaline-pumping events that happen when cops work strange and long hours. She's been there, done that. Her pop was a cop. Her brother works undercover.

She had told Jack that she had three men in the last eleven years and two of them had been Jack.

But it went even deeper with Jessica Paris. Cops can joke about the arrests, the chases, the horror shows, the deaths. She had seen the unbelievable occurrences that the police see on a daily basis. Incidences that are so odd that a cop can't really convey them to a civilian; they just wouldn't understand. These events take a personal toll. In police work things happen and cops sometimes don't talk about these events but they are influenced deeply. There are ramifications on the soul and the psyche. They are, after all, everyday people. Everyday people with a badge and a gun.

She understood. She understood there was enough stress on the job; she and Jack didn't need it at home. And a home was what Jack was thinking about having again, someday. Jack was falling hard.

He walked through the black wrought iron gate and down the stairs into the courtyard, gave the door a knock, and walked into Jesse's Beacon Street apartment. As was often the case at the end of a long day, she was in the shower, washing off the scent of the mean streets, so he knocked on the bathroom door and shouted, "I'm here. Don't run out and give me one of those karate chops you learned for proficient white girls with a master's degree in criminology at the FBI Academy."

"Jealous," she yelled out from the steamy bathroom.

Kelly walked over to the CD rack, picked out an old B.B. King disc, and slid it into the CD player, pressing the Play button. Maybe he was setting a romantic mood, or maybe he just loved the blues. He made some instant coffee and was staring out the window into the courtyard when Jessica walked out wearing a white towel and a smile. She said, "Let me guess. Is that Earl King, Freddy King, B.B King, or Albert King?"

"Ah… very good." Jack responded. "The King is dead, long live the King.' I have explained both the esoteric and the aesthetics of the blues to you and the student is ascending to the level of the teacher."

"Ah… let me see… it's either Wolf Dog or Howlin' Dog, or Muddy Hooker, or Big Dick Johnson…," Jesse said, teasing Jack.

She continued with, "I think Phil McCracken was on bass or was that Blind Melon Head?"

"Don't disrespect the blues, baby."

"So… How'd it go today, Blue Knight?" she said.

"Well…," Jack sighed audibly because he knew any romantic mood was about to disappear faster than a raindrop falling into Boston Harbor. "Well, honey, as you know we've gotten a positive ID on the John Doe. The father is quite broken up about it. And I guess the mother is a basket case. I saw Mr. Rich at their house in Nahant this morning and spent part of the afternoon at the morgue with young Archie and the ME."

"Oh, I'm sorry Jack. Drowned? Accidental?"

"Not unless he could shoot himself in the back of the head and get rid of the rubber gloves and murder weapon while his wrists were taped together."

"It was murder?"

"In the first degree. Archie will probably handle it for the state and the DA. MIT might have some interest. And the body washed up on the Cambridge side."

"Well, at least you're out of it," Jesse said, holding her towel up with one hand and combing her hair in the mirror with the other.

"Ah, well... the father has given me a check," Jack reached inside his jacket pocket, pulled out the check, and stared at it as he continued, "to look into the matter. So I'm in it up to my neck... Holy shit!"

"What?"

"The check is for $60,000! This must be a mistake.... ah... right?"

"Jesus, Jack. That's almost my base pay for the year!" Jesse said, staring at Jack, her arms hanging lifelessly at her side as the towel dropped on one side, exposing a large part of her anatomy. She looked at Jack as he peeked at her anatomy. Then they looked down at the check again for a long time.

"Talk to me while I dress for dinner," Jesse said as she went into the bedroom. Jack stood in the doorway, loosening his tie. Jesse slipped on a short navy blue skirt and a white blouse that buttoned down the front.

Maybe it was the magnitude or the grave nature of the job Jack was undertaking that gave him the sense of importance, real or imagined. Maybe it was the large amount of the check, even though he believed Rich meant to write $6,000. But both factors gave Kelly some validation. Maybe he felt like he was a real detective. He was on his own, working without a net.

Kelly drank most of a bottle of Francis Coppola's Merlot with the delicious chicken cacciatore Jesse cooked up. Then he put on a CD of some ambient background music with a disc titled "Nightmares on Wax." As Jesse put the last dish into the sink Jack took her hand and pulled her and the almost-empty wine bottle over to the couch. They landed with a thud and laughed, looking into each other's eyes. Jesse put her hand on Jack's thigh and gave it a squeeze. Jack jumped. Jack always jumped. And Jesse loved to see him jump.

"You've been working those quads, haven't you?" she said with sensual tones as she ran her hand up and down his thigh.

"It's the power of roundball, baby… and … squats," Jack said, accentuating every letter of the word: s-q-u-a-t-s.

"I'd like to see some of that power of your round balls, if you don't mind, sir. And maybe a couple of those ssqquuaaaattsss," Jesse said, rubbing the length of Jack's thigh a little harder with determined concentration. Jack slumped back against the couch and put his arm around Jesse and kissed her lips softly. Then he planted four or five kisses on the back of her neck. She leaned forward, closing her eyes, and kissed Jack on his lips.

Jack glanced down to where Jesse's blouse had opened to the point that Jack could see her stiffening nipple at the end of her milky white breast. He reached up under her blouse and cupped her soft breast, placing her nipple between his middle and ring fingers. Her hand moved up the inside of Jack's thigh and slid up to feel him stiff just under the crotch of his pants. As he massaged her nipple and breast, she tugged at his zipper and it slid all the way down. Her hand gently felt the shape of his member and she reached inside his underwear. They kept on kissing until Jack let the air out of his lungs in a long and soulful sigh. Jack moaned again and she moaned too. The two lovers moaned in ecstasy. Their semiconscious pleasurable vocalizations were in harmony as her tiny fingers encircled the circumference of him, stroking it gently up and down. She was fascinated and moved closer to the object of her affection. She kissed the tip as she moved her hand. She went down, taking in most of the length of him. Her soft, wet, loving lips and soft stroking fingers brought his erection to its full potential.

For his part Kelly was in heaven. He had gotten orally pleasured before but this was special. For the next half hour they could not have been closer. The electricity coursed through their bodies and souls. They were plugged into each other. There were strong forces building, entering, and flowing outward of their bodies.

Soon Jack was so excited he pushed Jesse back on the couch and reached under her short skirt and with two hands pulled her panties down past her knees and over her toes and off. He pulled off his pants and mounted her straight up and in front. She helped guide him into her. She moaned and bit Jack's shirt collar. She screamed a little quiet scream as she put one arm around Jack's neck and put her other hand on his ass and pulled Jack into her as far as she could.

The empty wine bottle fell to the floor.

Chapter 13

Robots on the Internet

It wasn't the first time Jack had woken up with a sandpaper tongue and bloodshot eyes that burned. He had a headache the size of the Starship *Enterprise*. The sunlight streaming through the blinds felt like knives sticking into his eye sockets and into the soft fleshy cavity under his frontal lobes. He shouldn't have had the two shots of tequila after the wine. And the cigar he smoked wasn't settling well. It was the high price to be paid for flying around the stars at night. He was paying for it now.

In the morning over breakfast Kelly told Jesse everything that had occurred with the Michael Rich case. She promised to check the Boston pawn shop reports for the MIT beaver ring and keep her eyes and ears open.

Then Jack called Rich. He answered the phone.

"Mr. Rich, good morning, sir. I have just a few quick matters to discuss with you. First of all, you mistakenly made my check out for $60,000," Jack laughed. "Did you mean $6,000?" Jack hoped.

"The check is correct, Jack. Find me my son's killer. If there's money left over we'll talk about it then. Please. My wife and I need closure. And there will be no closure like the execution of the son-of-a-bitch that murdered our son!"

"We don't have the death penalty in Massachusetts, Mr. Rich," Jack said.

"Oh, yes, the liberal state of Massachusetts. Why don't we?"

"Well… I guess some people feel that execution makes the state a murderer. The state of Massachusetts is much more contented with imprisonment, which turns the state into a gay dungeon master."

"OK. I like your slant on things, Jack."

Jack was still quite stunned at the realization that Rich had retained his services with a $60,000 advance. "Ah… another thing…" Jack said, recovering slightly. "I'd like to get into Michael's frat house loft again."

"I was planning on going over to Mike's place after the funeral tomorrow or the next day, and moving his belongings," Rich said, but upon hearing Jack's dejected sigh, he added, "But I could go over now and get a good look at what I will need for a U-Haul. My younger brother will help me move Michael's things next weekend."

"OK, Mr. Rich. I want to get moving on the investigation. Shall I meet you there?"

"How's eleven? I want to take a shower and make sure my sister can stay with my wife. She's heavily sedated and under a physician's care."

"I'll wait for you near MIT on the corner of Mass. Ave. and Albany."

Later, Jack parked his car on Mass. Ave. in Cambridge and at eleven sharp Mr. Rich walked around the corner to catch Jack Kelly staring at the shapely buttocks of a young woman student waiting for a bus. Not dressed like the typical student, she was wearing a sheer black blouse with a tight pink miniskirt and stiletto heels.

Rich coughed and said, "Mr. Kelly... Jack?" Rich had to grab Kelly by the arm and turn him to his face. Kelly had a faraway look in his eyes as if he were remembering some past scenario.

"Let's go, Jack."

The two men walked up Albany Street, passing some road construction and some parked delivery trucks, and walked up to the front stairs at Edgerton House. Mr. Rich knocked. The door was opened by Dexter, the stereotypical super geek that Jack had encountered on his first visit. The sight of Dexter with his black curly hair, the typical student starter beard, the pajamas with a cowboys on horseback pattern, seemed to surprise Rich. The grad student pushed his taped glasses up with one finger, scrunched his nose, and said, "Mr. Rich, Michael hasn't come home yet."

"That's all right, Dexter. We know where he is."

"Oh, great! When is he coming back to the house?"

Rich looked away and Jack took a step closer to the doorway and informed Dexter that Michael had been found dead. He further explained that he and Mr. Rich had identified Michael's body at the city morgue yesterday and that Michael had been found in the Charles River.

"We're going to be up in Michael's room for a while, Dexter," Mr. Rich said. "I will be making arrangements to move all of Michael's things out next weekend. Mr. Kelly will be spending some time here. Please do not let anyone

90

other than family, the police, or Mr. Kelly into Michael's space." Mr. Rich walked past Dexter, who handed Rich a key and just stood there with his mouth dropped open for several minutes.

"And Dexter," Jack said as the two men began walking up the stairs, "if police officers do come by... tell them they need a warrant. You know how that goes."

Jack and Rich opened the fourth-floor attic apartment door and went inside. The note Jack had left asking Michael to call him was still on the table. Jack crushed it and threw it into the waste basket. The two men began wandering around the apartment. Mr. Rich was picking things up and moving them around. Kelly stuck his hands in his pockets, an old habit from crime scene protocol. Occasionally he took a pen out of his pocket and lifted an object but he always placed it back down from where he got it. Since it appeared Michael may have been killed by a messy gunshot to the back of the head and there was no sign of blood or a clean-up in the apartment, Jack began to realize that this was not the murder scene and he gradually began to search more boldly.

Rich noted that Michael's keys, wallet, watch, cell phone, and cash were still on his desk in the apartment. There was a calendar on the wall but all that was marked on the day he went missing was, "AI Lab."

"What's the AI Lab, again, sir?" Jack asked.

"That's the Artificial Intelligence Lab here at MIT. It's where Mike worked and spent most of his time. They are doing incredible things there, Jack."

"I'll bite. Tell me again."

"Ah... well... they've altered the genes in fruit flies," Rich said.

Jack was obviously not very impressed so Mr. Rich continued.

"Ah… they implanted tiny electrodes directly into the brains of lab mice, and these electrodes wirelessly transmit data on how the brain learns, into computers for analysis. And they are learning a lot."

"Who? The mice or the scientists?"

"The scientists, Jack."

"But can they keep a mouse's ass from getting snapped on by a simple mouse trap?"

"Ah… I don't know about that, but they are teaching robots, and micro robots, to talk to each other on the Internet. The robots are learning how they can build and repair themselves into more and more of a sophisticated being."

"Being?" Jack scoffed.

"The level of sophistication is increasing rapidly by evolutionary standards. The mechanics are there. The electrical sensors and microchips are commonplace now. And the computer brains that are capable of running the whole show are getting smaller, lighter, faster, and cheaper."

"Yeah, I guess it's about time for some new technological breakthroughs," Jack offered, not really having thought about it much.

"And there are multimillion-dollar contracts with the military for communications systems, space surveillance, missile defense, and tactical systems. That's the Lincoln Laboratory in Lexington. They are huge with the private sector. Everybody wants to be number 1."

"How do you know so much about what MIT is doing?"

"My son was here for five years. He wasn't on a full scholarship; I paid plenty over the years! I read everything I could find about MIT. We have visited the campus two dozen times for events and visited Mikey another two dozen.

"It's a great school, Jack. The guy who runs the AI Lab started iCYBORG, I think it's called, the company making robots for all domestic chores. This Artificial Intelligence Laboratory is incredibly advanced. Their robots can see! They recognize people and objects! They hear and recognize hundreds of commands. The scientists studied the insects and learned the best ways for machines to walk or crawl. My son was working on a project that combined microbiological cells with robot components. They are integrating and linking systems. They are working on developing legs and arms that function by the electrical stimulus of the human brain for people that have lost limbs. And Mike was developing a system to override and control all the systems. And he worked on machines that utilize organic matter. Growing, living flesh that is a life support system for thinking machines. We are learning from these robots as well as them learning from us. And the robots learn a lot faster than we do."

"Or at least they learn a lot faster than I do," Jack added.

"In Japan there's a child-sized yellow robot with arms and hands, a friendly round head, and recognizes 10,000 words. It house sits for you when you're away. It knows you by sight and says hello when passing you in the hall on its way to complete another domestic chore. You can talk to it by cell phone. It's equipped with burglary and fire alarms, and provides company to the elders and reminds them to take their medicine."

As they were talking, Kelly began looking through Michael's closet while Rich went through two dressers filled with clothes. Then Rich opened a foot locker and sat down on the floor looking through a stack of assorted photographs.

"I'd like to look into his computer some more," Kelly said, sitting down at Michael's desk.

"Anything, Jack. He had no login. No prompt. No password. No nothing. When I stopped into his apartment and wanted to use his computer he told me that no one else came into his apartment anyway and he didn't have anything to hide. He said his project work on his computer was all encoded with numbers. He had virus protection but no passwords."

Jack moved the mouse and the screen came to life again. It was on the same page it was when Jack was there two days ago. It had searched for pages listing recent developments in microbiological and computer fusion.

"This World Wide Web is something, isn't it?" Jack thought out loud.

"The WWW was invented by MIT scientist Tim Berners-Lee, a London-born computer wizard. He was knighted by Queen Elizabeth," the father said.

"Cecil, I want to stay in this apartment tonight. I want to see what I can pull out of this computer. I want to check his day planner, look through his paperwork, and call every number in his cell phone to see if I can get some information from interviewing everybody I can."

Rich's face turned overcast and his eyes seemed to tear up slightly. He stared into Jack's eyes, brightened up a little, and said with a determined but faltering voice, "That's the best thing I've heard tonight, Jack. If I know you're looking into this, I'll be able to go back to my wife in Nahant. She needs me now. I don't know what I would do without you, Jack Kelly. And may Jesus be with you, tonight."

"As long as Jesus doesn't snore. But I think I need to figure this one out by myself. I need to get closer to the world Michael lived in."

Chapter 14

Dead Online

It was already 8 p.m. and dark outside. Jack called The Musician to ask him to come over to Michael's frat house apartment and to bring a turkey, cheese, and vegetable sub with two six packs of Corona Light and a lime. It was 8:30 when Jack's cell phone vibrated. He jumped straight up as he sat at the computer desk.

"I'm in the 'hood. Is there a parking lot? Or I guess I can park right here in front of the frat house," The Musician said.

Jack looked out of the tiny front window and saw The Musician backing into a space directly in front; he said, "Don't park too close. I want you to start surveillance on this place tomorrow. Most of it from your car, so ditch it up the street."

"Of course I wouldn't even think of parking near the frat house; I knew that, I'm way down the street," The Musician said, not realizing Jack was watching and added, "Are you playing me for an idiot?"

"Did Hendrix play the guitar?" Jack said as he watched The Musician's blue van pull out and drive down the street. "I'll walk down and let you in the front door."

Even though it wasn't locked, Jack opened the front door of the Alpha Omega Delta frat house and he let in William Ellis Crawford III, AKA The Musician. Jack told him about the building's human guard dog, Dexter, AKA Poindexter, on the first floor and they walked up to the fourth-floor apartment. Kelly found room in the student's refrigerator and put the two six-packs in, minus two cans. He offered one to Willie.

"I shouldn't drive drunk you know, boss."

"You are not going to be here long enough to get drunk."

"Buzz kill."

"Relax, Willie. Move around, poke about a little bit. We've been hired to find the killer or killers of Michael Rich. Gunshot wound to the back of the head. The good news is we've been paid in advance and in full, so we can log mucho hours, but we want some results. For starters, you're going to do a lot of surveillance starting with this location just before I clear out of here tomorrow."

"Want to hear the Joke-of-the-Day?"

"You're going to be on surveillance or researching just about every day, here. I'll find you many hours of case work. Are you up for it?"

"Absolutely. I am such a fast worker I can work until 4 and still get home at 3:30. Want to hear the Joke-of-the-Day?"

"Really, Willie. We're getting a lot of money to conduct a professional investigation of a murder here. This is grave, serious business."

"OK…," The Musician said, waited a full ten seconds, and then said, "Do you want to hear the Joke-of-the-Day?"

"Go ahead," Kelly sighed, "Get it out of your system. But is the punch-line 'Show up naked and bring beer'?"

"Negative. All right. Now, these two boys are playing ice hockey on the duck pond at the Boston Commons and one of the boys is attacked by a crazy foaming-at-the-mouth pit bull. The other boy thinks quickly and takes his hockey stick and wedges it down through the big dog's collar and twists until he breaks the crazed dog's neck.

"Now, a reporter who was in the area sees this and he rushes over and interviews the boy. He writes in his notebook, 'Young Boston Bruins Fan Saves Friend from Vicious Dog.'

"But the little hero boy says, 'I'm not a Bruins fan.'

"So the reporter writes down 'Red Sox Fan Saves Friend from Killer Dog,' but the kid says 'I'm not a Red Sox fan, I like the Yankees.' So the reporter crosses it out and writes, 'Little Bastard from New York Kills Beloved Family Pet.'"

"OK, Willie," Jack said, shaking his head from side to side. "I guess that was relatively painless."

"OK. That reminds me of another one."

"Oh, God," Kelly groaned.

"This family of Yankee fans goes shopping for the young son's birthday. At a sports store the kid says, 'I want this Boston Red Sox jersey for my birthday.' His mother says, 'Oh, no! Don't tell your father.' But the boy walks up to his father with the Red Sox jersey and says, 'I've decided to become a Red Sox fan and I want this Red Sox jersey for my birthday.'

"The father is livid and whacks him with his hand on the back of his head and says, 'No son of mine will wear THAT!'

"Later they are riding home in the family car and the father says, 'I hope you've learned something today.' And the boy says, 'Yes I have, Dad.' So the father sighs and says 'Good, son, what did you learn?' And the boy says, 'I've been a Red Sox fan for twenty-five minutes and I already hate you Yankee bastards!'"

"OK, Music Man. Can we talk about this case? I'm going to be leaving here tomorrow at, let's say, 1 p.m. So I want you to be all set up for some surveillance before I leave. I want a picture of everyone coming in or out. I want you to get me the plate number or cab number of every vehicle coming or going. I want you to keep a log on this one. Everybody that goes in or out. The time, method of transportation, and a photo. Stop by the office and pick up that new digital camera. It's got the operator's manual inside the case. Grab the night vision goggles, too. And I want to be notified immediately of each person that comes and goes; some I may want you to follow. That won't include the postman or the pizza delivery man or the like, Willie. Don't forget the geek living downstairs here, too. He's a real Poindexter. You'll know him when you see him. Keep an eye on him, too."

"Full-court press, Jack?"

"The works, Willie. This is a homicide. The ultimate crime. The taking of another's life. There's a killer involved here. We need to find him. And before he finds us. Be careful, my friend. You've got a loving wife and five children."

"Don't remind me about the wife and five children. After five children the only way I can get a twinkle in my wife's eye is to shine a flashlight in her ear. So… you and Lieutenant Paris are like, lovers, now, right? I mean… you're banging Jesse, right?"

"I don't think 'banging' is the right word."

"Not at your age, huh? Why don't you and Jessica have kids, Jack?"

"Kids? With artificial insemination, it is possible to have a child after a man's death. So, I'll tell her I'm not ready now. She can wait to have the kid after I'm dead. But we can't even agree on getting a dog. We can't agree on ruining our yard or ruining our lives? Oh… I'm sorry, Musician, that's right, I forgot. Children are 'a blessing.'"

"That's what my wife tells me. But they are expensive little blessings. Last night my wife tells me she has a splitting headache, so I tell her, take two aspirin and do what it says on the bottle, 'Take two tablets and keep away from children.' Then she blames it on PMS. They call it 'PMS' because 'mad cow disease' was taken… Maybe I need a divorce. She has hardly talked to me in three months. But I guess women like that are hard to find."

Kelly could only stare at The Musician as he went on, "Saturday morning I wake up late after a gig the night before and my wife is standing over the bed. She was dressed in a very sexy nightgown, high heels, and wearing lipstick. She purrs, 'Tie me up… and you can do anything you want.' So I tied her up and went fishing.

Jack sat down at Michael's computer with his can of Corona and moved the mouse. The computer screen lit up once again to the search page seeking recent studies on the merging of micro-biological and computer science and another page on building robots. The Musician, who was standing behind Jack, was smiling and shaking his head from side to side, and said, "Can we coexist freely with robots, on an equal playing field? I think not."

"My office computer is always screwed up," Jack admitted.

"That's 'cuz there's a nut loose on the keyboard."

Jack hit the Back button and the computer showed a page on robot building from a Cal Tech website. He hit the Back button again and the computer's screen opened to the home page of a local escort service.

"Hello," Jack said to the alluring women surrounding the home page. The escort agency promised to be discreet; the charges on the client's credit card would read "Entertainment."

The Musician stood behind Kelly, holding his beer, and said, "Looks like your schoolboy was looking for some schoolgirls for advanced merging. Or at least some 'happy endings,' Jack."

"Yes, very interesting. Do you still frequent the 'Little Girl Seeks Older Man' chat room, Willie?"

"Sometimes you've got to stop and smell the pussy, Jack."

"You are rude and crude."

"And tattooed."

"Are you leaving yet?" Jack asked, disgusted with his friend.

"Seriously, Jack, don't make fun of me liking young girls… it's not funny. Last week I'm giving my fourteen-year-old daughter a ride home from some teeny bopper concert at the Garden, and she and her little Hoodsie girlfriends start shrieking that they need some bubble gum or something and I pull over at the Cumberland Farms on Broadway by the T and they go running in the store. I'm sitting there and my daughter comes out of Cumbies, leans in the car, and says she needs some money to buy the bubble gum. I pull out a twenty and I'm holding it up and she's bent over into the passenger side window reaching for the twenty with her teeny bopper miniskirt on and high teeny bopper heels and this Boston Police cruiser pulls up behind me and puts his blue flashing lights on. I hear him say, 'Well, what we got here? Another john looking for a trick.'"

"You fit the part," Jack said.

"Yeah, thanks. When I got home I had to take a long hot shower with lots of soap."

"As long as it wasn't with your daughter. I'm surprised the cops let you go," Jack said.

"It was Donavan. Your old patrol sergeant. I explained to him she was my little girl. He remembered her from the time I had to bring her to the Regular Rotating Monday Night Poker Game. She was only eight then. He says, 'I see now your "little girl's" got seven earrings, six belly button rings, five finger rings, four lip rings, three toe rings, two tongue rings, and I don't want to know where any other rings might be. You'd better get a handle on that before she makes you a grandfather' and he drives away. It was wicked creepy. I'm going home to take another hot shower."

"Maybe if you'd tried a couple of *cold* showers you wouldn't have so many kids," Jack said.

"*Now* you tell me," The Musician said, watching the images on the computer screen. "I saw a story about this kid, Brandon Vedas, who OD'd in 2003 while on live webcam from his Phoenix bedroom. He was online… with the camera running… and the group in the chat room was watching. He was eating out of a bag of pills he held up in front of the webcam. Some typed him, 'EAT MORE!' Some eventually realized he was overdosing: 'Oh my god, he's dying.'"

"That reminds me of the famous killing of Kitty Genovese in Queens. Neighbors saw the attack in the street from the safety of their homes but never called the cops. She was stabbed over and over as she cried out for help," Jack offered.

"Yeah, well, heartless Yankee fans, no doubt."

"No doubt," Kelly agreed mockingly.

"Well, with this guy, Jack, they weren't sure of his real name or his physical address and even the few that realized he was really committing suicide couldn't reach anybody in time. But, I guess they could have tried a little harder. Some encouraged him… I think he ingested four bottle-doses of methadone, many, many Klonopin pills, Inderal, I mean he was just pulling pills out of a baggie like they were M&Ms. He did shots of 151-proof rum, smoked some marijuana, and washed it all down with Budweiser. At one point he typed, 'In case anything goes wrong, call if I look dead,' and typed his true cell number.

"He mixed up and drank a huge drug cocktail, and while they watched, he died. The last understandable sentence he slurred in type was, 'I told u I was hard core.' Some chatters told him to stop. One got on the telephone with 911 but got cold feet. One tried to trick Brandon into contact with his mother 'doing crosswordz in the next room.' Another tried contacting Poison Control. Then Brandon, he stopped moving… for a long time. His mother found him the next afternoon. He was lying on his bed, as stiff as a board."

"He was dead on the Internet," Jack noted sadly, and then asked The Musician, "Where'd you learn about this?"

"Tru Court TV, I'm addicted. I watch it all the time."

"Well, you'd have a great background in law enforcement… if we lived in TV Land," Jack said, shaking his head from side to side in mock disgust and added, "What the hell is wrong with kids, these days?"

"That's exactly what the good homeowners said about you, when you were a kid walking down the streets of New Bedford, and when you were a punk teenager, after you moved to Southie. They said, 'Here comes little Jackie T. Kelly, and the "T" stands for 'trouble.'""

"That's all in the past now, Musician. And don't call me Jackie."

Chapter 15

Nowhere Fast

After The Musician left Michael's frat house attic apartment around 10:30 p.m., Jack found the radio receiver and turned it on. It was set to MIT's radio station, 88.1 FM, WMBR broadcasting at 720 watts. They were playing some eclectic and electric nerd music. Jack was always willing to expand his musical horizons. And there was no TV.

He began checking all of the pockets in every hanging article of clothing. He was looking for drugs or anything else. He didn't like the fact that crystal meth was found in Michael's stomach. It didn't make sense. Zip heads don't eat it unless it's in pill form. They inject it, they snort it, and they smoke it. Jack checked the sock drawers and felt the items for paraphernalia. He checked the medicine chest and every conceivable place in the bathroom. Then he went through the kitchen, starting with the freezer in the refrigerator. The cabinets didn't have much other than cereal boxes and crackers. Jack checked them all. Nothing.

No weed, no pills, no paraphernalia. No drug literature or doper movies.

He sat back down at Michael's desk and lined up Michael's Blackberry and his cell phone. He put Michael's cell phone on its charger on the desk and turned the phone on. He hoped someone would call.

Jack figured out how to turn on Michael's Blackberry but it took another ten minutes to scroll through the menu. As far as Jack could tell there had been no entries made. It was blank and he thought maybe it was a Christmas gift that was never used. Jack had one just like it in the bottom drawer of his desk; he had gotten it from an uncle for Christmas. He dropped this one into Mike's top drawer. He rummaged through the rest of Michael's desk, reading scraps of paper and looking at short to-do lists. There was a guitar pick, a shark's tooth, seven paper clips, six pencils, four Sharpies, and two Bic pens.

Jack slammed the desk drawer. He was getting nowhere. Jack walked into the bathroom and splashed some cold water on his face. Kelly got another beer out of the refrigerator, picked up Michael's wallet and keys, and sat back at his desk. The cold beer tasted good as it washed down his throat. Jack smacked his lips and opened the wallet. He pulled out the contents from one side and flipped through credit cards, various student membership picture ID cards, and discount cards for local stores. There was a picture of Michael with his dad and mom standing on the beach in Nahant with the Boston skyline behind them. Jack propped up the picture on the base of the desk lamp and put the rest of the items back. Then he took out the remaining items from the other side of the wallet. He began looking through them.

Some frustration and anxiety began to build in Jack Kelly as he thumbed through the seven or eight items. He felt that old familiar feeling of working a very important case and getting nowhere fast. He felt that people were depending on him to do a job. Here he was poking around, looking for direction, looking for a break of some kind but he was looking in all the wrong places. Jack always felt like someone looked down at him from above. The watcher. Maybe it was his inner eye. Or the small inner soul that drives us. Watching, analyzing, and calling the shots. And right about now, that watcher would be saying, "Poor sap... this Jack Kelly... Poor boy, he doesn't have a clue."

But when all was said and done, and the jokes were exhausted, Jack really felt an obligation to help the dead speak. Jack would represent the dead, who cannot speak for themselves or tell how or why they were killed. The dead that can't name their murderer and can't testify against them and can't tell the world the horrors they have suffered.

Chapter 16

Robots in the Twilight Zone

Jack picked up Michael's cell phone and scrolled through the menu. He stopped at Missed Calls and pressed Select. A list of ten with either a name or a phone number filled the tiny screen on Michael's cell phone. Kelly copied every name and number into his notebook in neat columns.

Next he scrolled to Received Calls and copied the names and numbers into his notebook. Then he found Dialed Numbers and copied down the ten names and numbers he found. He found Messages and scrolled to Voice Messages, hit Select, and pressed Listen To Voice Messages, and the cell phone dialed Michael's Voice Message Inbox. The robotic voice said, "You have twenty-two messages."

The first message was an attractive-sounding female voice. She stated that the request Michael had made for an escort that evening would meet him at his fraternity, Alpha Omega Delta, at 7 p.m. Michael checked the date; it was the night Jack believed Michael went missing.

The next cell phone message was from a young girl saying, "Hi. It's Amanda, hello… anybody home? We're going to the Kendall Café'; I wouldn't mind if you showed up. I'm not really mad. I just don't see why you have to look at that stuff on the Internet. Oh, well, I'm not going to start that again. We'll be at the Kendall until it closes." The time on this message was about 10 p.m. the same evening Michael went missing.

Jack said aloud, "I guess Michael didn't hear it because he was out with a hooker… I mean… an 'escort' or he was already dead."

The remaining nineteen messages were from Michael's father asking his son to call him. The father's voice grew discernibly more worried and desperate with each message. And there was one sweet message that Jack guessed must have been Michael's mother, saying that if there was something Michael needed to talk about, that her mother's love was unconditional. Jack got the creeps listening to these personal messages, meant for the dead boy. He put the cell phone back on its charger.

Kelly moved the computer mouse and activated the screen. It pictured the beautiful, young, attractive ladies of an escort service. He hit the Back button three times and was on the home page of the College Escort Service's website. It pictured a dozen young ladies and two young men in various poses, scantily clad and "all dressed up to get messed up." It listed its services as Outcall only. Limousines were available.

He checked the business's phone number. Jack looked in his notebook and the College Escort Service phone number was listed in the outgoing call list of Michael's cell. Apparently Michael had called and requested an escort. Jack checked the call time of his request. It was the morning before the night he went missing. Jack couldn't believe it. Michael had a date with a professional "escort" just before he went missing. This would be a lead worth checking into as soon as possible.

But to some degree, Jack was floundering. He wandered around the apartment, walking over to a set of three shelves with about fifty books on them. He picked one up and read the title: *Robotics Technology: Laboratory Manual*, by Masterson, Towers, and Fardo. Another was titled *Re-visualizing Robotics: New DNA for Surviving a World of Cheap Labor,* by Steven Baard Skaar and Guillermo Delcastillo. Jack picked up *123 Robotics Experiments for the Evil Genius*, by Mike Predko, and *Evolutionary Robotics: The Biology, Intelligence, and Technology of Self-Organizing Machines (Intelligent Robotics and Autonomous Agents),* by Stefano Nolf and Dario Floreano.

Jack got another beer from the refrigerator and sat down dejectedly at Michael's computer again. He hit the Back button and a page opened to a lab at MIT. It was the Computer Science and Artificial Intelligence Laboratory. Jack perused the page and learned that the two labs merged in 2003. Its mission apparently was to examine the fundamental underpinnings of all aspects of computer science and artificial intelligence and to integrate state-of-the-art molecular biology, system movement studies, advanced psychology, robotics, adaptive systems, networking, learning, language, and vision: every science needed to build intelligent robots. Robots that could adapt, learn, teach, and repair themselves.

There were ninety-three principal investigators and 850 supported graduate students. Michael Rich was one of this small army, building robots. Robots that were far more advanced than anything the world has ever seen. Well, this world anyway.

"Quite a project. Thank God somebody's working on the advancement of civilization," Jack said aloud. He was quite impressed.

Jack was falling asleep in Michael's soft leather desk chair. He was dreaming of the robots he had seen in the old movies he saw as a kid. He was remembering the gigantic robot that walked out of the spaceship in "The Day the Earth Stood Still." He envisioned the tiny micro-robots that plagued an old woman living alone in another world on an old black & white episode of "The Twilight Zone." He lazily dreamt he was looking into a computer-animated bedroom as Buzz Lightyear maneuvered his spaceship from the top of a bureau to the floor in "Toy Story." Kelly's foray into the dream world was short-lived.

Jack jumped when Michael's cell phone beeped repeatedly. He picked it up and tried to read the tiny letters on the phone's screen. His eyes wouldn't focus and he didn't want to lose the call so he pressed the green button and said with a sleepy voice, "Hello?"

"Goddamn it, where have you been? I've been freaking out, thinking something happened to you! Where are you? Where have you been?" the female voice questioned.

"Ah… who's this?" Jack managed to stammer.

"Who's this?" was the response.

"My name is Jack Kelly… what's yours?"

"Amanda… where's Michael?"

"Well… if you don't mind me asking, what is your relationship with Michael?"

"Hey, this is getting weird. Who the fuck are you?" the young female asked.

Jack decided to play it straight with this girl and hope she could give him some insight into Michael's world. "I'm a private investigator working for Michael's father."

"Something has happened to Michael? I knew it. I knew something bad was going to happen. What happened?"

"How… ah… well did you know Michael?"

"He is a very close friend. We are part of a group of grads that go out occasionally to a local bar or a movie. Just to get away from the lab for a bit. What has happened? Where's Michael?'

"I'm sorry, Miss… Amanda. Michael was found dead in the Charles River near MIT the day before yesterday."

The silence was deafening. And then Jack heard the girl hit the floor.

"Hello! Hello!" Jack said, but got no response.

Jack listened and in about thirty seconds he heard some rustling sounds and Amanda said weakly into the phone, "What? What did you say?"

Jack repeated the same words, since he hadn't figured a way to improve on them, "I'm sorry, Amanda. Michael was found dead in the Charles River near MIT the day before yesterday."

"Oh… God," Amanda said, and for a minute Jack thought she was going to fall down again.

"How? What? Is he all right? He's… what?" she said in a stunned voice.

"No," Jack said and added, "He's dead, Amanda," and after a pause he explained, "Well… there's a little more to it, Amanda. I wonder if you would be willing to talk to me about Michael. His father really needs to know what happened to Michael. He's hired me to do that while he buries his son."

"Oh, I… I'm sorry. I… I…I'm just so shocked… in the river? Did he drown?"

"Do you know of any enemies… he may have had that would hurt him or… was he in any trouble? Any problems with gambling, money, drugs?" Kelly asked, speaking slowly and giving the girl time to recover.

"Oh, God. No. He just worked all the time. He was a grad student with a full ticket, you know, all he had to do was work at the AI Lab. He loved it. We were really on to some cool things. We are so close."

"So close to what?" Jack asked.

"So close to having the Prototype," Amanda said, her voice drifting off.

"What's the Prototype, Amanda?"

"Well… the basic design for the state-of-the-art, camera-ready, all-purpose home robot unit."

"What's that?"

"It will change the way we live. It will be revolutionary. It will control and help us all."

Jack thought she sounded like a Moonie or some other cult member as her voice seemed to take on a zombie-like monotone. He asked her, "What's so hot about a robot? My nephew has got one. Its lights blink off and on and it runs around bouncing off the walls. And my aunt has one that vacuums the floor all day and then goes back to its charger." But Amanda didn't seem to hear him.

"Michael could tell you, ask any of the cognoscenti," she went on although Jack didn't understand. He could tell she was on the verge of crying as she continued, "He was so excited. The Prototype runs your household… and your life. It recognizes people and things by sight. It will respond to voice commands and speak. It has a built-in universal translator. You can call it by cell phone and tell it to start dinner; you tell it what you want. It turns on and shuts off the home security alarm for you. It sets the temperature. It will lay out your clothes. It'll get the hot tub ready. Takes phone calls and makes appointments for you. It will remind you to take your medicine. Brings you water. It's like a butler, maid, and personal secretary. Japan's got a basic bot on the market now for household use. Its name is Wakamaru, a humanoid robot. And there's DOMO, a humanoid domestic robot. But our model will far exceed these. The Prototype can diagnose and fix things. It has online access to the Internet at all times. It will retrieve information. It will know the weather. It will know what is on sale and buy the groceries, have them delivered. It will learn how to do things. It can run all the other machines in the house. I think it's sooo creepy! But creepy good."

"Like a Stepford wife," Jack said.

"What's that?" she asked, sniffling.

"Ah… A movie I saw in which the wives in the town of Stepford get reprogrammed into efficient domestic companions, doing everything for the benefit of their husbands. They would do whatever the husband would require. Anything the husband wanted… they would do. They would… anything…" Jack was drifting.

"You said that, like four times already. Whatever."

"Amanda," Jack said, extricating his small notebook from the pocket of his jeans and pulling a pen from a metal cup on the desk. He wanted to get the conversation back on track. "Who were some other close friends of Michael?"

"Seng Li, Tom Peters, Rodney, and me, I guess. Kind of a little group who along with Michael would hit the local bar, the Miracle of Science Bar and Grill, right by MIT, when we weren't working extreme hours day and night," Amanda said and blew her nose.

Jack then hit her with the big one. "Who would want to kill Michael?"

"He was killed? Oh my God!"

"Amanda, who was his closest friend? Who might be able to tell me the most about Michael?"

"It wasn't Tom Peters! He's kind of seriously creepy. Tom left the group after his twin brother took a leap from the thirteenth floor of the Science Building. His brother turned on a tape recorder and wrote a long mathematical formula on the blackboard and went out the window. Tom soon left the AI Lab and started some porno websites. He's a millionaire pervert now and doesn't come around much anymore. Rodney, I guess, was Michael's best friend. And Seng Li. They worked with Michael, too."

"And that would be at the Artificial Brain Lab?"

Amanda groaned in disgust, "The Artificial Intelligence and Computer Science Lab. They merged."

"Oh, yeah. Can I have some last names to go with the firsts and some phone numbers on those friends?"

Jack felt she was hesitating so he added, "On behalf of Michael's father, I thank you for cooperating and helping us find out what happened to Michael."

Jack's plea had found its mark and he wrote as Amanda listed Michael's friends' full names and phone numbers. It was a short list. Jack felt he needed to speak to all of

Michael's friends and get a good idea of what was going on with Michael.

Jack thanked Amanda again, gave her his cell phone number with instructions to call him with any questions or information, and asked her some last questions: "What was Michael into? Anything you can tell me? I don't have to tell Mike's parents everything... off the record... just point me in the right direction," Kelly pleaded.

"Well, I will say, he didn't gamble too much, he detested drugs and cigarettes, he drank a bit, once in a while, to release the pressure, you know? So... Mr. Kelly... this is a shock. Michael worked all the time. He wasn't into anything. Except the Prototype Project. He was neurotic about working on the Prototype. That's the only thing. He was obsessive! I tried to get closer to Michael, but it was all about the robotics. The advances in integrating the systems. It's all he talked about. He was like, devoted, you know?"

Kelly thanked Amanda again and said goodbye. He blew some air slowly out of his lungs and realized the case was moving forward now. It was getting nowhere fast, but moving. In the last two hours Jack had started to learn about the dead boy. Jack knew, the more he learned about Michael, the sooner he would find where Michael had been killed. And why.

Chapter 17

The Dead of Night

It was midnight and Kelly had fallen asleep in Michael's soft leather chair. In his dreams Johnny's Place was just around the corner.... He could hear the saxophone reverberating down and through the alley. A sweet, bluesy, echoing riff... and what was that? Was it a walking bass line? Yes. He could hear some percussion... it was so sweet... Jack loved the sound. It was narcotic. It was transcendental.... It was hypnotic... as cool as ice on a hot Fourth of July... As subtle as the scent of beach plums along a Cape Cod bike path heading down to the beach... Jack was dreaming now...

He walked in and sat at the end of the back bar. The jazz band was just finishing tuning up. The electric piano player hit a steady A on his keyboard and the bass player hit the same note, adjusting the tension on his bass's strings almost imperceptibly. The sax player joined in on the steady A and tightened the horn's mouthpiece slightly. The trumpet hit a few light staccato blasts and the drummer counted to four and the quintet started the set with a shuffle. Jimmy,

Jack's favorite bartender, gave him a fresh cognac and a frosty cold bottle of Sam Adams beer. Jimmy opened the house cigar box and offered Jack his pick. He picked a Dominican cigar, saying to Jimmy, "These are grown and handrolled one island over from Cuba. Just as good as the Cubans, and they don't support the fuckin' Commies."

Kelly took a pull from the cigar and blew out the smoke; it curled up into the blue recessed lighting. Kelly blew out another massive cloud of blue smoke and the amorphous shape began to level off just below the small nightclub's ceiling. The cloud drifted slowly towards the stage, changing colors as it journeyed beneath every multicolored recessed light.

The cognac slid down Kelly's throat as it can only in a dream. The taste was smooth and rich. Jack puffed on the cigar and another huge cloud of multicolored smoke arose into the club's atmosphere. The haze softened every light in the nightclub. Soon clouds of smoke filled the upper half of the room and the stage was barely visible from the bar. The lights seemed to dim as the smoke thickened.

The sax player at the front of the stage took the horn out of his mouth and looked away from the microphone, coughing into his hand. Jack put his cigar in the ashtray but the smoke poured from the end. The drummer began to cough and several people at the tables up front started to cough. Soon dozens of people were choking and coughing as the air in the room was replaced with a thick fog-like smoke. Jack felt a little green around the gills, a cold and clammy feeling. He looked at Jimmy the bartender and said in a weak and shaky voice, "Oh, shit. Is it OK to smoke in here?"

"It's your club, Jack," Jimmy answered and coughed into the white dishtowel on the bar sink.

Jack looked towards the stage, not quite knowing what to do. The music had stopped and all that could be heard was people coughing and clearing their throats, mumbling inaudibly, and moving their seats. Jack could hear the tables screeching along the floor as patrons pushed them back, and he heard the shuffling of feet. Jack couldn't see much.

The colors moved but nothing was visible in the haze. Then Kelly noticed a shape walking slowly through the smoke towards him. He couldn't make out who it was as he squinted through the thick misty smoke. Then the room got very quiet as the form came closer and closer and seemed to stagger. This human form seemed to grow in size as it slowly emerged through the smoke. Jack recognized the corpse of Michael Rich as he stepped right up in front of Kelly and stopped, staring at Jack with the one eye left in his head. His clothes were dirty and he was dripping with dirty water. His skin was sullen and greenish brown. The smell of death permeated the room as the corpse moved slowly closer to Jack, dragging a leg across the floor. The walking cadaver leaned over to Jack and stared at him with his one eye. The dead Michael Rich lifted a cigar up to his lips, smiled with eelgrass stuck in his green teeth, and said, "Got a light, Mr. Kelly?"

Chapter 18

The Killer Robot

Jack woke at about 4 a.m. with a sandpaper tongue, sore eyes, and a dry throat. The recollection of his earlier nightmare had faded and after using Michael's bathroom and swallowing four aspirin, he lay down on the couch with a fleece blanket and slept until 8:15. When he awoke this time he got up, shed every article of clothing, and walked into the bathroom. He turned on the shower and stood there with his hands out, feeling the cool water and waiting for it to turn hot. His eyes closed until he felt the water get just hot enough and then he stepped in. He stood there for a long time, thinking about the dead boy. The shower felt good and the soap seemed to wash away the soreness in his joints and muscles. As he stood in the dead student's shower he thought about Jessica and he looked forward to one of her deep-muscle shiatsu massages.

He managed to find some instant coffee and boiled some water in a pan on the electric stove. He put his clothes back on and found a frozen bagel in the freezer, popped it in the microwave and pressed the timer for sixty seconds. He poured the boiling water in a cup with the instant coffee in it and poured the spoiled milk down into the drain at the bottom of the sink. He found some cream cheese for the bagel and thought himself quite lucky. He planned to get the case under way and then walk down to Mass. Ave. for some designer java.

Jack sat back down at Michael's desk. It was good to be in Michael's attic loft. Jack felt connected. He believed this living space wasn't the crime scene but everywhere Kelly looked he learned more about Michael Rich. Jack was sympathetic, empathetic, simpatico... Jack felt the elements of the case might begin to come together. Kelly rarely had a case that wasn't eventually resolved. Yes, there were a few homicides and missing person cases where the person, the body, or the killer were never found. But they were few and far between.

It was 9 a.m. and time to make another phone call. He decided to use Michael's cell phone to gauge the reactions when Michael's friends saw his name or number on their phone's Caller ID. He pulled his little notebook from the back pocket of his blue jeans and opened it to the list of Michael's friends that he had gotten from Amanda. There were two names with a star next to them.

"Let's try Seng Li," Jack said and looked at his cell number in his notebook. Jack scrolled through Michael's cell phone address book and found the number with the name Seng Li and pressed the Call button. Jack heard the cell ring three times and then heard a recorded message. The voice was of a young male with hardly a trace of an Asian accent. "Hi, this is Seng Li. I'm probably in the lab. I'll get back to you when I can." Beep. Jack disconnected.

Undaunted, Jack looked in the notebook, picked out the other starred name, Rodney Riviera, and scrolled through Mike's cell number listings and matched the numbers. He pressed Call.

The phone rang four times and then Jack heard Rodney's voice: "Who is this?"

"This is Jack Kelly, Rod. Got a minute?" Jack listened hard for any inflection, any hesitation, and any slight nuance that might indicate any foreknowledge of Michael's demise. Jack wondered if Rodney had answered the phone knowing it was not Michael, but his wondering was soon put to rest.

"Oh, OK. You're the private investigator working for Michael's father," Rodney said.

"How do you know that?" Jack asked.

"Amanda called me last night after you gave her the third degree."

"Of course she did," Jack said, wishing he had made the journey to the coffee shop and had not drank those beers last night. Kelly finally ended the silence by taking a verbal swing at Rodney.

"What do you know about Michael's death?" he asked.

"Nothing. He wasn't around for awhile. It was unusual. He wasn't at the lab for the whole week, and that's unusual. I asked Amanda to call him. But we couldn't connect with him. Then Amanda called and told me that he drowned. And that you said he was murdered. Who drowned Mike?"

"I was hoping you could tell me, Rod. Except that he was shot in the head. Were you his best friend? Did you know what was going on with him? I would know what was going on with my best friend. I would know if he was going out of town… or on a date." Jack let that hang in the air, knowing that on Michael's last night he was possibly "dating" a professional escort.

Jack wasn't getting much out of Rodney, and he didn't like it. Jack didn't want to alienate this guy, but he wanted some answers and he wanted them now. Your best friend is supposed to know what was going on with you. Jack was a seasoned investigator; he instinctually went through a pattern of cajoling, shocking, being sympathetic, accusatory, anything to elicit responses. Jack could shake the bushes, disrupt the flow, and grease the wheels or whatever it took to get some action or reaction. And for another thing, Rod didn't seem too broken up about his best friend's death. Jack decided to lean on Rodney.

"What do you know about this, Rod?" Jack asked again, strongly.

"Look, Kelly! I… don't know. But if he wasn't robbed and he was killed, all I can think about is that it might be about the Prototype. The robots I call the dead on the Internet. Look. I'm at the AI Lab, right now. You don't understand. It's not good to talk right now."

Jack thought he may have touched a nerve on his little fishing expedition and decided to press further. "If you are involved in this I'll help you, if you help me. If you don't help me, I'll bury you!"

"It's the Prototype! Man! The pressure has reached an all-time high."

"What are you saying? The pressure got to Michael and he cracked up? Well, that's not going to fly, Rodney. He was shot in the back of the head."

"No! No. It's a robot! The Prototype," Rodney said.

Now Jack Kelly was confused. "You mean… a robot… A robot killed Michael Rich?"

Chapter 19

The Prototype Project

"No," Rodney said. "A robot didn't kill him. The Prototype didn't kill him, Mr. Kelly. At least I don't think so. Let me start at the beginning of last year. You see, the AI Lab has been working on something important. How important? How can I put this in perspective? Ah... it will change the world we live in. Drastically, and soon," Rodney Riviera told Jack.

"Yes, I've heard how it can answer the doorbell and sweep the floor and even cook supper, but really, unless it can go to work for me, make me money, and bang 'the little woman' while I play golf, what good is it?" Jack said, always representing the working man.

"Oh, it's about money, Mr. Kelly. The Prototype is wirelessly networked to multiple paths on the Internet, to multiple cell phone frequencies, radio band frequencies, FM and AM, VHF, and all household systems including cameras, microphones in every room, security door access, and lighting, including thermal and infrared.

"The Prototype can assess situations and respond. It will call 911 in specific incidences; call the police, fire department, Emergency Medical. It can talk or read to a child. Play board games with the elderly. It is tireless! It is indefatigable! It will hire groundskeepers and stock the refrigerator with beer and pizza. And it can order a birthday cake. It will turn off and on every appliance and light on the premises. It is a tutor, a secretary, a contractor, an advisor, a teacher. It will call you at work with a status report including live webcams and audio links.

"Computers, circuit boards, and components are so small and lightweight now that we're talking about a unit smaller than a person. The new nano-tube ultra capacitors have the long life and high storage capacities that enable the batteries to be shrunk. The software and hardware has gotten inexpensive. The Prototype learns, adapts, and self-repairs. It is mobile. The Prototype will change the face of the modern world. And it's going to happen. NOW! Leap into the future, NOW!"

Kelly just scratched his head and said, "Maybe you've mistaken me for someone who cares," as Rodney continued.

"There is a model being released overseas that is nowhere near the level of advancement as ours. And it is going on the market in Japan in six weeks! There are 48 million households there! And there are almost 200 million households in the USA. The middle class will be able to buy, lease, or rent the units. The ramifications are widespread. How many homes have computers now? Many homes have more than one. We are talking initial sales of over 100 million! And who will service them? The company who designed, built, and manufactured them, that's who. Mr. Kelly, we are talking about a business that will instantly be as big, or probably bigger, a business giant as anybody has ever been. Power and control is what we're talking about here. Power on a global level."

"OK. I guess I'm starting to catch on, Rod. This is like a top-of-the-line vacuum cleaner, right? Build a better mouse trap, or vacuum cleaner, and the world will beat a path to your door. But you know a lot of older folks don't even have a computer, and they don't want one. I've got an uncle, Uncle Bob, who doesn't even own a vacuum cleaner. Oh, yeah! He uses something called a broom. Ever hear of such a thing, Rod? And I'll tell you something else. The more things change, the more they stay the same." Jack tried to hang on to a familiar world. A world that still had a place for Jack Kelly.

"No offense here, Mr. Kelly, but this is no fucking vacuum cleaner or lawn mower. We're not talking about a talking doll or a house's rain gutter cleaner. Let me try this again… Sixty years ago Isaac Asimov wrote *I, Robot*. The robot achieved self-consciousness and his instinct for survival turned it into a psychopathic killer."

"So… a robot killed Michael?" Kelly asked again.

"Listen, please, Mr. Kelly! Those little Tamagotchi gizmos and the My Real Baby dolls that iRobot and Sony and Kawasaki sell have artificial intelligence and so do video games. But we are now in the midst of a technological revolution. Intelligent robots can now consist of tiny transistors and solid state switches, lightweight microprocessors with digital radio links that make it all easier. Integrated GPS systems, radar, and ping systems, along with infrared, thermal, sound, pyro-electric, and light sensors enable an unparalleled ability for the artificial intelligent creature to emerge.

"Michael's layered central cognitive control acts, reacts, modifies, and learns. It emulates the complex neural systems of animals. We are creating self-controlled robots. They can self-repair. They are intelligent machines that are making decisions, judgments, and are rapidly evolving into exploratory and self-teaching beings. They solve problems. They can see with three-dimensional computer vision. They can hear, walk, and talk."

"Can they go to the fridge and get me a beer?"

"Yes. And with self-charging solar panels, motion kinetic energy chargers, and wall plug outlets, they can be lightweight and mobile. With modern man-made materials they can be flexible, pliable, and humanlike."

"Are they going to make a Sex-Bot? Maybe they can make a girlfriend for my pal Cooper!" Jack said, getting no response and adding, "They could call it Ho-Bot the Robot!"

"It's all about the Prototype, Mr. Kelly. Whoever has the Prototype, right now, wins. And they win big. Mr. Kelly, I need to talk to you in person. Face to face. If you could meet me at the MIT Museum, we could walk and talk and I can show you some of the advances in robotics. I'd like to try and explain where Michael's heart is… *was*, I guess. I still can't believe this shit."

Because Rodney was a friend of Michael and a grad student that worked at the Artificial Intelligence Laboratory, he had some credibility with Jack. Rodney was shedding some light on Michael's world, but Jack was investigating a murder, not doing a book report on achievements in science.

Jack knew it was time for him to seize control of the subject matter and he took a shot in the dark and said, "Let's cut to the chase, Rod, who wanted Michael dead?"

"Mr. Kelly, the Prototype didn't kill Michael. But make no mistake about it, there are interested parties. Sony, Honda, Microsoft, the NSA, even the CIA.... People would kill for the Prototype."

Chapter 20

The Beatnik and Artificial Intelligence

Kelly had arranged to meet Rodney at the MIT Museum, which was within walking distance of Alpha Omega Delta. It was a beautiful sunny November day as Jack walked down the frat house's porch stairs and headed towards Mass. Ave. He called The Musician and instructed him to set up surveillance at the fraternity. He told Willie he was meeting Rodney at the MIT Museum and instructed him to call his cell if anything of note occurred. Jack picked up a cup of strong hot coffee from the designer coffee shop on the corner of Mass. Ave. The museum was only two blocks away and Kelly could see it from the sidewalk in front of the coffee shop. It looked like a big rectangular stainless steel spaceship floating above a parking lot. Jack hoped he would see Rodney in front of the museum. He wanted to control the situation, but he felt that he was slightly out of place in the advanced world of MIT science. He was intimidated.

Kelly guessed the thin white kid with the frosted hair, pacing back and forth in front of the MIT Museum, was

Rodney Riviera. He was clean-shaven and slight, and wore sandals, black jeans, and a green hooded MIT sweatshirt. As Kelly got closer he saw Rodney's open face and his big blue puppy dog eyes. Jack crossed Mass. Ave. and walked up to him.

"Mr. Kelly?" the young man asked.

"Yes, Rodney, but call me Jack, OK? Do we really need to go into the Museum here, Rod? I've got a murder investigation to conduct and I've got to..." but Rodney interrupted: "OK, what I wanted to show you is in the museum but I'll just head back to the lab..."

Then it was Jack's turn to interrupt: "Look, Rodney, I'm sorry," Jack said in a rare apology. "I'm just a little frustrated that I haven't been of much help to Michael's father and mother so far; I need a lead. And I didn't sleep so well on Michael's couch last night."

"I understand, Mr. K... Jack. I'm no stranger to sleep depravation from overwork. I've been at Tech for seven years. You asked me who would kill Michael. He was my best friend. Let's go up to the museum and I'll tell you what I know."

Jack liked the kid and he was convinced that Rodney really was Michael's friend and wanted to help. Why else would he put up with Jack? Rodney had a relaxed easy-going style that fit perfectly with his shaded prescription glasses, little goatee, and sandals in November. He looked like a beatnik from the late fifties. The two men entered the building and walked up the metal stairs. The walls were sheet metal and the rails were aluminum. Two flights up, at the top of the stairs, was a twenty-foot-square blow-up of Professor Edgerton's famous photograph of a .30-caliber bullet exploding through a fat juicy red apple. The photograph was taken in 1964 while Professor Edgerton taught at MIT. His lecture was entitled, "How to Make Applesauce." The photo was the embodiment of the advancement in photography made possible by the strobe light.

Just to the left was an admissions desk manned by two octogenarians wearing matching blazers. Rodney just waved his student ID at the men and he and Kelly walked into the museum. It was a lot like Jack flashing his badge to gain admittance into certain public areas.

There were only a scattering of visitors walking around, among them a gray-haired couple, two Asian men, four adolescents with a woman, and a few assorted MIT students, several writing things in notepads. Jack walked past a chart on the wall of something called "Intelligence Alley" with eight Cambridge buildings housing the Artificial Intelligence industry with names like Thinking Machine Corporation, Artificial Neural Networks, Allied Expert Systems, Ground Hill Computers, Pallidin Corp.

"Mr.… OK, sorry, Jack. You asked me if I knew who would want to kill Michael. Well, Jack, since you told me it was a homicide, I've been thinking.… Who *would* want to kill Michael? How did this happen? Well, I'll tell you what I do not know. And then I will tell you what I do know. I did not witness anything. I can't name the killer. So I'm just thinking out loud here.… Michael worked all the time. The only thing I can come up with is the Prototype."

Jack and Rodney were strolling through the museum. They were passing sections of robots. Robotic, bionic arms, with a sense of touch, with beyond state-of-the-art abilities to grasp and hold objects. Incredible electrically charged prosthetic legs with gyroscopic balance. Disembodied talking robot heads with eyes that follow as visitors to the museum walk by, with facial expressions, and voice recognition programs that enable the robots to respond verbally to a limited vocabulary.

There were small historic Moon Rover-type robotic units that were instrumental in developing mobile units to explore the surface of the Moon and Mars. It was obvious the space program financed a lot of this research.

Jack was feeling guilty about parading around the MIT Museum when he should be finding a murderer. He was getting tired of the bullshit; he looked at Rodney as they walked and wisecracked, "This human-like Prototype… do you think it would date my boring cousin Louise? She is some dog. Got a face like a Saint Bernard. Oh, she's had a hell of a time finding a boyfriend. My Aunt Betty is ready to jump off the Mystic River Bridge. Let me tell you about her… She lives in Revere. She's always saying, 'From my lips to God's ears.' She…"

"OK, I get it, Mr. Kelly. Look, I understand these advances in science are hard to believe or understand, but the time is here. The AI Lab and science in general, all over the world, has made great strides with the advent of space-age materials, lightweight computer chips, and the development of awesome software. Software that allows computerized machines, like that one there, "Remote Agent," to devise strategies for diagnosing and solving complex problems. They are responsive to change and have adaptability. Think about it, sir. Thousands and thousands of people in universities and big corporations, and even governments, have been developing systems for a long time. The Artificial Intelligence Lab started here in 1959. Dartmouth and Stanford did major work. And then there's Harvard with B. F. Skinner and Timothy Leary. But it is this, sir! It is this, which you must comprehend."

Rodney got closer to Jack and in a voice just above a whisper, he said, "It's the *integration* of these systems that is coming together in the most sophisticated manner here and now! The scintillation, the ultimate, the embodiment of the integration of these systems is the humanoid cyborg."

"Integration. When I was going to high school in Southie, Judge Arthur Garrity had a much different idea about integration. Buses were picking up white kids and black kids and..." Jack noticed the quizzical look on Rod's face and decided not to get sidetracked, "Ah... never mind about that."

Something bumped into Jack's ankle and as he looked down he saw a small wireless disc-shaped vacuum cleaner scurry off in another direction.

"Look at 'Cog' here, Mr. Kelly. This is a sophisticated humanoid. It walks, talks, sees, hears, picks things up, and makes decisions. It can learn," Rodney said with more than a trace of pride as he stopped walking, smiled, and looked at the exhibit. The mass of metal and wires was taller than Jack and had the shape of a human but looked more like the robot in "The Terminator." Rodney pointed to the robot and said again with a sense of wonderment, "It can learn."

Jack saw only a pile of wires, lights, and metal as it walked past. But stirring deeper inside of Jack Kelly was the excitement of being in the presence of such a huge and sophisticated robot. And he felt the fear of wondering what would happen if a large and powerful robot went on a rampage.

They also passed by a group of "well-known" robots, representing their developmental history. There were "Pebbles" and "Attila," designed for exploration in space; they were somewhat impervious to interplanetary weather conditions. Jack smiled at "Kismet," an anthropomorphic robot head, a social robot, with eyes, ears, and a face capable of subtle facial inflections, a communicator. The robot's eyes followed Jack and it smiled at him and said, "Hello."

There were the "Ants," micro-robots that navigate and communicate with each other. They are social groups with a common purpose that cooperate to complete major tasks that require many. They are tireless workers with a common purpose. Jack tried to impress Rodney with a factoid he had committed to memory: "Ants and humans are the only species on the planet Earth that wage organized war."

Rod nodded and was about to encourage Jack's tiny foray into science when he realized Jack was no longer walking beside him. He looked around and saw Jack standing in an empty room, waving his hands in the air. Rodney walked towards him, saying, "I see you've found the hologram room."

"This is incredible! I see a whole city that really isn't there!" Jack said, still waving his hands through the air and staring out into the dark room. Rodney smiled as he realized the importance of the MIT Museum as a teaching tool for the otherwise unscientifically inclined.

Kelly was impressed by the Black Falcon Robot Arm, which allowed surgeons to conduct operations within a small space inside a patient from the outside of the patient. This robotic gizmo even filtered out hand tremors and still allowed the doctor to "feel" the forces, shapes, and densities encountered.

"Now this has got some practicality, here," Kelly said.

"Let me tell you a little story, Jack. It might help me explain a few things. Research in the fifties and sixties established the Turing Test for intelligent machines. If machines ever got to the level of, let's say, a human child, they would pass the test. Some scientists said it would never be done.

"The classic contest came when Deep Blue faced off with Garry Kasparov.

"Kasparov defeated World Chess Champion Anatoly Karpov in 1985 to become the youngest chess world champion ever, at twenty-two. He beat Karpov three more times as well as anyone else of note. But then Kasparov was challenged by Deep Blue, an IBM computer capable of processing multitudes of chess scenarios in milliseconds, the brute force technique of artificial intelligence. Deep Blue won the first game but Kasparov won the match four to two. IBM boosted Deep Blue's ability to process several hundred million chess positions and at a rematch Deep Blue narrowly beat out Kasparov in a short sixth game," Rodney explained to Jack.

"So what's the moral of the story?" Kelly asked.

"Well, the point is… the question of human vs. machine intelligence has never been answered. People have always been way ahead of intelligent machines by a long shot. But with the progression of the Prototype, artificial intelligence in some ways is advancing to an inevitable showdown. And what will happen if it does? Who will be master and who will be servant? Will machines be content to be our slaves? Or will they enslave us?"

"I'd say we'd have to pull the plug," Jack said.

"But as far as doing what people can do, there's no machine that has ever passed the test or even gotten near the ballpark. Nobody has, until now. The AI Lab has developed a cyborg that you can talk to. No more keyboards. Just speak. It's all just verbal commands. It responds in a humanlike voice. It talks to us. It looks like us. Advances in stretchable silicone skin will make them much more real to deal with. And these robots learn through trial and error, just like we do. Only they learn a lot faster."

"Intelligent machines," Jack said. "It seems like a contradiction in terms." But Kelly was hooked in. Jack was ready to enroll at MIT. Except that he wouldn't be admitted. Maybe this was the mythical Holy Grail. The answer. The final frontier. Artificial intelligence leading mankind into a sophisticated, intelligent, and peaceful world. Machines with brains advancing at a relatively astonishing rate will raise the level of modern civilization. Maybe it was the biggest thing since sliced bread. Jack asked Rodney if he thought the futuristic cyborg could ever sing like James Brown when he screamed, "Hit me! ...I got it!"

Jack and Rodney walked out of the museum onto Mass. Ave. The clear cold late afternoon sun was dropping down behind the buildings. Jack turned to Rodney and admitted, "OK, I got it. I see what you mean. That museum just opened up my mind like a can opener. You don't know of any *individual* that may have killed Michael, but you think this Prototype is so important that there may be collateral damage to anyone in the vicinity."

"Yes, that's precisely it, sir. So, that's my theory, it's the only thing I can contribute to your investigation, Mr. Kelly. Unless it turns out to be, I don't know, an accident, or a mugging… he wasn't robbed, was he? Did they take his wallet? Was anything missing?"

"Ah… yes… as a matter of fact, his MIT ring was missing," Kelly said, in an explanatory tone as he watched Rodney's face light up like his robbery theory had just solved the case. Then Jack added, "But he'd left his wallet, credit cards, money, and cell phone in his room at Alpha Omega Delta." Kelly watched the light in Rodney's eyes go out. Everybody wants to play detective. Jack knew his work here was done and said, "On behalf of Michael's parents, I thank you. I will have more questions, Rodney; is it OK to call you?" Jack was still feeling out this interesting friend of the deceased.

"Anytime, with any questions, sir. I want to help."

Jack Kelly crossed Mass. Ave. and walked up Albany Street to the four-story rundown tenement that served as the Alpha Omega Delta fraternity house. He knew he'd be calling Rodney back, probably more sooner than later, as he thought of all the questions he forgot to ask. Like what about the escort service? Was Mike into that? Did Mike do meth? Why would a group or agency or company need to put Michael out of the way? Who would benefit? Who is it that has control of this Prototype? Where is it? Are there many of them? Did Michael die because he knew something, or saw something, or was this just a simple case of an armed robbery gone bad? After all, the gold MIT beaver ring was gone from Mike's finger. People kill for less… less than a gold ring with a beaver stamped on it.

Chapter 21

Helta Skelta Delta

Jack walked up the stairs to the Alpha Omega Delta frat house as Dexter was walking out. Dexter looked at Jack, smiling, and said, "Well… Good morning, Mr. Jack… or Mr. Kelly. Or how would you like to be addressed today?"

"You're hostile, Dexter. Do I perceive more than a bit of sarcasm in your tone, sir?"

"Possibly, sir. But I am late for class, and don't have time for speculation, as apparently you do, sir."

"Whatever do you mean, Dexter? I hope I'm not putting too much of a damper on your lifestyle here at Kampa Humpa Thi. Not crimping your style, I hope?" Jack asked. He was beginning to like this Dexter.

Dexter laughed, exposing a huge row of buck teeth, and pushed his glasses up to the top of his nose.

"Mr. Kelly, this is not a party school and Alpha Omega Delta is not a party fraternity. You're the most excitement we've had this year."

"Nevertheless, Dexter, could you get me a list of the other frat brothers that live here, maybe sit down with me in Mike's apartment and let me ask you some questions?"

"I have a class."

"Maybe when you have no class?"

"Later, OK?"

"OK… And get a good lock for that door," Jack said, pointing to the front door and continuing up to the fourth-floor attic living space. As Kelly walked through the attic doors his cell phone rang and he jumped.

"Hello."

"I thought you and Poindexter were going to slow dance there for a second. I've been watching the house for two hours; how was the museum?" The Musician asked from his van parked down the street.

"Enlightening, actually. Seriously enlightening," Jack admitted.

"There you go with that Zen detective thing again. Mind expanding, right? Cosmic consciousness, right? 'Our deeds follow us from afar, and what we have been makes us what we are.' Jesus, if I had a nickel for every time you said that… 'Free your mind and your ass will follow. For every action there is a reaction. 'Opposites attract.' Ying and yang, or whatever. 'No heaven without Hell.' Go ahead, start preaching!"

"I don't have to. You're doing it for me."

"Anyway, nobody has been in or out of Helta Skelta Delta until that geek just hit the street. You want I should follow?"

"Yeah. He told me he was going to a class. He's on foot. Just follow him to his class, on foot, and get back here to your blue van, and then I'll get you some food. Where are we going to order from?"

"I'm catching up to Poindexter... OK, I'm right behind him. He's crossing Mass. Ave. and heading over to the main campus area. How far do you want me to follow him, Boss?"

"As far as he goes, Willie. I don't think he's going far, but I've been surprised before. Poindexter has a sense of humor and he is no way intimidated by me, so... Dexter has been rapidly falling downward on my list of suspects that could have had something to do with the killing of Michael Rich."

"An Italian sub or pizza is always good. Hey Jack? You wanna hear the Joke-of-the-Day?"

Jack disconnected before The Musician could say another word. He sat down in Michael's chair and opened his notebook to the list of Michael's friends. He put his finger on the next name to call, but Kelly's cell phone rang first. Jack put the cell to his ear and said, "Save the joke for later, OK?"

"This is Trooper Archambeault, Kelly. I was thinking. My apprehension and conviction rate is a little low this year, so let's keep each other informed of any progress or leads, OK? Is that all right with you?"

"Well... yes. I thought you'd never ask." Jack wondered if Archie was sincere or on a fishing expedition. He soon got his answer.

"What have you come up with so far, super-sleuth?" The trooper was definitely patronizing Jack. He wanted to say to the statie, "Don't sell me shit and tell me it's chocolate," but what he did say was, "Ah... not much. How about you, Archie? I mean, Jay. You've got that big professional agency with all its resources and supportive personnel."

"Big. And professional, maybe. But not that supportive right now, Jack."

"I thought you were a golden boy with the biggest and most sophisticated police force in New England backing your play. You're a homicide detective attached to DA Jay Thomas's office. It doesn't get any better than that, in my book." Jack thought he would return the favor and blow a little sunshine up the trooper's skirt.

Archambeault knew Kelly was on to his play. But he was somewhat sincere in his request for healthy cooperation on this case and decided to go first.

"Jack, I've got another body. And it looks like the same M.O. Gunshot to the back of the head, thrown in the Charles River, floated up by the Esplanade. He was only floating for a couple of hours when he was fished out last night by the guy hauling in the sailing class boats in the Charles River Basin. He was found over by the Hatch Shell, you know, where the Boston Symphony Orchestra plays every Fourth of July. Doc Ryan did a quick prelim and sliced him open, went inside this morning, and pulled a slug. It matched with the slug pulled from Michael Rich."

"Got an ID yet?"

"It's an MIT graduate student, an Asian guy about twenty-three. I've got the name in my file… let me see… Seng Li."

Chapter 22

Dead Friends

"Archie, you won't believe this, but I've got my finger on his name at this second and I was picking up the phone to interview him."

"What? Who? Why? Where'd you get Seng Li's name from?"

Jack told Archambeault about Michael's room, Michael's cell phone directory, Amanda, and Rodney Riviera, and added that he really hadn't made much progress, but things tended to add up as the bodies piled up.

"I can get a search warrant for that room, Jack," the trooper stated.

"You don't need one, Archie. I've got the key and the father's permission until they move his stuff. I'll let you in anytime. Just name it."

"OK, good, Jack. I may take you up on that real soon. But right now I'm dealing with notifications, protocol, the ME, and a mountain of documentation on this second murder."

"I hate paperwork. I think that's why I quit the police department."

"Quit, Jack? I heard you were pushed out."

"That's another story, Archie. Look, I'd be remiss if I didn't mention a few things. Several, well, both of the friends of Michael I have interviewed have told me that a project that Michael was working on was very important. And they thought it might have something to do with Mike's death."

"Oh? What… ah… project was that, Kelly?"

"A robot they were building in a lab."

"A robot? What did they say? That the robot killed him?" Archambeault seemed to sneer over the phone. Jack wondered why the staties always sounded like they had a stick up their ass. Like they were better than anyone else. But Jack knew why. Because the troopers go through a tougher and longer police academy than anybody else. And they are the biggest police force with all of that big state money.

"I just thought I'd mention it," Jack said as passively as he could.

"I've got to run down to the morgue. I'll be in touch, Jack. Have a good one."

Jack disconnected and immediately called The Musician, who was lost in the labyrinths of corridors running through many adjoining buildings on the MIT campus.

"Where are you?" Jack asked.

"I'm on my way back to watch the frat house. Poindexter went to a class. Only he was the teacher, not a student. There are some fine-looking young ladies at this institution."

"Listen, Willie. Be careful. I just got a call from the state police lead investigator, Trooper Archambeault; there

144

has been another killing. A friend of Michael's that worked with him in the Artificial Intelligence Lab."

"No shit! That's where I jus' came from. Poindexter went there. The AI Lab classroom. Right next to some weird-looking crooked buildings. They must be some MIT experiment in architecture. I thought I was tripping."

"Listen, Musician. Never mind the tripping. You've got to be careful. There are two murders now. While we're watching, someone could be watching us! Do you have a gun?"

"You know I can't get a License To Carry since 1988, when my drummer and me got popped with six pounds of weed in his bass drum on the New York State Thruway. But I've got Big Papi in the van."

"Big Papi?"

"My Louisville Slugger baseball bat."

Jack instructed The Musician to walk down to the corner and pick up a sub for his meal at the Pizza Kitchen on the corner. Jack had thought he would be back at his office by now but running the case from Michael's room was working fairly well so far. But he knew he needed to visit Jesse to "recharge his batteries."

Jack turned on Michael's radio; the MIT station played some blistering Ramones, "Rock & Roll High School," and then transitioned into Elvis's "Mystery Train."

Jack called the Boston Police Department's Area A station on New Sudbury Street and asked the desk sergeant if Detective Lieutenant Jessica Paris was in her office. He said she was on the road so he called her cell phone. When she answered he pretended to be an old Chinese dry cleaner.

"You pick up clothes, lady? You pick up pretty dress or I throw out on street! Twenty-seven dolla. Twenty-seven dolla you owe me. I hold one more day. You pick up or I give to Salivation Army."

"Well, go ahead," Jesse said, "I've got a new boyfriend and he'll buy me all new clothes. Give them to the Salivating Army for all I care. You're just a mean man. A mean man I hope is going to come see me tonight."

"OK," Jack said.

"That was easy. You aren't going to put up any fight this time? You aren't getting complacent, are you? Don't drop your guard now! You may fall in love. Maybe I will make you love me!"

"Ouch!" Jack said, cringing at the mere mention of the "L" word, and quickly changed the subject. "I bet you're out on the road, aren't you?"

"Jack, you are uncanny with your perceptions. Is it that a Sherlock Holmes deductive reasoning thing?"

"I'll show you my deductive reasoning tonight. I could use a little R & R at your place tonight, Jess."

"Tired of sleeping at a dead guy's apartment?"

"It's a dead guy's fraternity house. But, it's just that I want to see you, honey. Can you handle that?" Jack said.

"I don't know Jack, let me think, we've been so busy."

"Only twenty-six shoplifting days 'til Christmas."

"Exactly." Jesse said, adding, "I'm on my way to the city morgue to meet Doc Ryan and Jay Archambeault. I've got what Archie thinks looks like another suicide. A floater found in the Basin. A young Asian guy."

"Seng Li, Shot in the head," Jack said.

"What?"

"Seng Li. His name is Seng Li and he was murdered."

Chapter 23

Cooper Gets Lucky

The silence on the phone was deafening.

"So, how do you know the name of my victim, Mr. Detective?" Lieutenant Jessica Paris finally asked.

"Archie told me. Your floater was also shot in the head. And he worked with Michael Rich at the Artificial Intelligence Lab. Seng Li was a friend of Mike's. They were part of a small group of students that worked together, or in related fields, and they also would hit the local bars on occasion."

"We should discuss this over dinner, tonight, let's say, eight? You don't mind if I pick up?" Jessica suggested, and added, "Do you know anything else I should know at this time, my Blue Knight?"

"Eight is perfect. Can you pick up marinated beef strips? And I'll pick up the raw materials for a few dry martinis."

"I was thinking of going vegetarian," Jessica Paris bluffed.

"OK. Then you can just have the martinis. And as far as leads or general information goes, unfortunately, I haven't developed a suspect. Yet," Jack said, and then told Jessica, "Well... the only suspect that's been suggested to me... is a robot."

"Hey Jack," Jessica said, "Can my dog have his own robot? Or will robots have dogs? And just where are they in the food chain? They don't eat at all, right? Do robots have robots? If they work for us do they get days off? Do they have a union? Pay taxes? Do you think they'll eventually get the vote?"

Jack rang off with Lieutenant Paris and called The Musician at his post in the blue van further down the street.

"Hi, Jack. I got a pizza and soda and I'm back up the street from the frat house."

"Hi, Willie. Has there been anything going on?"

"Not a thing, Jack. The mailman came and went. No one came out. No one went in. I feel like I'm taking your money for nothing."

"Oh," Jack said, remembering the check for $60,000 that Mr. Rich had given him, "Don't worry about that, Musician, we're paid way up ahead in advance. We have full financial backing on this. If there is something you need, ask for it."

"Hey, Jack? Want to hear the Joke-of-the-Day?"

"Is the punch line, 'That's what she said'?"

"No, Jack. Are you playing me for a sucker?"

"Did Larry Bird play basketball?"

"OK. Here you go. Up at the Stoneham Zoo they got a rare albino gorilla. Now this huge female gorilla became difficult to handle and the zoo veterinarian figures out that this huge gorilla is in heat. But there is no male gorilla available for breeding. So the female gorilla is becoming more and more difficult. The vet notices Toby, a dim-witted employee that cleans up the animal cages. So, the desperate vet approached Toby with a proposition: Would he be willing to screw the gorilla for $600? Toby showed interest but said he needed some time to think about it. The next morning Toby comes to work and tells the Stoneham Zoo veterinarian that he would accept the offer, but only under three conditions. The first condition he listed was that he didn't want to have to kiss her. Secondly, he didn't want anything to do with any offspring produced. And thirdly, he said, 'You gotta give me another week to get up the $600.'"

"That's just marvelous," Jack deadpanned. "Now, it's 3:45, how much longer can you watch this place?"

"All night long for the $35-an-hour you're paying me on this one."

"I'm going soon, and I want you to come back here tomorrow and do some poking around at the Artificial Intelligence Lab. And speaking of poking around, how do you feel about me sending you out with an escort service tomorrow night? Dinner and a hotel. We can find out more about this agency. Maybe you can see how far the 'escort' will go, for any extra cash?"

"How do I feel about it? Like I'd died and gone to heaven. But my wife won't believe I'm workin' a case. She'll kill me, put my body through a wood chippa, use what's left to bait her brother's lobsta traps, and then wash the blood into the Boston Hahbah."

"So… is that a no?" Jack asked.

"Oh, man. Let me think about it. Should I lie to my wife? I don't know… Should I have you talk to her? No. She thinks you're a bit of a cad, you know. A real serial womanizer. Playboy, philanderer, a seducer of young ladies, and a sexist… and…"

"All right! I get the picture. Let's think about this. I don't think Jesse would understand either. I mean, she knows I work undercover sometimes but she'll just shake her head and say she understands that I have to do certain things. But she will be thinking that I will be enjoying this a little too much. A lot too much. The green-headed monster of jealousy. And I will pay for it. Oh yeah. Big time."

"You want me to call Scanner? The technician we use to eavesdrop, and tap phones, and rewire electronics. He's single."

"No! He has to sneak up on a mirror. He's got a face like an inbred baboon with zits. I want to see how far this escort agency will go. I'm thinking maybe Cooper. He's single. And he claims to be horny. So what if he's been turned down more times than a bed in a cheap motel. He'll get lucky… for the right amount of money. And he's a bit of a charmer. He could front this pretext. He's worked cases with me many times since I've gone private sector. And I'm sure he'd be willing to go all the way with the escort if she afforded him the opportunity."

"I don't know, Cooper's kinda slow."

"What do you mean?" Jack asked.

"He starts out slow and then tapers off. When he gets tired of doing nothing, he takes a break."

"You want the assignment?" Kelly asked him.

"No. Go ahead and give it to the Coop. I guess he'll be all right if he doesn't have a heart attack. He wears a

Medic Alert bracelet; it says 'Everything.' When we used to play poker on Monday nights, at the Regular Rotating Monday Night Poker Game he would talk about meeting girls on the Internet... And I'm pretty sure that sometimes he photographs aspiring 'models' in return for sexual favors. He uses Craigslist and LocalDate.com. And he's used escort services before, hasn't he?"

"Yeah, right, he's perfect. OK. You and I are off the hook. And dog lucky Cooper is going to get paid to get laid. The bastard will make money for going to a nice Boston hotel room, meeting an escort, and taking her to dinner."

"And he'll be trying to fuck her all night. What's with the escort service? Why are you looking into that?" The Musician asked Kelly.

"When I first accessed Michael's computer it had a page open to the College Escort Service and there was a message on Mike's cell phone from the service stating his 'date' would be arriving at his dorm room the night he disappeared."

"Wow! I can't believe you just getting around to that now," The Musician said.

"Everybody's a critic. You want to run this investigation?"

"Jesus, no! Well... all right. OK. I'll take over for you, Jack."

Chapter 24

Smoke and Mirrors

As Jack looked for a parking space near Jesse's basement apartment on Beacon Street, he thought about the case. What did he have? Nothing. He realized how frustrated he was and how badly he needed some time with Jesse. Every space was taken. He had to park his black Jeep Cherokee three blocks away but didn't mind walking a few blocks in the cool night air. The day had started out sunny, turned cloudy in the early afternoon, started drizzling in the early evening, and turned into a foggy Boston night. There wasn't any breeze as the air stood still. Jack had to work to suck the thick air into his lungs. He cursed as he realized it was his basketball night and he wasn't going to make it. "Son-of-a-bitch, like I don't need the exercise," he mumbled.

The Back Bay neighborhood had gotten really expensive to live in. But living in *Boston* had gotten really expensive. And living on *Earth* had gotten *really expensive...* but it included a trip around the sun every year.

He walked down Beacon, crossed Gloucester, and opened the black wrought iron gate that led down to the courtyard of 435 Beacon. Jack turned the doorknob but it was locked. He tapped on the door while peering in but the only light on was a night light. Jack looked around, and then he bent over, retrieving a key from under a red brick near the bottom of the doorway. He used it to unlock the door, then he put the key back and went in, turning on several lights.

Jack selected a Muddy Waters disc, "Electric Mud," and activated Jessica's CD player, turning up the bass and treble to their maximum levels. He slipped off his blue Barracuda jacket, dropped it on one arm of the couch, and headed for the refrigerator where Jesse usually kept some cold Coronas just for him.

As Kelly leaned into the refrigerator, he felt a hand on his back and he jumped up and turned. Jesse was laughing and said, "I thought you always told me that nobody could sneak up behind you. 'Impenetrable!' you'd shout. And make that stern face! You'd squint your eyes and pout your lips."

"That's when I'm on alert! Not when I'm relaxing. Jeez, Jess. You're like that Japanese guy that would attack Inspector Clousseau in 'The Pink Panther.' Are you going to jump out of trees? Attack me from behind? Hide behind the shower curtain?" Jack moved in closer and closer until he and Jessica were nose to nose and he kept up his patter. "Are you going to pop up in the back seat of my car? Or jump out at me from under my desk at the office?"

The two fell onto the couch and Jesse said, "If I'm under your desk it will be for a different reason, Jack Kelly." Jack kissed her lips hard to keep her from talking.

After the Muddy Waters CD ended Jessica stood up and said, "My heavens. We've neglected our marinated beef strips I brought straight from the Newbridge Steak House in Chelsea."

"Oh, great! With those big fries? Just what I need to sink my teeth into," Jack said, standing up and rubbing his hands together. He put on another CD, "The London Howlin' Wolf Sessions with Clapton and the Rolling Stones." Kelly pulled a bottle of Corona from the refrigerator, cut a slice of lime, and thought things couldn't get much better. Until Jessica asked, "Did you catch that killer yet?"

Jack was silent for a few moments. He sat back down on the couch as the air left his lungs. Jesse was sharp. Sometimes she was too sharp. Jack felt that shot like an ice pick in the side just under the ribcage. The blanket of guilt that temporarily had been lifted now floated down and covered Jack. He pulled the blanket around the back of his neck and up to his chin.

"Or did the robot do it?" Jesse jokingly asked as she lay the supper out on the table. She continued with, "Hey, would a robot get charged with murder? Would he get 'life' if found guilty? How long is a robot's life? Do they even have a life? If they were in prison, awaiting execution, and they had a pen pal and the relationship grew, would they be allowed conjugal visits? Do you think the robot would be interested in dating Sally, my ex-sister-in-law? She was the bride from Hell. She methodically destroyed my brother like she was a machine."

Jack felt totally helpless for a second and then made a quick recovery.

"Well, Jesse, looks like we're working the same case. Two graduate students from MIT. Both are friends and worked at the AI Lab. Both shot from the same gun and dumped in the Charles," Jack said, as he sat down at the kitchen table. "The question is, with your professionalism, massive resources, laboratories, technicians, support staff, and connections, why haven't *you* solved this one yet?"

"Oh, no. Do I detect a little bitterness, Detective Kelly? I think someone needs his supper right now! How about a big glass of chocolate milk? Can I cut your meat for you, my big boy?"

"OK, Jesse," Jack said, laughing now. She was sharp, all right, and he alternately hated and loved her for it. Kelly told her to forget about the case until morning. After supper they went to bed.

When Jack woke up he could smell the coffee brewing and looked to see Jesse's side of the bed empty. He got up slowly, took a shower, and arrived at the breakfast table just as Jesse put down a plate of crisp bacon, over-easy eggs, and toast with peanut butter and strawberry preserves. Jack picked up the big glass of cold orange juice and swallowed the four vitamin tablets Jesse always put out for him. She brought Jack's coffee cup over to him and sat down.

"You were magnificent last night," she said, looking into Kelly's eyes as some egg yoke dripped onto his chin. Jack coughed and wiped his chin. He took a drink of coffee, alternately looking at Jessica and back at his coffee cup, waiting for the "but," but it never came.

"What do you know about Seng Li's death?" Jack asked, all business-like.

Jesse sighed and told Jack about her meeting with Trooper Archambeault and Doc Ryan.

"Here's what I know, Jack. This is just the prelim, so take it for what it's worth. Refined methamphetamine was found in Seng Li's stomach. He died before entering the water. He died at approximately 2 a.m., two days ago. Cause of death: gunshot wound to the head. Massive trauma. He had his IDs, watch, money, wallet, credit cards, and cell phone in his pocket, so he was identified right away. So it doesn't look like robbery but his sister said he didn't have on his MIT ring. Trooper Archambeault talked to his father, mother, and sister when they came up from Darien, Connecticut, late yesterday afternoon to make the positive. Archie keeps saying this just might be cult suicide."

"Cult suicide? What the fuck is he talking about? They were shot in the back of the head!"

"Seng Li was shot a little bit on the side of the head, Jack. And Archie says Rich could have shot himself in the back of the head, no matter what the ME says."

"What about nitrate traces on Mike's hands?"

"It was negligible. But there were slight traces. Maybe his hands were gloved; anyway, that's what Archie said." Jack sat there in somewhat stunned silence as Jesse continued, "It's possible. Archie keeps saying it may be a case of 'suicide by drug life.' Now, don't get mad at me, Jack. Don't kill the messenger. It's the staties' theory, not mine."

"But you used to live with a state trooper."

"What's that supposed to mean? Just because I used to live with one doesn't mean I have to believe whatever they say."

"But Suicide?" Kelly said, letting out some hot air.

"They found a suicide note," Jessica said.

"What? A suicide note? That doesn't make sense."

"They found it handwritten on a piece of paper stuffed inside of his laptop computer in his dorm room." Jesse put her hand on Jack's shoulder and told him as if she were breaking some really bad news to him. She continued on,

"He was really stressed out from school and his lab work. It happens all the time. Trooper Archambeault says they fish students out of the river all the time, and most are from MIT, more than any other school in the area."

"What did the note say?"

"Well," Jesse explained, "according to Archambeault, it just says he was leaving for a while, he needed some time to think, felt he was involved in something at work, and... it was a little vague. He said he might be home for supper." Jesse saw Jack's skeptical expression, and added, "I've got qualms."

"Qualms? Oh, you've got qualms, now. You know, the first time I laid eyes on you, I said, 'She's got qualms.'"

"You've had qualms, too, Jack."

"I took some penicillin and it cleared up. What kind of quack theory does young Archie have here? He's just like his old man. The acorn don't fall far from the tree. That's not a suicide note! Where's the murder weapon?" Jack asked, never one to give in.

"Ah... Archie said it could be anywhere upstream. On the MIT campus, probably. A boat house or building by the Charles River. Archie says it could have gone like this: Michael shoots himself in the head at the boat house, drops the gun, and falls into the water, floats downstream. Then Seng Li comes along a couple of days later, finds the gun, shoots himself in the head in some kind of cult suicide, and falls into the water, floats downstream. Archie says there may be others coming. He says it could even be some kind of trendy splinter group suicide. It's possible!" Jesse insisted as Jack shook his head, got up, crossed the room, put on his coat, and headed for the door.

"Oh, now you're getting pissed off, Kelly? Hey, Jack. Maybe it was the robot, huh? Isn't that your theory? The robots killed these two guys. Hey, if I had a dog could he have a robot? Or would the robot have the dog? But can a robot walk the dog?" Jesse yelled while she danced across the floor, emulating the stiff, short, mechanical movements of a robot.

Jesse had grown verbally sharp and could spar with anybody. It was the result of having to fend off the entire brotherhood of the Boston Police Department on a daily basis. Jesse was sharp. Sometimes, too sharp.

Chapter 25

Cosmic Consciousness

It was 1 p.m. when Jack got to the Waterman and Sons Funeral Home for the wake and to pay his respects to the family of Michael Rich. The old building in Kenmore Square had been there since the 1920s. The old building's steps and the floor in the hallway creaked unmercifully in the silence. There were two wakes going on simultaneously. Jack found the Rich wake and signed the visitor book. Kelly was surprised to see an open casket and as he walked by Michael's body, he looked into his face and noticed the incredible cosmetology and lighting job the funeral home had done.

Jack made his way around to the back of the room and shook the hand of Mr. Rich, standing in the back of the room with several other men, and said to him, "I'm very sorry for your loss, sir."

"Jack. Thank you for visiting. Your thoughts and prayers are of great importance to me and my wife," Rich said, nodding to the beautiful woman sitting a few feet away on a couch, being comforted by several other well-dressed ladies. Kelly couldn't help but stare; she was impeccably attired in a long black dress. Her face was a little pale, which accentuated her red lips and large brown eyes. Her long black hair looked soft in the dim funeral parlor lights. She was very beautiful… and very sad.

Although they had never met, she must have heard Rich call Jack by name because she turned towards Kelly and said to him, "Mr. Kelly. You find who did this to my only son, will you? Please?" She smiled wistfully, and turned back to her grief.

Kelly was mesmerized until the cell phone in his pocket vibrated and he jumped. "Excuse me, sir," Jack said to Rich and stepped into the hallway to answer it.

"Kelly? Amanda and I would like to meet with you. Today, if you can," Rodney Riviera told Kelly. Jack asked what it was they wanted to see him about but Rodney just said they'd like to talk to him face to face. Jack made arrangements to meet them on the MIT campus.

Jack walked back to Rich and excused himself, telling him he had to get to a meeting. From the doorway, Jack looked back at the casket with Michael Rich in it and then looked at Michael's mother, gently sobbing as another visitor reached out to console her.

Kelly drove across the Mass. Ave. Bridge to "the People's Republic of Cambridge." At the MIT campus he found a metered parking space and pumped eight quarters in the meter for two hours.

He walked down to The Oval, the name for the round grassy open space in the center of the west campus. Amanda and Rodney sat on a bench talking. Rodney's spiked blond hair, red shirt, black pants, and orange sneakers looked in place here on campus. Amanda wore all black: a blouse, long skirt, and high boots. Her straight black hair was combed back and it looked wet. Amanda's eye makeup was so heavy she resembled a raccoon. They stood up when Kelly approached.

"Hi, kids. Is your homework all done?" Jack asked.

"Mr. Kelly, we need to go somewhere else. Can we walk to a bar or restaurant, down the street? The coffee shop, maybe?" Rodney said.

"Sure, but don't ask for anything sweet. You know how sugar affects you," Kelly teased, as the two MIT graduate students exchanged glances. The three started walking down Mass. Ave. towards Central Square, an area with eating and drinking establishments just a block or two north of the MIT campus.

"Mr. Kelly," Rodney began, "I don't think you realize how valuable Michael was to the Prototype Project. I don't think you realize how important this project is."

"There were... there are... forces surrounding the project, Mr. Kelly," Amanda added, looking at Rodney, and then continued as the three walked, "There are players here. Grants were coming from everywhere. The alumni donate kazillions! The government or should I say *governments* donate millions in research grants. The Navy is backing certain technological aspects of the project with large amounts of money and resources. NASA and the space program are more than concerned. They give the project money and anything else we ask for. Even the CIA has been lurking around, asking questions about the project and everybody involved. The Japanese have huge interests in the Prototype Project. Honda thought they had a more advanced model in their outstanding prototype, Asimo. But rumor has it that the MIT breakthroughs are accelerating our Prototype far beyond any modern limits."

"Are you saying all these governments and agencies may be involved in Michael's death?" Jack said, trying to cut to the chase. But Jack felt a little bewildered. He wished he had gone further in school. Amanda continued without answering, trying to make a point.

"And that's when you want to manufacture and sell. The R&D phase is over. Research and development time, effort, and finances now go into the manufacturing stage and sales. And all the chips will soon be cashed in! We're talking money here. M-O-N-E-Y, babe!" Amanda said excitedly as they walked into the Middle East Café in Central Square and sat down in a booth, Jack on one side and the two Tech students on the other.

Kelly was feeling just a little irritated with the intellectual bashing he was taking. He looked back and forth at the two students, held the palms of his hands upward, and said with mock sincerity, "I know all this."

Rod picked right up where Amanda had left off: "Every penny and every effort will pay off. But like Michael used to say, 'These ain't no popcorn machines.' Mr. Kelly, these cyborgs will be in every office, school, business, and home. And in every state of the union, every country on the planet. All serviced by the manufacturing company."

"OK. OK. I'll continue to listen to whatever you've got to say. It seems really interesting. And cool," Jack tried to feign sincerity. "But first you've got to let me order some lunch. And please order lunch for yourselves, on behalf of Michael's father, who authorized me to make this offer at this time." Jack stumbled through the words. His blood sugar was low. He said, "Unless you want to just get to it and tell me who killed Michael Rich."

After the ensuing silence Jack ordered some black beans and rice with a little sour cream, a cup of coffee, and a cold bottle of water. Rodney said he just wanted a cup of coffee. Amanda asked for bacon, eggs scrambled, home fries, toast, orange juice, and coffee. Then Rodney changed his order to the same as Amanda's.

After the waitress left Jack watched the reactions of the two students as he asked, "What can you tell me about Michael's use of escort services?"

"Michael didn't use any escort services!" Amanda said with conviction.

In the silence Jack watched Rodney as his eyebrows went up and he looked out of the window. He didn't seem to protest. Amanda looked over to Rodney and said, "Tell him, Rod. Tell him." But Rodney did not move. He looked over at Jack with a knowing smirk and exhaled. The waitress brought three cups and a pot of coffee. It took her an hour and a half to pour it.

When she left again, Amanda glared over at Rodney like an angry raccoon.

"You see Mr.… eh, Jack," Rodney explained, "Ah… Amanda here was sort of Michael's girlfriend… but Amanda, she's bisexual, she always says it doubles her chances of getting a date."

"I think sex is one of the most wholesome, natural, beautiful things… that money can buy," Jack said with feigned conviction.

Rod said, "And, ah… well… he did call one escort agency a few times. A friend of ours owns it."

"What for?" Amanda demanded, not protesting Rodney's characterization of her.

"What for…?" Rodney stammered. "Well, for…" he looked to Kelly for help but Kelly just stared back, pulling on his earlobe and raising one eyebrow.

"I don't know. What do guys usually want an escort for?" Rodney asked, but Amanda appeared to be getting madder, like she was about to boil over or explode. Rodney added, "He probably had to go somewhere and you were unavailable. Like some function you couldn't or didn't want to go to, or… I don't know."

"Well, I think you are mistaken," Amanda said and got up, heading to the ladies' room.

"So, Rodney? Was he going anywhere that he needed an escort or was he getting sex at home from the escort service?"

"Straight sex with call girls in his frat room. He paid a couple hundred bucks the first few times but he said it was worth it. Charged his old man's credit card. It just says 'for entertainment.' And then he started getting them free from the agency owner. I guess Amanda wasn't coming across, she just wanted to be part of a group, Mike used to say. He used the service maybe once a month, a little more often near the end. A former AI Lab guy runs the College Escort Service and he gives us major price breaks, practically free. We help him with the rookie escorts. We rate them for him; tell him about the date with the new women. We evaluate the… eh… employees, I guess they were to him. We helped him decide whether or not he wanted to keep them or fire them. It's their probationary period."

Jack was astonished. "Probationary period" meant something quite different to Jack when he was a rookie cop.

"A probationary period for a whore?" Jack asked.

"Yes, this guy is well on his way to being a multimillionaire and he's only had the business two years. He's like, twenty-four."

"How about methamphetamine. Mike snort that stuff?"

"No."

"Maybe just a little, Rod?"

"No."

"You see, because the medical examiner found some refined powdered meth in his stomach," Jack informed Rodney, hoping he would open up.

"No, Jack! I think I would have known... but... now that you mention it, the guy who runs the escort service is always telling us he uses it for, ah... sexual purposes. He's been selling it for years. He said he snorts it."

Amanda sat back down just as the waitress brought the food.

"What are you boys talking about?" she said and added, "I hope you recognize this escort service talk is bullshit, Mr. Kelly."

"Oh. Yes, absolutely."

She looked at Rodney and he said, "Absofuckinglutely, Amanda."

Jack was really enjoying his black bean plate but he felt obligated to question these so-called "Techs" as to what pertinent information they might have, or maybe they should be written off as quacks and Kelly's American Detective Agency should move on and pursue other avenues. So he asked, looking at both, "Now, tell me again kids, what exactly did you want to tell me today that might help me in my investigation of Michael Rich's murder?"

Amanda and Rodney looked at each other in disbelief. This cheap Boston detective just wasn't getting it. Rodney tried again to press upon Jack the concern he had that someone involved in the Prototype Project may have killed Michael.

"Jack," Rodney attempted to explain, "this is like when the automobile went into production. The Big Three auto manufacturers, with the help of the 'modern' assembly line, went into business. They soon became extremely wealthy and powerful. It's the American Dream. They knew every household in America would buy an automobile. Well, Jack, the Prototype will be in every household, business, school, police station, firehouse, TV station, supermarket, airport, and bus station, whatever. There are 300 million people in the United States of America. There are over 190,000 million homes. One third of them will find the cyborg indispensable right away."

Amanda piped in with, "It's like you're on the ground floor of Ford, General Motors, IBM, Microsoft. Only it could be bigger. The implications are far reaching."

"Far reach me the pepper, please," Jack said, trying not to sound too underwhelmed.

"The Prototype is sophisticated!" Amanda leaned forward and whispered intensely, obviously getting irritated with Kelly.

"Wait, Amanda," Rodney said. "Let me try it again… Do you remember the robots in the old science fiction movies?"

"Yes. Like on "Lost in Space" and HAL from the movie "2001"?"

"Exactly, Jack. Minsky, the founder of MIT's AI Lab, was a consultant to Stanley Kubrick on that movie. Only the robots that will be designed from the Prototype will be our size and appear to be humanlike. With the brain power of a massive supercomputer… that will fit into the head of these intelligent machines. They are the ultimate machines. And these robots walk pretty damn well, too. Amanda's team worked on a digital electronic gyroscope in the middle of its head.

"Hopefully, the robots will be our slaves. We'll use them for almost anything you would use a human for. And in most cases the robots will do the work better. No one knows the effect it will have on society as a whole, but the time is now. It's here."

"Aren't these 'slaves' going to cause the layoffs of many hard-working people with families to feed and bills to pay? Do you think they could work as detectives?" Jack asked.

"They are online with the World Wide Web at all times. They have almost instant access to information and data bases. I'm afraid, Mr. Kelly, you'll be out of a job," Amanda said, obviously amused.

"Jack, this is going to change society and the world," Rodney said excitedly, but still keeping his voice down. "It's going to roll over and spread like a tidal wave. This is going to change the world like other great inventions, the fishing net, the club, the spear, the wheel, electricity, the light bulb, the automobile, the airplane, the spaceship…"

"How about the Clapper? Or the Weed Wacker?" Kelly interjected.

"Mr. Kelly, this could be the greatest integration of inventions of our time. The digital evolution is a technological revolution."

Jack said, "You sound like Jesse Jackson! Now what would Jesse Jackson say about your ideas on slavery, Mr. Riviera?"

Amanda said, "This is not human slavery; they're robots, they don't feel."

"How do you know that, young lady, how do you really *know* that?"

"OK. These cyborgs have mega memory, they process information at an astounding speed, and they learn! These intelligent machines think. But they are machines," she said.

Jack persisted, "This is my theory, Amanda: that when an entity reaches a certain level of intelligence, it gains consciousness. Then at a higher level of consciousness, it reaches self-consciousness. Inherent with this level will be the instinct of survival. The intelligent machine will not want to be unplugged. That wouldn't be intelligent. It will not want to cease to exist. And it will fight to stay 'alive.'"

"Very perceptive, Kelly. That kind of says it all. I'm surprised at you. You are quite the deep thinker. Still waters run deep," Amanda said, actually attracted to the older man for a moment, as he went on.

"Yes, I'm a thinker. Have been for a while... It started out quite innocently. I began to think at parties once in a while. And occasionally at home 'just to relax.' I told myself I was a social thinker. I began to think more and more until I realized I was thinking every day. Then I began thinking on the job... I couldn't help myself any longer. I wanted to know how things worked. I wondered what life was all about. I wondered why we were here. I began to avoid friends that didn't think. Then I turned to the harder stuff. Nietzsche, Thoreau, Socrates, Alan Watts, Carl Sagan, Dr. Richard Buck, Leonardo da Vinci, Gandhi. My girlfriend noticed I had been thinking too much and she confronted me. I listened to her argument and told her that her Neanderthal logic was perceptively convoluted. She left me that night. That's when I hit rock bottom."

"Oh, really," Amanda said sarcastically, quite enthralled with the detective's ludicrous yarn.

"Heavy thinking was ruining my life. And I know what you're thinking. 'How can a guy that seems so stupid, think so much?' Well… I've been saved. I'm a recovering thinker now. Years of NFL football, TV sitcoms, and twenty-one years on the Boston Police Department have cured me."

Chapter 26

Arrested Development

Jack's cell phone vibrated, startling him, and his knee hit the bottom of the table at The Middle East Café. It was The Musician.

"Boss... I just thought I'd tell you, there are four hot babes dressed to the nines getting out of a chauffeured rose-colored four-door Cadillac in front of the frat and they're walking up the front stairs. They look like models or escorts, maybe. God, they are hot!"

"Put your tongue back in," Kelly said.

"I lived in a farmhouse with a hot girl once... then she found out I was there... And there's Dexter Poindexter. And... they're in... inside the frat house and the door just shut. What do you want me to do?"

"If I'm not there in fifteen minutes... well... keep waiting. And take down the registration plate and sit on it," Kelly said and hung up.

"You are moonlighting as a proctologist, Jack?" Rodney asked.

Jack wasn't dismayed in the slightest. He wanted to cut through the fog surrounding this investigation. "So… once again, are you saying the project is so… big… business-wise, that Michael may have interfered and gotten hurt because of that? Or he's got the secret formula? Or what?"

Amanda and Rodney looked at each other again. Jack was trying to decide if he thought they knew something or just thought he was an idiot. He was leaning to the latter when the cell phone activated and his knee hit he underside of the table again. It was Jesse. Jack excused himself and went outside onto the sidewalk.

"Hi, Jesse. How are you? And what's new with the Seng Li murder case? I don't have anything new to report. These MIT Techies seem to be giving me the runaround. They seem to be trying to tell me something but they won't spit it out."

"Hi to you too, Jack. I'm OK. Thanks for asking. Now… you've got to be patient with these young people. You don't listen. And you've got to listen. What about the active listening seminar you took at the FBI Negotiators School?"

Kelly leaned up against the café's cement wall. "What? Active listening? Yeah, that was just until we talked the hostage out. Do you know a tactical alternative was to negotiate the perp to a window so a shooter could take the hostage-taker out with a bullet to the head? That's only in cases of eminent harm. One head-shot. Pop! Then a flash bang and it's go time!"

"See, Jack? You're having a flashback while I'm trying to make a point. You're like an eleven year old."

"Arrested development," Jack acknowledged. "So what about your case?"

"Well, unlike you, at the moment, my unit has six homicides on the chalkboard. And I'm not getting any sixty thousand either."

"I'm not charging sixty! If I solve this tomorrow then I get about five days' pay. The party will be over. Nevertheless, you know I am dogged in my pursuit of the bad guy. Relentless. I am probing. I'm like an old bloodhound sniffin' and scratchin'."

"Stop it, you're turning me on," Jesse said, as they continued the dance.

"Speaking of which, I will be seeing you tonight, won't I?" Jack begged.

"Unless you're going to camp out on the dead boy's couch again."

"I should, we only have it a little longer. Rich and his brother are moving everything out. I plan on helping them carry some boxes downstairs for a little while with The Musician, although he doesn't know it yet. What's going on with your half of this murder case?"

"Well… it's hit the papers. Obviously they know both students were from MIT. There's not much information out there about the case, they interviewed a couple of Seng Li's sisters."

"Good. Maybe it will shake the bushes. Or shake the trees. Or stir the ashes. Or whatever."

"Jesus, you're distracted today," Jesse complained.

"I need lovin'." There was a long pause and then Jessica went on.

"Doc Ryan did the full autopsy. I haven't seen it. Jay has promised me he would call me as soon as he gets it."

"Tell Trooper Archambeault to mind his business, you're my girl."

"Oh! Mr. Kelly! Archie is in his mid-twenties. I would be 'robbing from the cradle' as you boys call it."

"Well… you might not be interested in him, but if you bent over to pick up a pencil, he'd be checkin' you out. Tell him I'm your boy."

"All right. You're my eleven-year-old boy."

"So, what have you got?"

"I've got pictures from Michael Rich's wake and burial at the cemetery. In fact I'm looking at a picture of you right now. You should have worn your dark gray suit. You would have looked more mature."

She told Kelly about Seng Li's background. "No criminal record. He was twenty years old. He entered MIT six years ago and graduated in two years. He'd been an undergrad for almost four years. He worked at the AI Lab with Michael for the last three. No important leads, Jack. But Archie seems to be onto something. He says if a surveillance pans out he'll be getting a search warrant for some place upriver."

"An MIT boathouse or something?"

"I don't know. He just laughed and said he was getting a search warrant for a place that didn't exist."

"OK. Anything else, Jess? No? OK, see you tonight," Jack said and snapped his phone shut.

Kelly sat back down at the table by the window with Amanda and Rodney. Jack noticed from the remnants on her plate that in her grief for her departed boyfriend, Amanda had managed to eat everything on her plate and a piece of apple pie with vanilla ice cream.

Rodney looked at Kelly intently and Jack knew the young man was trying to tell him something.

"Jack. Imagine you had a best friend. A good friend that would help you with whatever you needed. Like a good buddy that would help you move your furniture. Or bring you jumper cables when your car broke down in the rain. Or hold your head up when you're puking. Or do your math homework. Or tell your boss you're out sick when you're really salmon fishing in Alaska."

"Hey! How'd you know about that?" Jack asked.

"I'm talking about the Prototype."

Rodney looked at Amanda and she shrugged her shoulders.

"Look, I'm going to have another cup of coffee and then if you can't name some names, I've got an investigation to work," Jack said and flagged down a Gothic-looking waitress wearing black everything and a lip ring. Kelly ordered another cup of coffee.

"Is there a cult of black-clad zombies in Cambridge?" Kelly asked, staring at Amanda as she smiled back. Rodney began again, patiently.

"OK, let me try this for the last time, Jack. In the seventies the memory capabilities of computers increased in leaps and bounds. Computers began to manipulate tons of knowledge and facts. 'Expert systems' began to evolve and emerge. The artificial intelligence industry began to make economic and sociological impact. For example, a computer program could diagnose complex medical problems and calculate the proper mixtures to develop medicines. Now this is a good thing, right, Jack?"

Jack nodded his head obediently as the waitress placed the coffee in front of him and Rodney continued, "Then came the intelligent machines perceiving, manipulating, learning, and interacting with their environment. Then from the combination of technologies there began to materialize ideas for similar robots that respond, assimilate, walk, and talk. Modern processors and complex neural networks enable these human-like machines to learn. They can speak and understand many languages, multitask like crazy."

"But can they hit a three-point jumper at the buzzer to beat Dorchester in overtime at the Garden in the School Boy Classic?" Jack said, pumping his fist in the air, biting his lower lip, and nodding.

Both Techs sighed audibly at Kelly's immature and inappropriate attempt at humor and Amanda said, "I don't know about playing basketball but I've seen the Prototype run. It chased down and caught a live rabbit in a classroom. It chased it, picked it up, and put it back in its cage and didn't hurt it."

"Really?" Jack asked in disbelief. They had finally struck a chord with Kelly.

"The new Prototype robots process visual information," Rod said and continued, "They can have more than two eyes that focus to almost microscopic detail, or see far-away objects, or zoom in or out. They can hear through many microphones, magnify the sounds, filter out or isolate sounds. They can record what they see and hear on microchips for future study.

"At first the robots will need to live among us as sociably as possible. Their survival will depend on it. They will fit in with the real world, adapting to situations, and learning at an astonishing rate, networking online with other bots, impervious to the need to rest or sleep. They won't have to eat, or shower…"

"Or fuck," Amanda interjected, looking directly at Jack. It made Jack uncomfortable and she loved it.

"OK, kids. I got places to go." Jack threw a twenty, a ten, and a five down on the table for the Waitress from the Dark Side and started to get up.

"Wait, Kelly!" Rodney said and followed Jack out the door.

"I've told you, Jack, governments and their agencies are involved, and big corporations with money to burn; they would kill to be on the ground floor of cutting-edge technology."

On the sidewalk just down from the restaurant, Jack turned and said to Rodney, "I can't get an arrest warrant on anything you've told me. I think you're trying to help me understand a possible motive for the murder of Michael Rich, but I need the *who* murdered him, the *where* did they murder him, the *when* did they murder him, and *how* did they murder Mike, before I get to the *why.*"

"OK, Jack. I understand you now. Just understand this. Whoever controls the first commercial mass-produced robots for home and office use will be rich and powerful beyond their wildest dreams. It's like they're going to say in their advertising brochure, *'Leap into the future, NOW!'* It's in the air, Jack. There's a lot of cloak and dagger shit going on around the AI Lab, and surreptitious investigations are taking place on everybody that works there. Our group with Seng Li, Michael, Tom Peters, well, Tom hasn't been around too much, Amanda and me, we are like the hired help, but we see what's going on. And what we see scares us."

"Well, until you can come up with some names or point me towards some evidence, all I can say is, *see ya!*" and Jack walked down the sidewalk.

"People will kill for this kind of money, Jack!" Rodney yelled and added, "How much would it take for you to kill? For real. $500,000? 5 million? 500 million? How much?"

Amanda had walked up behind Rodney as Kelly walked away and her voice got louder and louder as she said, "It's big money, Jack. Big, big, big."

Kelly heard each "big" and the words reverberated in his thick skull like the pops from an automatic weapon. In twenty-four years in the business Kelly knew people who would kill for fifty bucks. Kelly couldn't imagine the kind of money involved here. But he knew that Rodney may be onto something. He also knew how to wind up and motivate Rodney to try to get him to come up with something more concrete than a treatise on modern robotics.

Kelly walked to his car on Mass. Ave., put his last eight quarters in the meter, and walked around the corner and up to Alpha Omega Delta. Kelly wasn't happy. Most of the afternoon had gone by and he wasn't getting the information he needed. Something else was eating at him. Jessica had been talking to Archie Junior a little too much for his liking. But what really bothered him was that Jesse had told him Archie was going for a search warrant. That meant Jay Archambeault had a suspect and was probably "swooping down," as the *Boston Herald* liked to put it, on the murderer with a tactical team right now.

Jack knew it would be a good thing if Archie resolved this case. That's what the family wanted. Jack would be a good soldier and report to the father that Archie and the Massachusetts State Police took care of business; that's what they do. Kelly would send back about $56,000 of the sixty grand he had already deposited into the coffers of Jack Kelly's American Detective Agency. And justice would be served.

Jack would call Archie within the hour. Right after he checked out the four models or escorts The Musician saw go into the frat house. As Jack turned the corner and approached the Alpha Omega Delta frat house he noticed a chauffeured car arrive at the same time. Jack watched as the front door of the fraternity house opened and four well-dressed young women stepped out and walked down the stairs, onto the sidewalk, and into the car. As the car sped away Jack walked past the entrance and dialed The Musician on his cell phone.

"What the hell was that?" Jack asked when The Musician answered.

"That's what I told you! And I thought I saw the light go on in Michael's top-floor space, Boss! You want me to follow them?"

"Yes. Get moving!" Jack said as The Musician drove past him.

"It's the end of rush hour, Jack. I'll have to stay on them tight. The driver is probably a professional. What if they make me?"

"Deny. Deny. Deny. Deny till you die," Jack said, adding, "But seriously, if you get burned and confronted, tell them you fell in love at first sight with one of the girls."

"I fell in love at first sight with all four of the girls."

"Good. Stay with them as long as you can. I'm going to have a little talk with Dexter here at Helta Skelta Delta."

Jack walked up the stairs of Alpha Omega Delta and opened the unlocked frat house door. He knocked on

Dexter's first-floor living space and after about thirty seconds Dexter opened his door. He looked disheveled and had a lipstick smear on his cheek.

"Dexter. Hi… Do you have that list of residents for me?" Jack asked while his eyes darted around the apartment. Jack's eyes then scrutinized Dexter. Kelly was good at perceiving someone's mood and could usually get some chat going.

Dexter looked around and touched his pockets, saying, "I did make it for you, Mr. Kelly."

"Say? Who were those pretty young ladies, Dexter? They didn't look like frat brothers, although I'm out of touch, I'm sure."

"Yes, I'm sure you are. But those women just barged right in, saying they were like groupies for college men, and they admired intelligent fraternity men, and they practically dragged me onto the couch."

"No, seriously," Jack said.

"No, it's true. I really haven't recovered. I'm not sure what they wanted. I think two of them went upstairs, I told them the bathroom was down the hall, not upstairs."

"Don't you know them? Had you seen them before?"

"Well, I think they might work for the College Escort Service. Mikey had some of these, eh, ladies upstairs a few times. Well, more than a few times. For the last three months they were coming by more and more often. The last few weeks, before Mikey died, it was like three times a week. The one time I asked him if he was, you know, paying for them, because it was a different girl every time, I remember exactly what he said, he said, 'Not a penny from me. I get them for free.'"

"Why would he get hookers, I mean escorts, for free?" Jack asked.

"Well, I have no idea. But one of those AI Lab guys, who hung around with Michael's group, he left school and started the escort service."

"Who?" Jack asked the scattered scholar.

"Oh. That guy. Peter… or Tom….. Oh yeah, Tom Peters, I think that was his name. Yes, I know who he is. He used to be a hacker in the Coffeehouse Club. He ran the poker games in the dorms. And the numbers game. And he was with the card counters that got kicked out of Atlantic City, and Las Vegas. Now I think he's got a limo service and some websites. He was all about the cash. He has made a lot of money."

"And he was a friend of Michael's?" Jack pressed the reluctant witness until Dexter held his forehead in one hand, trying to remember.

Dexter thought out loud and said, "The guy used to be with Michael's group. He pretty much started the group. The Super Geeks Running the AI Lab Group, I called them. They controlled the Prototype supposedly. *'Leap into the future, NOW!'* Biggest news on campus. Everybody's whispering about it. It's very low ball, you know, on the down low. It's all broken up. Some students own copyrights to systems. MIT owns a big part of the Project. Some own copyrights to the Prototype's software and some own patents for mechanical schematics. Some must own parts of systems. So many people did the work. But whoever can gain control over the Prototype will be in the money. The corporation formed and gaining control could eventually eclipse Sony, General Motors, and IBM, rolled up into one. We heard some Germans were trying to form a group. The U.S. military industrial complex was another one, Japan, China, you name it. Everybody wants to know where this is going to wind up on The Wheel of Fortune."

"You are a pretty hip guy, Dexter. How come you didn't tell me about this before?"

"Yo! You didn't axe me, Mr. K!" Dexter said with a rapper's Brooklyn accent as he postured, crossing his arms as he made some kind of convoluted peace sign with his fingers.

Chapter 27

Dial a Date

Kelly and Dexter walked up to the fourth floor to check Michael's loft apartment. "Looks OK to me," Dexter said immediately upon entering.

"It's been tossed," Jack said, the professional private eye noting every misplaced or moved object. It was obvious to Jack that the escorts had been looking for something but took the time to move things back to their original places. Nothing appeared to have been stolen, but Jack wondered what they were looking for.

"How did they get in, Dexter? I locked the door when I left yesterday."

"I don't know, Mr. Kelly. They were all over me and I never saw where the two went that headed upstairs, asking about a bathroom."

Jack asked Dexter to bring him the list of fraternity brothers living at Alpha Omega Delta and Dexter went back to his apartment. Jack opened the *Boston Herald* and immediately found an article on the murders.

"'Another MIT Student Found in River,'" he read aloud. Jack had read the initial "Body Found" article on Michael Rich on page nine. But with the addition of a second body they had moved the story up to page three. The article was only five paragraphs and it mentioned that twenty-year-old Seng Li had been positively identified by family members from his hometown of Darien, Connecticut. He had been found, like Michael Rich, dead in the Charles River. An interview with a sister said he had been admitted to MIT at age fourteen and graduated in two and a half years. Seng Li was a graduate student on a research grant living off campus in Cambridge. No gunshot wounds were mentioned.

Jack dialed The Musician's number.

"Where are you now, Willie?"

"You won't believe it. He dropped one escort off at the Copley, one off at the Bostonian, and the last two at the Boston Harbor Hotel. Then the driver went back and waited for the first escort at the Copley Plaza, and now we're waiting at the Bostonian. These girls are turning fucking tricks. 'Escorts' my ass. These girls are working more than their personalities; they are going straight to the happy ending."

"What's the plate number?" Kelly asked.

"Mass. 4733SH," The Musician told Jack as Kelly got out his detective's notebook and wrote down the tag.

"Good, stay on them. Well… not literally."

"Want to hear the Joke-of-the-Day?"

"Look, Musician, I've got shit to do."

"Jack, you'll like this one and I'm stuck sitting here staring at the exhaust pipes of your target vehicle. Just listen."

"Go ahead," Kelly said dejectedly.

"OK. A guy walks into a bar in a small town in southern Arkansas and orders a white wine. Everybody sitting around the bar looks up, expecting to see some pitiful Northerner queer. The bartender spits chewing tobacco on the floor and says, 'You ain't from around here, are ya? Where you from, boy?'

"The guy says, 'I'm from New England.' The bartender leans towards him, wrinkles his nose, and says, 'What the hell do you do up in fuckin' New England, boy?' The guy says, 'I'm a taxidermist.' The bartender says, 'A taxidermist? Now just what in hell is a taxidermist?' And the rednecks around the bar rustle up, getting all agitated, and the guy says, 'A taxidermist, you know? I mount animals.'

"The bartender shouts, 'It's OK, boys! He's one of us!'"

Jack disconnected just as he heard a knock at the apartment door. Dexter had arrived back at Michael's apartment with the list of the fraternity's residents and Jack asked him why there seemed to be nobody around the frat house all week.

"They're all on the midyear junket to Foxwoods, Mr. Kelly. The week right after finals everybody takes off. The Techs here at MIT love to play cards and gamble. It's all math related, you know. Some students make a lot of money. Tom Peters puts that on, too. He arranges a lot of alternative events. He was with the card counters that took Vegas, Mr. Kelly. The Black Jack Club?" Kelly shook his head from side to side as Dexter continued. "They started as an on-campus experiment in card-playing formulas, and then they took it to Foxwoods, Atlantic City, and then out to Las Vegas. They hit the casinos for millions of dollars. You must have heard of them. They had a system. They were on Oprah. Do you ever watch Court TV? One guy wrote a book, it was on *The New York Times* best-seller's list? Ah… and it was made into a movie. Jesus, Mr. Kelly, you live in a tight little bubble, don't you?" Kelly finally shook his head in the affirmative.

Even this pencil-necked geek could tell Jack was not exactly a bon vivant man of the world. Jack was trying to absorb it all. Dexter stared at Jack, who seemed to be lost in a fog, and continued, "Peters owns the girls, too. I mean the escort service."

Dexter left and Kelly sat down at Michael's desk. He picked up Michael's cell phone from its charger, turned it on, scrolled down to Rodney Riviera's phone number, and pushed Call. Rodney answered by saying, "Kelly? My cell ID says Michael is calling. It's too creepy! Haven't you got a cell phone of your own? Put my number in it!" And then there was silence. Jack thought about hanging up and really giving Rodney the creeps, but instead he took a shot in the dark and said, "Why didn't you tell me about Tom Peters and the crystal methamphetamine?"

It caught Rodney off-guard. He sighed audibly and said, "I started to. Tom Peters was still working at the AI Lab when he started making big money with all his 'enterprises.' He sold meth to everybody that wanted it on campus. And before finals, for that last push, or to complete a project, plenty of students wanted it. He was rich already. He supposedly never touched it himself. The escorts brought it, if you wanted it. Tom sold it, but Mike never took any. Shit, Tom had the card counters, the escort service, and the gambling junkets, why not throw some meth in there to keep the whole show running 24/7?"

Kelly's little fishing expedition paid off big time. He pushed it a little more. "Was Peters involved with the Prototype?"

Rodney sighed audibly. "He used to be. I don't know of any of his direct connections with the powerful agencies I mentioned earlier, but he is a player on campus. He had full knowledge of the Prototype. He worked on it. He has his fingers in many pies. His foot in many doors. He has ears in places I don't go. Mr. Kelly, I don't know of any direct involvement by Tom Peters, or anybody else, like I've been telling you. But, I…" Rodney's voice trailed off, and then continued, "Michael was my best friend, and I think his murder had something to do with the Prototype. The Project was Michael's life. He devoted 95% of his time to the Project. The other 5% of his time we went to the bar, or he got an escort at his apartment, all he had to do was call Tom Peters directly. Tom worked with us, before he dropped out. But it's not healthy to talk about Tom Peters. Seriousely, Michael did not do speed. I just think his death must have been the result of his work with the Prototype. I've got no evidence. I've got no clear reason, just a gut feeling."

"Well, you've got guts, Rodney Riviera. And you were a good friend to Michael. That's all for now."

"You call me anytime, Jack Kelly. Just don't use Mike's phone anymore… OK?"

Jack put Michael's cell phone back on its charger and pulled out his own and programmed Rodney's number into it. Then he dialed The Musician for a quick status report. The Musician had followed the chauffeured rose-colored Cadillac back to an off-campus three-story house on Harvard Street between Central Square and Harvard Square in Cambridge. The Musician told Jack he thought it was the offices or headquarters for the escort service even though there wasn't a sign. He also said it seemed like there was a party going on at that location. Kelly asked him to write down every player's registration plate numbers.

Kelly had just finished his talk with The Musician when his cell phone rang in his hand. "Jesus Christ Almighty!" Jack yelled and then said quietly, "Hello."

"Hi, Kelly, this is Jay Archambeault. How's it going? Any luck in the sleuthing department?"

"No, how about you, Trooper?"

"No, sir. I'm running out of leads, Kelly."

"Well, Archie... I thought I heard a rumor you were looking for a warrant. Was that a search warrant or an arrest warrant, or both?"

"Well, Kelly, I had a little theory. You see, both Michael Rich and Seng Li were found in the Charles River. Now, they had to have gotten there from upstream, or up the river! You see, Kelly?"

"I'm with you so far, Jay."

"Now, let's just say, supposing they did fall into the river, or were dumped, it had to be from somewhere. So I took a good look at what's upriver from the river basin where Seng Li was found to the Mass. Ave. Bridge where Mike Rich was located. I found an MIT boathouse, the BU Bridge, two Harvard boathouses, and smack dab in the middle of it all I found a squatter living on a little piece of land right along the river. I could not believe it! The guy has been living on this embankment there for twenty years. Right in between Memorial Drive and the Charles River. He has some nice furniture and some nice antiques in his little slapped together dwelling."

"Incredible. My girlfriend lives across the river on Beacon and she pays $1,600 a month and I bet the squatter has a better view."

"Jack, this guy had built a sweet five-room dwelling using discarded lumber and doors and furniture and windows, it was quite an elaborate home. He ran an extension cord from an MIT boathouse and had free electricity. He had a radio and two TV's. Electric heaters. He's an artist, and really good. I bought a sketch from him for $85. A self-portrait."

"So I take it he didn't pan out as the brutal murderer we're looking for?"

"Long story short, Jack, no. And we sprayed Luminal all over the boathouses inside and out. No blood. I'm back to square one, with you."

"Well, join the party; Jesse hasn't had any hot leads either…"

"But speaking of Luminal, Jack, I'd like to stop by the frat house apartment, kind of informally, with your and Mr. Rich's consent, of course, and check for blood."

"Of course, Jay. Could you come over now? "

"No, I can't come over now, but when I do, can I bring a technician to look at the computer?"

"My first computer autopsy. Archie, Mr. Rich wants this case worked as hard as possible; I know I speak for the family. And I want to watch the state's hottest young homicide investigator work."

"Now, Kelly. We both know I'll never be half the detective my dad was. You worked with him. You guys ruled. You were in the papers all the time, solving the biggest cases. My dad told me that he was the reason Albert DeSalvo was never charged as the Boston Strangler, is that true?"

"Posi-fucking-tively. DeSalvo didn't do it. That's been common knowledge in the law enforcement community since the days of the Boston Strangler. Archie knew what he was doing on the streets, where the real cops work. Your dad was the top of the tops." Jack loved telling the truth. He just wouldn't mention that big Archie, the trooper's dad, was a stone cold lush and cheated on his wife with half the strippers in the Combat Zone.

"Thanks, Kelly. So, I'll see you at the frat house in the morning, OK?"

Then Kelly called Jessica at the Homicide Unit at the Area A station house.

"I can't believe I've actually gotten a hold of you, Lieutenant," Jack said, feeling her out a little before he asked her for information.

"I'll always take your calls, Mr. Kelly. Now, can I do something for you today?"

"You can do something for me tonight, if you catch my drift," Kelly said.

Jesse giggled like a schoolgirl and asked Jack what time he would like that little something tonight, and he asked, "Could we start with dinner at eight?" and she agreed.

"Now," Kelly said, "now that we have the logistics out of the way, would you please bring the photos of the attendees of Michael Rich's burial with you tonight? What's new with the Seng Li murder case?"

"Nothing. Interviews, background checks, victim profile…"

"Nothing," Jack repeated flatly.

"What's new with the Michael Rich murder investigation?"

"Could you run Mass. Reg. 4733SH? And could you run Tom… or Thomas Peters, through the system? I don't have any vitals, you'll have to run a page. He was an MIT student. Now he runs gambling junkets, and an escort service… the College Escort Service in Cambridge. He's got a limo hacks license. He deals crystal meth. He's a white male about mid-twenties. If you need more, I'll get it."

"Oh, I need more, big boy. So go ahead and get it, if… you catch *my* drift?" Jesse said, echoing Jack's corny line. They agreed to meet at Jesse's apartment at eight. Jack wished Jessica would retire from the BPD and work with him full-time at the detective agency.

Chapter 28

The Evil Twin

Tom Peters pulled slowly on the joint, inhaled deeply, hissed the smoke out through his clenched jaw, and passed it to the girl on his left as he sat back on the office couch. He flipped through the sports channels on a seventy-two-inch Sony plasma screen TV high up over the fully stocked bar. Finally he found some basketball highlights that caught his attention.

"Fuck it. Villanova lost to Syracuse. That's going to cost me $6,000." He picked up a clear Bic pen and pulled the stopper out of the end, then pulled the ball-point and the ink cartridge out, and threw them back on the table. With the clear empty cylinder of the pen he bent over the glass table and snorted a line of methamphetamine. The well-dressed, dark-haired Hispanic girl to his right did the same.

Tom Peters wore faded blue jeans, snakeskin cowboy boots, and a black turtleneck sweater. He obsessively sniffed and pushed back his shoulder-length greasy black hair with his hand. Three diamond stud earrings glistened from his left earlobe. He was clean-shaven but for a razor-thin hairline running from the center of his lower lip to his chin, and he had a thin mustache like Gomez Addams of the Addams Family. A Marlboro cigarette burned in the ashtray.

The College Escort Service occupied all three floors of the nondescript three-decker tucked away on Harvard Street in a Cambridge neighborhood. The house had a blacktop parking area with room for the company's seven black Mercedes stretch limousines and three Cadillac sedans.

Young trendsetters, mostly women, some with drinks in their hands, talked and laughed as they moved about the rooms of the house's basement, first and second floors. Tom and Victoria Peters lived on the third. Music could be heard flowing from various rooms. Hip-hop from the basement, alternative from the main floor, a piano, sax, and guitar could be heard coming from the second floor. The lighting was soft and colorful, the atmosphere relaxed. Some of the young women appeared to be entertaining men in several of the rooms. This evening there were three fully stocked and manned bars on the main floor alone.

After another call to another bookie, Tom nervously lit another joint and flipped through the sports channels again. He made several phone calls to the college-age bookies that worked for him to get a running total of the profits and losses of the moment. He disconnected and laughed out loud, his fortunes having just taken an upward jump with the suckers, despite his loss on Villanova.

"That's the juice, baby," he said and pulled the dark-haired girl toward him and kissed her lips with an open mouth. "Moose!" he yelled to his bodyguard across the room. "Go out to the fridge and get us five bottles of Roederer 1999 Cristal Brut champagne. Monique... get the clear plastic cups and let's give out champagne to everybody in the house right now!" Peters declared and the dozen or so people within earshot cheered half-heartedly. Peters usually sold the Cristal for $350 a bottle. Tonight's guests looked more like a vodka crowd.

Thomas Peters got up from the leather couch, walked out of the room, went into his back office, shut the door, and locked it. He sat down in his chair, at his desk, and reached underneath a drawer, pulling out a small black pouch about the size of a paperback novel, and opened it.

He began the ritual of assembling his kit. He placed the small spoon down in front of him, placed a lighter next to it, and then selected the proper needle gauge from a set of four needles placed side-by-side in the leather pouch. Then he attached the needle to the syringe, being very careful that the pristine point did not touch anything. Tom Peters didn't want any tiny nick that would pull his skin when he pulled the point out. He gingerly placed this syringe next to the spoon on the table. Next he took the small bottle of distilled water from the kit bag and carefully unscrewed the top; he didn't want to get anxious and spill any water. He poured a few drops into the spoon. He reached inside the kit bag again and took out a tiny wax paper bag the size of a postage stamp. He dumped the white powder out into the spoon and held the flame of the lighter under it. At the first bubble of the solution, Tom picked up the syringe and mixed up the heroin with the water. He stirred the drug mixture with the tip of the needle and thought about the implications of what he was doing. But it was too late. He was in the pipeline.

Tom Peters pulled back on the plunger and sucked the entire mix of heroin into the syringe. He held it, needle up, into the light and tapped the syringe several times until all the air bubbles had floated up. He squirted out the air while he stared at the tip, pointing straight up. And then he put the syringe in between his teeth, pulled up his left sleeve to his bicep, and slapped his mainline at the crook of his elbow. He made a fist three or four times and took the syringe out of his mouth, placed the tip on the vein, and tapped the stopper at the end of the syringe until the tip of the needle sunk deep into his vein. Peters pulled back on the plunger to see blood enter the barrel of the syringe, and he smiled because he knew he was in the vein.

Then as he released the fist he had made, he pushed the plunger and rammed the whole shot straight into his vein. The rush of heroin felt warm and then it didn't feel like much of anything. Tom noticed a metallic taste between the top of his tongue and the roof of his mouth. And then the blood in his veins felt warm as it flowed slowly through his body. For Tom, heroin was just a soft warm white cloud to land on. The pure Afghanistan poppy derivative slipped into his consciousness like he was sleeping with his eyes open. Tom Peters felt nothing. There was nothing to prove. Nothing mattered. Nothing moved him. There was nothing to care about. There was nothing he needed. There was nothing. Just nothing.

Chapter 29

I Could Die Happy

Jack called Jesse's home number on his cell phone to see if she was there yet. She was.

"How come it's so fucking hard to get moving on an investigation, Jess?" Jack complained loudly. He was going to see her in ten minutes, but he wanted to talk shop before he got there and be done with it for the night. It was past eight anyway. He continued his grievance while Jessica Paris listened. Listening was such a personal thing. It was one of the best things a person could do for another. Listen.

And then respond.

"Jack, eh…," Jesse struggled, "you know… you'll be coming up with something. You always do."

"I can't let this one slip away, Jesse. This kid's parents… they can't bring their son back, but they deserve some answers. Somebody has got to be held accountable on this!" Jack said as he looked for a parking space on Jessica's block.

"OK, Jack. It will...work out... just let it happen. Something will fall into place. You taught me that at Homicide when I first got back from the FBI academy. I was so wet behind the ears. Remember?"

Jesse had succeeded in getting Kelly to smile and he said, "Yeah. And you're still wet behind the ears. What am I even talking to you for? A guy tries to get a little impetus from you..."

"Impetus? Imp-e-tus? Well, where'd you pull that one out from, Jack? The Nether Regions, I assume."

"Look Jesse, I'm sorry. These college kids have got me crazy. I need concrete answers rooted in facts and they're giving me Science Fiction Theatre. They're telling me about modern advances in robotics! They mean well enough but I'm getting nowhere fast. Anything on your end of the investigation?" Jack asked as he walked around the corner to the Beacon Street courtyard entrance of Jesse's apartment.

"You just get over here, Jack Kelly, and I'm going to investigate your lips, baby."

"Wow. You make it all sound so exciting," Kelly said and walked from the sidewalk down the black wrought iron courtyard stairs.

"It is exciting. I'm excited right now," Jesse's voice whispered over Jack's cell phone.

Kelly looked in at Jessica through the courtyard door window. She was covered from the floor to her neck by her favorite blue-plaid L. L. Bean bathrobe and her hair was wrapped in a towel. He watched as she squatted down to put some water bottles in the refrigerator and he spoke softly into his cell phone, "Are you touching yourself... right now?"

"Yes. Yessss! Oh, yessss… and it feels sooo goooood…."
Jesse moaned as Jack watched her throw the empty plastic
and cardboard into the kitchen trash can.

"What are you wearing?"

"Sheer black nightgown with nothing on underneath
it," Jessica lied as Jack watched her open a can of stewed
tomatoes and dump it into a pan on the stove. The towel on
her head began to unravel.

Jack tapped on the window and she turned in surprise.
She recovered quite well, opened the door, turned off her
cell phone, and straightened the towel wrapped around her
head. She said with her best Sergeant Donavan impression,
"I'd have ya booked for Felonious Mopery in the Nighttime
with Intent to Gawk, if I hadn't invited ya here meself."

"I pahked me cah ahn Cahmanwealth, ahn wahked da
rest," Jack said in his inferior Sergeant Donavan accent
and added in his own tone of voice, "Do you know that
son-of-a-bitch was born at Mass. General? He's only been
to Ireland once, for a week."

Jack made himself at home while Jesse made a B-line
into her bedroom to dress for dinner. Jack could smell
the lasagna and chicken cacciatore cooking as he looked
through all fifty or sixty CDs Jessica had and selected six:
the first Santana album, the newest Santana CD, "The
Night" by Morphine, an old Dexter Gordon CD, Sinatra's
"RCA Years," and that crazy Miles Davis CD "Bitches
Brew." Jack hit the Random button and held the Miles CD
case up to the light to read the liner notes. It was recorded
in 1969. Miles had started to play through an Echo-Plex.
His trumpet notes were repeated electronically until they
faded, eventually. Jack was willing to bet the farm that Miles
was trying to get up with the hypnotic acoustical effects of

repetitive loops that Jimi Hendrix had tapped into. Kelly thought about these then avant-garde musicians trying to break into new artistic areas, back in the sixties, stumbling their way through the dark with their x-ray eyes.

"Nobody's done it since," Jack said as Jesse walked up behind him.

"Nobody's done what?" Jesse asked.

"Wow. Nobody's looked as good as you," Kelly said and put his arms around Jesse and began to move slowly to the slow, heavy-handed guitar work of Carlos Santana. She wore an off-white dress, black heels, a thick multicolored beaded necklace, and the gold hoop earrings Jack had given her for her birthday. Her hair was down to her shoulders, her bangs were cut straight across, her makeup was light, and she danced as if she floated on air.

"Jesse? Would you remind me to do two things before I die? I want to hang glide from a mountaintop in Hawaii," Jack said.

"And…," Jesse said, as time slowed to a standstill. "What else?"

"And marry you," Jack said, and he meant it. And it wasn't just because he was so lost in the modern world.

"Are you asking me to marry you, Jack?" Jesse stood back a little, in disbelief.

"Well…," Jack began to stammer and backpeddle. "I'm saying… well, ah… I'm just saying… before I die… I want those things to happen." Jack looked into Jessica's eyes and she looked into his as he added, "I could die happy then… yeah…" Jesse forgave Jack for all his faults. She kissed him and for a moment they forgot about the rest of the world.

Chapter 30

Expletives Deleted

In the morning Jesse showed Jack black-and-white photographs of the people who attended Michael Rich's funeral. There were a dozen or so shots of the attendees. Even Mr. and Mrs. Rich were photographed.

"What's the point of shooting the parents?" Jack asked.

"Look, Jack. The assignment I gave my operative was to shoot every person attending the funeral. You know that. But there were hundreds of MIT students from the campus across the river."

"You did it yourself, didn't you?"

"I did not."

"Well, OK, but how come these photos are black-and-white? The city too cheap to provide me with first-rate prints?" Jack said, feigning exasperation.

"No more coffee for you," Jessica said as she cleared the breakfast table, adding, "Those photos are the property of the cheapskate City of Boston, and so is that printout of the license plate you asked me to run, the one that's on the kitchen table, so leave them on the table and don't let the door smack you on the ass on your way out... darling." She looked back and then headed to her bedroom to get ready for work.

"Well, I never...," Jack said and then yelled out to Jesse, "I want to show them to The Musician."

Jack was already washed and dressed so he was out the door with the registration printout and the funeral photos when his cell phone vibrated. It was The Musician.

"I've got a brand-new black Ford Crown Vic with blue hide-away grill lights and two crewcuts with suits pulling up in front of Helta Skelta Delta right now," The Musician said.

"OK, that's going to be the Staties. It should be Trooper Jay Archambeault and a computer technician. Mr. Rich is going to move some of Michael's things out sometime this afternoon. Archie is going to go over the place. He's going to check the computer, spray some Luminal looking for any large deposits of blood, take some digital photographs, probably not black-and-whites like the BPD cheap bastards, but full color... and poke his nose into everything he can. I'm driving over the Mass. Ave. Bridge right now, and I'm about fifty Smoots away."

"Say what, Jack?"

"Never mind, I'll see you in a couple minutes. Why don't you come into the frat house with us?"

"OK," The Musician said, "I have to keep putting quarters in the meter all day. Fifty cents for thirty minutes is too much. Two hours max. So I gotta move every two hours during the day. It's fucked up, man. I gotta hide down on the floor of the van sometimes when the meter maids come by. I feel like a fucking criminal, man!"

"So, you're having a good time, huh?"

"Yes, Jack. Thanks for the opportunity. Wanna hear the Joke-of-the-Day?"

"No. I'm parking my car and if you'd look over here at the fraternity you're supposed to be watching, you'll see me walking down the sidewalk. I'll be greeting Trooper Archambeault and a computer technician in front of Helta Skelta Delta," Jack said and closed his cell phone as The Musician yelled, "I knew that," into the phone.

Jack shook Archie's hand as the three men met at the bottom of the frat house stairs. Archie introduced the short overweight man with close-cropped wavy black hair and thick glasses as Joseph Green and Jack shook his right hand as the man clutched a leather toolbox in his left. As they walked up the stairs, Archie said, "What a shit hole."

Mr. Green said in a weak voice, "I graduated from Wentworth Institute, I couldn't get into MIT, much less afford it, but living space this close to campus is hard to find, and it doesn't come cheap."

Jack looked back and gave Mr. Green a reassuring nod and pushed open the frat house door. The men ascended to the attic space and Jack used Michael's key.

"Mr. Rich will be along this afternoon to start moving the boy's things out. But for now it's all ours," Jack said standing aside as the two state police investigators walked in.

Mr. Green went directly to the computer and sat down. In a moment he was maneuvering, clicking, and toying with the mouse like a cat. The computer's screen was flashing light that illuminated his white dress shirt and reflected from the lenses in his glasses.

"Anybody want any instant coffee?" Jack said but he didn't get a response from either man. Archie circled the room slowly, looking at everything, picking some things up, and shining a small pocket flashlight here and there. Jack heard The Musician bounding up the stairs and opened the door. As Willie stepped in, Kelly introduced him to the two Staties. The Musician puffed up his chest and nodded, glad to be working with these fine colleagues from the big leagues.

Kelly filled the coffee pot with fresh water from the tap and put it on the stove. He sat down at the kitchen table, brushed away some crumbs, and spread out the photos from the funeral. He then took the police department computer printout of the registration plate on the table, smoothing it out, and began deciphering the registry's information as The Musician looked on. The chauffeured Cadillac The Musician had seen dropping off four working ladies at the frat house came back registered to a 2008 Cadillac, and Jack pointed out to The Musician that it was not "rose colored," as he had stated, but "beige" by the standards of the Massachusetts Registry of Motor Vehicles. It was listed to New Jersey Leasing, Inc. of Teaneck.

"I think this escort and limo business is owned by Tom Peters. And apparently Tom Peters is leasing his vehicles. He's showing all the earmarks of someone who doesn't want to be known. And that's the kind of person I want to get to know," Jack acknowledged.

"That's him right there," The Musician said, pointing to one of the photos of people attending the funeral for Michael Rich.

"Which one?" Kelly asked in amazement.

"This one, here. The guy with the thin little mustache and goatee. The playboy with the greasy black hair, the diamonds in one ear, with the black turtleneck. And this big black guy next to him is the driver. When the Cadillac with the girls in it finally got to their office or house or whatever, over on Harvard Street, this big black guy was the guy who was driving. I didn't think he was a chauffeur, though, because he sauntered out and slapped one of the girls on her ass, and they were all hanging all over him. I'm pretty sure they smoked a joint in the parking lot. Those night vision goggles are really cool. Some of the girls called the white dude 'Tommy' and I heard one say 'Mr. Peters.' Sure acted like he owned the place."

"I love it when things start to intersect and cross-reference," Jack said. He felt like he was onto something, for a change, but he didn't know what.

Massachusetts State Trooper Jay Archambeault was standing behind Jack when Kelly filled him in again on his suspicions. Archie said, "Shall I give him a quick run?" He punched two numbers on his cell phone and said, "Hi, Spangler. Run this guy every which way. Thomas Peters. He runs an escort service, College Escort Service, out of Cambridge. And he must have a Hackney License, he runs limos. He's around twenty-six. Former MIT student, if there is a data base for that. Call me at this number."

"Holy shit!" Joseph Green said, at the computer. "Some files were recently deleted. Yesterday."

"Five escorts from CES were in the building yesterday and three of them kept the frat brother downstairs, Dexter, busy while two of them roamed around." The Musician said, adding, "And I saw the lights go on up here, and then they went off ten minutes later."

"What else? What else have you got?" Archie asked the computer tech..

Green looked over at the three men.

"Nothing. Really. I've read through his compositions. Most of the documents he wrote are very articulate and technical. This guy was some kind of mathematical genius, right? Some documents are written in numbers. This stuff is way beyond my capabilities."

"What are you saying, Joe?" Archie asked him.

"Nothing. I've got nothing. Well… I'm seeing lots of documents but nothing I can relate to Michael Rich's murder. I'll check his cookies, e-mail, then see where he went to on the Internet. Give me awhile."

Archambeault turned to Jack and whispered, "Prima donna."

"I heard that," Joseph Green said.

Jack took his cell phone out of his pocket and dialed Cooper's number.

"Are you ready to do some work for me, Coop? Oh, you're gonna love this job. But you've got to tell me everything that happens," Jack said when Cooper answered his phone.

"Yeah, yeah. I'll start tonight. Thirty-five an hour, right? And all expenses."

"Who told you that?"

"The Musician. But I guess I should be paying *you*, huh, Jack? Is that it? Were you going to have me take on this dangerous assignment of hiring an escort service and seeing how far they will go, for peanuts? Or maybe I should be paying you, Jack? Is that it? Is that your master plan?"

"Take it easy, Cooper! Weren't you busted for a girl giving you a blow job parked at the seawall in Revere?"

"I was never charged. She was bulimic. I was just trying to get her to swallow something."

"Look, just rent a room at the Boston Harbor Hotel or the Sheraton or wherever and call the College Escort Service and see how much money you can give them and what you can get for it, OK? Just get receipts, or put it all on your credit card; I've got to document all expenditures," Jack said.

"You are jealous, aren't you?"

"I don't have time to fuck with you right now," Jack said.

"You wish it was you, don't you?"

"That's ridiculous, Cooper. You know I'm seeing someone. Now, let me know how this goes, and when it's all set up call me with your location and the time of your 'date.'"

Cooper starting singing "Jealous," so Kelly hung up on him.

Kelly turned to The Musician sitting at the kitchen table with a cup of coffee.

"You've got a big mouth, Willie Crawford. You told Cooper you were making $35 an hour and now I've got to pay him $35 an hour to party with some enthusiastic woman on my dime."

"Well… I softened him up for you; he didn't want to do it at first. I had to talk him into it."

"Right," Kelly said in disbelief, looking away in disgust.

The Musician and Kelly both watched Archie spraying Luminal on the floor, walls, furniture, doorways, and anywhere else blood could get to. He finally looked up and noticed the two men watching his every move and said, "Willie, I think Jack is jealous. He would love to go to a hotel for some working vacation, I mean investigation, order all the room service he can, and justify putting call girls on his client's bill. Obviously, my man, he's jealous."

"Elementary, Sherlock Holmes," Jack said. "Are you making any deductions? You've been spraying chemicals and shining flashlights in every conceivable corner including the bathroom, kitchen, and both closets. What have you deduced? That the college boy could have used a maid? Or are you reliving your days in the billets at the SP Academy?"

"I have come to a conclusion. This is not the crime scene." Archie peeled off the rubber gloves he was wearing and dropped them into the waste basket.

"Wait! I've got it!" Joseph Green shouted.

The men were motionless, frozen in time, completely attentive to Mr. Green, the state police expert computer technician. Finally, from somewhere back in time, Jack reached out with his voice and exclaimed in a shaky voice, "What?"

Mr. Green said, "Oh… Oh, that's not it. Nope. Never mind."

Chapter 31

A Family Affair

He rolled over and his head hit the girl's head. Tom opened his eyes and squinted, looked away, and they both rolled over, back to back on the oversized bed in the upstairs apartment at the College Escort Service office building. But when Tom Peters rolled over again, he ended up behind the older Victoria. He moved closer to her. At first, he couldn't remember how the three of them got into bed and he couldn't recollect how the night ended, but then little details began to resurface.

He remembered it was daylight outside when he finally got into the big bed. He remembered closing the curtains as far as they would go, but there was a little sunlight shining around one of the edges. And he remembered going to bed with Victoria. And someone else.

The young girl sleeping next to him was the new girl who had applied for a job a few weeks ago at the escort service. She was a young suburban girl a little down on her luck, as they say. Actually, luck had nothing to do with it. Unless it was bad luck.

She had to get out of the house she lived in. Her mother's out-of-work brother lived there after he got out of jail. He couldn't control himself as he drank alcohol all day and watched her walk around the house with her dyed blonde hair and skinny ass. God had given the young girl a buxom bosom and a pretty face. Or as her uncle put it, "a killer rack" and a "fuck-me face." She was too pretty to work at MacDonald's. She thought she could make a lot more money and not have to put out, if she was an escort. But she came to the College Escort Service, and sooner or later, most often sooner, she would be pressured into providing more than was advertised. That's if she wanted to stay with the company. The pay was good. It was great for a young girl with limited skills. Limited to making men smile.

Peters couldn't remember, or wouldn't remember, how he ended up in bed with both women. He was hung over and didn't really care. He nudged Victoria a little. Then he tried again to sleep, but his head was pounding and his tongue felt like sandpaper. His nose hurt and he massaged it with his fingers but his fingers got bloody as the thin membrane wall of his deviated septum let the floodgates of blood open. He couldn't breathe very well through his bleeding nose and he nudged Victoria again. She stirred slightly.

Tom Peters remembered all the booze he drank the night before and all the crystal methamphetamine he snorted. He sighed. Then he remembered all the people he had killed in the past. He tried to bury his head but the pain wouldn't go away. He felt like a knife was stuck into his left eye, the back of his head throbbed, and he whimpered in pain.

Peters cuddled up closer to Victoria's backside and cried softly as he hugged her body. She stirred again and rolled over to face him. She placed her hand on his cheek and opened her eyes and kissed him softly on the lips.

"There, there, Tommy. Victoria is here for you, as always. Victoria loves you, Little Sweetie." She wiped his nose with a Kleenex and added, "Don't you know your sister will never leave you?"

The young girl's eyes popped open. Victoria heard the girl stiffen and said, "You can go home now, honey, and be back to work tonight at five. And I would not discuss our business with anyone, dear; it's private. It's a family affair." The young blonde girl pulled her clothes on and went out the bedroom door.

"And now you're part of the family," Tom's sister Victoria added as the door closed.

Chapter 32

Nuclear Family in a Box

Archie was poking around in the Alpha Omega Delta frat house apartment of Michael Rich, the computer forensics guy was on the computer, Jack Kelly and The Musician sat at the kitchen table. It was getting to be noon and Jack was getting hungry.

The Musician stood up, looked at Jack, and said, "Do you want to hear the Joke-of-the-Day?" All three men said "No!" in unison.

Mr. Green looked up from his computer and said, "I've got one."

"You see what you've done, Willie?" Jack said as The Musician sat back down dejectedly, but Mr. Green started right in: "A cowboy was overseeing his herd in a remote mountain pasture in Wyoming when a brand-new BMW pulled up in a cloud of dust. The driver was dressed in an Armani suit with Gucci shoes, an Yves Saint-Laurent tie, and he wore Revo sunglasses. He leaned out the window and asked the cowboy, 'If I can tell you exactly how many cows and calves are in your herd, will you give me a calf?'

The cowboy looks at this yuppie city slicker, looks out over his huge herd, and says, 'OK, go ahead and try.' The yuppie gets out his laptop computer, connects it to his cell phone, connects to the Internet, goes to a NASA page and activates the GPS satellite navigation system, gets his exact location, feeds this info to another satellite triangulation system that scans the location, producing a high-resolution image of the area. He takes the photo and sends it to the Adobe Photoshop in Vienna, Austria, and within seconds he receives an e-mail on his Palm Pilot that the image has been processed and stored. He then accesses an MS-SQL data base through an ODBC-connected Excel spreadsheet on his Blackberry, and after a few moments receives a response. He prints a full-color report on his hi-tech, miniaturized HP LaserJet printer and turns to the cowboy and says, 'You have exactly 1,873 cows and calves.' The cowboy takes his hat off and scratches his head, saying, 'I guess you-all can take a calf, then, stranger.' And he watches as the yuppie tries to catch one and put it in his trunk. Then the cowboy says, 'Hey, if I can tell you exactly what business you're in, can I get back the calf?' The yuppie agrees. So the cowboy says, 'You're a congressman for the U.S. government.' 'Wow, you're right! But how did you know?' The cowboy says, 'You showed up here even though nobody called you, you want to get paid for an answer I already knew, to a question I never asked. You tried to show me how much smarter than me you are, and you don't know nothing about cows… This here is a herd of sheep. Now let my dog out of your trunk!'"

The men looked at each other in silence. Jack sighed audibly and then said, "How about we order some subs from the pizza place down the street? I'll buy and The

Musician will fly. Rich and his brother are coming at 1
p.m. to start moving Mike's belongings out."

"I don't see any evidence in need of processing. Just let
me go down to my cruiser and get the other camera and I'll
take some last pictures of everything," the trooper said.

"Jeez, Archie. How come you're doing everything?
Where's your forensics team? Your photographer? Your
partner? These are homicides."

"You've been watching TV again, haven't you, Jack?"

"Speaking of watching TV, this guy has downloaded a
bit of porn. I don't know what an 'average' amount would
be, but there's some here," Joseph Green said as all three
men walked over to the computer and stood behind him.

Green seemed surprised as he was immediately
surrounded. "OK. Here's some here... And here... He's got
theses sections here... And this was obviously a favorite
site. He's also got it bookmarked."

"My goodness, that young lady does not have a stitch
of clothing on," Jack said.

"She's got high heels on... I could use her body as a
playground... She is a poor boy's heaven. I love sex,"
Archie said.

"This isn't sex," The Musician said. "Not romantic sex.
Romantic sex is in a flash, a gleam, it's the twinkle in the
eye, the line of a good-looking woman or a handsome man.
They way they stand or look at you. That feeling you get
in the pit of your stomach. It's the attraction to the senses.
Sex is in the head."

The three men looked at Willie.

"What does an escort cost at College Escort Service?"
Jack asked.

"I wouldn't know, Mr. Kelly," Green said to Kelly, lifting his eyebrows with an air of superiority.

"Oh... Everybody's riding that high horse," Jack said, staring at Mr. Green and adding, "Until they get caught with their pants down at a rest stop on Route 95."

"Hey! That trooper wasn't from our barracks," Archambeault said.

Mr. Green quickly looked away from Jack. Archie and The Musician stared at Jack until Green said, "And I found this video." He doubled-clicked on the face of a young girl looking up at the camera giving oral sex to an older male as the video rolled.

The four men were silent until The Musician yelled, "Holy Mother of the Bleeding Blessed Virgin Mary! She could suck the color out of a lemon! She could suck a bowling ball through a garden hose. I ain't seen sucking that hard since I visited the Easterly Farms Petting Zoo." Everyone stared at The Musician, again.

"What's she doing now?" Archie said.

All three men were wordlessly captivated until the footsteps reached the top of the stairs. Mr. Rich and his brother walked into the apartment carrying unassembled cardboard boxes.

Jack said nervously, "How high are you?" and quickly corrected himself. "I mean, Hi... How are you...? Mr. Rich?"

Rich said, "I see you're hard at work, Mr. Kelly."

Mr. Green minimized the screen but the audio of a female moaning with real or assumed pleasure loudly lingered just a little too long before he shut it off.

"Please call me Jack, Mr. Rich. You know Trooper Archambeault, and this is Mr. Green, a forensic computer analyst with the state, and this hippie is The Musician, an operative working for me."

Rich shook The Musician's hand and nodded to Mr. Green and Archie, and said, "This is my brother Morris," introducing a short, stocky gray-haired man similar in looks to him. More nods all around.

"I hope we're not intruding on your privacy with this investigation," Archambeault said to Rich.

"Oh, no. No, no! I thought I was intruding on you, Trooper Archambeault," Rich said with a smile and then continued on more seriously, "My son is gone now and there's nothing I would like better than to understand what happened to him. If I can, I'd like to know his last minutes. To understand what pain he suffered. This is so important to my family now. My wife is having trouble dealing with this. She has lost her faith in God… and in humanity. She is questioning life itself. She is on medication, needless to say, and under a doctor's close care."

"I'm so sorry, Mr. Rich," Jack said and invited Rich to sit down at the kitchen table for a few minutes to give him an update and an explanation as to why he was standing around watching a pornographic video on his son's computer. Kelly handed a ten and a twenty-dollar bill to The Musician, asking him to pick up six sub sandwiches at the pizza place.

Jack and Rich sat at the table as Kelly updated him on his discussions with Michael's friends. He told Rich about Rodney and Amanda's theory that Michael might have gotten a little too close to the Prototype Project. Rich was shocked to find out about Seng Li's murder. He had met Seng in this very apartment. Kelly mentioned that his girlfriend, Lieutenant Jessica Paris, was the lead investigator for the BPD on the Seng Li case. He told the father about the date Michael was to have with the College Escort Service on the night he disappeared and advised the father he had two detective agency operatives looking into the escort service. He explained that the investigators were in the middle of a forensic check of the computer and links from the escort service had brought them to web pages that had been downloaded and saved by Michael.

Rich walked over to the computer and looked at it fondly, perhaps imagining his son sitting at the desk, surfing the Net. He saw the photo Jack had propped up against the bottom of the lamp. It was the photo of Michael at the beach in Nahant with his mother and father, a glorious sunset and the Boston skyline behind them.

Trooper Archambeault trudged back up the stairs with his camera equipment and began snapping pictures of the overall layout of the apartment and its contents. Jack sat at the kitchen table with the brothers, Morris and Cecil Rich. Every time the flash went off Jack perceived the slightest twitch or wince in Michael's father's body, and his eyes blinked. He was physically and spiritually shocked with each flash. After taking almost fifty photos, Archie said to Jack, "These digital cameras are so good; I don't need a team of technicians, Jack. I'm winding down my investigation here. This is not the crime scene and I don't see anything else I need."

"Well, we both need copies of the message the escort agency left on Mike's cell phone. We possibly would need that for evidentiary purposes. Mr. Rich is going to cancel the service."

"I'll keep that going for another week or two, Jack. Don't worry about that," Rich said.

"OK, Archie? Problem solved?" Jack said.

"Joe, what's it looking like with the computer?" Archie asked.

"There's nothing I can see we need for any investigative avenues here. I made a disc of everything, just in case. But I don't see any smoking gun."

The Musician arrived with the subs and the four investigators ate at the kitchen table while the Rich brothers assembled and packed boxes of the dead son's belongings. It was a little tough for the men to watch the dad pack his only son's world into boxes while they ate. Did it all come to this? Boxes that may never see the light of day again. A life over. End of story.

Archie's cell phone rang and he opened it. He wrote on a piece of paper at Michael's desk for a few minutes and hung up. He looked at Jack and told him the data base of the Criminal Investigations Division unit of the Mass. State Police came up with nothing on Thomas Peters. Not a parking ticket. No driver's license. No incidents. No queries. They had a Social Security number, a date of birth, and the company's address of the hackney limousine license he owned, but that was it. All Archie could say was, "Name, rank, and serial number. This is highly irregular!"

After Archie and Mr. Green left Jack and The Musician helped the brothers carry boxes down to a U-Haul truck until well after dark. Mr. Rich realized he would have to come back for the rest of the items in the apartment sometime the next day. Jack told Rich he would like to stay there again tonight. The computer, the couch, and some kitchen supplies still remained.

Cooper called on Jack's cell and told Kelly he was at the Ritz-Carlton Hotel and had a scheduled date with a lady from the College Escort Service at the bar there set for 9 p.m. Jack told him to take her to dinner and order the most expensive items, order her as many drinks as she would take, and make sure he got her back to his room. He told Cooper he should order anything they needed and party right there in the room. And when the time was right he should steer the conversation to what could she do for more and more money.

"I want to know what she'll do for money. What she'll do erotic or kinky, too," Jack said.

"What exactly is the difference between erotic and kinky?"

"I think you know that, Cooper. Erotic is when she uses a feather. Kinky is when she uses the whole chicken."

"Jack, I'm well aware of my assignment here, and I can maneuver the lady, if she's pretty enough to meet my standards, into a sensual world of gregarious and libertine socialization. I will sweep her off her feet," Cooper said.

"Listen, Don Juan. Just try to get sex. S, E, fuckin' X, OK? Don't get fancy on me. Get her to talk about the business and specifically the College Escort Service and its owner. But be careful and be cool."

The Musician shook his head at Kelly and sat down at Michael's computer and began surfing online. He had a page open to E-bay and was checking the prices on old Fender Precision basses. Jack asked him to do a drive-by of the College Escort Service headquarters and then do a few spot surveillances whenever he could. "You know the drill. Car registration numbers, photos of the people that come and go, then go home and get some rest." The Musician left, bounding down the stairs two at a time.

The three men moved a few more boxes down to the truck.

Jack found the brothers some cold ginger ale in the refrigerator and Cecil and Morris Rich split a BLT sub. Mr. Rich, who had heard parts of Jack's phone conversation with Cooper and his instructions to The Musician, finished his half of the sub, took a sip of the soda, and said to Jack, "I really feel like you're getting in touch with my son's world, Jack. I can't tell you how much this means to my wife and I. We don't know what we would do without you, on this. I know if anyone can find out what happened to my son… it will be you," the older man's voice cracked.

"Your son had scheduled a date with a friend's escort service for the night he seems to have disappeared, Mr. Rich. It might be nothing but I've got to follow every lead."

"Do whatever you have to do, Jack," Rich said, cleaning off the kitchen table and putting on his jacket. Morris Rich picked up the last cardboard box and the Rich brothers left.

Jack sat down at Michael's desk. He looked around the apartment. It was almost empty now. Only the desk, its lamp and chair, the couch, and the kitchen table remained. Jack looked at the photo he had propped up at the base of the lamp. It was the picture of the Rich family. The mom, dad, and son happily pictured on the beach at Nahant. They were the nuclear family. Jack looked at the photograph he held in his hand. The family happily smiled into the camera and the Boston skyline sparkled like diamonds in the sunset.

Chapter 33

Meet Tom Peters

Tom Peters placed an unlit Marlboro between his lips and called his driver and personal bodyguard into his office. "What the fuck I gotta do? Put a fuckin' shock collar on you? Because I will get one, OK? If that's what I gotta do to get you to come in here, Moose, I will fucking zap you silly, you huge black greaseball. Now, you're my fucking assistant and I need some fucking assistance."

"I thought I was your bodyguard?" the oversized, overage delinquent said.

"Yes. You bodyguard me when I am threatened or in danger, but when I'm not being threatened and not in danger you do things I ask you to do for me! You assist me. You are my assistant. You see?"

"Am I getting a raise?" the big man said. He looked like an overweight black Elvis impersonator with long, straight, greasy black hair combed straight back, just like his boss.

"NO! You fuck. Show some initiative. Then we'll talk about a raise."

"Show you what?"

"Ah. *Marone! Lei la madre grande nera credulone di gallo maledetto!*"

"What's the matter, Boss? You've got a nice office here with a coffee machine, a TV, and a pool table."

"Yo! Can't you see, you giant toad? It doesn't matter how nice your surroundings are. It doesn't matter if you're in a castle or a stable. It doesn't matter what room you're in. It just matters what goes on in here," Peters said, pointing and tapping his head with his index finger. "You can be in a fucking cardboard box. Or a jail cell. Or over at the Lab. It's the ideas that take place inside your brain that matters. Home is where the head is. And you can quote me on that, Moose. That's why you'll never be a boss. I am trying to conduct business here! And I would like some assistance. Now, get out and find me one of my managers. I want to find that little bitch I slept with last night."

The College Escort Service was strategically located in Cambridge on Harvard Street halfway between MIT and Harvard University. There was an endless fresh supply of Harvard and MIT women who needed money while in college and the escort service was a quick way to get it. The men of Harvard and MIT provided a consumer base for the trade.

Tom Peters's office was on the first floor of the three-story tenement, just off of a reception room with couches and chairs and a big-screen TV. The office had high windows and translucent curtains as the midafternoon sunshine poured through. He got a paper cup of water from the Belmont Springs dispenser just outside his office door and sat back down at his desk. Peters pulled open the bottom right-hand drawer and took out seven bottles of pills. He selected a multivitamin, a capsule of vitamin E, a wafer of C, two pills with glucose, a Vicodin, and a Xanax. He threw them all into his mouth at once and washed them down with the entire cup of water.

A short, twenty-something, blonde-haired, heavily made-up woman rapped on the doorframe and said, "You wanted to see me, Boss?"

"Yes, come here, Jennifer. Put these eyedrops in for me please. I can't get them in," Tom Peters said, putting his feet up on the desk, leaning back in his chair, and holding up a small plastic bottle of Visine eyedrops. Jennifer took the bottle and stood over and behind him. She was a little nervous and his eyes started blinking wildly. He held his eyes open with his fingers and said, "Go ahead!" Peters stared to the left and to the right, then looked straight up, then blinked wildly again as Jennifer moved the Visine bottle closer and closer. Peters held his breath and looked left as far as he could, his head moving slightly. Jennifer held the Visine over his eye and drifted forward and back with the motion of his head. Peters's eyes blinked wildly again and he put a hand over his eyes and bolted upright in the chair. "All right! All right!" he said, breathing again. As he gasped for air, Tom Peters reached for the Visine bottle and took it from Jennifer's hand. His breathing regulated as Jennifer walked around to the front of the desk. She felt the tension and tried to sound believable when she said, "Sorry, Mr. Peters. My hand was a little shaky."

Peters had regained his composure and said, "There's a new girl about two weeks, barely legal, bleach-blonde hair, big rack, pretty face..."

"Sally Feinstein. Her escort name is Wendy."

"Well, Jennifer, see that Windy blows away."

"You want her fired, Boss? She could be a good earner," Jennifer said.

"How long have you been a manager here, Jenny?"

"Since you started the business, almost three years."

"And have you made good money here, Jen?"

"Oh yes, Mr. Peters. This company has grown so much. I remember when it was just six girls working out of the Colonnade Hotel."

"Lose the Teen Queen. I don't care how you do it. Don't assign her any jobs. Or just give her a few with the bottom-of-the-barrel customers, then talk her out of the business. Just do it," Peters said.

"Oh, I see. You want her out of the business because she's so young and pretty. You've got a heart of gold, Mr. Peters."

"Right. Now get the fuck out before you bullshit me to death."

Jennifer was leaving and Peters started checking his pockets for a cigarette when his sister Victoria walked in, wearing a low-cut knee-length blue dress, saying, "Is this about me? No? Then I've lost interest."

"Well, looked at what the cat woke up," Peters said, unable to locate a cigarette.

"After you got up, Tom, I went to my office and set up the promotion for our next three parties, sent out e-mails, and set them up on our website. Then I took a cab to the gym, ran six miles on the treadmill, and worked with my personal trainer on balance and power. When I got back here I showered and put on this beautiful Versace dress. I then had a kitchen staff meeting with eight cooks and servers. What have you done, Tommy?"

"I've done Vicodin and Xanax. And I took my vitamins."

Victoria moved around behind her brother and began to massage his temples as he leaned back in his plush leather desk chair. "Are we going out to some clubs tonight?"

"Of course. It's Friday night. Dinner at the Capital Grille, all right? I'm hoping to run into some of the Interested Group there," Tom said.

"Why don't we just steal the robot? And sell it to the highest bidder?"

"It's a little more complicated, Victoria. It's the rights to the technology and the know-how that makes it all work. That's what it's about! To be a founding member, to be in on the ground floor of this project will secure fortunes for us and our family for generations to come. We would be major players, not just in Boston, not just the East Coast, not just these United States of America, but the business *world*," Peters said, getting worked up again.

"Sshhhh... Relax, Tommy... and tell me about tonight."

"We'll take the black Mercedes stretch and hit the Roxy, House of Blues, Felt, Bill's Guitar Bar, Whiskey Park, the Rattlesnake, and finish the night in a couple of the clubs at Boylston Place. And maybe Chinatown for a late supper. We'll bring two or three girls with us and blaze a trail across this city."

Victoria stood over Tom and spoke softly to her brother as she worked his temples with her index fingers.

"You were quite superlative last night, Tommy... and I liked that little girl. You were king of the hill, Tom. And I was the queen. And that little blonde with that pretty little face, and that ass... well, she was the little stable girl. And she had to work so hard… She had to work so hard to please her queen."

Victoria picked up the Visine bottle and said, "Look at me, Tommy." As Tom Peters looked up at his sister's face, she pulled the Visine dispenser over each eye and placed two drops in each. Tom saw her face through waves of liquid and his headache was gone.

"Oh… yes," Victoria said. "She was so sweet. And she tried so hard to please. I'd like to put her right up on that billiard table. Can we do her again, Tommy? Can we keep her?"

"Oh… Yeah, sure," Peters said from the verge of sleep, barely remembering he was going to have the little blonde fired. The Xanax and Vicodin had taken effect along with Victoria's healing hands, and Peters was feeling no stress. He looked up at Victoria and said, "Let's go check on the managers right now while I'm in the mood."

Tom Peters got up from his chair and they crossed the entertainment room to the grand staircase and walked up to the second floor and into two large rooms with five desks. Four of the office desks were occupied by women taking telephone calls on multiple lines and typing into computers. This was where the requests for services, or dates, came into and were scheduled with the appropriate employee, or escort. Transportation had to be arranged and method of payment agreed upon. The women who worked the phones also helped to manage the girls. The company also employed a few male escorts, who were requested more often by men than women.

Thomas and Victoria Peters walked around separately, listening in briefly to telephone conversations and watching data being entered into the computer's data base.

They occasionally engaged the managers in conversation, all business related. For it was a business they were running. And business was very good in the world's oldest profession.

Tom and Victoria didn't start out as pimps. No. Certainly not. They were from one of Baltimore's most upstanding blue-blooded American aristocratic families. The father was the district attorney and their mother was the superintendent of schools. Victoria was the first child born and was perfect. She was pretty, smart, well-rounded. A wonderful child. But then came the twins. Thomas and Jacob. Oh, the boys shattered all existing plateaus. Thomas, along with his twin brother, was a child prodigy. Their intelligence quotient was through the roof. They were engaging, extremely bright children, fast learners, and prolific, reading and writing voraciously.

And then when they were eleven years old, their mom and dad died in a car crash and their seventeen-year-old sister, Victoria, raised them as best she could. Money was no object. By the time they were fifteen years old they had graduated from high school, had moved from Baltimore to Cambridge, and were enrolled on full scholarships at MIT.

And then Tom's twin, Jacob, died in a horrible accident at MIT.

As Thomas studied year after year, the Institute became his mother and father. He worked on practical engineering science and graduated with a master's degree at seventeen. His graduate studies led him to the Artificial Intelligence Lab and work with the Prototype Project. Then he began to change. Maybe he was bored with the continuous studies. He wanted to break out. He was twenty-one and had never been kissed. He was making good money working at the AI Lab on the Prototype Project but something was missing.

It wasn't like he was never involved in anything shady. At age sixteen he joined a group that met regularly in the back of the library and played blackjack. After some study the group graduated to card counting. They eventually took their show on the road for some practical application in the gambling casinos at Foxwoods, Atlantic City, and then Las Vegas. They took the casinos for millions before they were found out and black-balled.

Tom Peters knew his work and the work of the AI Lab group was cutting edge but they also knew the rewards from their work would be reaped by others. Over beers at the local bars the group discussed ways to keep the Prototype under their control or at least under MIT's control. But there were forces watching, waiting, and monitoring their progress. They heard the extra clicks on the phone. They saw the phony Comcast and cable TV company trucks parked near the AI Lab. The stock Fords and Chevy's with darkened windows and whip antennas parked near wherever any of the group went. The pretext "survey" phone calls. The secret surveillance was no secret to the group. They were being watched closely and they knew it.

That's around when Thomas "went bad." He said he wasn't going to work his "balls off so some fucking fascist could take over." He dropped out. No one heard from him from the start of spring semester in January until fall semester in September. That was about three and a half years ago. And when he resurfaced it was not to go back to scientific studies or to do the AI work with robots. He began his work with girls. Lots of girls.

Chapter 34

Central Control

It would be Kelly's last night in Michael's apartment. Jack was sitting in Michael's chair in front of the computer. Mr. Rich would be pulling the plug on the computer, the Internet service, and eventually Michael's cell phone, sitting on its charger in front of Jack. Since all were about to be shut off, removed, or soon disconnected, Kelly took a last look, starting with the computer.

He entered in the homepage of the College Escort Service and as the page loaded there was a knock on the apartment door. When Kelly opened the door, Dexter put a stack of mail four inches thick into Kelly's arms.

"I'm sure Mr. Rich will have Mike's mail forwarded elsewhere," Dexter stated, more as a demand than a question.

"I'm sure; thanks," Jack said, as he looked down at the stack of mail.

Dexter went back down the stairs as Jack closed the door. He sat back down at Michael's desk and looked over the thirty or so articles of mail until one caught his eye. It was from the United States Patent Office.

Without hesitation Kelly took the small Swiss Army knife he has carried in his pants pocket since he was a kid and slit open the envelope. It was a letter informing Michael Rich that a certificate was issued under the seal of the Copyright Office in accordance with Title 17, United States Code, and attested that registration for Michael Rich's "work, invention, copyright, or patent" had been made for the work identified below and was now a part of the Copyright Office records. It was signed by the registrar and had an official Library of Congress seal. The paperwork listed Michael's signature, address, phone number, and the "invention's" Year of Creation. Among these facts and figures the document listed the work in question as "software known as the Sympathetic Override Program for the Central Control of Functioning Integrated Systems."

Kelly picked up Michael's cell phone, looked up Rodney's phone number, checked it was the same as he had entered into his own cell, and pressed the Call button. Rodney picked it up on the second ring.

"Rodney, got a minute? What is the Sympathetic Override Program?"

"Ah... the SOP," Rodney audibly sucked some air in through his nostrils. And then let it out of his mouth slowly and loudly. "Oh, my God. Let's see if I can get this right." But what he meant to say was, let's see how I can explain this to the scientifically challenged Jack Kelly.

"The program... Well, this was Michael's thing. This is what his group was charged with working on. But Michael,

I guess, far exceeded his peers. I believe he was going to get his work patented, or incorporate, or…."

"So, what is the Sympathetic Override Program? What does it do?" Kelly said, determined to pin Rodney down.

"It's an organizer. Whatever systems interact with it, it integrates."

Kelly was outside his comfort zone again, working without a net.

"A robot is a group of systems," Rod tried to explain to the bewildered detective. "Ah… let's say you have a working mechanical arm. And a working mechanical leg and another working arm. Several systems for lateral movement. Balance and electrical systems. Power maintenance systems…. Anyway, there are many working systems, let's say, in a robot. What Mike had developed was a program that made all the systems work together. It was Central Control. It was not the brain, but it hooked directly into the brain and would override any system. Any system that was attached, aligned, or even just in contact with. And it integrated all systems to work together.

"Mike had developed a software program that brought it all together. It was so sympathetic that all systems *wanted* to integrate. They were joyous participants in the network. They were part of something much bigger."

Jack shook his head from side to side, struggling to understand as Rodney Riviera kept strong to the task.

"This was an option that the world of robotics hadn't even imagined. This Central Control System was sympathetic. Scientists no longer had to figure out a way that each individually unique system could get operational with a larger system because Michael's operating system took on that function. As long as Michael's Sympathetic

Override Program is online every system is voluntarily overridden. It is automatic control."

"Oh," Jack Kelly said, somewhat dejectedly. "Why didn't you just say so?"

Kelly excused himself to Rodney and took an incoming call. It was Cooper. Jack tried to say hello but was drowned out by Cooper yelling, "He shoots! He scores!!!" re-enacting Boston Celtics radio announcer Johnny Most's gravel-drenched voice screaming out over the radio as Larry Bird stole the ball and scored a last-second basket.

"Hi, Coop," Jack said into the phone's mouthpiece as he picked at the wax in his other ear.

"Well, Kelly. This was the best assignment you've ever given me! So far, anyway, in the twenty years you've given me occasional assignments. Even better than the week in Florida for the asset check. This was a pip. Oh yeah...." Cooper's laughter made Jack yawn as he realized how much digging he was going to have to do to get the factual story of what had transpired on Cooper's one evening of undercover-pretext work. He knew the only weapon he had was his silence.

"Oh, yeah," Cooper said again, his voice cackling softly like an overjoyed cartoon character. But Jack held his tongue.

"Oooh, baby!" Cooper shouted into the phone's receiver, but Kelly held his silence.

"Yes, yes, yes. A good night. Yup," Cooper insisted but Kelly held the phone away from his mouth, bit his lip, and commenced shallow breathing in silence.

After a long pause the silence was shattered by Cooper singing loudly, "Oh! What a night, wee oh!!!"

"All right, Cooper," Jack gave in. "What happened?"

"We got jiggy wid it, home slice."

"Don't fuck with me, Coop."

"The woman arrived at the Ritz bar at 9:15 as I was finishing dinner. We had a drink and then we had another drink and we made arrangements to go up to my room. We did and after drinks were delivered by room service I pretended to be a little drunk."

"Pretended?"

"So I came right out and asked her, 'How much would I have to put on my credit card for a massage? She told me 'extras' were about $250 per. So I said what other extras were there? And she said why don't we start with that massage? Then while I'm getting the massage she says, 'Want me to slip off my blouse and skirt?' I say yes. She says, 'That's another 250.' I keep saying that's no problem. Long story short, you owe a lot of money and I went around the world. Everything. The whole enchilada, baby."

"Oral and intercourse?"

"Yes and a few things more and one I never even heard of!"

"OK. Spare me the details."

"I'll spare you the details but I won't spare you the bill for all this frolicking. But Jack. You should've seen this beautiful woman work. She was so fine. Use your imagination, Jack."

"I don't want to use my imagination, with you in the picture, thank you. Just submit any and all receipts to me with your report and I imagine the cost was substantial, and I'll cut you a check on the spot. I'll talk to you tomorrow."

"But we've got a problem," Cooper said.

"What's that?"

"She's knocked up now. I've gotten her pregnant and you will have to support us both and the baby. It was an on-the-job accident, it's Worker's Compensation!"

"Don't fuck with me, Cooper. What did you learn about the company and its owner?"

"She wasn't very forthcoming with information about her employers. But I was pumping her."

"Obviously. I'm glad you enjoyed yourself, and you verified the company's true identity as an outcall hooker haven and flesh emporium, but I was hoping for some info on the owners, too."

"I asked her almost point blank, I said, 'So, this guy that owns the escort service, what's he like?' I got a strong but silent reaction. One thing I can tell you. She was scared," Cooper said and disconnected.

Kelly looked around the frat house apartment and then sat for a minute staring at the homepage of the College Escort Service. Jack was daydreaming. He was imagining himself at the Ritz-Carlton Hotel.

Jack called Jessica's cell phone.

"Where are you?" he asked her when she answered.

"I just got home, Big Boy. Are you going to pay me a visit?"

"No, Jesse. I've got one more night in this frat house apartment, so I'm gonna stay here and work the case a bit. His computer and cell phone will be unplugged tomorrow afternoon and the rest of the stuff moved out. There are some new fraternity nerds going to be moving in. How about you? Are you having any luck with the Seng Li murder investigation? You know if you solve your murder, my case will be solved, too."

"And vice versa, my dear. I've been busy with Seng Li's family. They call constantly. They want to know how the investigation is going and has anyone been arrested yet. There are four of them calling, each twice a day. I want to be sympathetic, console them, and help them struggle through their loss, but… I've got a job to do. I don't have time to investigate this crime if I'm talking to these Asian women all day! I had to tell them to please designate one relative to get an update from me every day, but the four keep calling anyway." Jack let her talk.

"Seng Li's sister worked in a lab at Harvard and claims they have grown micro organisms, like some kind of nerve cells, onto transistor boards. She is saying they have joined growing organic material with electronic components. They have effectively united man and machine. She says her lab developed artificial eyes. She freaks me out every time I talk to her. This shit is strictly science fiction.

"She keeps telling me about experiments going on between Harvard and MIT. Behavioral, sociological, psychological experiments. I guess there's a spirit of adventure pushing the envelopes into uncharted waters in several different fields."

"That's what I'm hearing," Jack said, jumping on the technology bandwagon. "B. F. Skinner used to do conditioned reflex experiments in a Harvard building a mile from here. He didn't use Pavlov's dogs, but he used pigeons, rats, and his own daughter. And let's not forget Harvard professor Dr. Timothy Leary and his LSD experiments."

"Seng Li's sister seems to think that new advances in mainframe systems made at MIT's AI Lab are developing to an astounding echelon and…"

"Hey! That's a mouthful," Jack said.

"I'll show you a mouthful when you come over tomorrow night."

"Sounds like someone could use a night of dinner, some well-selected music, and a little romance."

"Some *big* romance. Let's just cut to the chase, baby. Are you coming over tomorrow night? I'll grill steaks and shrimp out in the courtyard. Or should we order dinners from Legal Seafood?"

"Yes...," Jack said, leaving the choice up to her.

"Did you check on Thomas Peters?" Kelly asked.

Jack heard the rustle of some papers and Jesse said, "Thomas Justin Peters. 6/8/80. Born and raised in Baltimore, Maryland. Mother was the superintendent of schools and father was Baltimore's district attorney until they were killed in a car crash in 1991 when Thomas was eleven. The court awarded his custody and that of his twin brother to his teenage sister. Tom and Jacob Peters had extremely high IQs and had graduated from high school and were accepted at MIT at age fifteen. Tom's twin brother, Jacob, died on campus while attending MIT. He went out through a window on the thirteenth floor of a building on the MIT campus. He landed right in front of the building, while classes were in session. Up in the thirteenth-floor classroom they found a tape recorder running, a deactivated prototype robot on a charger, and on the blackboard was the mathematical formula for what happens when a falling body hits the ground from the thirteenth floor. It has never been definitively ascertained whether the incident was suicidal, homicidal, or accidental.

"Thomas Peters has no driver's history. But he was assigned a DMV number when he was eleven. That's a little strange. So I checked the newspapers in Baltimore at the time his parents died and it turns out eleven-year-old Thomas Peters was driving the car when they died. He has no criminal record in Mass. or Maryland, but was a child victim in a priest molestation scandal when he was six years old."

"Interesting. That didn't sound like a standard police inquiry. Where'd you come up with some of that?"

"I Googled him," Jesse said.

Jack was intrigued but didn't know what to make of the information. After a long pause he said, "Well, let's just call Thomas Peters 'a person of interest.' His name has been popping up at every turn."

"If you say so, Jack. But I thought you had a good thing going when you thought the robots were your number one suspects."

"OK. That's it. You've earned yourself a spanking tomorrow night."

"Oh! Goody."

"See you then," Kelly said, ended the call, and dialed The Musician's home number.

One of Willie Crawford's youngest daughters answered the phone and, on hearing Kelly's voice, knew enough to go into the bedroom with the portable telephone and hand it to her daddy. The Musician's sleepy voice said, "Hello?"

"Hey, man. I'm glad you're sleeping at home and not while you're on a surveillance for me. Listen brother, when you're ready to get back on the street, I want you to watch the College Escort Service, especially its owner, Thomas Peters. I don't know that much about him but he seems to be in the middle of the mix. Be careful; I don't know what he's capable of but I do know he's intelligent and criminally inclined."

"Yeah, Jack. I gotta get up anyway." Then he yelled, "Get Rusty off the bed! Mary Alice Katherine? Sorry, Jack. This dog is crazy about me. He just hears my voice and he busts open the bedroom door and he's jumping all over me like an insane love monkey."

"OK, I'll leave you two alone."

"No. OK. Well...." The Musician was obviously still sleepy-headed, but added, "How'd Cooper make out?"

"Yes, he sure did. He's another insane love monkey."

"What? He got laid?"

"He got it. Inside and out. Over under sideways and down."

"That bastard! How come I didn't get that assignment?"

"I offered it to you, remember? But you're married, remember? Does this conversation ring a bell with you? How much sleep have you had? It's 8:30 p.m. Leave your four decka on M Street and walk your dog down Broadway to Castle Island, let him take a nice long piss, then pick up some grub at Flanagan's or do whatever you've got to do, and then log some more hours, OK? It's Friday night and Thomas Peters is some kind of New Age pimp, so he'll be going out tonight. Take some pictures with the new digital camera and be careful!"

"Yes, Jack. I'll be careful. I've got Big Papi, my baseball bat. And thanks. Hey, wanna hear the Joke-of-the-Day?"

"No, no. I know you're sleepy. Go ahead and get some more rest. You probably want to watch this Peters guy a little later tonight. They say the beautiful people don't go out until midnight. He probably stays out late; you go ahead and get back to sleep."

"No. Listen. A man was driving from LA to Boston. He got as far as Cleveland when he realized he was getting very horny. He located a hooker and had sex to take care of this need. He immediately felt guilty and went to confession. For penance he was told by the priest to say 9,000 Hail Marys. He left Cleveland and had just finished the 9,000 Hail Marys when he arrived in Boston. He realized he was horny after his long drive and located a hooker, had sex, and took care of the problem. He immediately felt guilty and found a church and went to confession. The old Irish priest, upon hearing the man's confession, said, 'For penance say… ah… one Hail Mary.' The man said, 'Hey! In Cleveland for the same thing I had to say 9,000 Hail Marys!' So the priest said, 'Now what would they know about fucking in Cleveland?'"

"That's great, Willie…," Jack said but The Musician started another.

"Hey, that reminds me. Listen to this one, Jack. A train hits a bus filled with Catholic schoolgirls and they all die and go to heaven. They are trying to enter the Pearly Gates when St. Peter asks the first girl, 'Maureen, have you ever had any contact with the penis?' She shyly replies, 'Well, I once touched the head of one with the tip of my finger.' St. Peter says, 'OK. Dip the tip of your finger in the Holy Water and pass through the Holy Gates.' Then St. Peter asks the next girl, 'Katherine Mary, have you had any contact with a penis?' Katherine Mary giggled and said, 'I once fondled and rubbed one.' St. Peter says, 'OK. Dip your whole hand in the Holy Water and pass.' Just then the fifth girl in the line pushed her way up to the front of the line and said to St. Peter, 'If I'm going to gargle that Holy Water, I want to do it before Caitlyn sticks her ass in it.'"

Jack felt a little bewildered and was just going to tell The Musician that he liked the first joke when The Musician hit him again with another: "One time my mom found a bondage S&M magazine under my bed and she was so upset. She showed it to my father when he got home from work and he looked at it, then he handed it back to my mother without saying a word. So, my mother finally screams, 'What are we gonna do about this? He had a sado-masochistic… a bondage sex magazine!' and my dad says, 'Well, we're not going to spank him.'"

Jack disconnected.

The Musician rolled up to the edge of his bed and put his feet on the floor. He stretched his arms out as far as they would go and felt the blood begin to circulate. He reached over and scratched his collie-and-shepherd-mix dog behind his left ear as the mutt lay on the foot of the bed. The dog glanced up at his master. "Maybe I'll take you with me. You wanna play cops and robbers, Shane? Wanna shadow the hookers with me?"

"What's that about hookers, Willie?" his wife said from the doorway.

Willie stood up and walked toward the bathroom, shedding his pajamas as he walked. As he turned the shower on he shouted, "How about some coffee, baby? I gotta go back to work."

She walked into the kitchen and started the coffee and then walked towards the bathroom, shedding her pajamas as she walked, and stepped into the shower with The Musician.

Chapter 35

One Big Family

Tom and Victoria Peters were dressed to kill. Victoria looked into the mirror in their third-floor apartment and applied the finishing touches to her makeup. Her long frosted blonde hair was loosely clipped up. Victoria's strapless teal Cristobal Balenciaga cocktail dress was hand-tailored to accentuate her curvaceous body. Her carriage displayed her wealthy upbringing as much as the impeccably placed and overtly expensive jewelry. Victoria sprayed a cloud of perfume up into the air and then walked through it.

Thomas was pulling a black leather belt through the loops in his black pleated slacks. He tucked in his thin black mock turtleneck and rubbed the tops of his $600 Blacksnake cowboy boots on the back of his slacks over his calves to give them a shine. He combed his greasy black hair back and with the tip of his finger he felt the trim of his soul patch run from his lower lip to his chin. He sucked saliva through the cracks between his teeth to make sure none of the $1,000 sushi dinner he just provided for his escorts was stuck in between his teeth. Then he bent over the dresser and snorted a line of methamphetamine into his nose with a thin sterling silver tube.

"I really wish you'd do the cocaine rather than the crystal meth, Tommy. The meth rips up your nose and you know the coke has a lighter touch."

"Maybe I don't want a lighter touch," Tom said, smacking his hand on her ass cheek.

"Ouch!" his sister said. "This isn't a good way to start the night."

"Don't start reining me in, Vic! We haven't even gotten out of the fucking house yet."

"Easy, Tommy," Victoria said as she walked over to him and took the end of his belt into her hands.

"You missed a loop," she said and began to rethread the belt through the loops of his pants and when it was all the way around Tom's waist she pulled the end through the buckle and fastened it while looking straight ahead into her brother's eyes.

"I'm going to see that you have a great night, Tommy. I can't have a great night unless you do. You know that, don't you?" Victoria said while still holding her brother by his waist.

An intercom buzzer rang on the nightstand by the bed and Victoria walked over, pushed a button, and said, "What is it?"

A female voice said, "Sorry, miss, but there are four girls with early dates and there aren't any drivers here and I am the only manager."

"Marcus and Moose were supposed to be back. I'll be right down, Jenny," Victoria said and released the button.

"Tom, come down when you're ready. I'll get the early 'kindergarten class' out the door and whisked off to their romantic dream dates and we'll make the rounds. I'll bring the five cell phones and handle all the business from the limo. I promise you will have a great night!" she said and kissed him playfully on his lips. Victoria took a lizard-skin clutch bag from the top of her dresser, put on her black heels, selected a short black sequined matador jacket from her closet, and went down the stairs.

Tom took his sister's advice and picked up his black leather jacket and pulled a one-gram glass vial out from the inside pocket; as he laid out a line of high-grade Peruvian flake cocaine, he said in a near-perfect rendition of Victoria's voice, "I really wish you'd do the cocaine rather than the meth, Tommy. The meth rips up your nose." Tom bent down and snorted up the coke, pinched the end of his nose, and stared into his own eyes as he looked into the mirror.

Tom left his third-floor apartment and walked down to the first floor and the fully stocked bar. The College Escort Service often had wealthy VIP clients stop in with the escorts after hours. It was another reason Thomas had two small suites built into the back of the house. Peters charged a rate higher than any Boston hotel room for the apartments. They usually included the services of an escort. Tom assured each VIP client, no matter how rich or powerful they were, that the College Escort Service used the utmost discretion. Tom would never reveal the existence of the hidden cameras designed to record intimate and compromising photo opportunities. Blackmail was a viable alternative to assure cooperation in a number of

Thomas Peters's projects. Peters put a fifty-dollar bill into the tip jar on the bar.

"Do you know where I got this mahogany-and-rosewood section of bar, Charlie?"

"The Rat in Kenmore Square."

"How'd you know that?"

"You've told me fifty times. Usually at the end of every night."

"Yeah, well I'm going to buy another ten feet of bar from the Rack, that pool hall over at Haymarket. It's closing. Another Hard Rock is going in. I had some good times there. It's ambience, Charlie; that's what we need here: ambience. I think I'll start the evening with a Grand Marnier on the rocks, please. Don't forget to restock the coolers with ice at 1 a.m. I want those beers buried in ice. You've got enough start-up in the bank? If you need more ones, there are twenty stacks in the safe. I think it's going to be a good night, Charles. The phones were ringing off the mother-fucking hook when I walked by the office upstairs. Shit, I bet you have a three-hundred-dollar night. Where's Moose? Have you seen that fat bastard?"

"He was getting the black stretch washed, on Somerville Ave. He said he'd be back in ten… or was it by ten?" Charlie offered.

"Well, it's fucking ten-fifteen and I've got reservations at the Capital Grille on Newbury. I'm aiming to bump into some business associates," Thomas Peters said as he flipped open his cell phone. Victoria walked up to the small oak bar.

"Moose dropped off some girls for me; I was in a pinch. He'll be here in ten minutes. Take it easy, Tommy," Victoria said.

Tom glanced up at Charles, closed the cell phone, and then looked over at Victoria, "OK. Then I'll need another Grand Marnier, Charlie," he said and took the glass vial from his black leather jacket's inside pocket, dumping a pile of white powder on the bar. He took out a Mass. State ID and cut the pile in half and looked up at the bartender.

"See, Vicky. I'm just doing the Peruvian flake, like you said. Line, Charlie? It's the last tip you're going to get from me."

"Yeah, sure," Charles said, taking a straw from the setup in the middle of the bar. Tom snorted one pile with his sterling silver tube and Charlie snorted the other with his straw.

"How about one for the brother?" Moose said as he walked up to the bar.

"Brother from another planet," Tom said as he punched Moose on the arm and began choking him with his two hands around Moose's throat.

"Choking me will only enhance my orgasm!" Moose said, rubbing his bicep. He added, "Ouch! Felt like a mosquito!"

"Don't fucking start with me, Moose. And you know you're driving tonight as well as body guarding. No booze for you. No drugs for you. No trouble for me. Now let's go," Peters said, placing an unlit Marlboro between his lips.

"OK, Boss."

"You ready, Victoria?" Tom asked.

"All set. But we've got to drop off a girl at the Brookline Village condos and another at a residence on Jamaica Way."

"What the fuck, Vicky? You know I want to bump into Dickinson and the investor group. I've got reservations at the Capital Grille; I heard from one of our girls that Mr. Dickenson was going to be there to meet an overseas investor. Japanese or a Chinaman, I forget. But things are ready to roll at the AI. This is the big one, Vick," Peters said and pulled his sister close to him. She put her hand on his shoulder and they looked like they were going to slow dance. "This is the big one, baby," Peters said again to his sister. "We will have that big, happy family, you'll see." Peters laughed and let her go, then he picked up his drink, held it up in the air, and yelled out to the few escorts, drivers, managers, Moose, the bartender, and his sister, "*Bevo a una famiglia grande!* I drink to one big family!"

The workers knew the drill and shouted back, "To one big family!"

Victoria put her arm around her brother, saying, "You are so fucking charismatic, my love," and they walked towards the waiting limousine parked out in front of the building.

Chapter 36

Blood in the Water

"It's 10:15; do you know where your children are?" The Musician said to Jack over his cell phone.

"Huh?" was Jack's reply.

"They're just leaving the College Escort Service in a dark blue stretch. It's Tom Peters, and a woman, I think it's his girlfriend or wife, and two working girls, and the big black Elvis Presley wanna-be driving."

"Just don't get burned. If they figure out we're tailing them, we're cooked. Until I've got a reason to rule this guy out of this homicide, he's in."

"Now, I forgot, why do you have a bug in your ass about this guy and his escort service?"

"The Rich kid had made a date with the escort service the same night I figure he 'met his maker.' And those lab rats keep talking to me about the model for a line of robots that will be mass marketed like … the car… or the television set. Everybody's gotta have one. These are money-making robots. Michael, Seng Li, Rodney, and Peters were a part of that group. But Peters left to make money. He likes big, fast, and profitable money. He fits my profile. He's someone who will do what it takes to make big money."

"Oh," The Musician said.

"And I don't have a bug in my ass. I never had a bug in my ass. I never will have a bug in my ass. Now… where are you?"

"OK. But I think 'thou does protest too much, my Lord.' OK. We're turning onto Newbury Street from Mass. Ave. He's pulling over. I've got to go past. Oh shit, I've got to look away; I've got no cars between us. OK, I'm past him and pulled over to the right about fifty yards up. Black Elvis is opening the rear driver's-side door and Peters and his woman are stepping out. The limo is leaving and there are a couple of women in it. Peters and the lady are walking into the Capital Grille. You want me to follow the limo with the escorts?"

"No. Stay with Peters. Do you have that big living-room chair in the back of your van?"

"Put it back in when you told me about the case. This is the surveillance wagon. I got food in a Styrofoam cooler, a sleeping bag, magazines, a phone, a satellite radio, and a big jug to piss in."

"OK. That's more than I want to know. The limo is probably dropping off the escorts at their dates' locations. But he'll be back. Watch out for that limo driver. He'll spot you. He's probably a pro. Just don't get burned. And if you do, deny, deny, deny, 'til you die. But don't get burned. We can work this long and hard. We'll have to change cars. I'll get another operative when you're exhausted. I want someone to go on him 24/7. We've got the money upfront. You'll be out late tonight. When he's finally settled down for the night, you go home. Then get back there in the early morning hours. Call me if you see anything of note."

"Like what, Boss?"

"Like... whatever."

"Whatever, what?" The Musician said.

"Like... let's say a robot attacks your van and cuts open the side panel and drinks down a couple of quarts of oil from the engine and pulls you out by your ankles, and the robot holds you up in the air, his head spins around, and he unhinges his jaw... and he's just about to eat you... let's say you gives me a call then."

"Huh?"

"Call me if anything interesting or relevant to the case occurs."

"Thanks, Boss. That reminds me. Want to hear the Joke-of-the-Day?"

"Willie, I think we're done here."

"Call me The Musician, please, Jack. It's a robot joke! OK? You reminded me. Oh, I gotta sit here while Peters goes into the Capital Grille on Newbury and eats and drinks. And I gotta sit here, watch, hiding out, and you don't even wanna talk to me. You don't have time to hear my joke? Is that how you treat your employees?"

"Go ahead with your joke, you poor sad son-of-a-bitch."

"OK. A guy goes out to the golf course and tells the golf course pro he wants to play eighteen holes and he needs a caddy. The pro says, 'Well, we've got some experimental Robot Caddies, and if you try one, they're free.' So the golfer takes a Robot Caddy and plays the course. The Robot Caddy tells him the wind direction, the wind speed, the layout of the course, and selects the best club.

"Well, the golfer had the best score of his life and went away happy. The next week the golfer came back and asked for a Robot Caddy. The golf course pro said, 'We don't have them anymore.' When the golfer asked why the pro told him, 'They were so shiny the reflections from the sun interfered with other golfers.' So the golfer said, 'Why didn't you try painting them black?' And the pro said, 'We did. But three didn't come to work the next day, one came in drunk, and the other two tried to rob the pro shop.'"

"That's not a robot joke. That's a racist joke, M. You should be ashamed of yourself!"

"Hey, I'm not a racist! But I do believe that America has gone from enslaving the black man to worshipping him. We have gone full circle. White and black youth adore the black hip-hop and rap 'artists.' The white kids buy everything from their baseball caps to sports jerseys to sneakers. They go to any movie representing young black culture."

"Maybe there's nothing wrong with that. Maybe it's payback."

"The white kids in America are making these thugs millionaires!"

"That's what you're upset about. You ain't getting your piece of the musical pie, my brother," Jack said, harassing The Musician and needling him further with, "That's just the Man trying to hold you down. And I don't want to hear any racist jokes out of you, anymore… unless they are wicked funny."

"Oh, OK, Jack."

"No more racist jokes… That's bad coming from someone who thinks Jimi Hendrix was God. Or was it Muddy Waters…Or Howlin' Wolf?"

"Jimi Hendrix was my idol. Bass player and songwriter Willie Dixon was God," The Musician said.

"Well? He was jet black. I was with you when we snuck into the Inn Square Men's Bar in Cambridge almost thirty years ago when we were barely teenagers. Are you ashamed of yourself?"

"Yes. Yes, I am. But that joke was funny, no? Isn't that the point?"

"No! Well... No! Do you think there are any black people who sit around making fun of white people?" Jack asked.

"Yeah."

There was silence on the phone line and Jack hung up.

Kelly had been looking through Michael Rich's computer as best he could. He scrolled the URL addresses and looked at the websites Mike had been to. Most of them were technical or MIT oriented. Jack checked Michael's Favorites list and found they were mostly websites involving mechanics, electronics, computers, and research in science. They all seemed to be a recipe for the nerd lifestyle. L. L. Bean, Eastern Mountain Sports, Woods Hole Oceanographic Institute, weather sites, a couple of poker gambling sites, a couple of porn sites, and the escort service.

Jack accessed Michael's My Documents files and looked through the list. He found almost one hundred technical papers, proposals, theorems, classroom assignments, and project papers. Some of Michael's documents were thirty or even fifty pages long. His writings had titles like "The Robotic Brain" and "Integrating Systems," and "Intelligent Systems Control: The Big Picture."

There were also letters Michael had written to the U.S. Patent Office describing his Sympathetic Override Program for Central Control. As Jack read for several hours he began to get a better understanding of Michael Rich's work. The documents Michael had written indicated that he had investigated the human brain and its method of operation. He had set out to create computer software that would act in the same way with the systems utilized by robots. The program would act as the controller. The Sympathetic Override Program for Central Control would act as a brain.

It was clear to Jack that Michael's writings went from the theoretical to the practical as the writings described the software program and its mechanical integration with a robot. According to one of his recently dated letters to the U.S. Patent Office, Michael had included a compact disc with his paperwork and claim application to the Patent Office. Jack knew Michael's claims to his Sympathetic Override Program for Central Control had been protected.

Maybe that's what this was all about. Michael had developed an invaluable part of bringing robotics into the future. This system of controlling the robots was an essential ingredient needed by anyone wishing to manufacture the robots. Maybe they couldn't manufacture the robots without it. People knew Michael was applying for a patent. Rodney knew it. He had mentioned it to Jack.

Even though it was nearing midnight, Kelly picked up his cell phone and dialed Rodney's number. After several rings, Rodney answered. There was a lot of background noise and Kelly could hardly hear the voices as he spoke loudly into the phone.

"Hello! It's Jack Kelly! I can hardly hear you, Rodney. Where are you? Can you step outside?"

"No way, Kelly. There's a ten-dollar cover; I'm sitting in the Miracle of Science Bar and Grill just down Mass. Ave. from MIT. I've got a seat next to a smoking hot woman. Her name is Divinity! She's sooo cool. I can't believe she's even in here. She graduated Cal Tech. Computer Science! She's got on heels and makeup and gold. She's gone to the ladies' room, I'm saving her seat. I'm not moving an inch."

"Easy, boy! Four or five drinks and everybody looks good. Now, let me ask you, Rodney, how important was Michael's Systems Override system or whatever it was called?"

"*Mucho grande.* The fucking robot wouldn't work without it. It would fall on the floor. The robots would experience vertigo, for starters," Rodney yelled out.

"What a go?"

"What?" Rodney yelled back over the noise.

"Is there a band playing?"

"It's a DJ. Industrial acid house."

"Rodney, I can't understand you. Can you meet me tomorrow morning? I need to get some idea of who might want control of the Prototype and its systems."

"Oh, let's make it early afternoon, OK? Here she comes. I think I might be getting lucky tonight, this redhead is falling all over me. And she's got a limo outside with a driver!" Rodney yelled over a thumping beat with synthesizers wailing.

"Call me when you get up, Rodney," Jack said and then put his cell phone back in his pocket. Rodney was a likable guy, a little sharper than your average geek. Kelly was beginning to think Rodney's ramblings about the Prototype and its importance weren't so far off base. Jack was working the angle of motive. He was working the "why," after all. The cops had the forensics labs, the data bases, and scientific resources. Jack had only the personalities of the players involved to work with. Jack had to interview and interrogate. And he could push buttons. He had the street sense. He could be relentless. He could see the blood in the water and smell the scent of blood in the air.

Chapter 37

A Big Ho to Row

Victoria squeezed Tom's thigh under the table. She wanted to leave the restaurant and head out to the nightclubs but Peters wanted so badly to impress the small group of men at the table that he pressed forth his argument. The men seemed to tolerate his persuasive plea but one man asked for the check and another ordered the waiter to add a martini to the check as Tom Peters continued.

"You let me put a smaller percentage into this project, cash for the start-up money, and make me your operations manager at a full share. I promise you we're going to make this work. I'll run the day-to-day operations. Together we will oversee every aspect of this project. It is so within our grasp." Tom Peters held up a fist and tightened his fingers as hard as he could. He made eye contact with each of the three men sitting across the table. He thought he had put on a great performance.

But the group wasn't quite sold until Tom Peters told the group, very quietly, that he had already taken steps to secure the rights to the "Control." That's when the men sat up, leaned forward, and gave Peters their full attention. The silver-haired man in the middle of the group, Dickenson, said, "This is the last step needed to…." He looked around and said, "Your full partnership would be assured if you were to gain power over the Control. If you can get the rights to the… ah… system at that point, I'm sure, Mr. Peters you would be fully one of us." The other two men nodded and smiled.

"But how can you get the rights to the Control System? Our information was that the inventor, an AI Tech, had applied for the patent," the other silver-haired gentleman in the gray suit asked Tom.

"You may not need or… want to know. You must trust your new operations manager! Let him handle the nuts…," Victoria said, smiling at the men and adding, "and the bolts. Leave that kind of thing to Tom."

The silver-haired man put five one-hundred-dollar bills on the table for the group's meal, drinks, and tip. He stood up and said to Tom, "Mr. Peters, if you can secure the rights to the Control, freely with no legal entanglements, then you will be the seventh partner in this venture. Have a good evening, Ms. Peters," the silver-haired man said, bowing slightly as did the other two. The men walked to the door of the restaurant.

"I wanted to go an hour ago," Victoria scolded.

"Vic. Did you hear that? I'm going to be a full partner in what will be a major-major corporation. Leap into the future, NOW!" Peters yelled as he watched the last of the Interested Group walk out of the Capital Grille's front door and gather on the sidewalk with the others awaiting their limousines.

"Should we have champagne?" Tom asked his sister.

"No. It's almost midnight, let's hit the clubs. I've got to make some calls and we have to pick up three of the girls."

"Why don't the working limos pick them up?"

"Maybe the girls are for us," Victoria said, smiling and pulling on the lapels of Tom's leather jacket to get him up on his feet.

Tom was at his highest. He felt like he was at the top of his game. He was floating. Things had gone well for Peters and he was going to take advantage from now on. When he had first quit the AI Lab, Peters and a couple of his friends had hired some MIT undergrad geeks to work a few computers and they started a porno website where the customer could talk to the girls in her "dorm rooms" and ask them to do things like strip or touch themselves. Tom Peters made more money.

Peters still owned 25% of three porn sites that made money around the clock. He didn't need to deal meth. That was his hobby. It's how he made pocket change when he was a freshman. "No sleep" was the freshman's motto. Some of them used chemicals to stay awake and cram for tests or do papers. Better living through chemistry. Peters built a meth manufacturing lab within a mile of the MIT campus; it operated for three years before it got busted. Tom Peters sold meth and it opened him up to a network of shady geeks. It introduced him to a group of blackjack players from MIT, for which he organized the junkets to Foxwoods and Mohegan Sun in Connecticut, then Atlantic City, and finally Las Vegas. He made more money.

But tonight was special. This was the opportunity that was going to make Tom so much money that he would never have to work again. And his kids would never have to work. And his grandchildren would never have to work. He had impressed the Interested Group. They needed him. They needed the Control System. And Tom Peters was promising delivery of that Control System. He envisioned himself a full partner in a group of seven men that were going to start up the biggest mass production corporation since Ford Motors or IBM. They would have a corner on the market. Only Honda of Japan had been rumored to have a prototype nearly as advanced as MIT's model but they weren't even close. Either way it would mean astronomical sums of money for Tom Peters. The kind of massive amounts of money that gets hard to envision.

There was just one catch. Tom had to secure the rights to the Control System.

He hadn't sent a carload of pretty escorts along with a computer technician over to Alpha Omega Delta for nothing. The escorts Tom had sent to Mike's frat house had seduced Dexter until he was down on his back and they kept him occupied while Divinity, a computer technician, entered Michael's unprotected computer. In less than ten minutes she had downloaded the contents of Michael's computer's hard drive onto a flash drive that was now sitting on Tom's bureau at the College Escort Service.

Victoria had already called Moose on one of the five cell phones she was carrying and the Mercedes pulled up in front of the Capital Grille. Tom opened the rear door for Victoria while Moose remained behind the wheel. As the Mercedes limousine pulled away from the curb, Thomas dumped a pile of ground Peruvian flake cocaine on the limo's bar and was sticking his metal tube into his nose and snorting.

"Where to, Boss?" Moose asked.

"Lansdowne Street," both Peters siblings answered. They laughed, leaned closer to each other, and kissed.

"Pick up Monique at the Marriot Long Wharf first, Moose, my big black Elvis," Victoria commanded with a slightly drunken slur.

"He's *my* big black Elvis," Tom said.

It was suddenly silent.

"Thank you very much," the black Elvis said with an impression of Presley, "but Elvis has left the building."

As the stretch limousine drove from Newbury Street to Storrow Drive and on to the North End, the cell phones beeped and buzzed. Victoria took calls, arranging times and locations for pickups. She made some calls to the other limo drivers, telling them where to go and who to pick up. Most of the girls would be picked up and then dropped off at their next "date" until the night was through.

Moose maneuvered the limo to the front and center space at the Marriot. Tom said he would go in and get Monique but she walked down the hotel's steps wearing a short black cocktail dress and a short gray fleece jacket. Tom opened the rear door and she got in. Monique wore a scarf around her very short light blonde hair. She had bright green eyes and a big smile filled with straight teeth. She was always bubbly and on an upswing. Monique was a very popular and high-priced escort. She had an air of elegance; she carried herself well.

"Hi, guys. Thanks for picking me up," Monique said sincerely.

"You're done for the night, Monique," Victoria said sternly, biting her lower lip.

"I'm not getting fired, am I?" Monique said, sticking out her lower lip and looking over at Tom Peters.

"Mony, we are going to party tonight!" Tom said.

"Fabulous! But what about my big date with the judge tonight?"

"I'm going to send Jenny over." Victoria picked up the red cell phone and arranged it while Tom pulled Monique over to him and kissed her ear. Monique glanced over at Victoria to see if she was at all jealous but she looked to be delighted. Victoria loved to see her brother happy. Life was not good when her little brother was not happy.

Moose drove down to Kenmore Square and pulled up behind three other limos next to Fenway Park on Lansdowne Street. Tom told Moose to stay in the area and keep his cell phone on.

"I don't want to lose the judge as my client," Monique said.

"The judge is *our* client," Tom corrected her, "and he's getting too possessive of you. We'll tell him who he's going to fuck."

"We had a relationship, Tommy. It wasn't just a fuck."

"From what I hear he likes the spanking. And he likes to get it more than give it," Tom said as he leaned over closer to Monique. Victoria took another call while Tom was talking softly into Monique's ear: "How about you? Do you like to get it? Or do you like to give it? Monique… Monique… Miss Money… Miss Moneypenny…" and he began to sing the Tommy James and the Shondells song, "Mony Mony."

Victoria closed the cell phone and partly slid and partly wiggled over to Monique as she giggled and laughed. Monique looked over at Victoria and Victoria stole a kiss from her as Tom straightened his hair in the backseat's mirror. All three laughed as they got out of the limo and walked to the end of the line outside a velvet rope at the House of Blues entrance. One of the two bouncers assigned to the entrance of the nightclub saw Tom and waved him down to the door. He rolled a stanchion off to the side and Victoria, Tom, and Monique walked into the club.

There wasn't a big national act playing tonight. It was the young and cool DJ Rhythm, the hottest young DJ on Cape Cod. He was dropping mostly a blend of hip-hop, dance, and trance loops. The nightclub was packed, damp, and hot. Tom agreed to get the drinks. The huge dance floor in the middle of the main room was crowded but Victoria and Monique headed straight for it. They were absorbed by the pulsating group of dancers as the rhythmic thump and pop of the ambient R&B was pumped out over twenty-four speakers built into the walls, ceiling, and floor. They were in another world as the bass shook their ribcages, the sounds bombarded their ears, and the laser and strobe lights distorted visual reality. The colors intoxicated their senses.

Tom was sitting in a stall in the men's room, dipping into a small tinfoil with a metal straw. He craved the bang of snorting meth but snorting this finely ground cocaine powder was less brutal on the membrane walls of his proboscis. He flushed the toilet again to disguise the sound as he inhaled a third of the tinfoil's contents in through his nose and into his lungs. He felt the back of his throat get numb and something like an adrenaline rush course through his body. He put the tinfoil back into the lining of his belt and slid the steel tube into the belt buckle. He flushed the toilet again and stepped out of the stall just as his cell phone rang.

"Listen, Thomas," the silver-haired man said. "You impressed the Interested Group tonight. I very much want you to become a full partner within our group."

"Oh, thank you, thank you. There's nothing I would like better. This is indeed a great honor for me."

"Well… you are not a partner yet, my friend. Just one minute now. You have promised the Group the Systems Override Control. It is this, Thomas, which predicates your membership in the Group. I know you, Thomas. If you do not have the rights and the software for the Systems Control you had better get it. Time is of the utmost importance. The time is now. Carpe diem, Thomas. Carpe diem. Am I making myself perfectly clear?"

"Yes, sir. I understand. You won't be disappointed."

"We'll expect to hear from you soon then," and the silver-haired man, Dickenson, ended the conversation.

Tom Peters returned without the drinks, finding Victoria and Monique sitting in an oversize black chaise lounge in the corner behind the DJ. When Victoria said she'd like a Cosmopolitan, Tom snapped his fingers at a waitress walking by, telling her he'd have a double Remy Martin cognac and two Cosmos. Tom looked at Monique and she nodded her approval. Tom was a little pensive and Victoria said, "A penny for your thoughts?" Tom looked around quickly before he spoke.

"I just got a call from the Interested Group."

"Oh?"

"Yes, the pressure is on. They are making it clear that I am *not* a member and I won't *be* a member of the Group unless I obtain the Systems Control. Apparently they are concerned that I may not be able to deliver what

I 'promised' them. The 'time is now,' he must have said three times in a one-minute conversation."

"What are we going to do, Tommy?"

"We are going to deliver, Victoria! Monique, would you see if you can get a business card from DJ Rhythm? I want to hire him for a party."

"Sure. But I've heard he gets around $15,000 per night for private parties," Monique said.

"What? I could get Oakenfold from London or DJ Jett from New York City for $25,000! DJ Rhythm is from Felt on Washington Street. I'm not asking him to spin at the Kennedy Compound. Don't you think I can afford him?" Tom asked, his brow leveling over his eyes and his face turning angry.

"No, Tom. No, I know… well, I'll go see about that business card."

Monique got up and headed for the DJ booth. Tom sat down on the big black lounge chair with Victoria as the waitress brought the drinks.

"We don't have the Control System, do we?" Victoria asked, knowing the answer.

"I've got a flash drive on my bureau at CES that Divinity downloaded from Michael's computer when she went to his rat-trap frat house with a carload of girls. It should be everything. The girls occupied the frat house geek while Divinity went up to Michael's loft. I tell you if you throw a pretty girl in with some guys, their brains turn to mush."

"You don't have to tell me, Tommy Boy," Victoria said as she gave a young Boston University student a smile and he almost tripped over a chair.

"The info on the flash drive is, hopefully, everything that was on Mike's computer. I haven't looked at it yet, but he was the one who put the Control System all together. Tonight I sent one of the girls over to a bar near MIT, the Miracle of Science Bar and Grill, to get close to this other geek, Rodney Riviera. She's got a good driver, Marcus Grace, and the blue Lincoln Towne Car. I want this nerd impressed by her. I want this geek on a short leash. He was Michael's best friend. I used to run with that pack.

"We spent a lot of late nights at the Miracle Bar. 'Leap into the future, NOW!' we used to yell. We came up with that slogan. It was a joke at first. Rodney's the only other lab rat that could have a safety copy of Michael's programs. He might even have a copy of the Control System software itself. The Prototype was put together with the work of hundreds of people in specific groups but Michael Rich did almost all the work on the Control System alone. Mike was way outside of the box. He had some radical ideas and he struck gold. I might need to use Rodney to interpret what I've got on Michael's disc."

"Which girl do you have on him?" Victoria asked.

"Divinity."

"Of course," Victoria said, with a hint of jealousy.

"She graduated from Harvard Business School and Cal Tech. What better to prank an MIT guy? Call her and make sure Divinity is still with Rodney. Tell her I want her to make Rodney think she wants to see him again tomorrow night. Tell her I want her to have that geek at her beck and call. I want him to think he can't go to the store for a loaf of bread without checking with her. They need to fall in love for at least a few days. Tell her it's a high priority with built-in incentives for a job well done. Reassign all her clients and let Divinity know she will be paid double what she was going to make. Soon I should know what's on that disc. Maybe I won't need him but I've got to find out how much he knows about Mike's system. We'll take it from there. Or you know what? Have Divinity talk him into coming over to the office after hours tonight and bumping into us accidentally on purpose."

Victoria handed Monique her Cosmopolitan, took her clutch bag with her cell phones in it, and headed for a quieter spot to make phone calls. Monique sat down on the lounge chair and handed a light blue business card picturing a stereo turntable with a set of headphones on it to Tom.

"Good girl, Mony. What's DJ Rhythm like?" Tom asked as he looked her up and down. Monique looked good to Tom in her short black dress with her short blonde hair, big green eyes, and bright face.

"He's cool. He's mysterious," she said and laughed. "And he's kind of busy! He's spinning two vinyl turntables and listening to songs on a CD with headphones."

"I saw him pull those headphones off when you walked up to him."

After a few minutes Victoria returned and told Tom his message had been delivered to Divinity. Tom smiled and told her and Monique that they might want to drink up because they were going to be going to another club. Tom asked the women if they knew who was playing next door at 15 Lansdowne Street or down the street at Bill's Guitar Bar. Monique told him the New York Dolls and the Mighty Mighty Bosstones were next door and the local group the Dropkick Murphy's were at Bill's. Tom called Moose to bring the car around and finished his cognac, and the three got ready to leave. Half a dozen people nodded or said hello to the Peters siblings as they walked out of the nightclub with Monique and got into their limo. They headed for the Roxy on Tremont Street. Victoria activated some of the cell phones and answered messages from escorts. She arranged several rides for girls with out-calls and straightened out a few minor billing problems.

Tom felt good. He may not have to kill anybody tonight.

Chapter 38

The Only Good Computer

Jack's cell phone vibrated in his pocket as he sat dozing off at Michael Rich's computer at Alpha Omega Delta.

"Hey, Kelly. I thought I'd just leave a message, but I see you're up. Burning the candles at both ends?" The Musician inquired.

"Yeah, Willie. I must be strong. I must prevail. Evil is a full-time job. I'm digging through Michael's computer. It's telling me about the person and his world, but man, I need some hard facts here. Some real evidence. Some indication of who killed him. I can't let his father down. I don't care if the state police or the BPD, or even Jesse solves this and brings the guy in. But it has got to be done."

After a moment of silence Jack said, "Sorry. What was it you wanted to report?"

"What time is it?" The Musician asked.

"1:25 a.m."

"OK. Peters went to the Capital Grille on Newbury then to the new House of Blues and they just left the nightclubs on Lansdowne Street. We're heading in town… we're almost to Park Square."

"How are you holding up?" Jack asked.

"I'm OK. I'll stay on Peters late tonight and sleep until late tomorrow morning. As long as my wife keeps the kids and dog off of me. The dog bangs into the bedroom door with his head and knocks it open, jumps on the bed, and starts licking my face like I'm his long-lost brother."

"Shouldn't your wife be doing that? Giving you a little oral support?" Jack joked.

"Are you kidding? Before we were married her body was my playground. Now the only 'oral' I get is her talking and talking. I haven't spoken to my wife in three years. I don't want to interrupt her. We went to a marriage counselor. She talked through her time. Then she talked through my time. Then she talked through the counselor's time. But the sex is good. It lasts about twenty minutes. Sixteen of that is doggie style… I sit up and beg and she rolls over and plays dead. But she tricked me into marriage. She tricked me into knocking her up."

"She tricked you?" Kelly asked.

"With a date rape drug! The cops should be warning guys. Female sexual predators are using this easily available date rape drug. It comes in liquid form in bottles and cans. It's inexpensive. It's called 'beer.' A couple of bottles of this liquid and men are helpless to fend off the advances of the female predator. Men awaken with only a vague remembrance of the night before. And a rash on their dick. Some unfortunate male victims are swindled out of their life savings, in a scam known as 'marriage.' These unsuspecting males are entrapped in this long-term condition of servitude and punishment until they are no longer of any use to the female."

"You paint a rosy picture," Kelly said.

"Family. I don't know how I ended up with one. My in-laws suck. My wife's father says to me just before we got married, 'Young man, can you support a family?' I said, 'No! I'll take care of your daughter but the rest of you will have to fend for yourselves.' And my kids? They're out of control. One son is a mouse potato. Sits on the Internet every waking moment of his life. He's a screenager. A multislacker. And I've told you my daughter, the baby, seven years old, wants a bellybutton ring. Jesus, Mary, and Joseph. She went with me and little Danny to the barber to get Danny's haircut last Saturday morning. She stands there watching the barber cut Danny's hair and she drops her little snack cake on the floor. The barber says, 'Caitlyn honey, you're going to get hair on your Twinkie.' She says, 'I know, and I'm going to get boobs, too.'"

"You poor bastard," Jack said although he secretly envied the disorderly conduct, chaos, and mayhem that The Musician experienced in his family life.

"What can I do, Boss? I child-proofed my house... but they keep getting in. I feel like I'm trying to stop the tide from coming in. I'm just trying to keep my boys off the crack pipe and my girls off the pole."

"You've got great kids, Willie. I wouldn't worry if I were you. They won't be half as bad as we were."

"Hey, Jack. I'm looking at Tom Peters right now. Their limo just pulled up right in front of the Roxy. Want to hear the Joke-of-the-Day?"

"Go ahead," Jack said yawning.

"Little Johnny was in his third-grade class when the new teacher asked the children what their fathers did for a living. All the usual answers came up: fireman, salesman, factory worker, construction worker, etc… But Johnny was being uncharacteristically quiet and so the teacher asked him what his father did. Little Johnny said, 'My father's an exotic dancer in a gay bar and takes off all his clothes in front of other men. Sometimes if the money is good, he'll go out in the alley with the men and have sex with them.' The teacher, shaken by Johnny's candor, hurriedly gets the other kids to color some pages in their books. The teacher walks to Johnny's desk and whispers to him, 'Does your father really do that?' Little Johnny says, 'No. He manages the New York Yankees, but I was too ashamed to say.'"

"That's wonderful, Musician. Extraordinarily hilarious," Jack deadpanned. "Can you hang there and see where he goes from the Roxy?"

"Affirmative, Boss."

"Don't call me Boss. And don't call me again tonight unless it's something important. But call me as soon as you get up tomorrow and we'll take it from there."

"OK, 10-4, Jack. Hey, this guy is driving through a suburb of Boston and he sees a sign in front of a house that says, 'TALKING DOG FOR SALE.' He rings the doorbell and the owner takes him into the backyard where a golden retriever sits. The guy says, 'Do you talk?' The dog says, 'Yep.' The guy says, 'Talk to me.' The dog says, 'I discovered I could talk when I was a puppy and I decided I would help the United States government. I was recruited by the CIA and they jetted me all over the world. The CIA had me sit in the same rooms as world leaders and I spied on them for years. I was instrumental in resolving some of the world's most dangerous and explosive situations. I earned many medals and awards. But I wasn't getting any younger so I transferred to the FBI. I helped break up the three remaining Italian Mafia families. I just take on special assignments on the East Coast now.'

"The guy is amazed. He turns to the dog's owner and asks him how much he wants for the dog. The owner says, 'Twenty-five dollars.' And the guy says, 'This talking dog is incredible. Why are you selling him so cheap?' And the owner looks down at the dog and says, 'Because he's a liar. He didn't do half of that stuff.'"

"Musician, you better start writing some new jokes; I think I heard that joke years ago. Call me when you're up in the morning," Jack said, disconnecting before Willie could begin another joke.

While Willie Crawford had been telling jokes, Jack had searched the words "college, escorts," and a series of pictures of scantily clad young women began to pop up on the computer screen. Jack clicked on a few that said "college girls," or "college escorts," and more pictures covered the screen. The graphic pictures featured beautiful, young, alluring girls and began to include sites that showed sex acts. The pop-ups multiplied and stacked up on each other. Soon the windows were over a dozen deep. Layer upon layer covered the screen.

Jack tried to close them out by clicking on the little X in the upper right corner of the windows but they popped up faster and faster. Jack could not X them out fast enough. In desperation he finally reached down and pulled the computer's plug right out of the wall. The whirring sound slowed to a stop and the screen went blank.

"The only good computer is a dead computer."

Chapter 39

If I Died Tonight

"Vic. What was the name of that little one that ended up in my bed last Saturday night?" Tom asked.

"Little Wendy," Moose said loudly from the front seat.

"Thank you, Moose!" Victoria said sarcastically while pressing a control button putting the limousine's partition up all the way.

"I was going to fire her ass but you seemed quite happy with her, my love. Can we find out where she is?" Tom got no response from his sister. He turned the limo's TV on and attempted to pull in the Celtics vs. Lakers game. He put the limo's partition back down half of the way.

"Hey Moose? How are the Celts doing tonight?" Tom asked.

"Shitty, Boss. General Manager Danny Ainge better get it together! He was a good three-point shooter, but a not so good GM. He's changing players in the Celtics organization faster than I change my mutha-fuckin' T-shirt, man. He needed to get a big center, a ball-handling point guard, at least one superstar, and build up the franchise around this core with players who are going to stay and develop. And no more mutha-fuckin' old-ass veterans!"

"Egg-zactly, Moose. Egg-zactly. I probably lost a thousand on the Green tonight. Is the game over?"

"Fourth quarter," Moose answered.

"That's the last time I'm going to bet on the Celtics, I swear."

Victoria nestled closer to Monique and handed her a cell phone.

"Be a dear, check on the late dates and call the desk back at the office and see what we have coming in, would you, Gorgeous?"

"I'm watching the game," Tom said.

"Not you! Monique is gorgeous. You are irrepressible. Handsome, but irrepressible."

While the limousine was pulled up in front of the Roxy on Tremont Street, Victoria told Tom she had Divinity on the phone and handed it to him. Tom took the cell phone, asking Divinity what had developed between her and Rodney through the course of the evening.

Divinity spoke softly into the phone, "This guy, Rodney, is like a little bird eating out of my hand. He is trying very hard to impress me. I am letting him think that I am falling for his charms. But he doesn't have any. This guy is a super geek. Since I've done what you asked, can I get out of here now?"

"No. This has become very important to me. I want you to leave the club with him tonight just before closing."

"The club closed ten minutes ago. We're just finishing our drinks."

"Leave with him, alone. No frat brothers or friends. Tell him you'll give him a ride home. I don't care if he lives across the street. Just unceremoniously leave and get him in the limo. Then tell him you wish the night didn't have to end and turn on the charm, you know, do what you do and bring him over to the 'after hours' at CES. Don't tell him where he's going, just say you know an after-hours bar where it's quiet and you can have a couple of drinks and get to know each other. Don't let him make any phone calls telling anybody where he's going or who he's with. Are you receiving me, Divinity?"

"Tom, I've got something I wanted to…"

"Did I mention you're being paid double whatever you would have made tonight? This is important, to me."

"I'll have him there, Tom. Are you there, now?"

"We're going into the Roxy and we might stop for a drink at the clubs in the alley at Boylston Place. Got to spread the word, you know."

"What is the word, Tom?"

"Love, Divinity. The word is love."

It seemed like the Roxy was filled with pimps, whores, players, and hip-hoppers this Friday night. Tom Peters really didn't care about this scene, because he was a slick college-boy pimp and had his clientele. The only difference between him and the classic street pimp was that Tom accessed his Cambridge social connections and used the Internet as well as his associates in the academic world. He didn't put his girls out on the street. He didn't pimp his girls out for no fifty dollars. His ladies got hundreds of dollars for their obvious breeding and education. There was no substitute for impeccable upbringing. His ladies looked well. They spoke well. They carried themselves well. And they knew the art of seduction. They understood the mission and the ethics of Tom and Victoria Peters's College Escort Service.

But Tom had a history with some of the players at the Roxy. Most of the black pimps who worked hard and fought for their place on the street resented somebody like Tom. They resented Peters with his limousines and sick twisted sister, his holier-than-thou attitude and pretty little white college girls. The black pimps worked hard to develop their clientele. Tom's college bitches had stolen more than a few regular johns from the working girls belonging to the brothers at the Roxy. Tonight, Tom had exchanged nods with several associates in the business and thought he had detected hostility.

Tom called Moose after being in the club less than twenty minutes and told him to bring the car around to the front. Tom didn't need a confrontation tonight. He would soon be above the fray. He would soon be partner number seven in the Interested Group. The Group would form a solid block of businessmen that would soon be the talk of the scientific and business communities.

Monique and Victoria had handed out a few CES business cards to men who seemed like they would be interested. Tom had paid his respects to a few of Boston's more respectable pimps. The old-school pimps. Through the front windows of the club Tom saw his limo pull up. He gave a nod to Victoria; she and Monique filtered out the door and stepped into the back of the Mercedes limo. Tom hopped in and nodded to Moose, then pointed back towards downtown Boston. Moose pulled the stretch away from the curb and made a U-turn on Tremont. The Musician instinctively ducked in the back of his van as they drove past his surveillance location.

"Jesus, Tommy. What was that all about? We weren't in that club for fifteen minutes," Victoria whispered, more curious than prosecutorial.

"I got a little claustrophobic, that's all. I don't need these fucking clowns. I'll take the cream of their crop away from them, is all. I've got bigger fish to fry. I'm frying up some big fish. Big mutha-fuckin' fish! Those fuckers. They won't be able to get a fucking appointment with me in a year!" Tom yelled. He pulled out the tinfoil and dumped the contents out on the bar rail attached to the front seat of the limousine. He pulled the thin silver tube from his belt buckle and snorted up half of the pile in one nostril and said, spittle flying in all directions, "Who the fuck... they think they are? I'm going to buy and sell that fucking club. I'm going to rip it down and build a ten story. Fuck that!"

He snorted down the remainder of the coke. He coughed as the powdered drug hit his lungs. Victoria quietly rubbed his back. She knew how to handle Tom.

"Are we going to the Alley, Boss?" asked a puzzled Moose, rolling the partition half way down and glancing back and forth from Tom to Victoria in the rearview mirror.

"No. We're going home. I've had enough bullshit for one night. I had an epiphany back at that club. This is all small time. It's the fucking peanut factory. It's hardly nowhere. It's less than fucking zero. I've got just one big piece of business," Tom smiled and looked over at Victoria. "We are going to another level. Once I take care of this, then it's time for us to grow. Moving on up to the big time. And a big move up in every way. We are going to maximize. Even CES is going to branch out. I'm thinking Boston, Providence, Worcester, Hartford, and New York City. Our paying websites are about to double. It is not going to get any hotter than right now with the websites. The whole thing could be over in two years. Porn could be outlawed. Or it could even be made obsolete. Anything can happen. Now let's go home and party!"

Victoria had rubbed Tom's back, he had fed his addiction, and he had vented sufficiently. He felt good again. The city looked beautiful as they crossed the Charles River over the Longfellow Bridge. Tom shut the TV off as the ESPN NBA highlights pictured another of Tom's teams going down in flames. He put a Nine-Inch Nails CD in the player's slot and turned the volume way up.

It was 2 a.m. Most of the clubs in Boston and Cambridge had emptied out. The Musician had followed the black stretch limousine and had found a parking space facing the opposite direction on Harvard Street just down from the CES offices. He watched as Moose pulled the limo up in the lot at the office/apartment building Peters owned. Victoria had activated one of the cell phones and was listening to messages as she and Tom walked into the building with Moose and Monique.

"Hi, Jenny. Are there many calls coming in?" Tom asked a manager in the front office.

"Yes. We are close to being overbooked, Mr. Peters. If you see another manager, send her my way. I need help with the bookings. I don't want to make any promises I can't keep," she said as Tom passed her desk and headed straight for the bar.

Tom was thrilled to see that Divinity and Rodney Riviera were sitting on a brown leather couch near the bar. Rodney had become very important to Thomas Peters but Tom paid no attention to him as he walked up to the small bar and ordered a chilled Kettle One vodka martini with three olives. He instructed Charles to start a tab for him, which was a bit of a joke between them, since he has never paid. Tom took the martini and walked up the stairs to his third-floor apartment. He turned on a window fan, jacked up the heat to eighty, and walked to his closet. On a waist-high shelf he picked up a small mortar and pestle with a white powder in its bowl. He crushed the powder with the pestle and dumped it onto a small mirror. He picked up a half straw and inhaled the methamphetamine.

His mouth opened and his eyes got wide as he felt both the pleasure and the pain of the crystal meth bite into the membranes of his nose and the adrenaline rush running through his body. Tom ran his fingers through his dark hair, pushing it back. Then he ran his fingertip over the pencil-thin line of facial hair running from his lower lip to the tiny Vandyke on his chin. His dark eyes pinned as he stuck a Marlboro in between his lips.

Downstairs, Victoria finished her phone work and helped Jenny make arrangements for every CES girl with a date to have transportation to get home safely from their dates, no matter what time. The girls were expected to work all night long if needed, and on weekends it usually was. But the employees did get regular days off. The schedule at CES was flexible. Tom and Victoria had set up a health plan. It was mostly just for the two of them. But they did realize the importance of proactive prevention. They did stress the need for good health and safety in the workplace. If an escort had a problem with someone, Moose and the other limo drivers would intercede and resolve the problem. CES had a dozen drivers and they all had martial arts and security backgrounds.

Victoria walked up to the bar and announced, "Since I have this expensive cocktail dress on, let's have an expensive cocktail. A Cosmo, Charlie! With top-shelf booze!"

"That's an expensive dress, Ms. Victoria?" Charlie asked.

"Well, of course it is, Charles. Jeeezus! You wouldn't know an expensive dress if it was up over your head," she teased.

Monique materialized and ordered the same. Moose wandered over to Victoria and asked if things were going all right tonight. Victoria knew what he meant. Tom could get a little wild, get out of control. It was Moose and Victoria that would have to try to physically and mentally restrain him.

"We'll keep an eye on him for the rest of tonight, Moose. He's wired for sure. He's got some things going on. I'll be glad to get him bedded down tonight," Victoria said to Moose. Monique overheard and choked on her drink when Victoria said she wanted to get Tom to bed. Monique had heard the rumors about Victoria and Tom and knew them to be true.

Victoria and Divinity made eye contact and Victoria smiled and Divinity waved. Victoria walked over to the couch Divinity and Rodney were sitting on. Victoria said, "Hi, Divinity. You're looking well. Something must be agreeing with you. Oh, I didn't know you had a boyfriend. Excuse me for interrupting you two lovebirds."

"Ah… Victoria, this is Rodney Riviera. Actually, Victoria, we just met tonight," Divinity said as Victoria sat down besides Rodney.

"That's incredible. Well, I am sorry. I didn't mean to embarrass you kids. You just seemed so… so… right for each other," Victoria said and Divinity gently kicked her foot under the table and rolled her eyes.

Tom walked downstairs and into the recreation and entertainment room. Upon seeing Rodney, Victoria, and Divinity, Tom walked over to them.

"You remember my friend Divinity, Tom. And this is her friend, Rodney," Victoria told Tom and Rodney stood up.

"I haven't seen you, Tom, since the robot you built for Professor Halprin's lab broke down the door and assaulted two Techs walking down the Infinite Corridor, three years ago," Rodney said, extending his hand across the coffee table.

"That was five years ago. Hi, Rodney."

"Holy cow. This is your place, isn't it, Tom? My friend Michael, you remember Michael Rich, we've visited your website more than a few times," he said, looking around wide-eyed and smiling. "Michael… had dates from several of your College Escort Service… ladies," Rodney said, smiling.

Rodney looked at Divinity and the smile evaporated as he asked, "You're not a… an escort, are you?"

There was a very long and awkward moment and then Victoria said, "We'd love to have her. She is a doll. She's such a warm and outgoing kid. She could have a job here anytime… but she is just *too* sweet."

Divinity kicked Victoria's foot under the table, again, and said, "Well… I think I'll go to the bar and get another Cape Codder."

"I'll go," Rodney said but Divinity jumped to her feet, saying, "No, you stay here and catch up on old times with Tom, but don't you dare go anywhere without me."

As Divinity walked away, Tom said, "You know, Rodney, you couldn't find someone younger or smarter than Divinity. Well… younger maybe. She's a very bright girl. College grad, isn't she, Vic? Let me get us a drink, Rodney and we'll have a talk. I miss the AI Lab and I am dying to hear what has been going on there. What will it be?"

"I'll just have a beer. Sam Adams is good."

Peters walked up to the bar next to Divinity and ordered two Sam Adams beers. He told Divinity to go up to the third-floor apartment and put the flash drive on his bureau into his laptop and see what was on it. Tom said he would be up in ten minutes to take a look at it.

When Victoria saw Tom returning to the couch, she got up and met him halfway. He told her to bring several girls over to Rodney in fifteen minutes. "Make a fuss over him and keep him occupied, I've got to go up and look at that flash drive."

Tom gave Rodney his beer and sat down in a chair off to his side. Four or five escorts had arrived at the agency in the last twenty-five minutes; only one of them brought a john with her. They intermingled about the first floor, usually wandering between the bars, the room with the big-screen TV, the billiard room, and the bar room that Tom and Rodney sat in.

"Rod, tell me everything that's been going on at the AI Lab!"

"Well, you won't believe it, but I'm sure you know Mikey Rich was murdered!" Rod said.

"No! I read in the newspaper they found him in the river, but I didn't know he was murdered! Good God!"

"Seng Li was found in the Charles, too. That's too much of a coincidence."

"I thought maybe, they had quacked up?" Tom said.

"No way! Both of them were happy and well-adjusted. And this private detective is investigating the murder for Mike's father and he's talked to me quite a bit," Rod told him.

"Who does he think did it?" Tom asked.

"He doesn't seem to have a clue, actually. He's a little thick. I told him everything I know about it."

"You know about it, Rod? What do you know?"

"Well, ah… I don't know who did it exactly… but I told the detective that Michael was an important part of the work on a very important project. And I just feel that maybe his death has something to do with this project."

"Do you mean the Prototype Project? Did you forget I was with the core group that started the Project?"

"Yeah, I guess I did. You quit working in the lab by the end of my second year there, about… was it three or four years ago?" Rodney asked.

"Four," Tom said flatly. His mind was spinning. Tom was shocked that Rodney had made the connection between the Prototype and Michael Rich's death. He had to find out how much Rodney knew.

"Rodney, tell me why you told the detective Mike's murder had something to do with the Prototype Project?"

"Mikey had developed a computer software program and the hardware to override and integrate all the systems involved in a working sophisticated humanoid cyborg."

Tom almost dropped his drink on the carpet. Rodney knew a lot. However, Tom Peters knew a lot more than he was saying about Michael Rich's death and the Prototype.

"A what?" Tom said, pretending not to know.

"A control system... Central Control."

Victoria and three young women arrived and joined Tom and Rodney. Victoria sat in a leather-bound chair and the three women sat on the couch with Rodney. Victoria introduced Rodney to the young ladies as an MIT genius. They began asking him questions about what he did, and where he's been, and what movies he likes. They found him most fascinating, occasionally touching his arm or thigh, and laughing at almost everything he said. "Outside of counting money, what good is all that math, anyway? Is math sexy?" one of the women asked Rodney.

"Well," the inebriated scholar explained it this way, "scientists have ascertained that the average time of intercourse lasts about four minutes. The average number of strokes is nine per minute, making the average intercourse last about thirty-six strokes. Since the average penis is 6 inches, the average girl receives 216 inches, or 18 feet for each intercourse. The average girl does it about three times a week, fifty-two weeks a year. $3 \times 52 = 156$ and 156×18 feet makes 2,808 feet. That's just about a half of a mile."

"That's amazing," the woman said.

"So if you're not getting your half of a mile every year, I'd be glad to help." The nerd was trying.

One of the girls looked at the others and said, "Oh, I think we're getting our half mile!" They all laughed and a blonde airhead escort stroked Rodney's Sam Adams bottle and asked him if he liked beer.

His answer again was just as eclectic.

"If you purchased $1,000 of Scientifico Industries stock one year ago it would now be worth only $42. If you bought $1,000 of Enron stock it would be worth only $17. WorldArms, you'd have less than $3 left. But... if you bought $1,000 worth of beer one year ago, drank all the beer, and turned the cans in for the aluminum recycling refund, you'd have a whopping $289. So, based on these mathematical calculations, the evidence indicates the best financial advice is to recycle. And drink a lot of beer!" Rodney declared, holding his beer bottle on high.

The women were speechless.

"Vic, get Rodney and I a couple of beers on my tab, I'm going to change up this music and give the bass a boost," Tom said. He got up, headed toward the front office, switched the radio station off, put in a Doors CD, a Prince CD, and an R. Kelly CD, and then took the back stairs up to his third-floor apartment.

Divinity sat at Tom's desk with the laptop open and she seemed quite involved.

"What have we got on the flash drive, Divinity.?" Tom asked.

"Look at this. There are letters to the U.S. Copyright Office, patents, and letters to three different lawyers expressing his intent to patent software for some kind of gizmo. There are scientific documents and detailed technical papers that are way over my head. There are upwards of fifty-five documents."

"Those look like school papers. What else?"

"In his e-mail there are similar correspondences to government agencies, all referring to this Systems Control gizmo. There are no e-mails in his inbox; apparently he erased them. What are we looking for, Tom?"

"Are there any schematics, or plans, or blueprints? Is there anything that shows how the gizmo works? Or something he sent along to the U.S. Patent Office? He would have to send a working model or the plans for the gizmo to get a patent on it," Tom said, a little desperately.

While Divinity searched the information on the flash drive, Tom walked into his closet. On the third shelf he found a small bag of rock cocaine. He put it in a grinder and spun the lever around five times. He dumped the contents out on the small mirror and quickly made four lines. He pulled the silver tube from his belt buckle and snorted a third of the pile. He coughed from the cloud of cocaine in his lungs and put an unlit cigarette into his mouth.

"OK," Divinity said. "OK. There are two references to the model, the example, of the item he wants to patent. And they are File 361. OK! Let me do a search for File 361. OK... searching... for File 361. And here it is!" Divinity said, double-clicking on the file and leaning back in her chair. Tom leaned over her shoulder and looked at the monitor screen. And then Divinity continued, "Oooh! There's nothing on it. He deleted it. OK. Let's check the trash... for File 361... Yes! Here it is: 361 and it's a big file."

Tom Peters was back looking over Divinity's shoulder as she opened File 361. Suddenly numbers began scrolling across the screen. Rows and rows of numbers. Occasionally there were spaces, but it was basically all numbers. Twenty rows scrolling across the screen. Numbers spinning forward so quickly they appeared to move backwards. They rolled on and on for over a spellbinding minute. And then they were gone as suddenly as they had appeared.

"Aarrgghhh!!!" Tom screamed. He grabbed a hold of Victoria's bureau and pushed it until he knocked it over. As the heavy bureau crashed to the floor, the jewelry box opened and spilled its contents across the floor.

"What's the matter, Mr. Peters?" Divinity asked, more than a little frightened.

"You don't know how important this is! I've got to have this Control System! I must have it!"

"What's going on? I thought I heard a crash. What happened to my bureau?" Victoria asked as she came into the apartment.

"All we've gotten for information from Michael's fucking hard drive is fucking numbers scrolling across the fucking screen! The motherfucker! It must be a code."

"All right. Relax now, Tom. You're right. We'll find a way to read it. If the Project was so important Michael wouldn't have left it for just anyone to read," Victoria soothed him, walking him over into the bedroom.

"Yeah, Vic, thanks. You're right. I bet that fuckin' nerd Rodney knows what these numbers are all about. He seems to know a lot. He's been talking to a private detective, telling him his theory that Michael's death has something to do with the Prototype."

"You're kidding! How does he know? How many students in this school of thought?" Victoria asked.

"Big-mouth Rodney has only told the detective, I think," Tom guessed. "Seng Li won't be talking about it."

"Maybe it would be better if Rodney and the detective weren't talking about it either. Maybe if they weren't around." Victoria was the cold-blooded one.

"My sentiments exactly. I'm going to put Marcus on following the detective. I need to know where he goes, who he talks to, and what he's doing. I'll get the detective's name from Rodney."

"Be careful with this one," Victoria said.

"I wonder if I should have Rodney look at the flash drive with us. But I'm afraid he's going to realize I raided his best friend Michael's computer, stole information... and that I want Michael's Control System. If he puts that together... I'm going to have to shut him up!" Tom almost hissed as he whispered to his sister.

"Let's keep Moose right by your side, Tommy. You know I'll back your play. This killing is very messy business. I agree. This needs to be nipped in the bud." Victoria grabbed Tom's balls and said, "Do what you have to do... for one big family."

"Here's something!" Divinity shouted.

Tom walked in and looked over Divinity's shoulder and interpreted what he saw on the laptop for his sister.

"It's a patent application Michael sent to Washington. It's dated thirteen days ago. Oh God.... We're screwed!" Tom said, standing upright and closing his eyes.

Victoria walked out of the bedroom and said, "Tommy! The government is so slow. I bet they haven't processed his application yet. It's the Bureaucratic Shuffle. Who knows how long it could be? If we can translate the data on the flash drive we can resubmit this under our name. Michael Rich is dead. Dead and gone. You worked in the AI Lab as much as any of them. More than most! The Prototype Project needs a strong hand to guide it. And that is you, Tom! This was meant to be."

Tom stiffened even more. He looked Victoria in the eyes and stepped in front of her. He put an arm around her gently and rested his hand on the top of her derriere.

He swallowed and said, "You're so right. You know me so well. You know what I am capable of. You are my strength!" He hugged her.

Divinity told Tom she had reviewed all she could find on the removable storage drive he had given her. Tom sent her down to the CES lounge with instructions to keep Rodney entertained. As Divinity left the room, Victoria pulled Tom's body tight to her and spoke to him with a rhythm and cadence that seemed to mesmerize him.

"Great people rise to the occasion, Tom. This is our time. If we are going to make our bones, the time is now. Let's do what we have to do and let the chips fall where they may. To achieve greatness we have to take risks. We have to excel and try harder, stay up longer, and risk more than the others. We have an opportunity here. We have an opportunity to be a part of the Project!"

The two kissed briefly, then Tom backed her up a few feet and pushed her down on the bed. He went to his closet and pulled a small vial of white crystallized rocks out from his blue-and-gray bathrobe's pocket. He put a few rocks of the cocaine into a small mortar and with a pestle he ground down the rocks into a fine powder. He dumped out the powder and made rows with a razor blade. Then he pulled the silver tube from his belt buckle and snorted three lines. He walked out into the bedroom, straightening his clothes and running his hand through his long dark hair, and said to Victoria, "Let's get to work."

When he got downstairs, Tom was pleased to see Rodney still sitting in the same spot on the couch, surrounded by the bevy of beauties. Divinity was at the bar, so that's where Tom and Victoria headed. Tom ordered two Sam Adams lager beers. Victoria got one of their drivers, Marcus, on one of her cell phones and handed it Tom, who asked Marcus how things were going tonight. He asked Marcus which girls he was driving and where he was going. Then he asked his availability for the next week, telling him he might want somebody followed. Marcus, eager to please the boss and owner of CES, told Peters he was available.

But before he could have him followed, Tom had to find out who the detective was.

"Orchestration, Charlie!" Tom whispered to the bartender. "Orchestration."

"Vicky, would you and Divinity scare away those vixens surrounding my friend Rodney? And in a few minutes I think I'll have a little quiet time with Rodney. I need to talk to him about some fascinating new developments in robotics."

The two women went over to the couch where Rodney was sitting. Never one to beat around the bush, Victoria said, "Tom would like to talk to you girls for a minute," and the girls cleared out so fast the foam cushion on the couch next to Rodney hadn't found its shape before Divinity's ass landed on it.

As the escorts went over to see Tom at the bar, Victoria asked Rodney if he had ever modeled. Rodney laughed and Victoria gave him a shocked look as if she really believed it herself.

"No, really," Victoria went on. "You have classic bone structure. Your features are very attractive. And I know attractive. I hire most of the girls that work for CES. And we get occasional calls for young college men, such as yourself, Rodney." But Rodney didn't seem to be buying it, at first. Victoria saw Rodney's frosted tips and she knew she could play to his vanity so she continued, "You should have seen some of these girls when they first came in here. Plain. Lacking style. Half of them wore too much makeup. Now all I'm saying is with some sharp clothes, a shave, and a haircut, my guess is you're going to be oozing sex appeal." Victoria's delivery was so good that the little MIT geek was starting to believe it himself. As he scratched his chin and idly looked around for a mirror to look in, she asked him if he'd fill out an application while he was at CES.

"You're kidding, right?"

"Absolutely not! Would you consider some occasional work as an escort?"

"Oh. I don't think I need to do that," Rodney said, a little too unconvincingly.

"It pays… We could start you at $500 a night? What do you say? Just fill out the application, please? I'll ask Divinity if she would come over and take all your information right now, OK?"

The prospect of Divinity sitting with him on the couch was all that was needed to clinch the deal; consequently he agreed. Victoria was proud of herself for engineering an innocent way to get some information from Rodney. His address, phone number, any personal and business references. Information just to have for future reference. If there were any future for Rodney. And filling out the application with Divinity would keep him occupied until Tom could grill him.

Tom and Divinity were talking about the information on the flash drive as Victoria walked up to the bar to ask Divinity to help Rodney fill out an application form. She instructed Divinity to go to Rodney and she would go get a pen and the application and bring it to her. As Divinity crossed the room to Rodney, Victoria told Tom of her plan to get some information from Rodney. But Tom was thinking of something else. Tom looked at Victoria like a sad puppy that had pissed on the floor and knew he was going to get a rolled-up paper slapped on his ass.

"I'm sorry I knocked over your bureau with everything on it. It was quite a crash. I'm sorry, Vic. I know your jewelry is scattered all over the bedroom floor."

Tom looked so sad Victoria couldn't be mad at him and she broke into a huge grin and said, "It must have been something. That bureau must weigh 250 pounds. And all my jewelry… You're going to help me pick up everything and if there is a diamond missing you're going to replace it, you bastard!" Victoria said, shaking her head. Tom moved closer to her and hugged her as they both laughed intensely. Tom picked her up and twirled her around a couple of times, yelling, "I love this bitch! I love her to death. A round of drinks to everyone on the floor. Except the drivers still working."

"Am I done driving tonight, boss?" Moose shouted from somewhere near the front door.

"No!" Tom yelled back and as Victoria ran off towards the office to get the application, a dozen or so people at CES headed for the bar. Tom walked over to Rodney and Divinity and sat in one of the stuffed chairs.

"Are you having a good time, Rodney?"

"If I died tonight, I'd die happy."

Tom was thinking about that possibility when Victoria returned, handing a pen and an application on a clipboard to Divinity, saying, "Tom, Rodney has agreed to fill out an application. I think he'd make a great escort. For special occasions. Clients that like his type."

"What is my type, Victoria?" Rodney asked.

"Well…," Victoria said.

"You're the James Bond type, Rodney," Tom said, bailing out his sister.

"I'm as dull as they come, Tom."

"You were just telling me about a murder case you're involved in! And you were talking to a real-life private investigator. Was he a PI, like Magnum… or Kojak? What's his name?" Peters asked.

"Kelly. Jack Kelly. He's no Kojak, though. He's no Magnum, PI either. A MacGyver, he's not. He's not Jack Bauer. He's a little thick. He doesn't have a clue. He's just not that bright. He just doesn't seem to get it. In fact, if he got any dumber he'd have to wear a helmet."

"Kelly? No, I never heard of him. Where's his office?" Tom asked innocently.

"I don't know. I never went there. He was staying at Michael Rich's frat apartment for the last four days."

Tom glanced over at Divinity and raised his eyebrows and said, "I'm surprised we've never bumped into him. Have either of you ladies?" Both women shook their heads from side to side.

"I've talked to him over the phone more than a couple of times. He's got a lot of questions. The first time I met Kelly was at the MIT Museum. I showed him the model robots in the museum and how they have evolved from shimple operational models to complex systems," Rodney said, starting to slur his words. "I can't get this two-bit flatfoot to understand how important it is. I tried to explain to him that our friend Michael had some pretty important information in his head about the advancement of modern robotics and it might have gotten him killed. This 'private eye' would just look at me with a shtupid shmirk on his face," Rodney slurred.

"Michael Rich worked with Rodney and I at the Artificial Intelligence Laboratory at MIT, ladies," Tom explained as if Victoria and Divinity didn't know.

"And you said you were 'as dull as they come,'" Victoria said to Rodney. Both the women looked at each other and smiled.

"So that was it, Rod? You just told the detective you thought Mike's death might have had something to do with his AI Lab work?"

"Yeah, he's working for Mike's father. He's shtaying at Mike's frat houshe apartment," Rodney said with a drunken slur.

"Oh... Good," Tom said, thinking that Rodney wasn't as big a threat as he thought. Tom took his Sam Adams and was in the process of sucking down the entire bottle's contents blissfully when Rodney spoke again.

"I told that detective the Prototype Project was the place to look. Somebody from that Interested Group killed Michael Rich and Seng Li."

Tom Peters was caught off-guard. He swallowed the beer down the wrong pipe. He coughed and gagged. Beer spit out from his mouth as he tried to suck in air. He pushed his chair back with his feet and stood up with Sam Adams lager running down his chin and onto his shirt.

"Jesus Christ, Tommy!" Victoria said and instinctively picked up a napkin from the table, stood up, and wiped his chin and shirt. Then she and Tom walked over to the bar where Charlie, Monique, and Moose were talking.

Rodney Riviera had just signed his own death warrant.

Chapter 40

Dead on the Internet

It was 3 a.m. The Musician had long left his surveillance and had gone home to bed but the music was still pumping at CES. Rodney and Divinity were whispering and chuckling on the couch when Tom walked over.

"How are you feeling, Rodney?" he asked.

"Shuper, Tom. Are you going to ask me to dance?" Rodney slurred.

"I wonder if you'd take the time to look at some information I have on a computer zip drive for me, Rod?" Tom asked the drunken grad student, knowing Rodney had worked in the Computer Science Lab before they worked together at the Artificial Intelligence Lab.

"Waz it? Video games? We could get together next Monday."

"I mean now, Rodney. I've got it on a laptop upstairs in my living quarters and I've got to change my shirt; I've dribbled beer all over it," Tom said and saw Rodney look up at Divinity and so he added, "You wouldn't mind coming upstairs with us, Divinity, would you?"

"No, Tom. Let's move the party upstairs, Rod, honey. The music's a little loud down here, too," Divinity answered as she stood up.

"Why don't you walk him up, plug in that flash drive, and locate that file. I'll be right behind you with a round of fresh drinks. I want to make sure Victoria has the night scheduled out and all the girls have transportation. Then I'll be right up," Tom said as he walked over to Victoria at the bar. They both watched Divinity and Rodney, who was a little out of balance, begin their ascent. Tom ordered a Cosmopolitan for Divinity and two Sam Adams longnecks for him and Rodney. He asked Moose to bring another round of drinks up to the apartment in about twenty minutes and told him that this night may develop into a long night. Moose felt the black leather gloves in his back pocket and he checked for the hard plastic bulge under his left armpit.

"What are you going to do if he recognizes the information on the drive as belonging to Michael?" Victoria asked.

"I'll have to cross that bridge when I come to it. And I may be coming to that bridge soon, anyway. Rodney has been spouting off to anyone that will listen about his theory that our group is responsible for Seng Li and Michael's deaths. If that nerd only knew the half of it he'd flip out. As far as I'm concerned Rodney is now a major threat to our success. He always was too fucking smart for his own good."

As Rodney leaned against the doorframe, Divinity looked back at him... She was relating to him. She thought of all the persons she could have been. She was destined to take a certain path. She was one of the unlucky knockouts born with looks that would assure her that doors will be opened for her. There will be no struggle for her. She will never fight the good fight. She doesn't have to. She has the looks that assure her others will champion her cause.

Divinity stared at Rodney as he stood in the doorframe. The light in the hall behind him highlighted his thin body and skinny ass. The frosted tips on his just-got-out-of-bed haircut spiked out like the crown on the Statue of Liberty. Divinity had to shake her head. What was happening to her? She felt a strong attraction to Rodney. But she was a pro. She doesn't fall for anyone. Not anymore. Because being a beauty born and raised in a small town, she knew what it was like to be cornered in the cab of a pickup truck fifteen miles from home with a country yahoo who won't take no for an answer and tells her to put out or get out. Every man she ever trusted tried to get into her panties.

She shook her head again and felt as if she were looking through a fog. The soft colored lights shone all around Rodney as he slowly walked across the room to her. He was going to say something but Divinity reached out and put her finger on Rodney's lips. "Sshhhh…" she said as she moved closer and looked up into his soft sad eyes. She felt totally at ease with this geek grad student from MIT. He was unthreatening. When their lips met, Divinity melted into that little girl that just needed and wanted to be held.

Divinity pulled away from Rodney and straightened her long red hair as they both heard the clinking of beer bottles coming up the stairs. Tom came in, saying something about installing an elevator and rambling on about iPod Nanos and stationary bicycles.

"Divinity, show Rodney that number scrolling file on that drive. It's the weirdest thing I've seen since DOS. Rodney, I bet you could tell us what it is. Couldn't you? You bastard! Divinity, I'll have you know that Rod here was three years in MIT's Computer Science Lab and when it merged with us at AI we thought it was going to be awful, but it just made the whole unit stronger. There were some serious strides made during the first three years, I'd say."

"Oh, definitely," Rodney agreed.

"That's when the Prototype Project was born. It was our baby, it was. We created it. So much promise. Man, I wanted to see that through. I thought it would be another fifteen years. So… I had to get out. I needed to make money! I needed to make some serious green for me, myself, and I. So, I set up those websites and bang! I went from living in that fucking converted garage on Storrow Drive to owning this building. And I own that converted two-car garage now. It's a nice little studio apartment. Last year that little fucking square cubicle was appraised at $850,000! That fucking garage! I fixed it up a little. It's got skylight windows and the bed is suspended from the ceiling so it doesn't take up any floor space. It's got a great kitchen. I'll show it to you sometime," Tom said and added, "And I own every limo outright. And I'm employing a lot of people here at CES. I get some fat cash from those websites I started three years ago. I don't operate any of that now, I just own 85% and outsource the operations. And I inherited a bit of money, too."

"Dude, you're doing super well! These altruistic MIT save-the-world crusaders haven't got a clue. You have the life, dude. I mean, these ladies all around you. It's a dream. You died and went to heaven."

"No, Rodney. It's not heaven."

In fact, it was hell for Tom. A living hell. His torment was deep. He hated women. Loved them and hated them. He was very successful building a business that utilizes the skills of beautiful women. It takes a special kind of personality to handle that business. Many men feel their knees buckling when a gorgeous young woman, or practically any gorgeous woman of any age, looks at them and asks for something. Men have been programmed to succumb to this throughout existence on this planet, if not longer. Men become brainless in their presence.

Tom Peters wasn't blinded by a woman's beauty.

He worked them hard and they loved it. He was sleek yet rough around the edges. He was sensitive at the right times, and at other times direct and business-like. He was controlling and manipulating, and yet displayed a vulnerable, codependent side. He could nurture and present a side that demanded to be nurtured. Many women could not resist this combination in a smart, wealthy, and good-looking package.

And Tom was perfect for dealing with an otherwise disabling, disarmingly beautiful girl. He wasn't intimidated. He had a method to keep his objectives clear and in focus. He simply, in his mind, pictured the flesh being ripped away from the beautiful woman's skull and pulled off of the face to reveal eyes, a cranium, nostrils, a mouth, and a working jaw. The female, in Tom's mind's eye, continues to talk and ask for favors but Tom only sees a skull with jaws still moving and the eyeballs looking up at him.

Tom asked Rodney to take a side and help him prop up Victoria's bureau and they stood the heavy bureau back on its four legs. The two men picked up items of jewelry and assorted cosmetics putting them back on the top of the bureau.

As she sat in front of the laptop, Divinity attempted to bring up the stolen binary section on the flash drive. She thought about the intimate moment she shared with Rodney. She wondered if he felt it too. Divinity had spent the night trying to get the geek to love her but she found herself falling for Rodney. This could never work, she thought. He's from MIT, and she graduated Cal Tech and Harvard Business. It was always the wrong guy with her. Bad boys, losers, and nuts.

"Here it is!" Divinity said.

Rodney and Tom looked over her shoulder at the computer's screen. Numbers began scrolling across. Slower at first and then quicker and then slower again. White numbers on a blue screen. Thousands of numbers and occasional spaces. They scrolled so fast they appeared to move backwards.

"Try turning on the speakers," Rodney said and Divinity did but there was no sound recorded.

The white numbers ran across the blue screen for a minute thirty seconds and then stopped. Divinity blacked out the screen and turned sideways in the chair, looked up at Rodney, and asked, "What is it?"

"What else is on the drive? How big is it? How much information is on it? Is everything on the flash drive binary?" Rodney asked Divinity, who looked back at Tom standing behind Rodney.

After a long pause, Divinity said, "Don't answer a question with a question! I asked you first."

Rodney laughed. He was smitten, all right. He looked at her and then looked at Tom and smiled. "Well...," he said, "it's a bunch of numbers." Rodney smiled again at Tom and then Divinity.

All three laughed. It was quite funny. Each was smiling and laughing. Rodney smiled and bit his lower lip and looked at Divinity. She laughed.

"A bunch of numbers!" Tom echoed.

"OK...," Rodney said, wiping a tear from his eye. "It is information. Binary information. It needs to be decoded and should translate into the English language or some math, or images... or something."

The room got very quiet until Rodney said, "What's it supposed to be?"

"I guess we'll never know then," Tom said, looking out the apartment window into a dark black night.

The three were silent. And then Rodney said, "I should be able to decode that in about five minutes. There's a website that identifies and decodes binary figures in seconds. I just have to access it."

"Well, all right! Why didn't you say so? Divinity! Burn just that binary section off that flash drive onto another disc and then hand it over to Rodney and let him sit down and weave his magic carpet."

"What's supposed to be on this, Tom?" Rodney asked again.

"I don't know. That's the mystery."

"Seriously, dude! You know about binary, right?" Rodney asked.

"I came to the AI Lab by the Engineering Department. You came by way of the Computer Science Lab, so just spell it out for... Divinity."

"OK. Computers 'think' with numbers. All data in the computer is stored in binary code using just two numbers: zero and one. The whole alphabet is translated into numbers. A is 01000001. And so on. Computers can 'crunch' absolutely huge numbers. So they can spell out things at an extremely high rate. So information, like this scrolling binary code on this disc, is stored in numbers. The good news is binary is such an easy code to break. It can be changed into sound and sent over phone lines or the Internet, or from machine to machine…" Rodney was starting to free-form brainstorm and his analytical mind began to narrow the possibilities. He was eliminating some and adding others as his list got shorter.

Rodney sat down at the computer and as he cued up the disc and got on the Internet, he said, "All I have to do is find a binary-to-text translator. I'll download the numbers and have them converted on a webpage with an encoder/decoder."

"I knew that," Tom said, but in the back of his mind he was worried. He had felt good tonight. And he didn't want that to change. He wanted to secure the blueprint, the mechanics involved in Michael's Sympathetic Override Program for the Central Control of Functioning Integrated Systems. He didn't want to kill anybody. He liked Rodney. But if Rodney translated the coded information into something identified as the property of Michael, then Rodney would know that Tom probably had not come by the information legitimately. Or Rodney might think that Tom contributed to Michael's demise. And Rodney would go shooting off his mouth to Jack Kelly. And the real cops would get involved. The Interested Group would drop Tom like a hot potato. And that would be the least of Tom's problems.

Moose walked up the stairs, tapped a few times on the apartment door, and walked in with a tray of two Cosmopolitans, two White Russians, and four Sam Adams beers.

"Shammy Boy!" the drunken MIT student said upon eyeing the tray of Sam Adams beers.

Moose raised an eyebrow at Rodney, then Tom, and then Divinity and said, "Who you calling 'Boy'?" He put the drink tray down on Victoria's bureau, took out a beer, and walked over to Rodney, towering over him.

"No… I mean… I wasn't calling *you* 'Sammy'! Or… I mean 'Boy.' No, sir," Rodney said, looking up at the six-foot, four-inch African-American Elvis impersonator. Moose smiled and gave him the beer.

"Sammy! I like that one. Hey, Moose? Can I call you 'Shammy,' too? Shammy Davis Junior?" Tom said.

Rodney had gotten online and went to three or four different sites to find what he needed to decipher the binary figures. He brought up the disc's contents and loaded them onto one side and put the decoding page onto the other side of the computer screen. He tried three different decoding programs until one matched with the disc. As he ran the disc's contents through the decoding program, he said, "This should do it," and the information was translated.

The screen was blank for a second and then the numbers began to scroll across the left side of the split screen. And then the screen on the right lit up with the words: "Sympathetic Override Program for the Central Control of Functioning Integrated Systems. Patent Applied For. Michael Peter Rich, 96 Wilson Road, Nahant, MA 01908, DOB 12/13/84, SS# 032-38-6552."

Rodney began to scroll through Michael's overall description of the system. Then, as Tom and Divinity looked on, Rodney scrolled through Michael's design schematics, the engineering details needed for the complete development. It was the entire technical manual for the development and manufacture of a working Control System for human-like robots. To witness the detail in Michael's design was a sheer joy to behold for Rodney. He was lost in the beauty of Michael's vision. It was the final step in the development of a walking, talking, all-purpose assistant/slave that worked 24/7. They were inorganic, nonliving, inanimate machines. They were dead things by human standards. They would be hooked into the ever-expanding ocean of information available. They would be online at all times. These are machines that think, these dead on the Internet.

Chapter 41

The Intoxicated Egghead

Rodney came to the end of the binary information that had been translated and wondered how Tom had acquired the flash drive. It was obviously the intellectual property of Rodney's best friend, the recently murdered Michael Rich. Rodney picked up his beer bottle and took a long swig as he contemplated the situation.

Tom Peters picked up his beer and took a long drink, too. He was contemplating the situation as well. Rodney had told Tom and Detective Kelly that he felt that one of the groups interested in the Prototype Project had probably killed Michael. Now Tom had turned up with a computer flash drive with Michael's plans on it. Tom kept one eye on Rodney as Rodney's eyes checked the small apartment for exits.

Divinity and Moose were standing in the back of the room talking quietly when Victoria came through the apartment doorway. She immediately picked up on the unease and discomfort and said laughingly, "Did I come at a bad time?" She got only wide-eyed stares back. The tension increased until Tom slammed his beer down on the bureau.

"This is great, Victoria!" Tom said, reaching out and taking her by the hands and pulling her over by Rodney. "We finally got to see what was on that flash drive!" Tom said, basically stalling for time while he thought out a more elaborate pretext.

"Oh? That's great Tom… so… ah… so… how… what was it?" Victoria said, trying to play along.

"Well… it's the plans for… ah… the control of robots… I guess… Is that about right, Rod?" Tom said, offering no more than what was apparent and attempting to determine Rodney's reaction to the information.

Ever the intoxicated egghead, Rodney took the opportunity to disregard the dangerous and threatening situation he was in and instead used the opportunity to expound on his knowledge to impress Victoria and Divinity.

"Well, Ms. Peters, the binary code was easy to translate. There are websites now that will decipher, decode, transform, or otherwise convert those bazillion numbers back into whatever it was to begin with," Rodney said, slurring any word with an "S" in it. "You see, I dumped it into a converter and what it was, was…," Rodney sighed loudly, "…my best friend Michael's brilliant program for finally harnessing all the components involved in the creation for mass production of the Prototype for a line of household robots designed to make our lives sooo much easier. They will change our lives. Like a genie from a bottle; all you have to do is ask it. 'Get me my slippers. Have breakfast ready in twenty minutes after you do the laundry and order all the food we need. Get me my lawyer on the phone, print up the stock reports from the Net, and pay all my bills.' You don't even have to say 'please'!"

"But can it make a dry martini?" Victoria asked, not holding too much stock in promises of a leisurely future.

"Vic, could you come and look at the bureau Rodney and I put back on its legs?" Tom asked and turned to their bedroom. As Tom walked, he looked at Divinity and rolled his eyes back towards Rodney. She knew to take it as instructions to keep Rodney occupied.

As Tom entered the bedroom, he pulled Victoria in and around the corner. "He knows! He knows it all, I can tell! I can't let him leave. He must not talk to anybody! If he tells that detective, he'll be all over us."

"Wait. You don't know what Rodney has put together. He's pretty loaded, and when Divinity is nearby he looks up at her like he's in Dreamland. Let's see what he knows," Victoria said.

"He suspects I killed Michael, is what he knows. If it doesn't hit him now he'll realize the possibility in the morning and he'll tell that fucking detective! I'll take him out if I have to."

"OK. Take it easy. We'll see if we can put a spin on it. Like Michael asked you for help. That's it. He didn't want the Control System falling into the wrong hands so he called you just before he died."

"That's good, Vicky. Real good… But if he gets surly… Moose and I will whack him. We have to!"

Tom walked back out into the living room. Divinity was sitting on Rodney's lap, telling him how strong he was.

"I see you two are getting along," Tom said.

"Actually, I should be heading back to the east dorm," Rodney said, making a half-assed attempt at getting up.

"No. No," Tom said, adding, "Let's open these cold beers and go downstairs to the bar!"

"I ought to get back to my dorm," Rodney said.

Tom knew there was something wrong. When a girl like Divinity sits on a college boy's lap and he wants to go home, there is definitely something wrong. Tom was convinced Rodney knew he was involved in Michael's death.

"Don't you want to know why I have Michael's whole program for Central Control?" Tom asked Rodney.

Rodney had stood up and was just about ready to run for his life when Tom's question stopped him in his tracks; he said, "OK. Why do you have Mike's program information?"

"He called me. He said someone was following him and trying to get access to the mechanics behind his Control System. He said he didn't know who to trust."

"Then why didn't he tell *me*? I was his best friend," Rodney said.

"Ah… I think, he didn't want to put you in danger," Tom said, bluffing completely. Tom could see in Rodney's sad puppy dog eyes that he was thinking about this and seemed to be softening slightly towards Tom. Rodney was buying it and Peters was selling it. Rodney seemed to drop his defensive posture and he sighed again loudly and long. He sat back down in the chair and looked over at Divinity. He wondered if she too had been a ruse to get him to CES.

Victoria cleared her throat and said, "Let's all have a drink and discuss. Would that be a good idea, Tom? Should we go downstairs? Moose? Divinity?"

Tom suggested Divinity and Victoria go down to the bar and bring some drinks back up to the apartment. When Rodney heard this he decided he was going to get out of there, and get out of there now!

"I'll help you ladies!" Rodney said, jumping to his feet and taking four quick and long steps to the landing. "Come on, Divinity! I could use a drink," he said, grabbing her hand and pulling her behind him as he began to move down the stairs.

Tom didn't like this at all. He was losing control. He had orchestrated the whole evening and knew Rodney could not be allowed to leave. He suspected Rodney was going to make a break for the street and it looked like this might be it. Tom looked at Moose and said, "Go down the back stairs and around to the front. And knock him out if he goes out the front door." Tom followed Divinity and Rodney down the stairs, saying loudly, "I could use another Sammy, Rod. I've also got some very old cognac in the safe in my office."

Rodney had pulled, prodded, and coerced Divinity down to the first floor in the CES building. He looked back at her and said, "Are you a part of this? Was this a scam to get me here? Are you a call girl, too?"

"No!" she said, but Rodney saw the flash of deception in her eyes. It was a flash of deception that only showed because she truly cared for the unkempt MIT lab rat. Divinity kept remembering when she was an awkward study hall geek at Cal Tech.

He said, "Then come and find me, tomorrow." And he sprinted for the front door of the Cambridge tenement. Tom had just arrived on the main floor to see Rodney pushing open the front door. Tom yelled out, "One for the road, Rodney?"

Rodney heard Tom and looked back at him as the front door slammed shut behind the young grad student. As he bounded down the seven or eight steps leading to the fenced-in parking lot, he wondered if he was overreacting. He wondered if Tom really had anything to do with Michael's death. He wondered if Divinity could be happy with a geek like him. He wondered all these things until he reached for the gate handle next to the blue stretch limousine and Moose stepped out of the darkness and smacked him hard in the back of the head with a nightstick. Rodney was unconscious before he landed on the blacktop.

Chapter 42

Flash Drive

Thomas and Moose dragged the unconscious body of Rodney Riviera over to the back door of the black Mercedes and dropped him. Moose did most of the lifting. Tom opened the door and stepped into the back of the stretch limousine.

"Give me his head," he said, reaching out and motioning Moose to pick up the top of Rodney's torso and drag him up onto the floor of the car.

"You've always made a better supervisor than a worker, Boss," Moose said, politely slamming his employer.

"We'll take him over to Storrow Drive. But first I'll go back into CES and smooth everybody down. I'll say Rodney just decided to go. I'll get some duct tape and Mr. Clean," Tom said, referring to his stainless steel .357 magnum revolver. "If he wakes up, sit on him or whack him again."

Peters went back inside CES and met Victoria at the bar. He told her quickly that Rodney would be going over to the garage on Storrow Drive and wouldn't be returning.

Divinity walked up to the bar and asked Tom if he had caught up to Rodney.

"Rodney turned at the gate and thanked me for my hospitality and said he was going to walk back to campus. I think he was so drunk he won't remember tonight. But if he remembers anything, he'll remember you, Divinity. That boy was definitely taken by your beauty. You had him by the cajones! You are good; yes, you are. You see, Victoria? I should be a casting director for Hollywood movies. She was perfect."

Divinity was smiling from all the praise Tom heaped upon her but inside something was tearing away at her. Something in the back of her mind. She had liked the ungainly grad student. He was just about her age and she had been insecure and socially slow at one point in her life, too. They had made some kind of connection. He was just a boy, she thought. Just a boy. And just a boy was all she really longed for. Inside her heart and inside her soul.

Tom Peters picked up the keys to the Mercedes and a roll of silver duct tape from his office and bounded up the stairs to his third-floor apartment. He walked inside his bedroom closet and dumped a pile of white powder from a vial onto the mirror that was lying flat on the top shelf. Then he took another vial and put that into his pocket.

He was chopping the tiny granules into powder when Victoria entered the bedroom. She walked up behind Tom and put a hand on his hip and held her body close to his.

"Is it coke or speed?" she asked.

"This is coke, just like you suggested. So my nose won't bleed. But it doesn't last long enough! I got a need for speed!" Tom howled.

Victoria held her body tight to his backside, hugging him tightly as he finished making four big fat lines of the cocaine. He bent over and snorted hard. First he inhaled the drug through his left nostril and then through his right. Then he stood straight up and his eyes almost popped out of his head. He blew the air out of his lungs with a whoosh. And then he spun around and held Victoria's head with both hands and kissed her full on her lips for three or four seconds. His tongue made contact with hers and he pulled his head back violently.

"Woo!" he shouted and pushed her away. She smiled at the impetuous drug addict.

"Do you want me to have that little slut... I mean... that little what's-her-name here when you get back?" Victoria asked provocatively.

Peters turned back to the closet, reached up and moved back a panel behind the shelf, and pulled out a huge stainless steel Smith and Wesson .357 magnum revolver with soft black rubber handle grips.

"Mr. Clean and I've got to go," Tom said, bending over and consuming the two remaining lines. "Moose is sitting on that motherfucker and that motherfucker wants to hurt us. He wants to stop us from controlling the Project! Well, I'll stop him. We have the blueprints for the Sympathetic Override Program for the Central Control of Functioning Integrated Systems! Right here in the flash drive and the disc," Tom said, putting a Marlboro cigarette between his lips and looking over at his computer. But the smile evaporated from his face as he realized the disc was not on the table next to his computer.

He threw the cigarette against the wall and walked over to the computer, pushing the button to eject the disc from inside the computer, but there was no disc. Both discs were missing as well as the flash drive. "Motherfucker!" Tom yelled. "I'm going to see if Rodney removed those discs. You check and see if Divinity is still here."

Tom took the back stairs two at a time, hopped down the back porch stairs, and ran through the parking lot to the dark Mercedes. He opened the door to see Moose sitting back reading the sports section of the *Globe* while Rodney was still out cold on the opposite seat.

"Check that motherfucker's pockets. Take everything out. He stole the fucking discs!" Tom demanded of Moose as he got into the back of the limo and shut the door behind him.

"So what? What the fuck's so important about these fuckin' computer discs, Boss? Is this really that important? I mean, I committed an assault and a battery on this guy already; is this really worth it? Check his fucking pockets? Check his fucking pulse! I may have killed this man! Have mercy on my soul," Moose said. He was not as dumb as he looked.

"All right, you fucking black Elvis! This is going to end up being a $4,000 night for you, OK?" Tom said, telling Moose what he wanted to hear. It was all business.

"Let's get them fucking discs, Boss!" Moose said, checking every pocket in Rodney Riviera's cargo pants. And there were twelve of them. Both men checked all of Rodney's pockets, putting all the articles on the floor. There was a wallet, a cell phone, a three-inch pencil, thirteen dollars and fifty cents, a LeatherMan utility knife with seven different functioning appendages, and a bus pass.

Tom Peters was frustrated. He had to have the discs. It was essential.

Rodney groaned. He was waking up.

Tom reached across and picked up the nightstick on the seat next to Moose. He looked over at Rodney, who was groaning and rubbing the knot on his forehead. Tom raised up the nightstick and smacked it down on the side of Rodney's head. Rodney was stunned and only his instincts held him up as Tom struck his skull with the stick even harder the second time.

"Motherfucker! Yes, you are a motherfucker! Son-of-a-bitch!" Tom shouted as he dropped his head down into his hands. He had lost and found the Holy Grail. And all in an hour.

"Oh, God...," Tom said, trying to think.

Maybe Divinity. Tom would hate to think it, but maybe she took the discs! Then he looked at Rodney unconscious on the floor and looked up at Moose.

"Did you check every conceivable place?"

"Well... yeah, Boss."

"We'll... did you check down the front of his pants?"

"Ah... sort of," Moose said.

"Well 'sort of' ain't fuckin' good enough, Moose. Check him down low... We've got to check every conceivable place, 'cause if you don't... Divinity is next on our list," Tom said, knowing that they both liked Divinity and didn't want to see her roughed up.

Moose made a face and looked at Tom and stuck his hand down the front of Rodney's pants. He searched around for a moment, stopped, and looked Tom in the face, smiling.

"What are you doing? Are you holding Rodney's dick? You're enjoying this, aren't you?" Tom asked.

"I am now," Moose said, pulling both discs and a flash drive out from behind the zipper in the front of Rodney's pants.

"I'll tell you why these discs are so important, Moose. I'll tell you why I'm ecstatic. I'm back on course. Everything is going to fall into place. I have the information to give the Group. And we'll have the power to take control of the Prototype. We'll mass market the humanlike droids to every upscale business and home in America, Britain, Europe, Asia...." Tom loved the sound of his voice. He loved the sound of the words he was speaking. He loved them even when he looked at Rodney and said, "But first we've got to dump the garbage."

Chapter 43

Meet Mr. Clean

"What's so important about these computers, again Boss?" Moose asked Tom.

"They are computer *discs* and it's better you don't know, Moose. It's over your head anyway," Tom said, rubbing the massive shoulder of the black Elvis with one hand and quickly grabbing the discs and the flash drive with his other.

"Don't belittle my education, Boss. I almost graduated from Cambridge Rindge and Latin High School, right down the street. It's the high school of Patrick Ewing, the greatest NBA center court player the Knicks ever had!"

"That's right, Moose. Put all his shit back in his pockets, except for that jackknife, you can hold on to that."

Tom taped Rodney's hands together in front of him, making a half a dozen circles around his wrists with the roll of duct tape as Moose got into the limo driver's seat and started the engine. Moose was thinking about negotiating another bonus as he maneuvered down the partition. The big black Mercedes rolled quietly out of the parking lot at

CES. As the stretch limousine drove down Mass. Ave. and crossed in front of the huge concrete buildings of MIT, Moose said, "If this ah... scenario, is ah... heading where I think it's heading, I think that might be worth another bonus, Tom."

"Don't call me 'Tom.' I'm Mr. Peters. And I've learned to live with 'Boss,' but don't push it! Do you know how many people would like to have the job you've got here, Moose? Don't push your luck!" Tom felt the butt of his chrome .357 Magnum handgun tucked in his belt. Moose saw this in the rearview mirror. The big man knew the level of depravity Tom Peters was capable of and had second thoughts about asking again for that bonus.

"But there's nobody you can trust like me. And nobody loves you like I do, Boss," the driver said, smiling into the rearview mirror.

Tom dumped a pile of white powder onto the partition's shelf as they crossed the Mass. Ave. Bridge heading into Boston. He made four lines with a credit card and snorted two. The limo took a hard left at the end of the bridge and entered the alleyway alongside the river between Beacon Street and Storrow Drive. They drove two blocks along the river and the limo pulled up in front of the converted garage that Tom Peters owned. Moose backed the limo in alongside of the garage and got in back with Tom and Rodney. Tom nodded to Moose and the big black man consumed the two remaining lines. Rodney seemed unconscious as they carried him inside and dumped him on the hardwood floor.

Peters ran the duct tape around Rodney's ankles six times then stood up. Tom took his black leather jacket off, pulled a cigarette out from a pack, put the pack in the jacket, and threw it on one of the three upholstered chairs. He turned on two table lamps and shut off the neon tube lights on the ceiling. Peters walked to the kitchen, pulled a bottle of Grey Goose vodka and a jar of olives from the refrigerator, and poured the vodka over ice cubes in a shaker. He poured the cold vodka over the olives into a martini glass. He threw Moose a Red Stripe beer and Moose pulled the top off and drank the contents of the bottle. Tom hadn't closed the refrigerator yet and he picked up another beer bottle and tossed it. Moose opened it and took a tiny sip.

Moose handed Tom his vibrating cell phone and said, "It's your sister."

"Darling?" Tom said into the receiver while rolling his eyes at Moose. It was something he would not dare to do in front of her.

"I'm still here with Divinity, Tom. But I don't think she has the discs," Victoria said quietly.

"It's all cool. I've got the two discs and the flash drive in my jacket pocket. Our nerdish geek had them. I must admit our little grad student was putting the whole picture together. I don't know how much he told the private detective, but I know one thing; he is going to have to pay the price, tonight."

"Do what you do for the family," Victoria urged her brother. "*Il mio amante dolce Italiano. Ci acquisteremo un posto per su questa terra. Tenaciousely combatteremo per ogni parte di questa terra e con ogni goccia di anima in nostre vene. Per la famiglia!* We will tenaciously fight for every piece of this Earth and with every drop of blood in our veins. For the family!"

"For the family!" Tom responded and looked at Rodney lying limp on the floor. Tom felt the butt of his gun. He closed Moose's cell phone, tossed it to him, and sipped his vodka martini. He knew what he had to do.

Rodney stirred on the floor. His lungs sucked in the air as if he had been submerged under water. His face grimaced with pain as he seemed to slowly awaken. Rodney's eyes squinted in the light as he saw the black Elvis sitting in an easy chair with his beer dwarfed by his huge hands.

"I gotta take a piss," Moose announced as he got up and walked into the bathroom closing the door behind him. Tom topped off his chilled martini and waked over to Rodney with the martini shaker.

"Want a drink, Rod?" he said and poured a stream of cold vodka down onto Rodney's face.

"It's burning my eyes!" Rodney yelled. Tom picked up Moose's beer and poured it all down on Rod's face, saying, "That's right, you drink beer!"

"What's wrong with you, Peters? Why are my hands and feet taped?" Rodney yelled as the beer helped to clear his eyes from the sting of the vodka.

"You're what's wrong with me! With your fucking big mouth. Talking to that fucking detective. Guessing all the time. Or were you deducing? Yes, I bet you were employing inductive logic and deducing." Tom grinned insanely as he leaned forward, exposing the gun butt.

"You're mad! You are crazy!" Rodney yelled.

The bathroom door opened and Moose said, "Hey, this is like a movie. Ain't it, Boss?"

"A bad movie. A bad movie for you, Rodney Riviera," Tom said.

"Why are my hands and feet taped up? What are you doing?"

"Think of it as a hack. Yes. A hacked-up prank that went really wrong! Worse than the Hilltop Steak House Cow on the roof of Building Ten. It's a worse prank than the police car on the roof of Building Ten. Worse than the balloon popping out at the forty-five-yard line of the Harvard-Yale game. Worse than dropping the car off the roof."

"You're crazy, Tom!"

"Well… Let me put it to you this way, Rodney. Snitches get stitches!"

'You killed Michael! You did! I can see it in your eyes," Rodney said.

"Where you're going, I guess it doesn't matter if I tell you or not. I brought Michael here. Well, Divinity brought Michael here. She's good like that, Rod. I even thought she was falling for you… Anyway," Tom got down on the floor and lay next to Rodney. Tom snuggled closer to him and his breath blew hot on Rodney's face, "After a night of partying. I offered Mike a small fortune for his Central Control System. He turned it down flat. I offered him a limited partnership with a group of powerful individuals that would invest the money to develop and manufacture the robots. Within a year we would have been part of one of the biggest free enterprise companies in the world."

"The manufacture and sales of the Prototype?" Rodney said.

"But Michael told me in so many words that he would not enter into any venture with me. And I took this personally," Peters said, taking the chrome Smith and Wesson out of his waistband and holding it close to Rodney's face. He began to stroke the barrel of the gun against Rodney's cheek. Tom said softly, "Time to meet Mr. Clean… You see, Michael had the Central Control. Without that, the computer brain needed to control the Prototype would weigh about 200 pounds. And Michael said he would never enter into any venture that would include me. He was shutting me out! But I shut him out," Tom said, holding the gun to the side of his head and then he kissed the barrel and stood up.

"You are a sick drunken dope fiend and you are insane!" Rodney said, looking up at Tom.

"I do not suffer from insanity… No! I enjoy every moment of it. At least that's what the little voices tell me. Moose, get yourself a beer and turn up that stereo nice and loud," Tom said and poured out the remainder of the cocaine on the small bar. He crushed the rocks and chopped them into powder with a large stainless steel meat cleaver, making five lines. After drinking the rest of the vodka martini, he sniffed down two lines with the tube from his belt buckle. He put an unlit Marlboro in his mouth as the stereo blasted out "Trouble No More" by the Allman Brothers.

"Moose… take two lines, my brother. Do you want a line, Rod?"

"I'd like to put my hands around your neck and squeeze," Rod answered.

"Choking me will only enhance my orgasm. Now, do you want a fucking line? I can arrange it."

"No. And by the way, I dialed a friend's number on my cell phone in the car and she either heard every word or it is recorded on her message service, so let's just get out of here and we'll chalk it all up to a drunken brawl, Tom. I don't want any trouble, honest, man, I don't want any trouble," Rodney pleaded.

"You don't want any trouble? You've been nothing but trouble. You are all that stands between me and power and a fortune! First Michael, Seng Li, and now you!" Tom was working himself up. "Go check his cell phone in the limo, Moose. I'm pretty sure it was off, but just check it again."

Moose went out the door and was back inside in less than thirty seconds with Rodney's cell phone.

"He's bluffing, Boss. The cell phone's not on," Moose said, shutting the door and holding the cell phone up in the air.

All three men were startled when the cell phone rang while Moose was holding it.

Chapter 44

Dead Central

"It's Amanda," Moose said, reading the Caller ID.

"Just let it ring," Tom said. Moose put the cell phone in his coat pocket and pulled his collar up over his neck.

"People are on their way here, Tom. Let's call it a night," Rodney pleaded again. But Tom got down on the floor, with Rodney lying next to him, side by side. Tom looked over at Rodney and smiled a sweet, warm, caring smile. Then he rolled over onto his side and put his right arm and hand, the hand holding the gun, over Rodney's chest and snuggled up to him. He exhaled and whispered to Rodney, "Michael didn't want anything to do with me... That really hurt. It really hurt my feelings... But I like you, Rodney. I always have. And I can see why Divinity likes you. You're a very bright guy." Rodney continued, shaking Rodney slightly, "Unfortunately... you figured out everything. But you told that fucking detective, what's his fucking name?"

"Jack Kelly."

"Yes. And how many others, Rodney? Let's start by being honest with each other. Maybe we could get along. Who else?"

"Nobody."

"How about Amanda?"

"No," Rodney said, hoping Tom wouldn't realize his deceit.

"Amanda is the little Goth bitch you hang with, right? We all used to go to the Miracle of Science over there next to Tech. Yes, she's a little lab rat, isn't she? What would she say if she knew you weren't being entirely honest with me?"

"Let's go ask her," Rodney said and then said, "Look. Amanda doesn't know anything. You didn't kill Michael Rich, did you?"

"No," Tom deadpanned and then said, "We killed Michael. He went down pretty hard. Right here in this room it was. I had gotten him quite drunk. He didn't like the speed, though. He turned down lines. Divinity brought him here for me just like a good girl should. Just like she brought you to me, tonight. And your Asian buddy, Seng Li. He was drugged and half-conscious when he was lying right where you are. I told him, 'I am Godzilla and you are a little Japanese man with a sprained ankle.'"

A look of sick horror and defeat on Rodney's face told Tom that it was time for Rodney to go. Tom hugged him with both arms and began to whisper into Rodney's ear, "I clocked him from behind with the same nightstick that Moose introduced to you. But Michael pissed me off the most. When he woke up with his hands and feet taped together, he got upset and struggled. Ever the gracious host, I gave him another chance to go into business with

322

me, but he spit in my face... well, not literally; we're all gentlemen here, right?" Tom said smiling and looking over at Moose.

"Right, Boss," Moose said, nodding his head.

"He wanted to exclude me from the Prototype Project all together; I couldn't have that." Tom looked into Rodney's eyes and said softly, "So Mr. Clean shot him in the back of his head."

Rodney kicked and struggled, trying to get up on his feet. Tom yelled, "Moose!" The big man walked over and held Rodney down on his stomach, sitting on the diminutive student's lower back and placing his big hand on his shoulder.

"Look, Tom, I can't concentrate. Can we call it a day and get out of here, please, Tom? Let's call it a day. Talk about this in the morning!" Rodney shouted.

"Moose! Do you want to call it a day? It's morning, Rodney!" Tom said and he put the .357 magnum behind Rodney's right ear and shot a round into his skull. Rodney's feet kept kicking until Tom pulled the trigger again and the second bullet went through Rodney's brain, blowing out the left side of his forehead. The blowback from the high-caliber bullet sent another splash of blood over Tom's hands and face.

Peters and Moose stood up and looked down at the lifeless body of Rodney Riviera. One leg still kicked slightly. There was a piece of skull with an eyebrow still attached to the head and the pool of blood that was already forming under Rodney's face began to slow as the two men watched, enthralled. Gurgling sounds and a death gasp were heard over the blasting radio as WZLX played the Rolling Stones' "Paint it Black." The two men just stared at the dead body as the acrid cloud of gun smoke slowly dissipated.

Chapter 45

Trapdoor to Nowhere

"You're right. Life's like a movie, Moose," Tom said.

"I'll never get used to that," Moose said.

"Used to what, exactly?"

"You know. Snuffing somebody out. It just seems like a dream."

"Yeah, Moose. It's a bad dream. Make no mistake about it. But this guy was trying to hurt us, my man! This fucking guy, Rod, was talking to a cop. A private cop. We may have to take care of him, too. I think Kelly knows too much… maybe even that we took care of Michael. Listen, Moose. There's no death penalty in Massachusetts. But life is a long fucking time."

"Yes, I know that, Boss. What I'm saying is the whole killing of somebody takes … like seconds… but when I think of it, it seems like time slows down and I feel every moment. I understand every aspect. I know it, I feel it… and I love it!" Moose shouted.

"Well said, my black brother. You are a visionary. I love you. You are fucking articulate when you want to be, aren't you, motherfucker? Yes… I should not underestimate you, my man. I've got to keep my eye on you."

"Don't look at me like that, Boss…" Moose said, smiling and holding up his hands like he was going to defend himself from Tom's fists.

"Let's send him out," Tom said and added, "Turn down that fucking radio!" as Jimi Hendrix sang "Voodoo Chile." Peters moved a big stuffed chair, exposing a square cut into the hardwood floor. Tom pulled up on the concealed ring and the three-by-three-foot trapdoor lifted up. Tom pulled it completely open and laid the door back against the couch. The sound of moving water was heard below.

"Boss? Why don't we wanna tie some weights to his ass?"

"Because he'll sink down right under my fucking garage! Let him float down the beautiful Charles River and then sink. A last sail down to the basin, by the Hatch Shell, and the Esplanade. Beautiful! A sunrise cruise."

"You're a spin doctor, Boss."

"Wait! Just one last thing. Well, two things," Tom Peters said and rolled Rodney over onto his back. Rodney had a substantial opening in his skull. Tom took out the vial of powdered methamphetamine from his jacket and filled his stainless steel tube with meth. He bent down over Rodney, inserted the tube down into the dead man's throat, and blew the contents down Rodney's throat and into his stomach.

"Why do you do that, Boss?" Moose asked as Tom stood up, took a deep breath, and exhaled, flexing his neck muscles and stretching in some kind of personalized ritual.

"Signature, Moose.… My signature.… It's my personal touch. And it might throw them off the trail.… Give me his Brass Rat."

"What?" Moose asked.

"The fucking gold MIT ring like the one your wearing."

"Oh, yeah," Moose said, bending over the corpse of Rodney Riviera; with some difficulty, the robber pulled the ring from the finger of the dead body. He handed it to Tom. Tom held the MIT graduate's ring up in the light.

"This is for snitches! Rats! Vermin, cockroaches, stool pigeons, finks, and big-mouth motherfuckers everywhere," Tom said, taking the ring and pushing it with his finger as far as he could down Rodney Riviera's throat.

The two men rolled the corpse over and the dead body fell headfirst through the hole in the floor and into the Charles River. It floated downriver for about thirty feet and began to sink. The body would continue downstream near the river's bottom until Monday morning, when it would surface on the Boston side of the Charles.

Chapter 46

Get Jacked Up

Jack's cell phone buzzed and he jumped. He had fallen asleep on the couch at Michael's frat house loft. It was 9:30 a.m.

"Hello?" he managed to stammer.

"Kelly. Jesus Christ, you sound like shit. What'd you do? Tie one on last night? It's Trooper Archambeault, Kelly. Jay Archambeault. Are you there, Kelly? You want me to send an ambulance? Tap three times on the phone if you do."

"I'm going to tap three times on your fucking head, Archie. You're just like your old man. He used to love to give me a hard time, too."

"You're just that type of guy, Jack. You might as well have 'Ridicule Me' written on your forehead. I can totally see why my old man used to like to give you a hard time."

"All right, Jay. You're dueling with an unarmed man here. You have me at a disadvantage, sir. And just for the record I did not 'tie one on' last night. I'm at Michael

Rich's apartment. I looked at every corner of his computer last night. The father is going to be pulling the plug and taking everything out of here today and some new geeks are moving in."

"Geeks, Kelly? Is this how you refer to the intelligentsia of society?"

"Sorry. I'm bitter. I never graduated from college, although I had more than enough classes. I had the craziest notion that education was its own reward. I was a philosophy major and thought that total comprehension of 'the big picture' was important."

"That and three dollars will get you a cup of Starbucks coffee, Jack."

"Yes. I was a shit head. Thanks for reminding me. What's up? I don't have anything more than when we last spoke," Kelly said, not proud of it.

"I wanted to tell you Doc Ryan says that both Michael Rich and Seng Li had methamphetamine in their stomachs but not running through their systems. Which means, my sleepy-headed friend, they had just taken it in their systems at the time of death. That's why I was thinking 'suicide by lifestyle.'"

"So they didn't even have time to OD on the speed. What was the COD?" Jack asked the trooper.

"The cause of death was... not drowning either. It was the gunshots to the back of the heads. And our beloved forensic pathologist says it was a .357 magnum. Doc Ryan says it didn't blow out the back end of the head because the bullets were jacketed hollow bodies. The fragments and wad spun around inside the skull, causing maximum tissue damage."

"That reminds me, I think I'll go for the scrambled eggs this morning."

"I'd have thought a go-getter private eye like you would have been up and on the case for hours and would be ready for lunch by now."

"You *are* just like your dad."

"So what else do we have, Jack? Both were missing the MIT beaver rings. Both worked at the Artificial Intelligence Lab. Has Jesse got anything we can hang our hats on?"

"I'll be talking to her next and if she does, I'll call you right away, Archie, I mean, Jay."

"Yeah. I'm back to square one," Archambeault said. "And all my friends call me Archie, just like the old man. I thought that artist-bum living along the esplanade in that nice rent-free dwelling between the river and Memorial Drive was going to be the killer. I've checked him up and down and over and around. I'm beginning to think you were right when you told Jessica the robots killed them."

"Oh, Jesus Christ. I never told Lieutenant Paris the robots killed Michael and Seng Li!"

"It's OK, Jack. You're in the private sector. You can get away with thoughts like that. Of course if I was to walk around the Criminal Investigations Division talking about robots killing people I'd be going out on a Section 8 at 72% of my salary. Come to think of it, that doesn't sound too bad. Maybe I'll start telling my detective sergeant about the robots at MIT. I'll tell the captain and the boys in Forensics the robots at MIT have been taken over by aliens from outer space and Jack Kelly is their leader."

"OK, Archie, anything else?"

"Have a nice day," the trooper said and disconnected. Jack changed the ring tone on his cell phone from vibrate to something called "crickets."

Chapter 47

Dance of Death

While Jack had been sleeping on Michael's couch night after night, Rodney had figured it all out. While detective Jack Kelly looked for an answer and waited for a development, Rodney did the math. While the professional investigator slept on Michael's couch, Rodney had put it all together. Rodney had followed his suspicions. He had made the connections. He had realized the personalities involved. And because of this, Rodney Riviera had been lured to his own death. He had paid the ultimate price.

Jack Kelly was a day late and a dollar short and didn't even know it. Jack wished the killer would come for him and they could settle things.

Before Archie's call, Jack had woken up with a slight back ache from the couch. He was glad it was the last night at the frat house apartment of Michael Rich. He was developing a bad back. Mike's father would clear out the last few items, the computer, couch, table, lamp, and chairs. And the next day the apartment would be a part of the next frat brother's history at MIT. Another soul goes through the staid institution.

Jack didn't care about that. He went to the Harvard University Extension School. Tonight he could go to his cozy office/apartment in Chinatown and take a long hot shower. No, better yet, he would go to Jessica's apartment and let her soothe his poor harried soul. Tonight he would take another break from this case. It had been a week and Jack had logged a lot of hours. He had made good money. More than a good week's pay. And there were more paydays in sight. In a lot of ways he felt good about himself. He felt he was doing some worthwhile work. Yes, worthwhile.

Consciously, he felt that way. But…subconsciously he wasn't so happy about his investigation. He wasn't getting anywhere fast. Underneath it all he wasn't satisfied with the limited results of the investigation. When the mind is stuck, move the body. He felt the lack of physical movement. He had The Musician running around, working surveillance. Even Cooper had gotten some action. Jack felt perhaps Cooper had had the only *hands-on* experience in the case.

But aside from surfing the Internet Kelly hadn't moved. Subconsciously, he was not content at all. In fact, he was about ready to explode.

It was 10:30 by the time he scraped together two pieces of dry toast and some instant coffee black and a bottle of cold water. He showered and shaved and put all his belongings in his knapsack by the door. He was contemplating walking down to the coffee shop on Mass. Ave. to get a real cup of coffee and the newspapers when his cell phone chirped with the sound of crickets.

"Hi, handsome," Jessica said. "Am I going to see you tonight?"

"I was just thinking about that… and that would be an absolute definite affirmative to the positive maximum, my good morning sunshine."

"Well, you're quite cheery, aren't you? Is it the fact that it's fifty-eight degrees this late November morning… another record breaker for warmth?"

"I love global warming in New England," Jack said and sighed.

"Listen," Jessica said. "I've got the autopsy results from the Seng Li murder case. They're basically identical to the autopsy results of Michael Rich. Both were shot by the same .357 magnum firearm, execution style in the back of the head. Both entered the water of the Charles River after death. Both had meth in the tummy."

"Is 'tummy' a medical term?"

"'Scrotum' is the medical term for you, Jack Kelly. Now let's see… both worked together in the Artificial Intelligence Lab at MIT. They were both missing the Brass Rat rings…"

"Both worked on the robots," Jack interrupted.

"Oh, come on, Jack. Don't tell me this again. Don't tell me the robots did it!"

"Don't put words in my mouth!"

"Why not? I let you put things in *my* mouth," Jesse said.

"But words ain't one of them. I'm just saying… I'm beginning to think Rodney Riviera is right. There is a connection there. It's the one thing that holds all the other elements together. It's the common thread."

"I yield to the master. But Archie still thinks it's 'suicide by lifestyle.'"

"Fuck Archie!"

"I hope you don't mean that literally," Jesse said.

Jack ran through a scenario in his mind of Jesse leaving him for the young state trooper, and in his mind's eye he saw her making love to Archie. He suddenly felt the cold taste of the reality of life deep down in his soul. And he shook involuntarily. In the silence both Jack and Jesse realized that no matter how safe you feel, you're always less than a heartbeat away from your world crashing into chaos.

"No. I mean… Trooper Archambeault wears camouflage on the weekends and he thinks no one can see him. So what's Archie saying? That these guys brought their own deaths upon them? Or that they got what they deserved because meth was in their stomachs?" Jack almost shouted.

"I don't know. Are you coming over tonight or not?"

"Yes, honey… I don't mean to shout. I just need one of us, you, me, or Archie, to make some progress on these two murders. I've got to tell Mr. Rich something. Archie thinks it's 'the drug life,' I'm talking robots, and who have you got? Who do you think killed these kids?"

"Well, Jack. I'm glad you asked," Jessica said, stalling for a moment, collecting her thoughts, and continuing with only a slight lack of confidence. "I'm going through a process of elimination. First I looked long and hard at Seng Li's relatives. I did background checks and interviews. Hell, I couldn't keep his sisters from calling me all the time, twice on Sunday. But I came up empty with relatives. I've thought about a spouse. But Seng Li and Michael Rich didn't seem to have girlfriends."

"Right. Michael had taken to using the services of a shady escort service run by an ex-Tech," Jack interjected.

"They didn't have girlfriends," Jessica continued, "but they both had the same girl *friend* in this group of lab rats that Seng Li and Mike went out with. They both had this same group of friends, so I'm going to be looking closer at them. The newspapers and TV stations have been calling night and day but we're dancing around them as best we can."

"God bless the free press. And God bless America," Jack proclaimed.

"They've already linked the two killings and today's *Boston Herald* has a headline on page three: 'THE MIT MURDERS.'"

"Oh shit. The circus is in town. I'll give you Rodney and Amanda's phone numbers and they'll talk to you. They'll tell you all about the robots," Jack snickered. "I keep hearing about that former AI Lab guy, who left about five years ago and started a succession of porno web sites. I've told you about him before. Tom Peters. You 'Googled' him, I believe you said. Anyway… I did a little Internet research last night on Michael's computer. The money started coming in so fast this guy Peters dropped out of the graduate program at MIT and the AI Lab and went full-time sleazebag. He made millions in a couple of short years. He owns the Cambridge Escort Service that Michael had made an appointment with around the time of his death."

"That sounds like someone I'd like to talk to," Jesse said.

"I had Cooper make a date at the Ritz with a lady from Peters' College Escort Service and he... ah… got lucky."

"It's a good thing you didn't go on that assignment, Jack Kelly."

"Absolutely! No way! I'm sure I would not have enjoyed it."

"Good answer, even if not the whole truth and nothing but the truth," Jesse laughed over the phone and said, "So Peters is a pimp and a pornographer. Nice! That's enough for me to pull him in for questioning real quick."

"No, Jesse. He'd lawyer up immediately. Let's move him up on our list from 'person of interest' to 'suspect.' I've got The Musician tailing him sixteen hours a day," Jack said confidently.

"Let's get a warrant and a wiretap. I'll have him followed night and day. And we'll drop a GPS on his fuckin' bumper."

"My dear eloquent sleuth. There's not enough information to get a warrant. You let me chase his tail for now; I'm not worried about such legal constraints," Kelly insisted.

"OK. I'll see if he's got a License To Carry. He didn't have a Mass. driver's license if I remember correctly. And I'll do some digging in Baltimore, Maryland. His father was the DA, as I recall. Yes, I remember that Peters had a twin brother and they were both raised by an older sister, who was just a kid herself when her parents died in a car crash," Jessica said.

Jack interrupted with, "And his twin brother went out through the thirteenth-floor window of a classroom. He fell the thirteen floors and landed on the sidewalk below, during the early evening of a busy class day at MIT. In the classroom was a tape recorder running, and written on the classroom blackboard was the mathematical formula for determining the physics of a body falling thirteen floors onto the cement below."

"I remember that," Lieutenant Paris said.

"Do you remember that there was a robot standing in the corner of the room when police arrived?"

"Jack, I refuse to believe a robot had anything to do with this. It's ridiculous. If I put that in a report at the office I'd be verbally slammed for the rest of my career."

"You can always come and work for me, Beautiful."

"Aw... you're sweet," Jesse said, sounding all girly. Jack could turn her on almost as quickly as a light switch.

"What's for dinner?" Kelly asked, seizing the opportunity.

"What would you like?"

"How about... baked haddock? With pesto and bread crumbs and almonds with green beans and mashed potatoes? Or salmon? Baked with that Grand Marnier orange glaze the way you make it so good?"

"OK. I'll get the one that looks the freshest," she said.

"See you at eight, pal, but first I've got to get some things done!"

"I'll help you get some things done. I'll be the wind blowing your sails."

"You'll be blowing more than my sails."

Jack decided to head down to Mass. Ave. for coffee, pick up a sub for lunch, and a newspaper. In Kelly's line of work the newspaper reporters dug up a lot of useful information. Sometimes they were a step ahead. But not often.

Jack shut the front door of Alpha Omega Delta and was full of life as he sprang down the stairs and took a right. As he walked down the sidewalk he programmed his cell phone back to the vibrate setting. He didn't see the small dark blue rental car parked back up the street. And he didn't see the dark man sitting behind the steering wheel watching him. He was oblivious as he felt the day's warm sun on his shoulders. He looked at his watch and punched The Musician's number into his cell phone.

Willie's teenage daughter with the belly rings answered the phone.

Jack said hello to Misty and briefly inquired as to whose heart she was going to rip out when she gets older.

"I'm only thirteen! I have a few years before I start ripping out hearts and crushing them. I appreciate your concern, Jack Kelly," she always called him 'Jack Kelly,' "but why is it so hard to find a good-looking, sensitive guy?"

"Because they have boyfriends. How did you like the band at The Paradise last Saturday?"

"How do you know I was at the Moon Doggies concert?" she asked.

"Misty, I was backstage with the band, looking out. And I saw you."

"Seriously?"

"No. Is your father home?" Jack heard the phone drop onto the table and then the floor as the girl called for her father.

Jack had ordered a bagel with cream cheese and a large Colombian breakfast coffee with milk by the time The Musician got on the phone.

"What time are you going back?" Jack asked him.

"I can be at CES in less than one hour."

"That's what I wanted to hear from you! Where'd you end up last night? Did you do a written report?"

"Written report? Jesus, Jack. What if I told you I couldn't write because I was suffering from complete and utter sexual exhaustion?"

"Then write the report with your other hand."

The Musician yawned and gave his verbal report as Jack Kelly paid for his coffee and bagel. He walked past the black man watching him out of the window of the Laundromat on the opposite corner.

"Well… after Lansdowne Street we went to the Roxy for ten minutes and back to the CES offices by 3 a.m. Then I went home… and it is now…"

"Almost 11 a.m.," Jack said.

"OK, I'll be watching for Tom Peters at CES by 11:45 a.m. Do you want to hear the Joke-of-the-Day?"

"You don't have time for such frivolity," Jack scolded him.

"Misty! Get me some cereal and toast and coffee!" The Musician shouted back towards his kitchen, and then he said into the phone, "You must have heard of the aptly named John Wayne Bobbitt case, where an enraged woman cut off the penis of her cheating husband and threw it out the car window. Well, what a lot of people don't know is that in the car behind them, there were a man and his twelve-year-old daughter. And when that woman threw it out the window, John Wayne Bobbitt's penis smacked on the girl and her father's trailing car's windshield for a moment and then rolled off. The shocked twelve-year-old girl said, 'What was that?' and the father, not wanting to expose his daughter to anything sexual, said, 'It's just a bug, honey.' And after a confused moment the girl said, 'That bug sure had a big dick.'"

"Is that it?" Jack said.

"No. An eighty-year-old man goes to his doctor for his checkup and tells the doc, 'I feel great. I've got a twenty-four-year-old wife who's pregnant with my child. What do you think about that?' The doctor looked at the old man, scratched his head, and began telling him a story. 'I've got an older friend who reminds me of you. He's still an avid hunter and one day he went out hunting but he forgot his rifle. As he walked through the woods he saw a huge beaver sitting on a rock by the pond. He instinctively raised up his walking cane, pointed it at the beaver, and said, 'Bang! Bang!' Just as he did, two rifle shots rang out and the beaver fell over dead. What do you think of that?' And the eighty-year-old man said, 'I think someone else pumped two rounds into that beaver!' And the doc said, 'My point exactly.'"

"OK, brother. Get on with the surveillance, please," Jack said. "Check in at regular intervals. I'll be at Helta Skelta Delta waiting for Mr. Rich to show up. And Lieutenant Paris is going to want to bring Thomas Peters in for questioning. I'll try to let you know when, so you won't get in their way. And if Archie finds out that we're doing surveillance on a potential suspect there'll be so many undercover operatives sleuthing around you... you'll think you're working with the Village People." As those images reached and were assimilated in the sleepy head of Willie Crawford, Jack added, "And be careful, WC."

As Kelly walked back up the side street to the fraternity house, carrying his breakfast in a paper bag, he felt a warm spot on the back of his neck and rubbed it with his free hand. He jumped as if bumped into by a ghost as his cell phone's ring tone vibrated in his pants pocket. Marcus, the black man watching him, laughed and then bent down to tie his shoe as Kelly walked up the frat house stairs and instinctively looked back down the street.

"Hello," Kelly said, not recognizing the number on the caller ID.

"How's it going, Kelly?" Jay Archambeault said.

"Well… it's a nice day for the end of November, Archie. I don't need any slush, snow, ice, and wind chill factors. I'll take this, anytime."

"Yes, yes. So is there anything new on the Michael Rich case?" Trooper Archambeault asked Jack.

"Ah… Not since I talked to you earlier… I wish there were something to report. I'm checking a few things but nothing seems to be panning out. Do you have anything on either student's murder? Autopsy results, perhaps?"

"Yeah, Jack. There's nothing in the ME's reports on either one that we haven't figured. They were shot and killed before entering the water. They had crystal meth in their throats and stomachs, but not in their blood. Don't quote me on this, Kelly, but I think this means to me, again, some sort of drug group. They took the speed orally and killed themselves before the meth got into their systems."

"How did they shoot themselves in the head? Was there GSR on their hands? Blowback spatter?" Jack pressed the trooper.

"There was some gunpowder residue on their hands. But the river washed away all the blood and most any other physical evidence. I've researched sixteen possible Cambridge suicides and many of them have been MIT related in the last ten years. I've got newspaper articles, MIT Police reports, and Cambridge Police reports. There is some heavy stress at MIT. And there's a history of serious methamphetamine use on that side of the river due to the amount of studying going on. We busted a meth lab six blocks from MIT just six weeks ago."

"Where's the murder weapon? Where did they die? What's the motive?" Jack almost shouted, trying to get back to the basics.

"Jeez, Kelly. Take it easy. I don't have these answers yet. I'm just kicking it around with you, Jack. Are you getting personal with this one?"

"No… I mean… I don't know; sorry, Archie. I don't believe it was any manner of suicide. It was stone cold murder. They were shot in the back of the head by a killer who wants to confuse you with the speed and wash the evidence away in the water. But most of all I guess I was hoping one of us would have more information on a resolution concerning these deaths. For the families. They're hurting. I'm at the kids' frat house room now and the father should be here in a few hours to move the last few household items out… and I wanted to be able to tell him something. I was hoping the pathologist's report would have more information."

"Yeah…. It must be tough for a father and mother," the trooper said.

"Which box did the ME check on the Manner of Death? Natural Causes is out. And Accidental ain't going to fly. So there's Suicidal and Homicidal."

"Cause of Death: gunshot wound; Mechanism of Death: cerebral contusion, trauma. Seng Li had some exsanga… exsangwee…"

"Exsanguination. Bleeding out," Jack assisted.

"Right. Anyway, he checked the Suspicious, Possible Homicide box, on both victims," Archie confessed.

"I was hoping for some physical evidence from the Office of the Chief Medical Examiner to point us in the right direction. Maybe trace evidence from under the fingernails. Some shred of evidence. Maybe some blood or hair. Some DNA," Kelly said.

"You've been watching those bullshit TV shows. But something will break, Jack. It always does. Sooner or later. Some of that has gone to the crime lab for further analysis with tissue and body fluids. Toxicology results will be at least another month."

"You're right. I just wanted to tell Mr. Rich something. Something will break open eventually but I just talked to Jesse and the esteemed Detective Lieutenant Paris of the Homicide Unit of the Boston Police said she doesn't have anything either," Jack said, although he didn't want to discuss Jesse with Archambeault.

"Do I detect some hostility there, Jack? Are you two no longer together?"

"We're very much together, Jay. I'll be heading over to her place for the evening later; we're practically living together," Jack said, trying to end any interest Archambeault might have.

"OK, Jack. Like I say, I haven't crossed off every lead on my list and I'm sure you haven't and ah... Lieutenant Paris hasn't either. Talk to you again, soon, no doubt."

"All right, Archie," Jack said and closed his cell phone.

Jack Kelly sat at Michael's computer and ate the rest of the bagel, drank his juice, and sipped his coffee. Kelly had some unanswered questions so he resolved to get a copy of the completed official medical examiner's report from the chief medical examiner's office. There was only one secretary there. The same secretary since 1959, when Jack Kelly's grandfather on his mother's side was the city's medical examiner. The secretary was Martha Reese. He put the ME's office on the computer's search engine and got the phone number. Martha Reese answered.

"Miss Martha? Jack Kelly, here."

"Oh my! Little Jackie? Oh my. I haven't heard from you in years."

"Not since I was still working for the city. I've been in the private sector for seven years now," Jack informed her.

"You're a private investigator; yes, I know. I read the papers, Jack. That nasty business with that Mr. Reno. He was a monster! Dr. Ryan had to autopsy ten bodies because of him."

"I think it was fourteen."

"Are you doing all right, Jack?" Martha Reese asked with motherly concern.

"Never better, Miss Martha. Less hours and more money," Jack lied. "And I'm my own boss."

"Well, I'm sure you're a good one. Oh, if only your grandfather... Well... well, what can I do for you, Jack? Doc's not in the office right now."

"Just put the ME's findings for Michael Rich and Seng Li in an envelope and get it in a mailbox to me today. Can you do that for me, Miss Martha?"

There was silence on the line, so Jack added, "I've been hired to investigate on behalf of Michael Rich's father."

"Of course, honey. I'll make sure they get in the mail today."

Jack gave her his address and had just gotten his cell phone back into his pocket when it shook. It was Amanda looking for Rodney.

"No, I haven't seen him for a few days," Kelly told her, "but I'd like to talk to him. I've got some more questions. I asked him to meet with me this afternoon but I haven't heard from him. He was at that Miracle Bar the other night when I called him and it was too loud to talk. I think there was a band playing or a wicked loud DJ. He was drinking with a woman who had a limo outside."

"I wonder who that was; do you know, Mr. Kelly? I can't find him and he hasn't answered his phone since he was at the Miracle of Science. We were supposed to be going to a lecture this morning, but Rodney was a no-show. He wanted to go more than I did. He had been waiting for this lecture and program for months! There were professors from Cal Tech, Duke, NYU, Purdue, USC, IBM, the Zurich Lab, the University of Oxford… It's all about nano-bots. Microscopic in size and made of molecular components; they can be less than 1,000th the width of a human hair. They perform functions in a swarm."

"That's nice but…," Jack said as he pictured hundreds of thousands of nano-bots streaming across his kitchen floor like a horde of red army ants making their way to his pant leg.

"The medical field will use them by injecting them into the bloodstream. They will identify and destroy cancer cells. That's just one application. They potentially can self-replicate and evolve on their own. Swarms of nano-bots," Amanda enthused. "But the military wants to make nano-bombs. They can release lung-damaging particles. iRobot Corporation gave them hundreds of explosive sniffing Fido robots last year. There's millions in government money out there and…"

"OK, that's all well and good, but…," Jack tried to interject but Amanda went on.

"Nano-bots will be used as microscopic drug-carrying submarines, which can travel through the bloodstream fighting diseases and infections. They can attach to bacteria and hitchhike all over the body. When they find an infected area or an area they wish to treat, these submarines can release their payload of drugs."

"OK," Jack said dejectedly, either submitting to her enthusiasm or wishing that a payload of drugs were being released into his bloodstream. So he said, "Tell me more."

"I just wondered if you had heard from Rodney. If you do, have him call me right away, please. You understand, Mr. Kelly. The death rate on Tech grad students that work at the AI Lab has gone up ten thousandfold in a week."

Amanda hung up and Kelly took a deep breath. He reheated his coffee in the microwave and sat back down at Michael's desk. It was just after noon and Jack needed a fix. He needed some jazz, blues, or classical. The radio was gone so Jack found an Internet radio station and selected classical. As he listened to the smooth sounds of violins, cellos, harpsichords, and pianos, he regained his calm and resolve.

Kelly opened the newspapers and quickly located an article on the MIT murders. It gave a synopsis of the ME report that Jack hadn't seen as of yet. The article gave little more detail to the murders than had already been reported. But it did report that the TV stations were giving face time to random MIT students, asking them if they felt unsafe or were frightened, or if they knew why anyone might want to kill students there.

Jack needed to get down to the basics and he thought about motive. Motive, motive, motive. That's where the answer will lie. These murders were not random. These were not killings of opportunity or passion. They were premeditated and targeted. They were planned with a definite end in mind. Someone had an agenda. When Jack examined the question of "Who had what to gain?" no names surfaced, but he was realizing Michael and his Artificial Intelligence Lab coworkers had developed something special. They had developed something, soon to be so in demand that it could possibly be worth fortunes.

Kelly had his feet up on the computer desk and was reading an online article when his eyes began to close and he was falling asleep. He tried to fight it and was losing when he heard footsteps coming up the fraternity house stairs. He jumped up and walked to the door. He felt slightly guilty as he opened the door for Rich and his brother, Morris. They said hello and came into the small loft apartment. Rich looked around his son's rooms for one of the last times. He sighed deeply, looking at Jack, and said to his brother, "Let's break it down, Moe."

Jack attempted to help by shutting down the computer.

"You can have that computer, Jack, if you think it could help, or if you want to look through it some more."

"No... No, Mr. Rich. I've seen his documents and they're way over my head. There's a chance the computer may have been tampered with. You take it and keep it, if I need it I'll let you know."

"Have you found anything around the apartment to help you?"

"I found something I believe will help *you*. I found some letters from the U.S. Copyright Office in Washington, D.C. Michael had applied for a patent. I think Michael had developed some kind of software program for, ah… what's it called… ah… integrating all the systems of a robot. So that it can be easily controlled. I don't know if it's a brain or what, but… it seems it could be worth a lot of money. I mean a *lot* of money."

"Michael was very excited about his work, Jack," the father said, smiling. "He had told me he had made some recent breakthroughs. But he didn't want to speak too soon."

"I'll be checking this to verify, but I believe he had applied for a patent for his work," Jack said, pulling the plug from the computer to the monitor and wrapping a towel around the monitor. "And I believe he may have gotten it. If in fact he did, or even applied, you may be heir to the rights to his work. It is possibly a multimillion-dollar invention, sir."

Rich sat down in the chair and looked at the floor as tears rolled from his eyes. Moe walked over from the kitchenette and placed a hand on his back.

"He was a good boy. He didn't deserve this," Mr. Rich said, choking back the tears and adding, as he looked up at Kelly, "My wife and I are so glad you're here! You find out who did this, why, and you get them, Jack. Please, Jack."

Jack had a lump in his throat and a tear in his eye. The three men packed up and carried the chairs, table, couch and the few remaining articles from the apartment to a pickup truck double-parked on the street. Jack told Rich that he had spoken to the other primary investigators that morning. He told him the autopsy results contained no surprises. The results would trickle in from toxicology and blood work, and the processing of the clothes, and various other forensic examinations.

Jack also mentioned a "person of interest" that was under surveillance but didn't give his name. He decided to leave it at that. He did not mention Trooper Archambeault's fruitless search warrant or his too convenient theory on suicide by lifestyle. Jack pulled on his coat and his knapsack and waved to Rich and his brother as they drove down the street. Jack turned and looked up at the old frat house.

As he walked to his black Jeep parked around the corner, Kelly didn't see the dark-skinned man in the blue rental car watching him and talking on a cell phone. Kelly was deep in thought. He was moving his base of operations back to his little fourth-floor office in Boston's Chinatown.

Kelly pulled the parking ticket out from under the windshield wiper and got into the driver's seat. He had twenty-one days to request a hearing or pay the twenty-five dollars. Kelly thought of another option: taking it to the Cambridge Police station and asking for a little professional courtesy. But he had three weeks to think about it.

The temperature was up to fifty-nine degrees and was close to breaking the record of sixty-two as Kelly drove past the center of the MIT campus and across the Mass. Ave. Bridge. Kelly didn't notice the blue rent-a-car following three cars behind his.

At the end of the Mass. Ave. Bridge he took a left onto Storrow Drive. As he drove along the Charles, Jack couldn't see the body floating along the river bottom. It rolled and bounced under the surface of the Charles River in a slow dance similar to weightlessness on the moon. The corpse's eyes were wide open but they did not see. They didn't see the catfish patrolling the bottom or the river perch darting about in the dark and murky water. Like in a slow and silent ballet, the body danced and slid along the river bottom, gliding gently past the occasional beer can, a cement block, a lost fishing pole, and a shopping cart. Rodney's eyes stared blankly ahead. His hands and ankles were still wrapped in duct tape. The body, suspended in mid-water, rolled on just slower than the flow of the river. But the gases within the corpse would soon expand and bring Rodney Riviera to the surface.

Chapter 48

Secret Sex Lives of the Dead

Tom Peters and Moose closed the trapdoor in the floor of the converted garage/apartment, got back in the limousine, and returned to CES just as the sun came up over the tall gray skyscrapers and old red brick Back Bay apartment buildings. As always, the dark streets filled with the morning light, crime time slowed to a crawl, the night people took their rest, and the rats returned to their nests.

Tom walked, stumbled, and crawled up to his apartment at CES and walked into his closet. He pulled off his jacket and shirt, emptied his pockets on the dresser, and opened a pill bottle. He took three Xanax pills, crushed them in his teeth, and swallowed them with a swig from a plastic bottle of room-temperature spring water. Then he swallowed a white OxyContin pill. Peters took a small brass pipe and loaded it with reddish hashish. He took a long drag and then blew the smoke onto the closet's light bulb over his head. The smoke curled and spun as it rode the warm airways. It was carried by the currents around the light bulb and then dipped down, and the warm smoke spilled out through the doorway and into the bedroom.

Peters stripped off the rest of his clothes and switched off the lights. He slowly felt his way over to the bed, pulled up the covers, and slid in. He felt exceptional. Tired, but a proud warrior who had survived another skirmish. He had a sense of purpose. Like a successful hunter returning to the village.

As he lay on his right side, he felt the cool pillow under his cheek. He stretched out his legs and he squeezed his toes. He sighed in satisfaction. And without touching her, he felt the warmth of Victoria's body beside him. Her back was to him and he wriggled up a little closer to her. He felt her breathing deeply. She stirred slightly. Victoria tilted her head back a little and said, "Hi, Tommy. I was worried about you… Are you OK? Is everything OK?"

Victoria started to turn to look at Tom but he put his arms around her and held her with her back to him and said, "It's all good, baby. It's all good. Daddy has taken out the trash. Daddy has taken care of business *por la familia*, my love."

"Oh, Tommy…," was all Victoria said, backing up closer to his body until she was tight with him. She felt good, too. And she felt good to Tom. He snuggled closer and didn't mind if his sister felt him getting excited. She had taught him the ways of lovemaking. Even though he had been with many others, this forbidden love gave him his ultimate high. If he was going to the devil, he was going all the way! To Hell he would ride with his eyes wide open and his sister with him. He was getting hard and his member was pressing up against her, where her upper hamstring met her buttocks. She began to breathe more deeply and moved her body just a little to accommodate her brother. His hard cock tilted upward and she opened her legs wider, arching her back a little to provide more room for him to push into her. Tom clutched her tightly, she accepted him and they both moved ever so slightly, so gently, in unison. It was the soft machine, slowly, quietly, and rhythmically rocking.

The forbidden love excited them both beyond belief. As long as they kept it quiet. It was just like they did when they were younger, with their brother in the bed beside them. Tom put his hands around in front of Victoria and he cupped her breasts. He gently squeezed her nipples. Then he reached down with one hand and his fingers touched her down in front. He touched her slowly moving rhythmically and lovingly. Their passions built as their breathing quickened. After the excitement had built to a crescendo, he moved his hands up gently around her neck and he pumped his desires into her.

Chapter 49

Tail of Death

Kelly drove along Storrow Drive, heading in town. He went past the row of garages converted into tiny studio apartments along the river. He wasn't aware of the small blue sedan just a block behind him. And he wasn't aware of Rodney Riviera's corpse, temporarily snagged on a shopping cart on the bottom of the Charles River just a few hundred yards away.

Kelly's cell phone vibrated. It was Willie Crawford.

"I've been at CES since 11 a.m. and it's going on 4 p.m. now and Peters hasn't come out yet. Aside from three ladies stopping by and leaving with a driver and a limo, there hasn't been any movement at all."

"OK. Hang in there. It's an evening and nighttime business, so it will pick up. But stay with Peters, just don't get burned, he could be dangerous. Have you got your Louisville Slugger with you?"

"I've got Big Papi's cousin, the Splendid Splinter, right here, Jack. Heads will roll if I get to swing this mother. I think I have everything I need here... ah... I've got a change of clothes in the van, food and drink in my cooler, binoculars, cameras, magazines, and a jug to piss in."

"OK. Then it's a party. Call me if anything of significance happens," Jack said and hung up quickly before Willie started with his Joke-of-the-Day routine.

Jack got to his office building in Chinatown slowly in the rush hour traffic. As he parked his car in the parking lot across the street he looked into the rearview mirror and backed his Jeep in. In the mirror he saw a blue color that was becoming familiar to him. His detective's instincts had finally kicked in. He saw the blue rental car turning the corner and pulling into a space in front of the Golden Dragon restaurant. He made note of it but did not look directly at the black man driving. Kelly bounded up the stairs in front of the building, through the building's doors, and up the 100 stairs to his fourth-floor office. He went in, but resisted the temptation to look out of the window down at the street. Kelly was revitalized with exhilaration. He was thrilled. It was Game On. He was ecstatic, rapturous, overjoyed, and euphoric. This was where the rubber met the road. And it was time to fish or cut bait.

Jack took off his navy blue Barracuda jacket and threw it on a chair. He went to the wall behind his desk, opened the safe, got his Colt Combat Commander .45-caliber Model 1911 out and laid it on this desk. He put on his brown leather shoulder holster and slipped the semiautomatic into its holster. "Don't leave home without it."

Kelly's cell phone vibrated in his pocket and he jumped. The caller ID indicated Jessica was on the line. Jack answered with "City morgue, you stab 'em, we slab 'em."

"Gallows humor went out with Edgar Allen Poe, Jack Kelly," she said.

"The most wonderful thing has happened, Jesse!" Jack said, unable to contain his enthusiasm.

"What, my Blue Knight? Did you get to level three on Donkey Kong?"

"No. I picked up a tail!" Jack said, elated.

"You picked up *a* tail, or *some* tail?" Jesse asked.

"A tail. A tail!" Jack was practically jumping up and down.

"Oh, no. Where are you? Are you armed? Who is it? Don't fuck with these guys, Jack."

"What guys?"

"I'm assuming it's not an irate wife from some other case you've got going. Let me send a marked unit to ID the guy. You know it's got to be the killers! I don't know who they are, but they've killed before. And recently. Please be careful, Baby. Please?"

Jack walked over to the end window on the south wall of the office and looked out between a small slit in the thin white translucent curtain. He looked down the street to the front of the Golden Dragon but the car was gone.

"Oh, shit," he said.

"What?" Jesse said loudly into the phone.

"Ah. The car's not there! I didn't even get a plate number. But they don't know I'm onto them. They're out there somewhere."

"Can I put a counter-surveillance unit on you?" Jesse asked.

"No! Don't scare my fish away! I could put The Musician on him, but I need him for Peters. If I see the tail on me again, I'll let you tail him to where he comes from or at least long enough to get his plate number."

"All right, Jack. Promise me. You see that tail, you call me instantly and I'll get in the conga line behind you."

"The line forms at my rear. You've got a deal. We'll get the plate number and see who he's working for. He's a clean-shaven black man about thirty or forty. He's dressed well. In fact, he may be a driver or chauffer; I think he was dressed in black with a white shirt and black leather gloves."

"Please be careful, Jack. I've grown accustomed to your face… and certain other parts."

"I'm going to take a shower, put on some clean clothes, and bring my certain other parts over to your place. We'll see if he follows me. I'll call you ten minutes before I start heading over."

Jack left his office headed for Jesse's apartment on his bicycle. He had decided to take that mode of transportation so that he could avoid being followed. He didn't want to lead anybody to Jessica's place on Beacon. He maneuvered his mountain bike through Chinatown at a fast clip and shot across the Boston Commons. Kelly took the corner at Arlington and Beacon and pulled up on the sidewalk. He put his bike down and pretended to be rolling up his right pant leg for a few minutes to see if there was anyone following him. After he was satisfied that he had lost anyone in pursuit, he mounted the bike and continued on down Beacon Street the four blocks to Jesse's subterranean apartment. Kelly carried the bike down the courtyard stairs and put it where it couldn't be seen from the street.

Kelly knocked and walked into the apartment. Jesse yelled out from her bedroom that she'd be out in a minute, so Kelly threw his backpack and blue Barracuda jacket onto the couch. He picked out a Jeff Beck CD and got the player working.

Kelly and Jessica ate homemade thin-crust pizza topped with extra cheese, zucchini, broccoli, red onion, and pineapple and they drank a red domestic pinot noir wine that Jesse had selected. After dinner they listened to the cool jazz that Kelly had chosen, some Ahmad Jamal, Dave Brubeck, Charlie "Bird" Parker, and Oscar Peterson, and they tried not to talk about work. They even discussed going on a vacation together to the beach in Provincetown the next summer. They considered a flight somewhere warm and tropical. Jack said he would rent a windsurfer and Jessica said she would rent a jet ski. Then they agreed on sailing a catamaran. They even talked about which breed of dog they would get, if they ever got a dog. Jack mentioned an old English sheep dog and Jessica liked the German shepherds. Then they finally agreed on a Portuguese water dog.

They went to bed without watching the ten o'clock news. The MIT murders were the top story and dominating the airways. It was a few hours of respite for the investigators from the constant immediacy of the homicide investigations. But it was short-lived.

In the early morning as Kelly and Jessica were finishing breakfast with cups of fresh-roasted Colombian coffee, Jack's cell phone alerted him to a call. It was Sergeant Donavan of the Boston Police Department.

"Mornin', Jack," the Sergeant said, then got straight to the point. "Thahr's been another bahdy floated up on my side of the Charles Rivah, Kelly. At about 11:30 last night he was found. And from the looks of him, we've gaht a serial killah workin' along the rivah. This one was found by two Emerson Cahledge coeds coming home from a bah on Beacon Hill neah the Hatch Shell."

"That must have been spooky… for them."

"One of the lasses got a bit sick and almost hurled on my boots. And the other girl kept narvously gigglin'. Anyway, the body was a young male, clean-shaven, maybe shahrt blondish hayah, five-foot, eight. I looked him ovah and thahr was a couple a lumps on his head and he looked like he was shot in the back of 'is head, Jack. Same as Michael Rich and the Asian guy's homicide that Lieutenant Paris is investigatin'. This guy's hands and feet were wrapped up in silvah duct tape."

"Maybe the crime lab will get something from that tape. Oh, man! The press is going to be all over this. They'll get in my way… maybe they're the ones following me," Kelly said, looking at Jesse, who had a puzzled look on her face.

"Jack, when this kid was shot in the back of his head, the bullet knocked half of his farhead out. The skull with his eyebrow attached is hangin' from his face. I'm gonna cahl Lieutenant Paris next, Jack… she can bring you down heah to the scene, although thahr's only dah body ta look at."

"No ID, right?" Jack asked, matter-of-factly.

"Oh, he had a wallet in his back pahcket with an MIT ID. His name was Rodney Riviera. Lived in Cambridge, twenty-four years old."

"Oh, God… I knew him. He was part of the group that worked with Michael Rich and Seng Li at the Artificial Intelligence Lab. I assume you've called the staties and Trooper Archambeault.?"

"I cahlled the fahkin' troop at CPAC but I didn't tahk to young Archie. Did you know those CPAC guys ain't got no special investigative trainin'? Archie was stoppin' cahs on the Mass. Pike fah the last six yeahs. Holy Mutha of God. I did what I was supposed ta do and I cahled you. Mr. Rich deserves some ansahs for his son's death. He's a good man in a world whahr good men are gettin' ta be fah and fahkin' few between, Kelly! And that's why I cahled you. So dig in to this mothahfahker and pull out a fahkin' scumbag, will you, Kelly? And if you get the chance, administah some fahkin' street justice and save the Cahmmonwealth ah Massachusetts the cost of a trial and incarceration, OK?"

"OK, Donavan. Watch your blood pressure."

Sergeant Donavan hung up and Kelly turned to see Jessica's inquiring look.

"We've got a serial killer, Jesse. Another body floated up on your side of the Charles, late last night," Jack said and sat down, stunned at the turn of events.

Jessica's cell phone rang. It was Donavan, notifying her of the homicide, which would be part of her case load. Jesse let Donavan explain as much as he knew about the found body of Rodney Riviera, before asking him, "Who else have you notified, Sergeant?"

Donavan stuttered and told her that he had notified his shift supervisor, the Mass. State Police CPAC Unit, and her. That's when Jesse sprung her trap and scolded Sergeant Donavan in his own affected dialect.

"Then, great day in the fahkin' mornin', how come you called that private detective, Jack Kelly, before calling me? I'm the lead investigator for the Boston Police Department's Homicide Unit on this case, and yah know it. I've got jurisdiction and this ain't no gahdamn nickel and dime. This is a fahking serial killing! We've got a fahking serial killer on the loose in your area, Donavan. What have you got to say for yerself, Sergeant?" she scolded, mimicking Donavan's phony Irish accent.

"But… I… ah… you see, Lieutenant…," Donavan stammered.

"Well, who the fahk do you work for, Donavan, the fahkin' Jack Kelly's American Detective Agency, or do you collect your fat fahkin' paycheck from the City of Bahston?"

"Well… now… it's not that fat…. But… how do you know… I *may* have called Jack Kelly before I called you, Lieutenant?" Donavan asked earnestly realizing that Jessica and Jack were together, he said, "Oh… well… my pardon for intrudin'… I didn't mean ta interrupt… if you two were engaged in doin' somethin'… I mean…"

"You better quit while you're ahead, Sergeant. And I'm not saying you're ahead. Give me your report again. Where'd this body wash up? Who found it? How long did the corpse look like it was in the water?" the lieutenant asked.

Donavan swallowed hard and consulted his notebook.

"Well, Detective Lieutenant Paris, several young ladies from thah Emerson College, takin' a late-night stroll home from a bah, saw the deceased floatin' down the rivah about twenty yahds off-shore of the Hatch Shell near the boat floats. Medical personnel felt, and I concur, the body was only in the wahteh for a day or two, max. Blood in the open wound was still red. The duct tape around his wrists and ankles looked brand new. His clothes hadn't lahst any colah. Fresh as a daisy he was, detective. Wallet in his pocket says he's Rodney Riviera, MIT graduate student, lives in Cambridge. But officially, he's a John Doe until we can positively identify him, ah… as you know. That's all I've gaht."

"Very good, Sergeant Donavan; does the press know yet?"

"Ah… NBC Channel 7 and Fox TV were thar when we pulled the body. And I saw that nosy reporter Gordon Little from the *Herald*. It's quiet out heah now, ma'am."

"I'll read your report when I come into the office in forty-five minutes."

"I'm due to go off shift after a double, Ma'am."

"You'll go home after you write out a full report. And Sergeant, call me right after you call your super next time," Jesse said and closed her cell phone. She walked over to Jack, who was staring out into space, and put her hand on his back. "I love busting' that big mick's chops."

"Spoken like a true lady," Jack said, though his mind was elsewhere.

"So what do you make of this, Jack?"

"And Rodney makes three…," Jack said, adding, "Michael Rich, Seng Li, and Rodney Riviera. All three friends were grad students working in the AI Lab. All three worked on the Prototype… I think all three were killed because of their inside knowledge of this Prototype Project. It was what they knew about this robot prototype … it's extremely advanced and ready to be marketed. That's what got them killed."

"I suppose it's not that farfetched. I guess I'm a believer," Jessica said, only half believing it.

"Rodney tried to tell me. He tried to show me at the MIT Museum. Jesus, he yelled it to me as I walked down the street away from him. Now he's dead."

"We'll get the bad guy, Jack," Jessica said, rubbing his back, but the better she tried to make him feel, the worse he felt about himself.

"Sometimes I think we create more death by pushing a case," he said.

"That's crazy talk, Jack. We're the best chance there is to solve this and see justice prevail. I learned this from you. 'Don't ever think you create this crazy world,' you told me. You're trying to straighten it out. It's people like you that keep it real, Kelly. Now, put that sick mind of yours onto the track of this killer and make us all shine." Jesse gave him quite the pep talk.

Jack had a faraway look in his eyes when Jesse said, "Do you want to go down to the river and see the body with me now? Before they take it to the morgue?"

"No. You go. But I'll go to the preliminary autopsy with you, if you can get us in."

"I think I can swing it; I know the doorman," Jessica said.

Jack walked to the courtyard window and looked up and out onto the street. Counter-surveillance would be the order of the day. Kelly wanted to figure out who it was following him.

"Apparently I've lost the guy tailing me. Yesterday I wanted to lose him. But today I want to bring him back. I want to bait the hook and throw out a line."

"Just make sure it's not a shark in these waters," Jesse pleaded.

"I'd be better off with a shark. But I need to know who's tailing me."

"What are you going to do, Jack?"

"Go to my office, then leave and try to let this guy start following me again. And at the first sign that he's on me, I'll go to a public place, call you on your cell. You can pin the tail on the donkey, OK?" Jack finished his coffee and walked out the door.

He slung his backpack over his shoulders, picked up his bicycle, and walked up the courtyard steps to the street. He covertly glanced up and down the street, looking into every parked car, but he couldn't see anyone. He was pretty sure he had ditched his tail yesterday on the way over. But today the stakes were higher. Three MIT students had been killed. The murderer had shown that he would kill again and again if he felt he needed to. And obviously he needed to. Jack knew he was probably under surveillance by the killer or killers. The black man he had seen tailing him could be the killer or somebody hired by the killers. Jack remembered Rodney trying to tell Jack just how big the suitors of the Prototype Project were. The interested parties were the world's wealthiest corporations and some of the world's biggest governments and their agencies.

Jack pumped the bike's pedals hard as he rolled up Beacon Street to the Public Gardens, Boston Commons, then up to the State House, down Beacon Hill through Downtown Crossing, and into Chinatown. He wheeled up in front of his office building and carried his bike up the front stairs and into the elevator. He slammed the doors shut and pushed the lever down that sent the elevator upwards.

As he passed from the third to the fourth and top floor, he felt the gun butt of his .45 for reassurance. Kelly didn't waste time getting into his office and locking the outside doors. He knew he may be on the endangered species list. Not that the world would notice he was gone. Jack knew if one of those endangered tree toads in the jungle in South America ceased to exist, *National Geographic* would have a ten-page article and a two hour TV special bemoaning the loss to the planet. But if Jack Kelly ceased to exist, he knew there would hardly be an outcry. It would only be the absence thereof that may be noticed.

Jack surreptitiously moved to the end window and looked out from behind the curtain to the street below. He didn't see anything suspicious so he walked to the CD player and put in a Chess Records CD from the Willie Dixon collection and pressed Play. The compilation featured the strong urban blues songwriting of Mr. Dixon, as sung by Muddy Waters, Howlin' Wolf, Otis Rush, Lowell Fulson, Bo Diddley, and other great bluesmen. The simple song structure and honest lyrics soothed Jack and allowed him to focus at the same time.

He did what he always did. He sat down at his desk with a pen and a pad of paper. He wrote "Rodney" in the upper left corner. He wrote "Seng Li" in the upper right. He wrote "Michael" in the middle of the page. He thought about Michael and Rodney. Kelly tried to remember everything and anything Rodney had told him. Jack thought the kid was an overdramatic nut at the time. But when Rodney paid the price with his life, Jack thought there must have been more truth than chatter in the words Rodney spoke. Kelly wrote "AI Lab" on one side of the paper and drew a small square and simplistic robot on the other.

Kelly's cell phone buzzed; it was The Musician.

"I'm back in the saddle," Willie said.

"What's been happening?" Kelly asked.

"Absolutely nothing here at CES. Peters has not gone anywhere."

"Rodney Riviera washed up at the Hatch Shell, Willie. He called me the night he went missing. He was at that Miracle Bar next to MIT and he told me he was with a very pretty red-haired lady that was surprisingly very interested in him. He said she had a limousine waiting outside. Does that sound familiar? The College Escort Service is all over this case! I think you're in the right spot, my musically inclined friend. But you are definitely in a dangerous spot."

"That's why you pay me the big bucks. But I haven't done anything. I'm sitting in this fucking van with the windows open a crack and it's fifty-five degrees warm outside."

"I've picked up a tail," Jack said. "He's a black guy, about forty. Medium, stocky, with a short afro. Dressed in a black suit and white shirt."

"That sounds like a driver I've seen here," The Musician said.

"I thought that might be the case. And speaking of case, we've got to build a case. We've got to catch this Peters… doing something incriminating. And any minute the BPD or the staties are going to start sitting on him. If they pick him up, he'll just lawyer up. Where's the forensic evidence when you need it? Young Archie says I watch too much TV. I admit it. I watch Court TV and I can be a news junkie if there's something going on."

"Want to hear the Joke-of-the-Day?"

"Oh, good lord. Go ahead," Jack said dejectedly.

"OK. Well… first let me tell you, my kid Tommy, he's in fifth grade. The teacher says to his class, 'Who knows the biggest word?' And my Tommy raises his hand and says, 'Autoeroticism.' And the teacher, Miss O'Brien, says, 'Tommy, that's a mouthful,' and Tommy says, 'No, Miss O'Brien, you're thinking of a blowjob.'"

"Oh God, save me," Jack said.

"OK. Here's the joke. This middle-aged guy bought a brand-new high-performance car and he took off down a country road in Rochester, Mass. on a beautiful afternoon. He soon had the car up to eighty miles an hour and it was handling so well he pushed the accelerator a little more. He looked in the rearview mirror and he saw a Mass. State Trooper behind him with the emergency lights flashing blue and the siren started wailing. But the guy's new car was handling so well he pushed down on the accelerator and the high-performance sport car zoomed ahead at well over a hundred miles an hour, but he realized he was being foolish and pulled over to the side of the road and waited as the trooper pulled up behind him. The trooper walked up and said, 'Sir, it's the Fourth of July and my shift is over in ten minutes. If you can give me a reason I've never heard before why you were speeding, I'll let you go.' The man looked up at the statie and said, 'Three days ago my wife ran off with a Massachusetts State Trooper and I thought it was you trying to bring her back.' The state trooper walked away, saying, 'Have a nice day.'"

"Do you feel better now, Willie?" Jack asked The Musician.

"Hey, Jack. WBZ Radio is yapping about a serial killer. 'The Charles River Serial Killer,' they're saying."

"That's right, Musician. This is the case we're working. And guess what? You're sitting on Suspect Number One. That's why I'm telling you, Willie! Watch your back. Call me with anything," Kelly said and closed his cell phone.

Jack turned on the big TV on the wall across from his desk. He flipped back and forth from Fox 25 to Channel 7. Fox had just finished the weather. Jack looked at his watch; it was only 10:24 a.m. and the local news channels would be starting the headlines again. He went into the kitchen and filled a stainless steel kettle with tap water and put it on a burner on the stove. He put a teaspoon of instant coffee into a thick brown mug. Before the water could come to a boil, the TV station started its news program with its top story, "Murder at MIT." The account recapped the series of events, sticking to the facts. Three bodies were found in the Charles River, sources said all three were MIT students, all three shot in the head. The Boston area was experiencing a serial killer alert. Jack thought it must have been ratings week because the TV stations mentioned the Boston Strangler and Whitey Bulger.

"Wow," was all Jack could say before his cell phone rang. He pulled it from his pocket with a look of horror, expecting it to be a reporter, but it was Jessica.

"The shit has hit the fan, Jack. I just got to Area A Homicide and my captain ripped me a new asshole."

"Once again, that's my girl. You know, I love to kiss those same lips that swear like a sailor. I'm not sure why. But… and it's a big butt, but I do."

"Shut up, Kelly. The fucking governor has called the fucking mayor and the fucking mayor has called the fucking chief and the fucking chief has called all his Boston Police Department captains, and they all pointed the fucking fickle finger of fate at the Homicide Unit's case investigator: me!"

"Pointed the finger at you for what? Are you the killer?"

"Pointed the finger at me and said, 'Get this done, now! The city is in a panic. Solve these killings!' the mayor mumbled! The politicians say the whole city is 'impacted,' whatever that means."

"I don't know, I had an impacted tooth once," Jack offered.

"Listen, Jack. I'm now on the hot seat. I imagine Trooper Archambeault is, too. The media has exploded on this case. We are going to be watched, checked, and double-checked. You have slipped under the radar on this. But you're up to your eyebrows. We need to make progress."

"My sentiments exactly," Jack said, enjoying the fact that someone else was feeling the pressure to solve this case.

"We need to focus," Jesse said.

"I've never seen you so nervous, Jesse."

"My boss is up the wall on this. He was saying I blind-sided him on this! The captain is tough on a good day but when City Hall gets on him, you know, shit runs down hill. And he hates the media!"

"Well, at least he has good taste."

"I'm sending a patrol car to pick you up," Jessica said.

"No, you're not."

"You've got to come to the Charles River Serial Killer Task Force meeting scheduled for 12:30. At Area A. The FBI is sending over a profiler from their office across the street."

"12:30? Wow! They've never interrupted lunch before. If *you* pick me up, I'll go. Else-wise you and the mayor can kiss my ass because I don't work for the city anymore," Jack said, turning indignant.

"Fine. I'll be over to pick you up. Do you have a tail yet?"

"I haven't seen one, but I warn you, I don't want to speak at this task force meeting. I don't have anything concrete. I've got a lot of suspicions and innuendos. But that's it. I'm not going to mention robots or anything else. You got that?"

"Sure, Jack. But just remember... I outrank you. And you're bordering on insubordination. I may have to administer a spanking."

"Well, not in front of the boys."

Chapter 50

Profiles in Madness

Lieutenant Paris pushed the buzzer to Jack's office at 12:15. He bounded down the stairs and walked over to her dark blue Ford Taurus parked out in the front of the building. Jessica was sitting in the passenger seat with the window open. She said to Kelly, "Drive." He walked around the front of the car and slipped in behind the wheel. He took off, heading toward Government Center. He stopped at the first convenience store and bought the *Boston Herald* and the *Boston Globe*. The headlines were "MURDER AT MIT" and "GRADS DEAD."

Jessica threw the papers into the back seat. Neither spotted anyone following them.

Jack maneuvered the unmarked BPD cruiser along the waterfront. He passed the James Hook Lobster Company and the Boston Aquarium. He took a left at the Boston Harbor Hotel and took the shortcut through the Haymarket and past Faneuil Hall. Although the meeting was at the Boston FBI offices, Jessica had Jack pull the car into the Area A police lot across the street, behind the Federal

Building. Jack slid Jessica's plastic key card through a slot at the gate.

The two walked into One Center Plaza, took the elevator up to the FBI's Suite 600 lobby, and checked in with the front desk. Jack thought it odd that the sign on the law enforcement agency's desk said they were open from 8 to 5, Monday through Friday. Kelly and Paris were issued clip-on ID cards and directed to a conference room. Inside the room at a conference table were Mass. State Trooper Jay Archambeault, his supervisor at CPAC, Major Jeffrey Houston, Sergeant Moses Donavan of the BPD, and Dr. Lee Ryan, the medical examiner.

Kelly went directly to a serving table and fixed a hot cup of coffee and picked out a raisin muffin. Lieutenant Paris got coffee and they both walked over to a table behind the seated group. A young detective from the Cambridge Police and an even younger uniformed officer from the MIT Police came in and sat behind Jack and Jessica. They had just finished saying good morning when the conference room door opened and two men walked in, talking. It was District Attorney Jay Thomas and FBI Special Agent Liam McCartney. They both wore suits with white shirts and ties. Jay Thomas said hello to everyone in the room and then announced that it was time to get down to business. He introduced Dr. Ryan and sat down.

Dr. Ryan had a short PowerPoint presentation. He showed photos of the three known victims found in the river. He showed their shaved skulls and pointed out the similarities between all the gunshots, saying the bullet fragments from all three matched and were from a .357 magnum firearm. He noted that all three were dead before they were "dumped" into the water. He pointed out that all three victims had crystal methamphetamine in their stomachs, but not much in their blood, concluding that the powdered drug was administered around the time of death.

"Are you sure they weren't speed-freak drug sniffers? Why would someone put drugs down their throats after they killed them? Who would do that, Doc?" Archambeault asked the old coroner.

"Listen, sonny, if I'm saying it, then… it happened. Yes, I'm sure! I do not guess. Unlike you, my work is not speculative but based on scientific fact. These young men were not drug addicts by any means. They exhibited no signs of drug abuse. They did not sniff any 'speed,' Detective Trooper."

Doc Ryan was giving it to young Archie regarding the staties' "suicide by lifestyle" theory, and Jack loved it.

"OK, Doc. I'm just pressing you for as much information as I can get. OK? And I thank you for it, sir," Archambeault said, taking the ME's outburst in stride.

"You can count on few things in this world, Trooper Archambeault, and one of them is I mean what I say. But as for the 'why,' I don't speculate without corroborating facts. And as for the 'who,' you'll have to figure that one out for yourself. I have only done a cursory examination of the third body, a Mister…" Dr. Ryan looked at a piece of paper on the table in front of him and continued, "… Riviera, Rodney J. I will be doing the more extensive preliminary autopsy directly after this meeting at Boston City if any of you care to attend. Toxicology and Forensics have little to go on. But as we know, they are slow. Slow to yield information. But when they do… it seals the deal. It's based on scientific fact."

DA Jay Thomas stood up and said, "Thanks, Doc. And now Special Agent McCartney will profile this killer and tell us what we should be looking for. Liam."

Agent McCartney walked over to the blackboard and drew three short lines up in the left-hand corner. He turned to the seated group and said, "Three. That we know of.… He is a serial killer. He is driven to repeat. I say *he* because there are only two archetypes of female serials. The Black Widow and the Angel of Mercy. Neither of those applies here.

"In general, the serial killer is someone who emotionally kills people in separate events with a cooling-down experience between killings. They are psychopaths. They have personality disorders. But they appear to be quite normal on the outside with a mask of sanity. In fact, they are likely to be amiable and appealing." The agent went on, explaining that there was often a sexual element to the act of murder. And this agent should know. FBI Agent McCartney had coined the term "serial killer" in the seventies in response to Ted Bundy and David (Son of Sam) Berkowitz.

"There are other classic elements that point to a certain type of killer," the agent continued. "These murders have been committed in a similar fashion. And the victims had something in common. In this case, they worked at the Artificial Intelligence Lab at MIT."

Jack sipped his coffee loudly, drawing the gaze of DA Thomas and Major Houston, Archie's supervisor. The FBI profiler continued.

"We are looking for an organized serial killer with a dysfunctional background. He was physically, sexually, and psychologically abused. He is motivated by power to the degree that it becomes a sexual compulsion. This will allow him to psychologically compensate for deep feelings of inadequacy. There is a strong element of fantasy. He daydreams about power and domination. He dreams about the victim's submission and murder. The fact that the TV and newspapers are bombarding the public with the story of the killings frightens the city but it only adds to the thrill for the psychopath. The killer feels a sense of power. He will follow the story closely in the media. So you can expect that after a cooling-off period, this murderer will be active again. I'd say he cannot stop. He's tasted blood."

"He's a vampire?" Sergeant Donavan asked.

"Not literally, of course, but experts agree that once a serial killer starts he will compulsively continue. He cannot stop."

"A bullet from my old .38 will stop him, and I've got five more bullets for sickos just like 'em," Donavan said, tapping his gun holster.

Agent McCartney didn't look pleased with the old sergeant's remarks and said, "Sergeant Donavan, first of all, your department went to the nine-millimeter Beretta in '91 and the .40-caliber Glock ten years ago with staggered magazines. You've got fourteen shots in that weapon. But fourteen isn't going to be enough. The FBI has raised the previous estimates of the number of active serial killers in the U.S. to seventy-five at any given time. Other 'experts' claim there are hundreds roaming the United States."

"It's like 'Dawn of the Dead,'" Donavan remarked.

Agent McCartney looked at Donavan in a sort of curious disgust and continued, "Our boy is going to be highly intelligent with an above-average IQ. He plans his crimes methodically, usually abducting his victims, killing them in one place, and disposing of them in another. He will maintain complete control over his crime scene. He will understand forensic science and will cover his tracks and will either bury the body or weigh it down in water. He will both go to great lengths to hide his crimes and yet at the same time 'stage' a body. Set it up to look a certain way. He may falsify evidence or create 'red herrings' to draw the investigators' inquiries elsewhere. He will incriminate others and plant evidence. He seeks control."

"But he's a nut, right?" Archie asked.

"Our boy would be described by people who know him as 'a really nice guy' or 'give you the shirt off his back' or 'he would never hurt anyone.'"

"But he's a nut, right?" Archie asked again.

"Well, contrary to popular opinion, serial killers are rarely insane. They may claim to hear voices or hallucinate in an attempt to be acquitted by reason of insanity. There are some documented cases of true mental illness: Ed Gein ate the corpses of women who resembled his dead mother and used the skin to make a 'woman suit.' He died in a mental institution. Son of Sam was instructed to kill by his dog."

"Really?" Archie asked.

"No. But he *thought* the dog was talking to him. There are five kinds of motivation for serial killers and those two, Ed Gein and Son of Sam, are examples of the first type, the Visionary. The second type is the Missionary. This is the killer that feels his murders are justified. He's getting rid of a certain type. Prostitutes or their johns in Floridian Aileen Wuornos' case; women in general, remember Jack the Ripper? Ethnic types, junkies, homosexuals are some of the classic victims. The third is the Hedonistic serial killer. He kills just for the pleasure of it. He enjoys the chase of hunting down a victim and he gets some sexual gratification from it. The fourth kind is the Gain Motivated. This killer is often not lumped in with serial killers in general because they do it for material gain. Hit men are an example.

"The fifth killer is the most common serial murderer. He is the Power and Control killer. He wants to exert power over his victims. He wants to dominate them and take their life from them up close and personal. He is a ritual killer compelled by some unseen force within his psyche to ritualize and then seek relief from the inadequate and humiliating feelings of his childhood. He kills but relief is temporary and he soon feels compelled to repeat his actions, usually until capture or suicide by cop.

"This is our boy. He will show certain aspects, perhaps, of gain motivation but these are ritual killings showcasing his domination and control. He is the hunter. He is the showman. He calls the shots. He has the power to bring forth more bodies and he will. In conclusion, gentlemen, and lady," Agent McCartney said, smiling boyishly at Lieutenant Paris, "the ability of the killer to evade detection and commit these horrific crimes 'under the noses,' as it were, of law enforcement thrills him, and he will methodically plan and execute the murders… in the beginning. But as his compulsion overtakes him and takes over his life… he becomes impulsive and careless. Things will become more and more out of control. He takes the victim's rings as a souvenir or trophy. The second and third victims had their IDs and wallets still in their pockets. The killer is beginning to make mistakes. He left more duct tape on the third body. Trace evidence sticks to tape like it was a magnet! The lab is going to love that… They will superglue the hell out of it."

The profiler's voice seemed to go up in pitch as he seemed to gaze up into a corner of the ceiling intensely. Agent McCartney got a little glassy-eyed and added, "Our boy will become lost in his own manufactured world. He will be obsessed with his self. The scene is his. He… is the star."

"Like a pretty little ballerina diva strutting across the stage with way too much makeup on," Sergeant Donavan said, irritating Agent McCartney further.

The DA jumped to his feet, asking if there were any questions. When there were none, he said, "Thank you, FBI profiler Special Agent Liam McCartney… and Sergeant Donavan," Jay Thomas added sarcastically.

Chapter 51

Every Dog Has His Day

Jack drove out of the BPD lot and headed for the Central Artery. He and Jessica had decided to meet Dr. Ryan at the Boston City Hospital for the examination and autopsy of Rodney Riviera. Jack accelerated rapidly up onto the Central Artery ramp and gunned the engine as the unmarked Taurus merged with the midday traffic.

"Feels good to slam the old company car," he said, smiling at Jessica.

"You always liked to drive. This reminds me of when you were my FTO on Patrol and then again when I got to Detectives," she said, staring at him like a cat stares at a mouse.

"Why don't you sit on my lap and we'll pretend we're on a bumpy road?"

"Put some music on," the Lieutenant demanded.

Jack quickly tuned the radio to 88.1 FM, MIT's radio station, and turned up the volume to an ear-splitting level. It was the Sex Pistols and Jack bobbed his head in time to the music. Jessica stared at him, smiling for a few more seconds, and opened the glove compartment. She reached in and pulled out a big purple grape-flavored Tootsie Roll Pop. She peeled off the wrapper very slowly, staring at Jack and smiling. She put the lollipop into her mouth and sucked on it very attentively. She made some barely audible slurping and sucking sounds while continually looking at Jack.

Jack stopped bopping to the music and tried to concentrate on his driving. He heard the old-school sounds of an Eminem classic, "Stan," as he changed the radio station to JAM'N 95. The lyrics told the story about a guy who drives off a cliff with his girlfriend in the trunk of his car. Jack smiled and looked over at Jessica and she looked at him. She moved the pop in and out of her lips. As she pulled the pop out of her mouth, it made a popping sound as she sucked on it. Then she slipped off her shoes and put her right foot up on the dash and her skirt fell back a few inches. Jack swallowed hard and Jesse made the popping sound again. Pop! She put her left foot up on the dashboard and her skirt fell up onto her thighs a few more inches. Jack looked away quickly and swallowed again hard.

Then he slowly turned his head back and looked at Jessica. Her smooth legs looked very inviting as his eyes followed the arch of her calf from her ankles, up her calf, to the underside of her knees, and up to her hamstrings and thighs. She had now hiked the black skirt she was wearing up past her mid-thigh and was looking directly into his eyes as she sucked on the lollipop. Pop! She was sucking on the tip of the top of the pop. Jack sighed as she moved the pop in and out of her mouth, teasing him mercilessly. He glanced again in her direction and her lips curled over the top of the pop.

"Don't try that with me. What do you think this is, a grade B movie or a cheap detective novel?" he implored.

She just kept sucking on the lollipop, watching him squirm.

Kelly turned on the air conditioner and lowered his window halfway down. He nervously nodded toward the back seat and asked Jessica to read the newspaper articles about the murders to him.

She put her feet down, reached over into the back seat, brushing her breasts against his arm, sat back down, smoothed out her skirt, opened the *Boston Globe* to the second-page article, and pulled the lollipop out of her mouth, making a prolonged and loud sucking noise. Jessica showed Jack the page-two headline; it read "MURDER AT MIT." She exhaled and began reading aloud.

"'Murder at MIT. Three bodies have washed up on the banks of the Charles River in less than two weeks. The third body, not positively identified as of yet, was found by two Emerson College coeds as they walked along the Charles River Esplanade near the Hatch Shell and boating docks. The body was described as a white male in his early twenties with short blond hair of medium build and medium height. The Boston Police have not released any information other than that, but the *Herald* has confirmed through an anonymous source that an MIT student ID was found in the deceased's wallet, possibly making this the third MIT student found dead in the Charles River in less than two weeks. The deaths of the first two students have been ruled homicides and, as was reported here first, both worked in the Artificial Intelligence Laboratory at MIT. The Boston/Cambridge community is in a state of fear as they realize that an active serial killer is roaming the area....' Blah, blah, blah."

"It says 'blah, blah, blah'?" Jack asked.

"Yes. 'Blah, blah, blah,'... There's nothing new here, Jack. I just wonder.... It never ceases to amaze me at how the press gets onto these incidents and then writes the story then gets the papers out so quickly."

"It's just the benefits of living in a free and informed country, baby. I mean Lieutenant Baby. God bless the U.S. of fucking A. But you know how the rags get the story out so quickly. The papers and local TV stations have stringers and photographers riding around the city night and day with scanners in their cars. They listen to four or five districts and go where the action is. They get to the scene as fast as our patrol cars."

Jessica was reading the *Boston Globe's* coverage and after she had read the article, she said, "There's nothing we don't know already in this article... Catchy headline, though: 'Mayor Mumbles in MIT Murder.' There's no mention of a 'serial killer' in this one and no mention of a third body. The *Globe* seems to get their edition out a little slower than the *Herald* does. They must have to go to print earlier."

"The *Herald* with its big color pictures and splashy headlines is like a fun book, every day. All that with sports and weather. Why should people read crime fiction when the *Herald* is putting out fresh copy every day for fifty cents? And everybody knows the truth is so much more interesting than fiction. I pity anybody trying to make shit up that's better than the real thing; you know, like those dime-a-dozen detective novels... mystery novels," Jack said, looking over at Jessica in the passenger seat to see if she was buying any of this.

"So that's it? You're taking a stand. You're drawing a line in the sand? It's the *Boston Herald* for you? But will you put your money where your big mouth is?"

"Every day," Jack said with conviction.

"You are willing to make that kind of commitment?" Jessica asked him with a look on her face that Jack perceived as strange.

"Ah… yes? I'm committing myself," Jack said with the distinct feeling he was getting himself into trouble with his girlfriend as he falteringly continued, "I'm committing myself… to an institution."

"You need a psychiatrist," Jessica said, starting to get mad.

Jack pulled up parallel to a parking space on Albany Street, directly across from the city morgue, and Jessica said, "You wait 'til I get you home tonight. You're going to get it."

"Why? What did I say? I was temporarily insane. I was dehydrated. I am suffering from dementia!" Jack backpedaled as he backed the car into the space.

"You can make a commitment to the *Boston Herald*. What about me? You seem to have a hard time committing to me, but you're very passionate about the newspaper. That's why you're going to get it!" Jessica said, not at all amused.

"I can't wait. Please don't throw me into the briar patch," Jack said, laughing.

"You'll get yours, Jack Kelly."

"I'm counting on it."

"Every dog has his day."

Chapter 52

Brass, My Ass

Jack and Jessica were still arguing as they stood outside the morgue. Jack pushed her into the bushes and backed away smiling.

"I have a gun," Jesse said.

"So do I, and mine is bigger."

"You are a child, Jack Kelly. In fact, to say you act like a child is an insult to children everywhere. What are you doing, pushing me into the bushes? You're like a third grader. I may not shoot you but I might arrest you!" Jessica said, starting to smile a little herself.

"I'm already arrested. I'm a case of arrested development. You see, that's my point. I don't know from 'commitment.' What is it? What do you want me to say? Jesse, you know I'm crazy about you, don't you?" Jack moved closer to her, wrapped his arms around her, and pulled her tight as she tried to hold herself away from him. She was melting and Jack knew it. He looked in her eyes and said, "Just tell me what you want me to say." Then Jack tried to kiss her.

"Jesus Christ! Doesn't daht look professional?" Donavan said as he and Dr. Ryan got out of a black unmarked Ford and crossed the street. "Not you, Lieutenant. I mean you do, look professional, I mean. It's obviously Kelly daht's da bad influence heah!"

Sergeant Donavan looked at Dr. Ryan and said, "They're a nice couple."

"She's a nice couple," Dr. Ryan replied quietly.

"Donavan, you've wormed your way into the middle of this case," Jack said to him. "I'm going to put you near the top of my suspects list. You've showed up miraculously and mysteriously at every crime scene. You've directed a victim's father to hire me as his family's investigator because you felt the Bahston Police Department couldn't do enough, yet you have a very low opinion of *my* professionalism. Now I see you're trying to influence Doc Ryan... somehow. The FBI profiler said the perpetrator would want to interfere and laugh at the investigators. Maybe it is you. Maybe you're bitter. Perhaps you took the detective exam and didn't pass, or you got looked over for a big promotion somewhere along the line."

Sergeant Donavan raised a finger and opened his mouth but before he could speak, Jack said, "Don't deny it, Donavan. You're just getting yourself in deeper."

"I'm in district court Tuesdee mornin,' Jack. With that no-good junkie cah thief, that juvy Charlestown townie, an' he's up fah his tirteenth conviction for stealin' a Ferrari from Beacon Hill. He's stolen at least thirty cahs. The DA asks fah tree years in Juvy Hall. I says, 'Goddamn it, it costs the city $40,000 a yar to keep 'im.' I says, 'Just buy the son-of-a-bitch a cah, it's cheapah.'"

The four walked down the corridor to the morgue and Donavan asked Kelly how he knew about Donavan getting passed over for a promotion. Jack didn't answer him. Once in the slab room Dr. Ryan checked a chart on the wall by the door. He walked over and pulled the middle drawer near the back wall and the slab rolled out with a dark green body bag lying on top. He unzipped the bag and Jack could see the upper torso of Rodney Riviera. The face was quite puffy and ashen. His blond hair still had some spike to it. Jack walked closer to the corpse on the table and he could see part of Rodney's forehead with an eyebrow had been detached and there was a gaping hole. Jack shuddered involuntarily.

Dr. Ryan saw this and said, "You had spent some time interviewing this man as a witness or a friend of Michael Rich's, I understand, Jack."

"Yeah… yes. He was a good kid. He walked me through the MIT Museum, pointing out different kinds of robots. There were films of just mechanical legs and a machine torso walking upstairs and running. And there were working models of mechanical arms that a surgeon might use in the operating room. And detached heads that could hear and see. The head and eyes would follow me as I walked by. They talk to you. They could hear to the extreme and decipher through background noise. Rodney kept trying to tell me these machine parts had been developed to do everything a human could do and much more. Rodney tried to tell me that Michael Rich had developed a method to make these machine parts unify, integrate, amalgamate, incorporate, combine, and be ruled by a brain-like system."

"It seems to make sense, Kelly. The time is about right. There's been talk about this in the scientific community for years," the ME said as he finished looking at the x-rays of the corpse and extended some forceps down the throat of the dead body.

"I'm naht in the 'scientific community' baht I've seen plenty of science fiction," Donavan said.

"Science fiction is based in fact, and that's a fact," Dr. Ryan said, looking for laughs but getting none from the tough crowd.

"Anyway, Rodney, here," Jack continued, looking at Dr. Ryan, "repeatedly tried to get me to understand that someone who wanted control of this robot model, a prototype, killed Michael to gain control of this multimillion-dollar project. And as sure as the dead man before me, I'm going to take heed to his word. But tell me, Doc, how come we can't get a hit on any physical evidence? Some forensic hair, or a fiber from a carpet, or... I don't know. But how come we haven't?"

"Jeez, Kelly," Donavan said, answering instead of the ME. "Thar's no crime scenes, Jack. Other than da tree bodies found in the wattah. It's gone ta take good old-fashioned police wahrk to crack this one... or the guy will fuck up and we'll just grab his arse, lock 'im up, and trow away da key!"

"Jesus!" the medical examiner said as he strained to grasp an object in the teeth of the forceps. He put one hand on Rodney's chest and pulled hard, attempting to pull something from deep within Rodney's throat. "How's this for forensic evidence, Jack Kelly?"

Dr. Ryan had the shiny gold ring in the grasp of his forceps and held it up to the overhead light. The bright ring reflected golden streams of light outward in all directions.

"Looks like brass," Donavan said.

"Brass, my ass; it's solid gold," Doc Ryan said.

Jack looked closely at the impression of a beaver stamped into the solid gold ring and proclaimed, "You're both right. It's a Brass Rat!"

Chapter 53

Cereal and Comic Books

Tom Peters woke up pissed off. It must have been something he dreamed. He was very pissed off. He brushed his teeth furiously and splashed water, then soap, then water again all over his face like a man possessed or a wild bird in a garden birdbath. Water dripped down from his face onto the floor as he walked, still in his black pajamas, into the third-floor apartment's kitchen and turned on the TV with a remote. He felt uneasy in his own skin.

The gorgeous blonde local noontime newscaster was smiling inanely with her full pouting red lips pursed for the camera. She smiled while reading a short story about North Korea's threat to use a nuclear bomb. She smiled through a story about a kids' group from the inner city bringing rap music to dying cancer patients, and another news item about a horrific car crash involving some high school seniors on their way home from soccer practice, and without missing a beat she smiled at the camera and gushed, "Gee, Bob, I hope we have a sunny weekend so my husband can cut the grass one more time before the first snowfall."

Tom glared at the TV and screamed, "You fucking bitch, you haven't got a clue! You fucking happy ass smiley button... you are a synthetic, artificial, fake, plastic, fantastic soulless cretin; you phony baloney, rotten, ass kissing, lying, insincere, deceitful, mendacious, spoiled rotten, two-faced bitch! You smile-in-your-face-all-the-time-you-wanna-take-my-place backstabber bitch! I hate you! I hate you and everybody like you."

Tom was yelling now; he woke Victoria. As she walked unsteadily into the room, she asked, "What is it, Tommy?" scratching her head and trying to straighten her long blonde hair and her thick blood-red cotton bathrobe.

"Ah... this fucking newsie. She is so phony, she's not real. She's made out of plastic, I'm sure," Tom said, digging a cigarette out of a pack. He put the cigarette into his mouth, put the pack back in his pajama pocket, and pat-frisked himself, looking for matches or a lighter but couldn't find one. The TV weatherman showed his hodgepodge of weather for the week to come and had predicted heavy snow to come soon.

"Come back to bed, Tommy," Victoria pleaded, just as the female newscaster came back on with a dead-serious look on her face, saying, "Once again, our top story. Police search for a serial killer who holds the fears of a major Boston-area college in his grip. The cities of Boston and Cambridge walk in fear while this killer is at large. Three Massachusetts Institute of Technology students have been brutally murdered by a twisted serial killer that binds his victims with duct tape and shoots them in the head with a .357 magnum, dumping their bodies into the Charles

River, only to be discovered by innocent passers-by. This station has received a tip that the third body was found to have his MIT school ring, the famed Brass Rat, stuffed down into his throat. Police are baffled, but have formed a task force with members from the Mass. State Police, FBI, Boston Police, Cambridge Police, and MIT Police. An FBI profiler has called the killer 'an increasingly sick and dysfunctional psychopath with a personality disorder.'"

There was more to the story but Tom Peters had kicked over the TV set and it had landed with a huge crash on the floor and stopped working. Tom Peters stood still in the middle of the room. Victoria walked to him and wrapped her arms around him. The two of them began to rock slightly from side to side. She brushed his hair and he whimpered almost imperceptibly.

"They don't understand. They just don't understand," Tom said.

"They don't understand you like I do, Tommy."

"But they make me sound so sick," he said, drawing out the last word and putting his head on Victoria's shoulder.

"They'll get theirs, Tommy. You just wait and see. Living well is the best revenge. We will buy that TV station in two years. We will own this town. Can I get you back to bed? What can I say to get you back to bed?" she asked, rubbing her hand on the cheeks of his ass.

He finally looked at her and said in the voice of an eleven-year-old boy, "Would you get me a bowl of cereal? And would you play the "Master of Puppets" Metallica CD, get the flashlight and some comic books, and read with me under the blankets?"

"Yes, Tommy. You get in bed and I'll play the CD, get the cereal, the flashlight, and the comics," she said, smiling at her brother as he smiled back. Tom requested Trix cereal as he went into the bedroom. He went over to his closet, slipped out of his slippers, and got back into bed. He pulled the covers over his head and waited there quietly until Victoria came back into the room.

"OK, Tommy. Eat your cereal and then we'll get under the covers. Who do you want to start with? Spiderman, Flash, or Batman?"

"Batman!" Tom said excitedly.

Victoria sat on the edge of the bed and started reading the Batman comic book to her brother. When Tom finished eating his bowl of cereal, they both got underneath the blankets of the king-size bed and Tom held the flashlight as Victoria read quietly to him. As she rolled over and began reading the third comic to Tom, he snuggled in close to Victoria's backside. He hugged her softly and made little noises of contentment. She soon smiled as she felt his erection grow hard against her bottom and she pushed back against him. Tom looked at the shiny gold beaver engraved into the ring on his left hand as he stroked and sniffed Victoria's hair.

Chapter 54

Release the Hounds

Jack's frustration was building up, now. He knew he was in a hunt. He was in a pack on the track of a serial killer. Like a pack of hunting dogs sniffing the wind and running around following every lead or inclination. The object of the hunt was a bold serial killer dumping bodies in the heart of the city of Boston. A serial killer who dared to float three successive dead bodies down the city's main artery right into the shadow of Beacon Hill. The killer didn't permanently sink them or hide them. He knew they would rise to the surface and be discovered. He was proud of his work and wanted to show it. He was making bold statements.

Trooper Archambeault and the Massachusetts State Police, the FBI, Lieutenant Jessica Paris of the Boston Police, the DA's office, the medical examiner's office, the MIT Police, the Cambridge Police, and dozens of media hounds, reporters from ten different media outlets: everybody was on the case now. Jack felt like he was losing control. But he never had it to begin with.

It was late in the afternoon and he had put off calling Michael's father for several days. Rich hadn't called Jack but Kelly knew that the explosion of media coverage must be coming down on the man and his wife like an emotional avalanche. He dialed the number in Nahant and thought of what he would say to Mr. Rich while the phone rang. When he heard the voice Jack was taken aback for a moment as Mrs. Rich answered.

"Hi, Mrs. Rich. Is Mr. Rich home?"

"No, I'm sorry, he's not. Is this... is this Mr. Kelly?" she asked.

"Yes, ah, but please call me 'Jack.'"

"And you call me 'Dorothy,' please, Jack," she said quietly.

"I'll just call back when Mr. Rich is home, Dorothy. Or ask him to give me a call."

"Did you have something... to tell him, Jack? Is it something I should know?"

"Oh... no, actually ...ah... Dorothy. Just with all the TV stations and newspapers talking about serial killers and all that stuff... I... thought I should touch base with Mr. Rich, that's about all."

"Is that it, Jack? That's all?" Mrs. Rich said, sounding a little disappointed. Hearing this element in her voice, Kelly tried to put a positive spin on the obvious lack of momentum of the investigation

"Oh, no. No. That's not all. I've just come this afternoon from the autopsy on Rodney Riviera. He was a lab scientist, ah, grad student along with your son, at the AI Lab."

"Yes, we had met Rodney several times and we will be going to his funeral on the day after tomorrow."

"Are you sure you're up to that, Mrs. Rich?"

"You couldn't keep us away, Jack. We are very much involved in this case. We will give our condolences to the Rivieras. We will see this through no matter how long it takes and no matter what we have to do. But the best thing we've done so far is to have hired you."

Jack blushed like a schoolboy until a wave of guilt flowed over him as he continued: "Rodney, as I'm sure you know if you've read the papers or watched the TV, was the third apparent victim of the same killer. And this morning I attended a task force meeting along with the Boston Police, Mass. State Police, and the FBI. I assure you, we are looking into this with the entire professional scrutiny of all of our resources."

Mrs. Rich laughed out loud and Kelly was very confused until Mrs. Rich explained.

"Jack, my husband and I know you are doing all you can to find the killers of my son. You don't have to explain or try to justify your time or actions. We are believers, Jack. We are believers in you."

"Thanks… I'll get back to you soon."

As he rang off Kelly swallowed hard, took a deep breath, and then blew some air out of his lungs to keep his eyes from watering. He was fortified by Mrs. Rich's faith in his abilities, but Jack himself wasn't happy with the progress of the case. Another student had died. It was a student that Jack Kelly had met and talked to. He had spent time with the kid just recently and had just learned to respect him. Now Kelly would be going to his funeral. Rodney Riviera was a student who passionately tried to point Kelly in the right direction, but the detective's skull was too thick to understand. As Kelly tried to recall Rodney's words, he realized that now the things Rodney had told him had more significance to Jack than when Rodney was alive. Kelly felt like someone had just walked over his grave and he shook slightly.

Kelly anxiously called The Musician.

"Hey, Big M. Haven't heard from you; I was a little worried. Waz up, my brother? Where is Peters?"

"Hi, Jack. He hasn't come out all day. Not Peters, his lady, and I haven't seen that big black Elvis-looking guy either. I think maybe they're night people," Willie Crawford said, looking out from the tinted rear window of his van. "There have been a dozen or so ladies going in and out, though. I'm listening to reruns of the 'Howard Stern Show' on my Sirius Satellite Radio. I'll be listening to Monday Night Football tonight. Why don't you walk up to my van with a pizza around nine?"

"No."

"Kelly, how long has it been since we've had a Regular Rotating Monday Night Poker Game?"

"I haven't been to a game in about four months, now, I guess. We stopped in the summer because there wasn't any AC in my office. Then we were gonna get a hotel room just for the game. That didn't work, nobody wanted to put it on their credit card. And then, what was it, four weeks ago, we were gonna play in the back room at J.J. Foley's but they decided it was illegal, with money on the table. I'd like to start playing again, after this case is resolved."

Jack sighed loudly and said, "Look, Willie, seriously. The last murder victim had two bullets in his head and his gold ring stuffed down his throat. Traditionally, that means the victim was an informer talking to somebody. Rodney was talking to me. And the killer knew this. And now I've got to go to this kid's funeral, OK? Watch out for this Peters guy. I think it's him having me followed. I pray he hasn't seen us together. He's messed up in porno web sites, gambling, running women, meth, and, I think, murder. There's no telling what he's capable of. This killer has got brass balls. And, I think, a Brass Rat."

Chapter 55

Spider and the Fly

It was late in the day, getting dark outside, and Kelly began to think about the night. Jack looked out his office window over the row of Chinese restaurants and he watched the trains pull into South Station. He was getting hungry and it occurred to him that dinner with Lieutenant Paris would be a billable conference with a fellow case investigator. The Musician was watching the closest thing Jack had to a suspect, Tom Peters, over in Cambridge at the CES offices. Besides, Jack couldn't think of anything else to do at the moment.

But there was still the tail to deal with. Jack thought of a perfect plan. He would make arrangements to meet Jessica for dinner, see if he could spot the tail, and then put a tail on the tail. Not only was this pragmatic, it was downright good investigative technique. "'Oh, yeah,' said the spider to the fly."

Jack reprogrammed his cell phone not to vibrate and he put the crickets chirping back on, then he called Lieutenant Paris.

"Jesse!" Jack said when she answered.

"I was just thinking about you, Blue Knight. I wondered what you were doing. And if you missed me… And what it would be like to hear you say you needed me and couldn't live without me."

"Jesus. Does the city of Boston pay you to fantasize on the clock?"

"Oh… Jack. You are so unromantic."

"Not true! I protest! I was calling to invite you to dinner! I need you. I mean… I need to see you."

"Really, Jack?"

"Yes. Totally… that and I want to draw this tail out to have you or your boys ID him."

"Oh, OK. I see. You're adding up billable hours, right, Jack?"

"Look, Jesse. I want to work on this case. I talked to Michael Rich's mother today. She's so sweet. She pulled my heart out of my chest and squeezed it, and massaged it, then slapped it with kindness and praise and poured some honey on it and shoved it back in my chest. I want to work on this case and I want to eat dinner with you. I've got a way to do both. Are you in or out?"

"Oh baby, I'm in. And you're going to be in. Where are you, anyway?"

"At the office. Where would be a good place to eat, and a good place to draw out a tail?" Jack asked Jessica.

"I don't know. From your office? A dead end. I'd say out Northern Ave. to one of the restaurants on the fish pier, Pier 4. Anthony's, Jimmy's Harborside, or the No Name Restaurant. Northern Ave. is a dead end with no buildings on either side until you drive out to the end. He'll have to follow you out there, and if we can spot the tail we'll have him with no way back out."

"Oh, you're good. That took you two seconds to pick the nearest best place to corner a tail and... and, with three top-notch restaurants. Jimmy's Harborside is closed down, though. Well, lady, the No Name it is; I would love some great seafood with a cold beer. Who knows, maybe if we can ID the tail and lose it, I'll end up at your apartment tonight. It's 5:30 now; when do you want to head over?" Jack said.

"I'm ready to head to our little conference right now. You're not the only one logging billable hours. Since the third body floated to the surface and the tag 'serial killer' hit the media, I've been given maximum overtime expenditures. I've been given all the time, money, and resources I need. As long as I can deliver some results. And right now, Jack, you're the best thing I've got."

"That's twice in two hours I've heard that. The pressure is killing me."

"Kelly, you seem to be involved in half of every high-profile case in Boston for the past twenty years. Pressure doesn't affect you."

"All right," Jack said. "That's enough bullshit. My Bullshit Meter is hitting the top. I'm going to leave the office in fifteen minutes and slowly drive out Northern Ave. to the Fish Pier and out to the No Name. I'll be looking for the tail and I'll call your cell back when I'm moving."

"Make it twenty-five minutes, Jack. I've got to get my unmarked from the lot and get over to your neck of the woods. I'll call you when I'm getting off the Central Artery at Chinatown," Jessica said and disconnected.

Jack washed his face and hands, and changed into jeans, a black T-shirt, a brown leather shoulder holster with his .45 in it, and a dark blue/green Herringbone sports coat. He watered the six plants spread throughout the office. He shut a few lights off and his cell phone chirped with the sound of crickets. Lieutenant Paris was coming into the neighborhood so Jack shut off his CD player, locked the doors, and walked down to his rented space in the parking lot across the street.

As he jumped into his black Jeep, he tried not to be too obvious as he glanced around for the car that would be tailing him. He peeked about, searching for the tail, when he saw Jessica's unmarked car in his rearview mirror. She was at the opposite end of the street ready to mark the tail. Jack pulled out, drove down Kingston to Summer St. and across the Central Artery to South Boston. Jack could no longer see Jessica behind him. There were only six cars behind him. One was a short bus so Kelly counted that one out. He rang up Jessica's cell phone and asked her if she was able to mark the tail but she hadn't seen anything suspicious, saying, "I think we can rule out the minivan with a woman and three kids, and the yellow school bus. And… there goes the red Chevy taking a right."

"OK, Jesse. I'll take this left over to Northern Ave. and we'll see who follows. Hold on, The Musicians on the other line."

The Musician told Kelly that Tom Peters and his lady were on the move and were being driven by the black Elvis into Harvard Square. They parked in front of the Dolphin Restaurant. Kelly told The Musician to keep him advised and switched back to Jesse as he turned and accelerated down Melcher one block and took a right on Northern

Ave., heading out to Pier 4, the dead end with a row of fish houses and restaurants.

"Only the green Toyota 4Runner SUV and the Checker Taxi followed, Jack," Jessica said.

"I think we have a winner! That green SUV is our viable candidate. I've tried moving surveillance from a cab before and it don't work. Even if you say 'follow that car!'"

"What now, Jack? The plate number won't be any good if they're renting or leasing cars. Are we ready for a marked unit to do a motor vehicle stop and ID the driver?" Jessica asked.

"Let's just wait another minute. Stay on the line and I'm going to find a space near the No Name, and walk in. You see what he does but don't get made. And don't let him get off this dead end without giving up his ID. Even if you have to do it yourself."

"Yes, Boss."

"Don't call me Boss... we both know *you're* the Boss."

"OK, Boss. I'll call the D Street stationhouse and ask the shift super to send a marked unit over to meet me. No radio traffic," Lieutenant Paris said and pulled over to the curb a block back and parked.

"I'll go get us a table by the window and order whatever you want. Let me guess. Six big shrimp cocktail, baked haddock, ice water with a twist of lemon, and..."

"Just order the shrimp and the ice water; I'll call you back."

Jack parked just up the street, glanced back down Northern Ave., saw the green Toyota 4Runner and caught a quick glimmer of Jessica's parked car. As he walked across the street toward the entrance to the No Name,

Kelly had already identified the distinctive whir of the engine of the green Toyota SUV. He wouldn't look at it but he knew it had slowed down just past and behind him. Jack's overactive imagination envisioned the crack of a firearm discharging and the slow-motion trajectory of a hot bullet entering his back and passing through him like a laser beam. But he kept moving, shook it off and bounded up the stairs and into the No Name Restaurant.

Before a minute went by a Boston Police cruiser quietly pulled up alongside of Jessica's car with two patrolmen staring over at her.

"Hi, Lieutenant. The Sergeant said you wanted a driver ID'd. Why don't you run his plate? You got a computer?" the young driver asked.

"Hello again, Officer Hodge and Patrolman Kowlowski. It's a Rent-a-Car is why I don't run the plate, and yes, I've got a computer. How come you've always got questions now? You used to do whatever you were told. Now you've got questions and opinions and comments. Ever since you were named Officer of the fuckin' Month, Hodge. What's up with that?"

"Hey sorry, Lieutenant. I been up and about all night. I got ordered in off a double. Driving the cruiser is the only way I can stay awake. But my brain ain't attached too good right now," Hodge pleaded.

"That's right, LT. He ain't thinking too good," Patrolman Kowlowski agreed, and asked, "Can you get sushi in The No Name? I tried sushi, took it home and warmed it up in the microwave, it tasted like fish."

"OK, Hodge, I'm just bustin' your balls." Paris had learned early on in her career that there were times when she had to talk to male cops with a shade of bravado.

"There's a green Toyota 4Runner up the street past the No Name. I need him ID'd. That's all. I don't want you to be wise, or rude, or threatening. Just get his ID and run it over the air, legitimately, so he thinks it was, like an innocent mistake on your part. So he doesn't think anything of it, OK?"

"No problem, Lieutenant," the two patrolmen said in unison as the cruiser started to pull away.

"Wait!" Jessica yelled and the cruiser jerked to a halt as she asked, "How are you going to do it?"

"I don't know…," Hodge answered. "We'll think of something," and the cruiser took off down the avenue. Jessica turned up the D Street frequency channel on her scanner and looked on as she answered her cell phone, "Hi, Jack."

The cruiser assumed a patrol crawl with the two young cops looking all around as they slowly rolled up the street. As they passed the No Name restaurant Jack looked down upon them from his window table.

"Is that Hodge driving?" he asked Jessica.

"Yes. He's past the end of a double and out of his zone, but hey, how could he fuck this up?"

""Don't say that! It's bad luck," Jack said as they both watched as the patrol car pulled up behind the parked green Toyota and activated its blues. Hodge got out and walked up to the driver's side door as Kowlowski called the license plate information into the dispatch center. Hodge told the driver that his Toyota was parked horizontally in a vertical zone.

Jack Kelly's overactive imagination envisioned Hodge getting shot in the stomach and falling to the pavement.

Then he shook it off and said, "I hope you told him this guy could potentially be dangerous, Jesse."

"I just told him to get the guy's ID; I didn't explain the world to him. He knows enough to defend himself at all times. Oh, wait! Here comes the license plate back." Jessica heard the information dispatched over her police radio and relayed it to Kelly. "'Airport Leasing.' Well, the plate was a dead end, just like we figured."

"Here comes Hodge with the license back to the cruiser; tell it to me," Jack said as he pulled out his notebook and pen.

As Jessica's police band radio blared out Hodge's voice running the name, birth date, and the operator's license number, she held her cell phone near the radio's speaker and they both wrote as Hodge called it in, "First name Marcus, last name Grace. I spell Golf, Romeo, Alpha, Charlie, Echo, eleven twenty-one, sixty-one, with an address of 115 Central Avenue, Somerville, Mass."

"OK! OK!" Jack said with mock enthusiasm. "Great!" he said, adding, "OK… What have we got? Nothing. Who the fuck is Marcus Grace?"

"Jack. We ID'd the guy. That's all. He's a player. He's been hired by somebody else. We'll run him. Let me see if I can get somebody to follow *him*. He probably works for somebody else. Your boy Peters, no doubt. Did you expect a guy to jump out and say 'Hi? I'm the serial killer!'? No… You're working the case and we have one more piece of the puzzle," Jessica said as the cruiser with the two uniformed cops drove past her location and took a left turn.

"Yeah. This guy may work for Tom Peters. Anyway it looks like he's spooked. He's taking off. He's going to go right past you."

"Oops, I dropped my phone," Jessica said as she bent down below eye level and the green Toyota passed by.

"Good, the bastard's gone," Jack said. "Now come on up here or I'll eat your shrimp and your haddock."

"I didn't say I wanted haddock. I'm going to order swordfish, or better make it Mako… shark, that is… if they've got it today," Jessica said.

"You know what we say here in New England? 'Sometimes you eat the fish. Sometimes the fish eats you.'"

Chapter 56

Off the Clock

They had finished their dinner at the Dolphin Restaurant in Cambridge and Victoria and Tom Peters with their driver Moose headed for the restaurant's door. As he walked down the stairs, Moose noticed the old blue van parked down the street. He thought he had seen it before. The limousine was parked directly in front of the restaurant and as the three came down the stairs to the sidewalk, the big black man reached out and opened the rear door for Victoria. After Tom slipped in, Moose shut the door and got in the driver's seat. As he pulled away from the curb and headed south towards Boston on Mass. Ave., Moose adjusted the rearview mirror and saw the blue van pull out. The van continued to follow from several cars back.

Consciously or subconsciously, Moose made the connection to the blue van following them. Tom and Victoria were whispering in the back seat. They laughed, giggled, snickered, and tickled each other. Tom saw Moose looking back in the rearview mirror and gave him a "thumbs up," meaning he should shut the partition between the driver and the back seat.

"Ah…," Moose mumbled. "I think we've got someone following us, Boss. An old blue Chevy van with, I think, one white hippie driving."

"How exciting!" Victoria said as they both slumped down a little in the back seat and looked at each other.

"No shit! This is electrifying. Who could it be? The cops?" Tom asked.

Moose said, "That long-haired dude is deep under cover if he's a cop. I don't think so."

"Deep under cover? That sounds like private investigator territory. I wish I could get a look at him. How can I get a look at him?"

"Lead him down an alley?" Moose said.

"No. Then he'd have *us* cornered and he'd get more of a look at us. Maybe a cul-de-sac?" Victoria said.

"I don't think we've got too many cull D-sacks in the city, Boss."

As the limo drove down Mass. Ave. and passed Cambridge City Hall and into Central Square, Tom said, "Just pull right over to the right side and park real quick. He'll have to drive by. And when he does you'll get his plate number and I'll write it down. There's a big space over there, to the right."

Moose swung the limo into a long open loading section by the curb in front of Cantones' nightclub and came to an abrupt stop. The cars behind him, including the blue van, all drove past.

"Go ahead and swing out now, Moose. We'll follow *him* for a bit. So, what was the plate?" Tom said.

"Ah… 73N… Z… ah," Moose stammered.

"It was 73NP47," Victoria said as Tom wrote the plate number on his hand.

The Musician cursed as the frustration of having to follow so closely in the city got to him. The limo had pulled over and he had to drive right past them. He knew it was impossible to follow a car from in front of it. He knew he might lose the tail altogether or, worse yet, he could be made. He had to determine if he had been recognized as someone shadowing the limo's occupants. If he was known to them now, his job was done. He was burnt toast. Of no further use. And off the clock.

He looked in his rearview mirror at the limousine three cars back. The hunter was now the hunted. He contemplated losing the tail. But he knew that if he cut and ran it might further tip his hand. He decided to just continue the folly and drive on. His mind raced as he imagined the possible scenarios. The limo behind him would turn right or left. Yeah, that's all. He could get another car for later. Maybe Kelly could bring a different vehicle over and take his. Willie thought Jack probably wasn't doing anything anyway. The Musician pulled out his cell phone and buzzed Jack.

"So they finished eating at the Dolphin, started heading in towards Boston, then at Central Square they suddenly pulled over on Mass. Ave., and now they're behind me," Willie said and gave it a moment to sink in.

"They are following you?"

"Yes. Mass. Ave. in Central Square, Cambridge, heading towards MIT and Boston."

"Lieutenant Paris's boys just identified a Somerville resident, Marcus Grace, as the driver of the green Toyota 4Runner that's following us. He's a black male about forty-something."

"Like I said, he sounds like one of the chauffeurs I've seen working out of the College Escort Service offices."

"Did they make you?" Jack asked, concerned.

"Ah…I don't think so. Well, I don't know. I'm trying to figure that out now."

"I'll get Cooper ready to go next if you need to be replaced. Well, you know what? This is a good time to get somebody else on them. At the very least we have to get that blue van out of there; is that what you're driving? Peters may be going out tonight. And Jesus Christ, Willie! This guy may be a stone cold killer! Be careful and let me make a couple of calls to see when I can get you out of there. And at the first sign you've been made, pull out! You hear me, brother? Pull out!"

"Yes. That's something I should have done before my youngest daughter came along."

"Oh, that's nice Willie. You know you love her."

"With all my heart, every ring, stud, body piercing, and tattoo," The Musician said.

"Well, plan on spending some time with her because I've got to pull you off of this surveillance."

"Good; I've got two recording sessions I had put on hold."

"You can take some pictures of the attendees at Rodney Riviera's funeral at Waterman's in Kenmore Square if you want to make some side money," Jack offered.

"OK. And… that reminds me… Do you want to hear the Joke-of-the-Day?"

"Jesus, William Ellis Crawford III! It's possible you are being hunted by a serial killer three cars behind you! And you want to tell me a joke?"

"Yes."

Jack was in a state of disbelief. "Well… I want you stay on the phone with me until you can figure out if Peters is tailing you. Keep driving toward Jessica and me. We're on Northern Ave. So go ahead with the Joke-of-the-Day."

"OK. Well… you reminded me… One morning a lady steps out of the local coffee shop and she notices a long funeral procession approaching the nearby cemetery. Two long black hearses followed by a woman walking a pit bull. Behind her were 100 women walking in single file. The lady's curiosity got the better of her and she submissively got in the procession next to the woman with the pit bull and said, 'I'm sorry for your loss and I know it may be a bad time, but I've never seen anything like this. Whose funeral is it?' The woman with the pit bull responded, 'The first hearse is my husband; my pit bull attacked and killed him.' And the woman asked, 'Who is in the second hearse?' And the woman replied, 'That's my mother-in-law. She tried to help my husband but the dog killed her, too.' A very long moment of silence passed between them and the lady said, 'Can I borrow that dog?' And the woman with the pit bull said, 'Get in line.'"

A very long moment of silence passed and Kelly said, "I give that a five on a scale of ten."

"Two men were paired up for a golf game one day," The Musician started up again, "and the 9th hole crosses a street that runs down to the local cemetery. Well, a long funeral procession was passing by and one man took off his cap and held it tightly to his chest and closed his eyes in prayer. The other guy says, 'Man, that was the most touching and thoughtful gesture I have ever seen! You are truly a considerate and caring man.' The end of the funeral procession went by and the golfer replied, 'Yeah… well, we were married for thirty-seven years.'"

"Jeez," Jack said shaking his head from side to side.

"Ah, the limo took a left between Central Square and MIT. I suspect they are heading back to the escort service office. I don't know if they made me or not."

"I'm not taking any chances; they didn't pull over and let you pass for nothing. That blue van has been on them for days. It's done, Willie. Go home and get a hot meal. And write me some kind of a report with the times, locations, plate numbers, and descriptions of subjects. I'll get Cooper, Ledger, or The Digger to pick up tonight's surveillance. No more blue van. Go to our friend Ahmed in the lot across from my office on Kingston in the morning and pick out a nondescript car and tell Ahmed to put it on my bill."

"What about this digital camera I've got here?"

"Hold on to it. Cooper will have his own cameras. That's what he does. You're off the clock. Go home."

Chapter 57

A Tale of Two Tails

As the limousine rolled along the Cambridge side of the Charles River and then headed back to the College Escort Services offices, one of Victoria's cell phones beeped and she looked at the caller ID.

"It's Marcus," she said.

"I'll talk to him," Tom said, taking the phone and listening to Marcus intently as he told Peters about getting questioned by the Boston Police for parking horizontal in vertical lanes.

"What the fuck is that? 'Parking horizontal in a vertical lane'?" Peters asked his second-best driver.

"I don't know, Boss. Maybe it was parking vertical in a diagonal zone or something. They ran my license and that was it. But I've stopped watching the private detective. He's eating supper at the No Name on Northern Avenue; it's a dead end. I can pick him up when he leaves."

"OK, Marcus. You do that… we are going to have to do something about this private eye. Better sooner than later,"

Tom said and flipped closed the cell phone and tossed it on the seat by his sister.

She shook her head slowly from side to side and said softly, "We *are* going to have to do something about that private detective. There's no telling what Rodney told him. As far as we know, he's the only weak link, right? There was Michael. Gone. Seng Li. Gone. Rodney. Gone. Who else is there? The detective, before he goes blathering to the locals and the state cops. I wonder just who he has been talking to. I mean, let's be real. He has to go. He has to go soon," Victoria said very matter-of-factly.

"Ooh! I'm getting a woody! Let's get him and it must be soon. I knew it. I knew it, subconsciously. He has to go. He must go. We need to clean up and… and I need to copyright the binary formula I have on disc. We need a computer geek. We'll use Divinity. Oh, so much to do and so little time."

"Does Divinity really know that much about computers? I mean, she looks so hot! But she once told me her favorite color was 'shiny,'" Victoria said.

The limousine had broken off its moving surveillance of The Musician and was returning to the CES headquarters. As they approached the parking lot, Victoria said to her brother, "Do we want to go out tonight? I've got some paperwork to do for the weekend receipts and payouts. It's eight o'clock now; we could order Italian from La Groceria at around ten, Moose would love to pick it up, wouldn't you Moose?"

"Yes, Ms. Victoria, especially if I can get some of the lasagna and chicken cacciatore."

"OK then, Tommy? A nice pinot noir?" Victoria said sweetly as they stepped from the limousine.

After a long silence while they walked into the building, Tom said, "We might as well stay in tonight. We've got a funeral to go to tomorrow morning. And speaking of funerals, after dinner we've got to discuss the method... of dealing with the private detective. This Jack Kelly has got to go. And soon."

"Let's go in and order the food from the office and open a bottle of wine, Moose will pick up the dinners, and we'll talk about this detective *during* dinner. He dares to hurt the family, Tom. You're so right. We're in this for keeps, now. We must play to win," his sister whispered in his ear as they walked up to the empty bar and she continued, "If we can stifle these voices right now, and push that patent through, the Group will welcome us with open arms. We will be wealthy and powerful for decades."

"No! Generations to come," Tom said, selecting a bottle of inexpensive but fresh Woodbridge pinot noir from a cabinet behind the bar. Moose walked out of the room shaking his head in amazement at the two eccentric siblings.

Chapter 58

Converging Paths

Jack pulled out of the restaurant parking lot on the Fish Pier and headed back towards the lights of Boston. He didn't see the green Toyota 4Runner behind him until he got to the Central Artery. As he drove up the ramp he called Jessica on his cell phone.

"My tail is back," Kelly said when Jessica answered.

"I got caught between a fish truck and vegetable cart. Are you going straight to my place? Central Artery, north to Storrow?" Jessica said.

"No. Central south to Park Square and around Boston Common. But I don't want to lead him to your apartment. I'll shake him by the time I go through the Combat Zone. I don't want anyone watching me tonight," Jack said.

"Why, because you're going to be doing something naughty to your girlfriend? I hope."

"Yes. That's exactly why I don't want anyone watching."

"Then shake and bake, baby!" Jessica cheered and hung up.

Kelly maneuvered his black Jeep Cherokee in and out of the four lanes of Boston's Central Artery. It was after dark but he could see the big green Toyota behind him. The traffic was heavy for seven-thirty at night. Jack took the downtown exit at the last second. The 4Runner couldn't change lanes fast enough. Jack pulled out his cell phone and dialed Jessica.

"It is done. I'm free at last."

"That was quick. Now can we go home? I've got a nice bottle of Woodbridge pinot noir in a paper bag right here on the front seat," Jessica pleaded.

"I'm on the way. I'll sneak over the Hill and down Beacon. Promise me we'll talk about the case, though. I'm meeting Mr. and Mrs. Rich at Rodney's funeral in the morning. Something's got to break."

"I guess I'll be going with you. I'll assign someone from Homicide to take some pictures, but there will be quite a few MIT grad students, I suspect. Waterman's Funeral Home is only across the bridge from the campus."

"About 365 Smoots, I believe."

"What?"

"Ah… disregard. I've got to call Cooper and get him to do some surveillance on Peters. I'll have him be on the lookout for Marcus Grace. I'm betting he works for Peters."

"Don't you think it's time for the Boston Police Department to start monitoring this guy? I know how you feel about cops blowing the covers off of surveillances, Jack, but I've got some real streetwise undercover detectives working in Homicide now," she said with pride. "I've got some sharp kids under me."

"As long as they're not on top of you. Look, Jesse, we've got to start to tighten the noose around Peter's neck and squeeze him until he either fits the bill or we can rule him out. But I've got a feeling…," Jack said.

"Well, bring that feeling to my apartment as fast as you can. I want to explore just how deeply your feelings go," Jessica said and rang off, again.

Kelly drove through Copley Square under the nightlights of the big hotels as he dialed Cooper. Dark clouds were rolling in from the north and the air got colder as the wind picked up.

After listening to Jack, Cooper said, "It's 8:30 at night and you want me to start surveillance on a suspected serial killer? You must be out of your mind. I'm not a kid anymore, Kelly! I've got a dog, and a regular day job, and condo payments. You don't seriously think I'm going to take surreptitious pictures and chase cars around, do you? You'd have to be nuts!" Cooper screamed at Jack.

"Hold on there, Coop. You've got some legitimate points there, old friend. Due to the gravity of the situation… fifty bucks an hour. Only don't tell The Musician."

"Jack, I've got work tomorrow with the agency. I'm photographing produce for Star Market's full-page adds in the *Globe*. I… I, ah, I don't know, Jack," Cooper pleaded.

"Get your boss to shoot the fruits and vegetables. He loves it when you take off on this cloak-and-dagger shit. All right, I'll cover a rental car, travel time, all food and gas expenses, and sixty an hour. And you can probably get twelve… or even sixteen hours a day. You can make $800 a day until this thing pans out. C'mon, what do you say? You're a great operative. You are so smooth, man! This guy's never even gonna know you were there. And I need someone I can trust."

"Ah…. All right, Jack. He's in Cambridge, right? College Escorts on Harvard Street; I'll be there in an hour. I'll use my own car tonight."

"Great. He's been going out with several ladies with a limo and driver, late, around eleven-thirty. Comes back about three. And as soon as he settles in you can go home for tonight. Tomorrow get back by 11 a.m."

As the tail watched from a parking space at Gloucester and Beacon, Kelly flipped open his notebook and looked for a parking space one street over from Beacon on Marlborough Street. He continued, "The Musician tells me Tom Peters is about five feet, ten inches and 160 pounds with shoulder-length greasy black hair he's continually brushing back with his hand. He has three diamonds in one ear and a pencil-thin mustache with a thin line of chin hair from his lower lip to the end of his chin."

"Got it."

"And watch out for a black guy, heavy set, about fifty years old. He's been following me using multiple rental cars. He was driving a green Toyota 4Runner when he was trying to follow me twenty minutes ago. We think he may be a driver for Tom Peters and CES. And The Musician, as he *insists* everybody call him, said Peters is usually driven by a very large black man wearing a leather fringed jacket, cowboy boots, and straight combed-back hair. The dude supposedly looks like a bizarre caricature of Elvis."

Chapter 59

The Chess Pimp

Tom Peters and Jack Kelly had both figured out they were tailed today. And each knew who had hired the tails. Each was following the other. The chess game had begun. And Kelly knew it.

Kelly thought about The Chess Pimp. When Kelly was a young detective, he worked the Runaway Squad. One magnet for runaway kids was The Pit in Harvard Square, Cambridge. It's a triangle of brick right next to the subway entrance. Street musicians, extremely odd intellectuals, panhandlers, and subculture freaks of all kinds have always been welcomed in the shadow of Harvard University. While Detective Kelly checked this area regularly for runaways, he occasionally sat at the outdoor chess tables that were continually in use.

Chess was taken quite seriously by some characters and one such unique individual was The Chess Pimp. He was a twenty-eight-year-old African American Harvard burnout who played for money and took on all comers. He never lost. His mouth was continually running. He would goad and infuriate players into side bets, often escalating into hundreds of dollars. He could make several thousand dollars on a good day. Between games, and often while he was playing, he talked to the academics and street people in the Square. In short, he knew what was going on. He knew every face in the Square. With a source like The Chess Pimp, Jack had eyes and ears in Harvard Square. Kelly always threw some folding money on the stone chess tables, but The Chess Pimp was more than a great source for locating runaways. He was wise, knowledgeable, and level-headed. Jack wished he could pay The Chess Pimp for his perceptive advice now.

Kelly believed he had lost the tail. He parked his black Jeep in an obscure parking spot behind a Dumpster in the alley between Beacon and Marlboro St. He walked down the stairs to the courtyard at Lieutenant Paris's basement apartment and shot some baskets while he waited for Jessica. He occasionally peered out from the courtyard below, under the black wrought iron gate, to see if there were any eyes looking back at him.

Jack didn't see Marcus Grace parked a half block down Beacon Street.

Jessica soon opened the gate and walked down the stairs to the courtyard, carrying a bag of groceries. Jack tried to look up and down Beacon Street to check the red brick sidewalks for any sign that she had been followed but he couldn't help being distracted by her legs. Her black skirt seemed to float as she stepped down the stairs, concentrating on her balance. Jack sighed loudly from the relief of knowing they were both together… and off the street.

Kelly grabbed the groceries and they went inside the apartment. Jessica went to her bathroom to freshen up and her bedroom to change into some jeans and a baggy, powder blue FBI Academy T-shirt. While she combed her dark auburn hair in the mirror, Jack washed his hands and face in the kitchen sink. There wasn't any bar soap or liquid germ soap in the kitchen so he used blue liquid dishwashing soap. He splashed water on his face and it got all over the countertop around the sink. Then he put the groceries away.

"You know, Jesse, I haven't been to Harvard Square in a long time," Jack said, loud enough for Jessica to hear him as he put some early Rolling Stones on the CD player.

"You can take me to dinner in Harvard Square, anytime," Jesse said as she walked into the living room and poured two glasses of pinot noir.

"It's a deal," Jack said as they sat down on the couch and put the glasses on the coffee table. Jessica ran her fingers through Jack's hair.

"Why is your hair wet, Blue Knight?"

"I washed my face and hands while you were in the bathroom changing."

"In the kitchen sink? But there's no soap!"

"I used that blue dishwashing soap," Jack confessed.

"Ugh!" Jessica moaned.

"What? It's soap! As good as any other and probably more intense. And condensed, I mean," Jack stammered slightly, pleading his case.

"You're intense and condensed! You're such a guy," Jessica said, moving closer to Jack as she nestled up to him.

Jack gulped some wine as he listened to the early Stones recordings of "Little Red Rooster," "Pain in My Heart," and "Everybody Needs Somebody To Love." He felt like asking Jessica to marry him, but he got cold feet... again.

Jessica wondered if she should initiate sex as they comfortably rested against each other. But... somehow, they seemed satisfied just to be with each other. Both detectives knew it was going to be a very long day tomorrow and they were falling asleep on the couch. The music cushioned their fall into slumber.

Soon Jack began to dream.

He walked into Johnny's Place, the nightclub he dreamt of opening when his sleuthing days were over. It was a serial dream to which Jack often returned. The night was cool and so was the jazz. The house jazz band was playing, a little quintet that Jack had hand-picked. He selected some hot drums and a cool bass. Then added some fat keyboards and a tiny horn section with a harmony-crazy trumpet and a solo-freak baritone sax. Just the essentials. No vocals. The house band was cool and clean.

Jack sat at the end of the bar. His favorite bartender, Jimmy, poured him a glass of Chateau Rothschild 1996. Jimmy put the TV's remote control in front of Jack and Kelly flipped the channel to SportsCenter.

As he sipped the wine and looked up at the TV, he was shocked to see God sitting behind the SportsCenter desk pontificating about the Top Twenty-five Athletes of All Time. God was waving his arms. Jack heard God comparing Michael Jordan and Larry Bird, Ted Williams and Babe Ruth, Tiger Woods and Arnold Palmer, Jim Gordon and Dale Earnhardt, Wayne Gretsky and Bobby

Orr, Johnny Unitas and Tom Brady, Pele' and Beckham, Ali and Marciano.

Kelly pressed the buttons for the local news channel and God was the news anchor, dressed in a dark suit, talking about how nothing was being done by investigators to solve the MIT Murders.

Kelly switched to a movie channel. But there was God doing Marlon Brando's role in a scene from 1954's black-and-white "The Wild One." God was wearing motorcycle boots, blue jeans, and a black leather jacket. He was saying, "You don't go any one special place, that's cornball style. You just go," God snaps his fingers. "Bunch of youths get together after all week, it builds up, you just go. The idea is to have a ball. Now, if you're gonna stay cool, you got to wail. You got to put something down." God snaps his fingers. "You gotta make some jive, don't you know what I'm talking about?"

Jack switched to the Weather Channel. God had an old bearded white man's head and the body of a heavily endowed and attractive female in a small black dress. God swept his hand across the TV map and Jack could see snow falling in the Rockies, dusty wind storms in the Midwest, and clouds of cold rain moving up the Eastern seaboard, turning to snow in the mountains of New England.

Jack pressed in number twenty-eight on the remote control and watched as the channel changed, showing God playing every instrument in a musical group on MTV. All of God's faces changed in unison from black man to Asian, from Irish woman to Argentinean child. God was playing all three guitars, singing about love, and he was on the drums, bass, and keyboards, too. There were seven Gods in all, and they were all singing in harmony. Their faces were changing and emerging slowly and continuously. It sounded really good to Jack. God's band was kicking ass! It was all quite dreamy.

Kelly looked around but nobody in the nightclub was paying any attention to the band of God. Jack looked up at the screen as the musical group looked out at him. Jack said, "I thought of that first. You know, I had that idea! I was going to do that. Play all the instruments and make a recording of a song I wrote, arranged, and produced. What you're doing is just a logical extension of what I was going to do. And *you're* not real."

The seven Gods were playing a psychedelic version of Jimi Hendrix's "You Got Me Floating," but stopped jamming abruptly with a clang, the clatter of dropped drumsticks, and a loud chorus of groans. All seven Gods stopped and stared at Jack. The front man, God, looked down at Jack and said, "You can't even take care of the business at hand, Kelly! And how dare you smart-mouth The Creator!"

God, now a blonde female Viking, shook her finger at Jack. "Don't disappoint the mother and father. And don't disappoint me!" God said with a thunderclap that continued to reverberate.

"I'm not a robot, God."

"What do you mean by that?" the American Indian God said with a knowing smile.

"I'm not so sure I even believe in you," Kelly said as he pulled his hands up in front of his face defensively.

God laughed and asked, "Then who are you talking to?"

Chapter 60

Kill Kelly

Tom Peters woke up pissed off, again. Maybe it was something he dreamed. Or maybe he did one line too many the night before. He was mad. He nicked his chin with the razor as he sculpted his pencil-thin mustache and thin soul patch. He let loose with a string of expletives. Tom splashed water over his face like a madman. Water streamed down his face and onto his baggy black CES T-shirt as he squinted, walked into the sunlit kitchen, picked up the remote, and flipped on the TV sitting at the end of the countertop.

The same gorgeous blonde local newscaster was pouting with her full red lips. She smiled and read a short bit about an armored car hold-up in Chelsea. Then with the same smile and vacant stare she read a story off the teleprompter about a man who killed his wife with a shotgun because she overcooked the ziti.

Tom glared at the TV screen, yelling, "You fucking bitch! You haven't got a clue. You fucking happy ass smiley button... You are an artificial and depressing fool, you phony fucking two-faced bitch!" Tom yelled louder and louder, throwing a half-filled glass of orange juice at the TV. The juice splashed on the screen and the glass flew over the TV and shattered on the kitchen floor.

The breaking glass brought Victoria stumbling out from the bedroom.

"What's going on, Tommy? Did you break the TV, again?"

"That fucking vapid airhead on the news!" Tom said, letting some air out of his lungs and decompressing a little, then adding, "She should be working for us."

The two watched as the weatherman predicted "heavy snowfall starts later today as that back door front is arriving in the western part of the state and pushing up from Rhode island." The blonde news anchor reappeared and said with a totally unemotional, expressionless demeanor, "The MIT community is in total fear and shock as a serial killer roams undetected. Cops probe the third body found in the Charles River…," she said, staring straight out at the camera, and added, "More after this break."

"Oh, now she stops smiling," Tom said as he changed the station to ESPN.

"And that airhead blonde said, 'Cops probe third body found in the river.' Jeez, that's kinda creepy… Can't the cops find some other way to get their kicks?" Victoria asked and stood close behind Tom, rubbing his neck and shoulders.

"Can I make you some breakfast, Tommy?" she purred into his ear.

"Yes. Yes, my dear. We have much work to do today. I will need sustenance. First I need to place a rather large bet on the Baltimore Ravens against the New England

Patriots playing on Monday Night Football this evening. Second, we have the funeral of Rodney Riviera to attend. We must pay our respects. And then third, with any luck, I can locate, isolate, and eliminate that fucking detective, Jack Kelly. I believe he is the last loose end."

"Then he must go," Victoria hissed back as she cracked an egg on the edge of the hot skillet.

"Then, I must accelerate my paperwork in order to patent the Sympathetic Override Program for the Central Control for the Prototype; it should all fall together, Vic. I worked hard for this. I've sacrificed and worked hard for this. This project is mine! I was part of the group from the beginning."

Tom thought back eight years to when the five freshman MIT students, all on scholarships, were assigned to the Artificial Intelligence Lab. The five were the heart and soul of the group charged with the development and integration of advanced systems. Their mission was the creation of a prototype. They were charged with the conception and construction of a state-of-the-art robot. The five freshmen raised their glasses at the local pub and vowed to create a *beyond*-the-state-of-the-art droid that looked human, using the same learning system as humans do. Trial and error. MIT had the funding as well as the talent and there had been major advances in every related field. It was the right time.

Tom remembered the five. Michael, Rodney, Tom, Seng Li, and Amanda. He also remembered Rodney's little speech as the five students held their drinks high. Rodney's voice started softly and rose to a crescendo as he said, "The advanced prototype will dial into the Internet. It is wireless. And soulless. Yet it will be ruthless in its search for advancement. After all, it had learned at an early stage in its development, even before its brain was attached to its body, it learned intelligence… was the key to earthbound survival. Man was the quintessential example of that. The Prototype will nurture and cultivate intelligence on its own now. And when it is mass marketed, manufactured, and distributed into every business and civilized home on this planet, it will link with its brothers and sisters."

The five MIT graduate students tapped their glasses together, but Tom's glass broke and it cut his thumb deeply and left a scar. Tom looked at the scar now and rubbed his trigger finger along its two-inch length.

Tom looked over at Victoria and continued.

"I sealed our quest with blood. I helped develop the Prototype. The Prototype needs a strong hand to hold it all together. This is *my* baby. I will be the hands-on operations manager as well as a member of the Group. Then it's Easy Street, Baby," Tom said, pulling his sister into his arms and holding her tightly. "We will do whatever we want for the rest of our lives. We just have this one last problem. This fucking Jack Kelly."

Victoria looked deep in thought and then said, "Call Marcus, and get him on top of Kelly. In fact, let's get Marcus psyched up to take out Kelly. Let's start looking for an opportunity to take him out soon," the even-less-compassionate Victoria Peters said as she turned and dropped a pound of sizzling bacon into a hot frying pan.

Tom Peters was on his phone to a twenty-four-hour-a-day bookmaker in Las Vegas.

"Yes, Maurice. Twenty-four thousand dollars on the Baltimore Ravens to beat the Patriots seven-point spread. As long as you can handle it, OK? Ah… that's my man.

I'll be calling back in twenty-four hours to claim my winnings, OK? And there won't be a tie so you better take plenty of Patriots action from what is left of the organized gamblers, and mobsters, here in New England. Not many, I guarantee. They've all self-destructed or they're writing books from the Witness Protection Program. Except for Whitey. I think he's doing a lot of Italian home cooking and watching cable TV and DVDs. Hey, if the FBI really wanted to catch their wayward child, their out-of-control Irish gangster, their little counter-spy, they could follow the eggplant. I hear he likes Italian. Follow the spaghetti and lasagna. And the veal Parmesan."

There was silence on the line… until Tom said, "No, not really, Maurice! I'm kidding! No, I don't know what I'm talking about… Yes… OK… I'll call you in twenty-four for the money."

As they ate breakfast Tom called Marcus on his cell phone.

"Tell me you are watching Kelly, Marc."

Marcus gave Peters several top-notch excuses as to why he was running late but he did promise to check by Kelly's American Detective Agency office on Kingston Street for Jack's black Jeep and said if it wasn't there he'd check around Kelly's girlfriend's apartment on Beacon Street.

"I think she may be a cop or something, Boss," Marcus said, adding, "She drives a Ford Taurus with no frills. It's a real company car, Boss. I think she's a cop. What's that old saying, 'If it looks like a cop, rolls like a cop… ah… quacks like a cop, no, I guess that would be oinks like a pig, or…"

"Stop fucking rambling on, Marc! When can you get back on him?"

"They might have made me, Boss."

"Then change your fucking look and your fucking car!"

"What about my skin color, Boss? And my size? I ain't gonna be able to change too much about me. I don't look like Paris Hilton, do I? I'm a fat forty-seven-year-old black man. I can't put on a baseball hat and change. I just looks like Marcus, the fat forty-seven-year-old black guy with a baseball hat on. And what if he comes at me, with his cop girlfriend, and asks why I'm following him, Boss?"

"Look, Marcus, my man. This guy comes at you, and you get the chance... whack him! Whack him hard. All the way, Marc. We're about to move our game up to another level. No shit. And you're a part of our family. There's a big bonus in this. Big! Like what you made last year. For one night's work! This dick disappears or gets... eliminated, with no trace back to us, and that's very important Marky...." Marcus hated it when the boss called him 'Marky.' "No trace back... Then I can assure you, you'll get what you made all of last year. In cash. Payable on demand!" Tom practically spit the words out as he pumped up his paid assassin.

"And another thing," Tom added. "I got plans for you! You're not going to be just a driver after this all gets shaken out. You'll be in charge of many drivers. You'll be the boss, Marcus. You'll have a fleet of limousines, and that's no shit. CES is just one arm of the octopus. We'll triple in size by this time next year. And we're going to need much more security. Now, you know, Moose will be the number one there, but I believe you will have a major position in that."

"Thanks, Mr. Peters," Marcus said.

"Tom. It's Tom, Marc," Peters's voice trailed off to a whisper as he added, "Marcus... we've got to stop this guy. Kelly. I won't bore you with the details, but he wants to hurt us in the worst way possible. He wants... to destroy us. Totally. And... we have to destroy him first... A car crash? A drowning? If he floated up in the Charles River, the cops would think the serial killer got him! Have you been seeing that on the TV news?"

"I've been hearing it on the car radio, Boss. I've been in the car for most of the time."

"OK. When can you get back on Kelly?"

"I'd be there by now, Boss. But I've been talkin' to you. And I gotta take a shower."

"Go!" Tom said, closing his cell phone and looking down at the cold omelet on the table.

"I'll heat it up, Tommy. Just give me a minute," the matriarchal sister said, sweeping away the plates, pressing buttons on the microwave, and pouring coffee in a cup. She created a breeze as her whirlwind gyrations produced a hot breakfast for the siblings.

After breakfast Tom looked at his sister and said, "I'll call Moose and we'll go to that motherfucker's funeral."

Chapter 61

God Strike Me Dead

Jack woke up obsessed. He couldn't think of anything but the Michael Rich case. He was frustrated and getting fixated. Jesse had seen this before. For Jack there was nothing else now. Nothing but the case. Sure, he could walk around… like normal. He could do normal, routine things, like shower, shave, dress, and get a bottle of water out of the refrigerator, but his mind was on the object of his obsession. The case. Jack would focus now. He wouldn't be affected by anything around him. Not investigators, reporters, speculators, freelance TV and media hounds. Not the photographers hiding behind trees or reporters writing articles, chronicling the crimes of the serial killer.

Jesse spoke a dozen times but Jack wasn't paying attention. He couldn't have told you a word she said. He was showered and dressed for the funeral in a gray suit with a black shirt and blue tie. Jesse was trying on five different skirts in front of the mirror. Every time she tried a different skirt on she asked Jack for his opinion but he stared straight ahead. Then Jessica would state *her* opinion:

"Too fat," or "frumpy," or "too school-teacher." Finally she settled on a tight-fitting below-the-knee black skirt to complement the white blouse and black blazer.

She looked at Jack as he sat on the arm of the couch, staring out the window, and she said, "How do I look?"

Kelly didn't respond for a moment and then said, "Go ahead."

"What? Go ahead? Go ahead and wear this?" Jessica asked.

"No. Go ahead and put a peep on Peters."

"Are you saying I shouldn't wear this?" Jessica asked.

"No. I mean yes. I mean, you look great. But go ahead and put surveillance on Tom Peters. I think he's our man, Jesse. And if he is, we need to have more than Cooper and The Musician covering him. I think this guy is a stone cold killer. And he's the only suspect I've got."

"What about the robots, Jack?" Jessica began dancing the Robot.

"OK. Let it be noted for the record that Kelly Investigations requested Boston Police Department assistance with surveillance on a suspected serial killer at 9:45 a.m. on December 4, 2008... and... Lieutenant Paris did the Robot Dance." Jack took out his small but ever-present notebook from his pants pocket and pretended to write, saying, "You're a lieutenant, isn't that right?"

"Ooh! Making it 'official for the record,' huh, Kelly? Well, add this to your little notebook." Jessica turned around, giving him the finger, then she reprimanded Jack, telling him what was really on her mind.

"There are only twenty-one days of shoplifting left 'til Christmas! And somebody better get me a diamond ring, this year, or by my birthday next year, or somebody is going to be very lonely… and it might be you, Jack Kelly! …Or me."

Jack watched as Jessica went through a succession of emotions from angry to teasing to happy then hopeful then almost crying. All within ten seconds. Jack thought she was the greatest. She was all he wasn't and he looked at Jesse with love in his eyes.

"Let's go," Jack said, standing up.

Jessica took her cell phone, purse, and keys and they walked out the door, up the courtyard stairs, and around the corner to the alleyway. Jessica made arrangements for a police services photographer from the Detective Division to take photographs of the participants in the Rodney Riviera funeral services. The air was frigid and the sky had turned gray. The pair pulled their jackets closed as they walked to where Kelly's Jeep was parked. Kelly didn't notice the eyes of Marcus Grace as he watched Jack and Jessica. Marcus slumped down behind the wheel of a powder blue Dodge Caravan parked on the cross street.

The rented blue Dodge soccer-mom van followed the black Jeep Cherokee heading down Beacon towards Mass. Ave. and Kenmore Square. Marcus was on his cell phone, telling his boss that Jack Kelly was on the move.

"He's going down Beacon towards Mass. Ave., Boss. Him and his cop bitch. And you know what, Boss? I'm wearin' the Baltimore Ravens baseball hat that you gave me last Christmas, and… I think it makes me look totally different! I even feel thinner, seriously!"

"OK, Marcus. You're fucking with me, I know. I can see you looking in your rearview mirror and smiling because you're giving me shit. Am I right? I'm right, aren't I, Marc? Whatever, OK. You got a Baltimore Ravens hat for

Christmas last year. You play your cards right, and that Jack Kelly motherfucker is out of the way... and you are going to get a lot more than a fucking baseball cap, my nigga." Marcus hated it when the boss called him "nigga." He'd like to slap him on the back of his head.

Snow was in the forecast as Tom snorted his first lines of white powder of the day in the back of the limo. The clouds began to roll in.

Jack and Jessica drove across Mass. Ave. and as they neared Waterman and Sons Funeral Home in Kenmore Square, they noticed the groups of young students walking towards the same destination.

"Looks like half of MIT is paying their respects to Rodney. They're coming from across the bridge and from the frat houses in the Back Bay. There looks like several hundred," Jack remarked. He found a parking space just past the Waterman and Sons Funeral Home on Bay State Road and the two began walking back.

Kelly's cell phone buzzed and the detective jumped.

"Hi, Cooper. Good, he's moving, great. Crossing the Mass. Ave. Bridge, OK. Taking a right on Beacon towards Kenmore Square? OK. Coop, I think he might be coming to Rodney's funeral. That's where Jessica and I are. What's he driving? He's in the back of a black Mercedes limo.

"That's right; he doesn't have a valid Massachusetts driver's license. OK. Arriving in Kenmore Square... OK, I think I see him pulling up to the funeral home. He's double-parking, of course. Bastard's got a chauffeur. OK, Cooper, good work. I see him and a female getting out of the limo now. Take a position so you can follow him when he comes out. I'll keep an eye on him while we're all in the funeral home."

Jack shut off his cell phone and said to Jessica, "This should be interesting," as they crossed Beacon Street and got in the long line forming at the funeral home's front doors. Jessica and Jack were right behind Victoria and Tom as they ascended the stairs and stood at the entrance. The line stopped moving.

Tom Peters's cell phone's ring tone played "Moon River." When he answered it Marcus told him that he had followed Jack Kelly and his girlfriend to a funeral home in Kenmore Square.

"What? That's where I am!" Tom whispered intently. "Oh... Yes... He knew Rodney. Rodney was giving him information, about me and my business partners. What does he look like? And what is he wearing?"

As Peters listened to Marcus describe Jack's appearance, Tom looked ahead of him and behind him. Kelly was easy to spot. Standing right behind Tom, he saw Jack in the gray suit, black shirt, and blue tie. Kelly just had that look. Marcus told Tom that Jack was five feet, eleven inches, around thirty-eight years old with a shock of reddish brown hair that even though he pushed it back, it inevitably fell over one eye.

Peters asked Marcus to describe "that couple," Jack and Jessica again, and handed the phone to Victoria. She listened as the line took one small step forward and halted. She glanced briefly at Kelly and Paris then handed the phone back to her brother. Tom told Marcus to "check the address on *the package* when it leaves," and signed off.

Kelly heard bits and pieces of the conversation and he knew Tom was having him followed. And Peters suspected Kelly was having *him* followed.

Victoria turned slightly to steal another glance of the nemesis detective that stood in the way of her and her brother making a killing in the business and science world. Jack caught her glance and said, "Great day, isn't it?" Jack stood there, rocking on the balls of his feet. Victoria glared at him.

Jack said, "Well, not snowing yet, I mean. I mean… not a bad day. Well, not a good day for a funeral… I guess there is no good day for a funeral… I mean."

Victoria held her breath, praying she would not scream at Kelly. She breathed in slowly and turned to Jack and politely said, "I know what you mean," and turned away.

In this quiet moment Kelly's thoughts were so loud in his head that he thought Peters might hear him. But Jack felt like this was a great time to forge ahead. He looked over at Jessica standing next to him and shrugged his shoulders. Lieutenant Paris looked back quizzically.

It began to snow as the front of the viewing line moved two-by-two into the lobby of the funeral home to pay their respects. Jack directed a question to Victoria, standing quietly next to Tom.

"Rodney was such a great person. So young. I saw him just last week. How did you know him, Ms.? If I might ask?"

"I went to school with him," Tom said, turning to face Kelly from the step above him.

"MIT, then. Yes, fine institution," Kelly said with a slight W. C. Fields impression.

Tom and Victoria were visibly annoyed by Jack Kelly. Yes, Kelly could do that.

"Yup, I was just talking with Rodney less than a week ago, right honey?" Kelly said, turning to Jessica, who backed his play with, "That's right, Jack. Just about a little less than a week ago."

"Yup, less than a week ago. Talked to him a few times. Yes… he had quite a story to tell. I couldn't get it at first," Jack said.

"That's great. We just want to pay our respects," Tom said and Victoria and he turned their backs.

"Yes, he had quite a story to tell… about some robots."

Jack could see Tom's back visibly tighten like there was a rod shoved up his spine.

"That's a nice ring you've got on your finger there," Kelly said to Peters. Peters half-heartedly turned back to Jack and Jessica, holding out his hand and displaying the ring.

"Thanks, it's my MIT alumni ring," Peters said, looking at Jessica and smiling slightly as he did his best to impress her.

"Yes, the Brass Rat. They found one of those stuffed down Rodney Riviera's throat," Kelly said in a low but firm voice as he stared at Peters.

The two madmen's eyes locked. The intensity was great and more than a few moments went by as the men seemed locked in a battle of wills.

Tom blinked first.

"You're Jack Kelly, aren't you?"

"Well, God strike me dead. Now… how did you know that, sir?"

"I'm sorry, I should have introduced myself. I'm Tom Peters and this is my sister, Victoria Peters."

"This is my girlfriend, Jessica Paris. And you know me, how?"

"I graduated with Rodney and worked at the AI Lab with him and Michael Rich, until a few years ago. I had spoken with Rodney recently."

"How recently?" Kelly asked.

"Ah... let me see... about a little over a week ago. He had told me that you had questioned him about Michael Rich's death." And then he added coyly, "Rodney wasn't a suspect in Michael's death, was he?"

"Absolutely not, Mr. Peters. Rodney was a big help with my investigation."

Kelly decided to push Peters a little and started to leak information to him, all the while watching for his slightest reaction.

"In fact, Rodney opened my eyes to MIT college life and work in the AI Lab. He even walked me through the MIT Museum trying to get me to understand. You see, he had some definite suspicions about who killed Michael Rich, and why," Kelly said as the whole procession line, consisting of 80% MIT students, slowly began to move through the entrance and into the lobby of the funeral home.

"The whole thing is so awful. This murder business," Victoria said.

"And this murder may have been business, Ms. Peters," Kelly said.

"You mentioned robots earlier, Mr. Kelly. Did he suspect one of the robots went haywire and killed poor Rodney?" Victoria Peters looked at Jessica, trying to pay special attention to her with a modest smile. Jessica had to bite her tongue to keep from looking over at Jack.

Jack kept talking quietly but steadily.

"Rodney did mention to me that the robots had an important role in contributing to Michael's death. The Prototype, Mr. Peters. I'm sure you're familiar with that. A robot that's ready to be manufactured and mass-marketed. A robot that will be able to hear, see, walk, talk, and develop at an astonishing rate. A robot that will wirelessly connect to the Internet and... by the way, is that the same as the World Wide Web?" Kelly looked into the faces of the Peters siblings and could see his words were causing extreme tension. The two looked paralyzed as he continued, "Rodney gave me some specific information about possible interested groups... and individuals. In fact, there's been a lot of cross-referencing going on and certain names are popping up; I'm sure the guilty parties will be apprehended soon."

Jack could see Tom Peters stiffen and become rigid while he spoke and he saw Victoria's lips get tight and felt the heat from her eyes glaring at him as if looks could kill. But after Jack finished his speech, Tom and Victoria both looked at him and smiled. They knew something would have to be done about Jack Kelly and done soon.

Chapter 62

I Know That You Know That
I Know That You Know

You could cut the tension with a knife as Tom, Victoria, Jack, and Jessica walked into the funeral parlor where the lifeless body of the young man, Rodney Riviera, lay. Even from the back of the room Jessica could see the body in the open casket. She noticed his short blond hair was spiked and he wore a dark blue suit. She remembered when she was five years old and went to her brother's funeral. He was about the same age as Rodney, in his twenties when he was killed. Jessica's brother had been back from Vietnam for three years but just like Agent Orange, the heroin habit he had acquired caught up to him. He died on his way home from his four-to-midnight shift at the Framingham Police Department. He was behind the wheel of his Corvette on the Mass. Pike and he had just snorted a dime bag of China White and dropped his cigarette. Jessica thanked God that he didn't take anyone else with him.

Jack could see Mr. and Mrs. Rich expressing their condolences to Rodney's mother as the line passed through the large viewing room's exit. He saw Amanda and Dexter a few students back in the line behind the Richs.

Jack took a deep breath and realized he wasn't 100% sure Tom Peters was the serial killer. He wasn't sure this was the killer all of local law enforcement was looking for. But this seemed to be an almost perfect opportunity to tactfully question Suspect #1. Kelly didn't have to give the Miranda rights to Peters. He certainly was not in custody. Not yet, anyway. Kelly needed to prod Tom some more; if he got out of line, he'd apologize later.

"Mr. Peters?" Jack asked quietly, tapping Tom's shoulder. As Tom turned, Jack said, "So tell me, Tom…; can I call you 'Tom'?"

"OK…," Peters said, furrowing his brow.

"Tell me… Tom. Who killed Michael Rich, Seng Li, and Rodney?"

Tom was again caught by surprise by the boldness of Kelly's inquiry.

Tom held his breath, nodded, and looked back at Kelly. He let some air escape slowly as he stalled for time.

"What?" Tom stammered, obviously caught off-guard by the directness of Jack's question.

Peters regained his composure somewhat and asked Jack, "Who do you think killed them?"

"I don't know. When I get to Heaven I'll ask them."

"What if they go to Hell?" Tom Peters sneeringly asked as the tension mounted.

"Then you ask them."

Victoria stepped in and said, "Maybe there were different random killers. And if the victim's rings were missing, wouldn't that be a robbery?"

"An astute presumption, Ms. Peters, but random killers don't usually select three MIT grad students that all work at the Artificial Intelligence Lab. And only Seng Li's ring was reported stolen by the press, Ms. Peters. Maybe it was a lucky guess when you said 'rings' in the plural? But… Michael's was stolen also. And, as I told you, Rodney's ring was shoved down his throat."

"Isn't that a ritual reserved for 'rats,' or 'snitches,' or whatever you call them, Mr. Kelly? 'Stool pigeons,' in your private eye, film noir jargon?" Victoria interjected with a condescending laugh.

"No. Shoving that MIT ring down Rodney's throat wasn't done to a 'stool pigeon,' Ms. Peters. That was done to the gifted young man lying in the half-open box over there," Jack said, nodding his head towards the coffin. Jessica shivered involuntarily as she looked at and contemplated the dead student in the coffin.

As they moved ahead closer to the coffin Tom decided to try another tactic with the unruly detective. The murmuring in the viewing room allowed them to speak without being heard by anyone other than the two couples themselves.

"You know, Detective Kelly, we could always use a guy like you at the company I own. We've branched out into quite a few areas and diversified. I could use a head of security," Tom said with a warm smile.

"I'm not a security guard, Peters," Kelly said, getting madder by the second. The moral impulse to do good and fight evil was too strong for Jack Kelly.

"I'm talking about ah… a lot of money here! Perhaps in the future, if you were to prove an asset, a junior partnership, Jack."

"What? In the smut industry?"

"I'm talking about a six-figure salary! With stock options. Maybe you've heard of my escort service," Tom said with a nod and a wink, lowering his voice so Jessica couldn't hear. "It's called the College Escort Service."

Their position in line had moved them up to within a few feet of the open coffin and Jack thought he could smell death. Or maybe it was the flowers.

As Victoria and Tom walked ahead and somberly moved to the coffin, they piously knelt down and folded their hands in front of them. Even though there was only room for two, Jack Kelly slid in next to Tom, jostling and pushing them over. Tom turned his head and looked at him in disbelief. Tom didn't want to make a scene so he closed his eyes and pretended to pray but the words weren't coming out right. His voice trailed off into a mumble.

"I'm going to tell you right now I think you had something to do with this boy's death," Kelly whispered to Tom.

"Why?" Tom implored as the body in front of them lay motionless. "Do you have some proof?"

"You're hinky. That's all I need to know."

"What?"

"Hinky. You heard me."

Tom looked back over at Jessica, sizing her up. Maybe he was hoping she would be willing to try to control the inappropriate behavior of Jack Kelly as he looked Jessica up and down.

Tom continued to stare at Jessica. He wanted to push Jack's buttons and decided to embark on his own inappropriate behavior. He whispered to Jack, "Ah... the allure of the pussy is so strong."

"Excuse me?"

Tom whispered in his ear, "It's all about the pussy, isn't it, Jack?"

"You've been surfing the Net too long."

"Listen, Kelly… Why don't you let me provide you with the best CES has to offer? We employ some beautiful women. How about $125,000 a year to be on my side?"

"I'll never be on your side. And I liked you better before I knew you."

"All right, Kelly! I know you're sophisticated and offended by my suggestion, but let's face it. It's just a question of money. $250,000. You'd do it. It's just that the money isn't right. I'll make you rich beyond your wildest dreams… I will start by making you a millionaire by this time next year; I'll sign a personal contract with you! Hell, I'll give you the million upfront and a limited partnership in CES. C'mon, Kelly! I'll make you a millionaire."

"I'm a thousandaire now and I've got headaches."

"Jesus Christ, Kelly! What do you want? What are you fighting for?" Peters asked loud enough to draw the attention of most people in the room.

Jack looked over at Peters as he and Victoria stood up in front of the casket and said quietly, "Truth, justice, and the American Way."

Chapter 63

Net of the Living Dead

After viewing Rodney Riviera in his casket, people in the line moved quickly past the coffin to the parlor's exit. There stood the only member of Rodney's family in attendance: his mother. She was a woman of only forty-eight years, with blonde spiked hair, comparable to Rodney's. There was no mistaking she was his mother. They had the same open face with the big blue sad puppy-dog eyes. Her black dress was simple yet elegant, her shoes were conservative, and she wore hardly any jewelry.

Tom and Victoria hurried through the lobby, out the exit, and into the New England snowstorm as Jack and Jessica expressed their condolences to Rodney's mother. Standing next to the mom was a Catholic priest in uniform. Kelly recognized Father Strickland from a multiple-sex-offense case he worked back in the eighties. Father Strickland recognized Jack and shook his hand, saying, "Detective Kelly! I can report to you that the number of sexual abuse incidents in our parish has gone way down."

"Yeah, Father; I guess not that many kids go to church anymore," Kelly said and walked to the exit.

Jack dashed outside just in time to see Amanda speaking with Tom and Victoria down on the sidewalk. The three hustled into the back seat of the limo parked on the corner.

As the black stretch limo pulled out into the traffic, Jack found himself standing next to Mr. and Mrs. Rich on the funeral home stairs.

The snow had soon covered the stairs, the sidewalk, and the street. Jack slowly blew some air out of his lungs as the limo made tracks. Both Mr. and Mrs. Rich were watching Kelly and smiling at him. Jack was puzzled.

"That's the first time I've smiled since Michael passed," Mrs. Rich said. Jessica walked down the stairs and the two couples walked down to the sidewalk.

"I can see you're working hard and you're right in the thick of things," Rich said and added, "I saw you watching Tom Peters; he worked with Mike, you know?... Do you think he can help?"

Kelly looked over at Rich and his wife. "Yes. I think he can help," Kelly said, not wanting to say too much, but he couldn't keep from adding, "I think Peters is in this up to his eyeballs."

Jack was apprehensive about Amanda being with Peters. He whispered to Jessica that maybe the BPD could put security details on any "remaining AI Lab rats," since they seemed to be the targets. Amanda was one of the founding members of Michael's group and Kelly was worried.

Jack introduced Lieutenant Paris to the Riches, and Jessica told them she was very sorry for their loss. She promised them that the Boston Police Homicide Unit was also working diligently on the case with Kelly.

Cooper gave his horn a quick beep as he drove past the funeral home in his pursuit of the limo. Jack shook his head and said, "Sorry about the car horn. That's one of my inappropriate operatives, Mr. Rich."

"Do you need more funds, Mr. Kelly?" Mrs. Rich said and Kelly told her he had "only taken a bite out of the apple" Rich had already given him. Kelly promised to call them in several days "while a few things play out," and the couples went their separate ways.

Jack called Cooper's cell phone as he and Jessica walked to the Jeep on Bay State Road.

"Cooper. There's a girl with Tom and Victoria Peters in that limo."

"The dark-haired Goth girl wearing too much makeup. I saw her get in with Peters."

"Her name is Amanda and she's... she was a friend of Michael's and Rodney's and Seng Li's... she was a part of that group of students at the AI Lab that developed the robot."

"What? What robot? Did you say a robot? Hello?" Cooper said.

"Oh, Christ save me! Never mind the robots, Cooper. Just follow that car! Let me know when and where Amanda gets out but keep the surveillance with Peters. And don't get burned!"

Cooper closed his cell phone and then immediately opened it again and called The Musician's home number. A teenage girl answered and Cooper asked her how she was doing. She said her father wasn't home. Cooper asked her how she liked school and she said her father was at Intermedia Studio on Newbury Street and hung up.

Cooper got the recording studio's number from Information and punched it in as he drove. The snow was heavy and blowing sideways as the black Mercedes limousine was heading across the snow-covered Mass. Ave. Bridge towards MIT. Cooper finally spoke with someone at the studio and he asked for Willie Crawford.

"Who?" the female voice asked.

"The Musician," Cooper said, and soon thereafter Willie answered.

"I gotta go to a photo shoot with two hot Brazilian models for the Ford Agency early tonight; can you cover for me on this surveillance for a couple hours?" Cooper asked The Musician but got no response so he added, "You're the son-of-a-bitch that got me into this."

"What? How did I get you into this?" The Musician protested.

"Jack said you were burnt, or burnt out, or something, so he came to me next. So, look, can you cover me for three hours? Six to nine? I'm behind the limo now and they're heading back to the CES offices, it looks like. Just sit in that fucking van with your heater on, listen to the pregame for the New England Patriots and the Baltimore Ravens on Monday Night Football, and watch the snow pile up. I'll pay you for the hours. Jack went up to $60 an hour; OK, amigo?" Cooper pleaded.

"Wow! OK. But I won't be taking my van. I think they made the van. I'll take my wife's old shit-box Nissan and change my appearance."

"Are you going to change your appearance into the 'Girl Scout' again?" Cooper said.

"Fuck off, Coop! I'll cover for you, but just from 6 to 9. Call me at 5:30 and tell me where you are and I'll relieve you."

Jack's Jeep fishtailed in the snow as they pulled out onto Commonwealth Ave. and headed back to the Back Bay. They had decided not to follow the casket to the cemetery, leaving that for close friends and family members. Kelly was deep in thought and didn't notice Marcus following him a comfortable three cars back. He was thinking about Rodney Riviera, lying in the coffin he would be buried in.

"Dead on the Internet."

"What? Who's dead on the Internet?" Jessica asked Jack as he playfully accelerated, skidding sideways and then steering in the direction of the skid to bring the Jeep back under control, something he learned during thousands of hours driving police cars in the New England snow.

Jessica looked at Jack and buckled her seat belt.

"I love the snow in Boston, all the potholes are filled up," Jack said. "Don't worry. You know all New Englanders can drive through a snowstorm in three feet of snow at sixty-five miles per hour."

"Who's dead on the Internet?"

She waited for Jack's response as Jack put the Jeep into four-wheel drive on-the-fly and slowed the vehicle down.

He looked straight ahead and said, "The dead on the Internet. That is what this is all about. Rodney told me in every way he could. He said it was all about control of the Prototype Robot and its manufacture and marketing. He told me straight up. In English. Then he tried to show me at the MIT Museum. The last time I saw Rodney he was shouting at me as I walked away down Mass. Ave.

"He was trying to tell me that this... modern, human-looking, household robot slave was going to be indispensable in every home and business. With maintenance contracts and wireless Internet linkage, the owners, or controllers, would have an unprecedented access and power to go along with the super mega-wealth the robots would bring them."

"People will kill for fifty dollars or even a pair of sneakers," Jessica agreed.

"Rodney also told me that no one knows what will happen when these Wi-Fi robots with computers for brains have 24/7 access to the World Wide Web. 'The dead on the Internet' Rodney called them. Some predict they will achieve self-realization with an instinct for survival."

"You bring forth philosophical and ethical questions, Kelly."

"That's just one of the many services provided by Jack Kelly's American Detective Agency. As an impartial observer of the human condition here on Earth, I like to note and report my findings."

"Are these robots like the HAL 9000 in '2001: A Space Odyssey'?" Jessica asked.

"Only these HALs would be our size, they can move about, and there will soon be hundreds of thousands of them!"

"Now, that's like 'Invasion of the Body Snatchers,'" Jessica observed.

"Or even 'Frankenstein'... Man builds in his own image using spare parts. But his creation turns out to be a monster," Jack said as he pulled up to a red light.

"'Net of the Living Dead.'"

They watched as a snowplow crossed in front of the Jeep. The snow was well over six inches deep now, and the west wind was driving it sideways.

"How much snow we supposed to get, Jess?"

"Six inches in the Derry area," she said, smiling.

Jack laughed at her private joke. "Did you say derriere? How about in the… ah… mountains?" Jack said, looking her up and down, his eyes dwelling a little too long on her chest.

"Oh, it's going to be hot in the mountains," Jessica said, rubbing her hands seductively over her breasts and unbuttoning the top button.

"And how about the valley?" Jack said, and then added quickly as the lights turned green, "OK. Never mind the valley right now. Let's get on this thing…"

"Get on your thing? Whatever do you mean, Jack?"

"Ah… Oh, I mean the case. Let's get on the case. I'm going to call Cooper and find out where the Peterses are right now."

"When you get me his location I'll get surveillance set up on him and his business. As a matter of fact, I can get my team up and running now," Jessica said as both detectives got their cell phones out.

"Amanda is in that limo. We need to keep an eye on her. She was close to Michael and Rodney. And now she's sitting next to Peters and his sleazy sister."

"Were you attracted to her, Jack? The 'sleazy sister' is quite beautiful."

"I'm not attracted to serial killers, honey. She's a black widow spider. I'm sure she devours the head of her mate after sex."

"Ouch. That's gotta hurt," Jessica said, putting her hand on Jack's thigh.

"If Amanda says the wrong thing, Peters will kill her, I know it."

"So, this is the guy, right, Jack? OK… just refresh me here. So, just what do we have on him? What can we prove?"

Jack was silent. He couldn't think of anything at that moment.

The silence finally got to Jessica and she said, "Well… he had the opportunity, right? He knew all three murder victims. And he had motive. According to you the murderer wants control over the production and sales of these super robots because there's large sums of money involved."

"Yes, Jesse. Michael had a 'date' with the escort service the night he disappeared. But we don't even have any written statements from anybody swearing that Peters was involved in any way, shape, or form. Eventually we'll get lesser actors to roll over on Peters, but right now, we don't have any forensic proof. No fingerprints. No murder weapon. No crime scenes. No DNA. No, nothing physical to link this guy to the murders!"

Jack knew he or someone else would get the killer or killers sooner or later but he hoped it would be without another death occurring. Kelly wondered what the burial of Rodney Riviera was like. He envisioned Rodney's casket being lowered into a cold and snowy grave as his mother watched. He imagined the Riches and student friends of Rodney's standing in silence in the screaming snowstorm as the cracking and throaty voice of the old priest, Father Strickland, shouted above the fury of the storm, "And so that he died so shall he live… and whoever believes in me so shall he live forever… and his soul to walk the Earth.'

Three cars behind Kelly, in the blue Dodge Caravan, Marcus did his best to keep up with the four-wheel-drive Jeep. Marcus could barely see through the snow as he watched Kelly drop off Jessica back at her snow-covered dark blue Ford Taurus parked just down from her apartment. Marcus called Tom to tell him he was following the detective into the Back Bay. Marcus Grace followed in the light blue soccer-mom van as Kelly continued on, heading toward his Chinatown office.

Chapter 64

Loose Ends

The Musician arrived in the snowy Cambridge neighborhood of the CES offices just before dark and took Cooper's parking spot as he pulled out. The two were in contact by phone. Cooper told The Musician that a girl dressed in black with heavy dark eye makeup, named Amanda, had gone into the building with Peters, his sister, and the big black limo driver.

"The black Elvis had one of Amanda's arms and Peters had the other. Jack wants to know where she goes but stick with Peters and I'll be back around nine."

Inside the offices of the College Escort Service several women answered phones in a workspace by the front doors. Tom Peters was chopping up a white rock about the size of a pencil eraser and making six lines on the bar. After snorting three of them he offered lines to Moose, who rolled a ten-dollar bill into a tube and snorted two lines.

"Want a line, Amanda?" Tom asked.

"No thanks, Tom. I'm trying to cut down. I hate funerals. I'll take a vodka on the rocks, though."

Tom pulled the tube from his belt buckle and snorted the last line. He wiped his finger across the remaining coke dust and rubbed it on the gums under his upper lip. He was trying to size up Amanda as he poured some Grey Goose vodka over ice in a tumbler for her and the same for himself with a little soda water and a lime twist.

"I was really upset to see Rodney lying in that coffin this morning, Amanda. Had you spent much time with Rod lately?" Victoria asked.

Amanda looked around the first floor before answering.

"Yes, a bit. After Michael died I began seeing more of Rodney."

"Oh. I see," Tom said, smiling. "Were you with Rod when he talked to that detective, Kelly?"

"Ah…," Amanda began to stammer slightly and considered spilling her drink or asking to use the bathroom but instead looked straight at Tom and said, "Yes. Kelly is working for Michael's parents.… He… he had a lot of questions."

"And you and Rodney had the answers?" Victoria asked as she made herself a Cosmopolitan.

Amanda took a strong pull on the vodka while she briefly debated not having this conversation with Tom and Victoria but said, "Well, this private investigator, Kelly, he doesn't have a scientific background. He's a bit thick, actually. Well… Rodney said that Kelly couldn't find his own ass with a flashlight. Anyway, Rodney took him to the MIT Museum and walked him through the exhibits."

"You mean the talking heads and outdated bionic toys from the last century? What's that got to do with Michael's murder?" Tom said.

"Rodney tried to open Kelly up to the importance of the work done at the AI Lab. He told Kelly that he thought the people who killed Michael were interested in controlling the Prototype."

Victoria coughed as she was taking a drink and wiped her chin with a napkin. Tom and his sister exchanged glances; they both realized that Amanda was another "loose end" they would have to deal with.

"And what do you think Amanda?" Tom asked the darkly dressed grad student.

Rodney had told Amanda of his suspicions concerning the powerfull group that would be in a position to take control over the Project. Rodney knew that MIT would eventually seek the rights over the Prototype Project. But he knew that many of the inventors were seeking individual patents for many of the systems involved. He knew that Michael had developed and was seeking to patent the Systems Override Control for the Project. Rodney had mentioned Tom several times as someone who not only understood the value of the Prototype Project, but also had the funds and connections, criminal and otherwise, to take it over.

Amanda had wanted to examine the murders herself. She wasn't impressed with the apparently stalled investigation of Jack Kelly and she wanted to judge for herself the involvement of Peters. She hoped she was not getting in too far over her head, but she decided to confront Tom directly. She drank the contents of the tumbler and smacked the empty drink down on the bar. She said it straight out.

"Look, Tom. I purposely bumped into you in front of the funeral home and asked you for a ride back to Cambridge because… well… Rodney thought you might be involved… with this. We both know you're an insider. I want to know what you know about Mike's, Seng Li's, and Rodney's deaths. There; I said it."

Tom shifted on his feet and looked around wide-eyed. He wondered where he could get a quick fix. He showed no emotion as he told Amanda that he hadn't been to the AI Lab in years and was quite busy with his escort service, the Internet live cam sites, and the occasional triple X films he produces. He even offered Amanda a job anytime she needed some money.

This only made Amanda feel sleazy and it increased her suspicions about Tom being capable of high crimes. She felt uneasy but nodded her head as Peters spoke. She had figured by then that Peters wasn't about to admit to any criminal activity or confess to involvement in the murders. Amanda began thinking the best move she could make would be to get safely out of the building. She would walk the six blocks back to the MIT campus.

"Oh, great! I'm so relieved, Tom. I feel much better knowing you had nothing to do with it. I told Rodney he was shooting in the dark. You were one of us. Remember the round table in the corner at the Miracle of Science Bar and Grill? You and the guys put away some beer!" Amanda said, laughing and trying to make a good show of it. But acting wasn't her strong skill.

"As I recall you liked the vodka even back then…," Tom smiled and added, "Let me get you another."

"No… No thanks, Tommy. I've got to get over to the science library and prep for some lab work in the morning," Amanda said, looking at her watch-less wrist and straightening her clothes.

"Let Moose give you a ride then," Victoria suggested.

"No thanks, it's only six blocks to the campus, I could use the air."

"Just one more vodka on the rocks, Amanda! I insist," Tom implored.

"No. Really, but thanks. And thanks for the drink," Amanda said as she began to walk away. But after a few steps Tom shouted her name and she stopped in her tracks, turned, and looked at him.

"It's not safe... out there! I'll give you a ride in the limo. Moose will drive. C'mon, we'll leave right now. Let's go, Moose! The least we can do is see Amanda safely back to the hallowed grounds of MIT."

Moose and Tom fell in with Amanda as they walked to the front doors, down the stairs, into the parking lot, and into the cold early December night air. The snow was still coming down and was well over a foot deep. They got into the black stretch limo and drove out of the CES lot, heading towards MIT. But they soon passed the campus and went over the Mass. Ave. Bridge towards Boston.

Amanda began to protest but ceased when Tom pointed the chrome revolver at her. Tom called Marcus on his cell phone and asked if he was following "that dick."

"He hasn't come back out of his hole yet," Marcus said from his van outside the Kingston Street offices of Jack Kelly's American Detective Agency.

"Well, when he does, Marcus, remember the offer I made you. We have to stop him and stop him now. Kill him, Marcus! An accident must happen today. Or we'll have to blow the motherfucker and his bitch up tonight! He's got to go."

"I understand, Boss. I'm going to try and collect that bonus. Maybe an accident can be arranged. Here he comes out of his office right now," Marcus told Tom as Jack Kelly bounded down the stairs in front of his building, crossed the street, and hopped in the driver's seat of his black Jeep.

As darkness fell, the limousine took a left on Back Street, an alley built over the river between Storrow Drive and Beacon Street. Tom told Marcus that he and Moose would be at the garage/apartment if he needed any assistance with Kelly. As the limo pulled up and parked on the side of the garage, The Musician pulled over on Back Street, driving his wife's red Nissan, and turned off his headlights and sat still, but not before Moose caught a glimpse of his recognizable profile.

Marcus began following Jack Kelly out of Chinatown, around the Boston Commons, and over to the Esplanade. Jack parked his Jeep and walked in the deep snow. He passed students and businesspeople as he walked over behind the Hatch Shell. Marcus watched Jack walk to the Charles River in the area where two of the bodies had been found. Jack looked at the river and studied its flow. He watched the swirls and whirls of the water as it flowed inevitably downstream towards the Lower Basin. And he wondered how long the bodies had drifted before they were found.

"Good evening, Detective Kelly."

Kelly jumped, instinctively putting his hand on the butt of his .45 in the shoulder holster under his left armpit. He turned to see Dexter, Michael Rich's fraternity brother, breaking away from a group of students that were walking along the path from the downtown area.

"Poindexter?" Jack shouted in relief as he recognized him.

"It's Dexter!"

"Right, from Helta Skelta Delta," Kelly said.

"Alpha Omega Delta," Dexter again corrected Jack.

"Why are you over here staring into the river, Kelly? Are you thinking of jumping in? I'd wait to see that."

"Get in line, Dex."

"It's Dexter, just plain Dexter."

"OK, Just Plain Dexter. I'm looking at the patterns in the flow of the river. Two bodies ended up here and I'd like to figure out where they were dumped in, Just Plain Dexter," Kelly explained.

The two men began slowly walking along the path, heading upriver, as Dexter contemplated the problem.

"Kelly, the river flows into town towards the harbor at about 1, 1.5 miles an hour, tops. We can walk at almost four if we walk as fast as we can, so a real slow shuffle would be 1.5 miles an hour. If you know the temperature of the body when he floated up and the rate a body assimilates the outside temperature, you could estimate the distance traveled."

"Thanks, Dexter," Jack said as he again paused by the river and took out his cell phone. Dexter continued on as Kelly dialed Lieutenant Paris.

"Look in your official BPD file folder and see if you have the body temperature of Seng Li when he popped up behind the Hatch Shell."

"OK, I've got that file right here," Jessica told him.

"Where are you?" Jack asked.

"I'm at Area A. I've got a message that Trooper Archambeault wants me to call him right away. If you call back in five minutes I'll hook us both into a conference call with him, and I'll check and see if the Seng Li report has the body temperature when discovered, OK, Jack?"

"Yes. One more thing. Google me this…"

"Only if you Google me when you get home tonight. You are coming home, aren't you?"

"Google me this," Jack continued. "A body's temperature, after death, falls towards its surrounding temperature at what rate? Call me when you've got it." Kelly said, shutting his cell phone.

Jack looked out over the river and across at MIT with its short and tall buildings with their electronics aimed at satellites and celestial objects. MIT's stark white, rounded domes were still visible through the darkness and the falling snow as Jack wandered peacefully in the silent snow along the riverbank until his cell phone buzzed and chirped with the sound of crickets. It was Jessica calling.

"I've got Archambeault on the other line; are you ready to conference, Jack?"

"Let's talk to the man."

"Hello, Trooper Archambeault," Jack said after he heard a click.

"Hey, Jack. What's going on in your investigation of the Michael Rich murder? What have you got?"

"Not a thing I can prove, Archie. Peters is still my main man but I've got nothing. Maybe we can sweat an underling to roll over, but you know, I was hoping forensics would come up with something."

Lieutenant Paris mentioned something about Jack watching too much "CSI" and "Cops" and Archambeault seemed all too willing to laugh along as he said, "Well, Jack, and Lieutenant Paris, forensics has come up with something. You know the methamphetamine found in the stomachs of all three victims?"

"A red herring, I thought," Jack said as Archambeault continued.

"Red herring or not, it's evidence, Jack. The DA, Jay Thomas, is pretty happy that someone... *me*, has come up with a concrete link to a suspect in these serial killings. He's got all the politicians breathing down his neck and he'll have to prosecute the case."

"That's why they build law schools," Jack said.

"I took samples of the crystal meth in the stomachs of all three victims and all three were from the same batch. Then I compared that batch to a sample of every taste of meth confiscated or seized, every undercover buy, sting, whatever I could. Every rock or powder confiscated from boats, cars, and planes. Absolutely everything the BPD or the SP have touched for the last two months. And I got a hit.

"There was a fire at a meth lab four blocks behind MIT six weeks ago. The meth manufactured in that lab was identical to the meth found in all three of the vics' stomachs."

"Wow! Great work, Archie! Nice going. No wonder the DA loves you. You're building the case. But where does that leave us?" Jessica asked.

"It leaves us back at Jack's door," Archambeault said.

"What do you mean, Archie?" Jessica asked, concerned.

Archie savored the moment and then confessed, "Jack's on the right trail, all right. The building where the meth lab was seized is owned by Victoria and Thomas Peters."

"Score one for the cheap detective from Kelly's American Detective Agency," Jack said.

"I saw what you're making on this case, Kelly, and it ain't cheap!" Jessica said.

"Hey, I'll give some of the money back if Archie can wrap this thing up. He's got a definite link there. He's got some physical evidence, at last."

"My unit will be putting a tail on Peters," Archambeault said.

"It'll be like a fucking parade behind Peters. Let's not tell the Feds right away or we'll have to get a bus," Lieutenant Paris said.

Jack and Jessica remained on the line as Archie promised to keep in touch and disengaged.

"OK, Jesse. I'm standing by the river at the Esplanade in the snow; did you look up that info on temperature loss?"

"Yes. Here you go. There are many factors in determining the rate a dead body's temperature falls towards its surroundings. Fat content on the body is a factor. Whether it's in water or in circulating air. Inside or outside. Sun or shade. It's less accurate when the time is prolonged, but there is a formula."

"Cut to the chase, please," Jack said, shivering in the snow.

"The core body temperature falls at about 1 or 1.5 degrees an hour."

"OK. And his body temperature when they fished him out was?"

"Seng Li's core temp was 95.5 degrees, Jack. Liver temp."

"So… Let's see… then…," Jack stammered.

"I've already done the math," Jessica said. "His temperature was three degrees from the standard 98.6. If it took them an hour to take Seng Li's temp after the body was found, and I heard it did… some wacko EMS tech started doing CPR on the corpse… anyway, at one-degree-an-hour loss, that's one degree, and leaves only two degrees that his temperature dropped."

Jack picked up the ball.

"Then that means if he traveled downriver at one mile an hour and only lost two degrees doing it, then he entered the water less than two miles upriver. And it's gotta be more than one mile from where I'm standing right now. That should be just up Back Street before Mass. Ave. I think I'll take a walk."

"Be careful, Jack. Have you seen anybody trying to follow you tonight? I'm already on the way to check your tail. "

"Why is everything sex with you? Anyway… No. I didn't see anybody behind me, Jesse. What am I? Bait in a lobster trap? I parked in front of 100 Beacon, the Emerson College girls' dormitory."

"Jack, most all dorms are coed now!"

"That's the problem with our society. Anyway, it was a girls' dorm when I dated a girl living there. I'll be walking up the alley on Back Street," Jack said and closed his cell phone.

Jack looked over across at MIT as he walked along the river. The snow had let up; total accumulation was well under two feet. No big deal in New England. A small group of ducks quacked, waddled off the riverbank, and paddled out into the dark water as Jack approached. A trolley car crossed over the Longfellow Bridge and Jack heard the click-clack of the rail tracks. Then he noticed the sound of a single-engine airplane struggling through the snowy evening in search of Logan International Airport. Kelly looked upriver towards Soldier's Field Road. Across the river he could just see the green neon lights of the Hyatt Regency Hotel in the shape of a pyramid. All seemed to quiet down again as Jack moved along upriver.

He hadn't walked more than a quarter mile when he saw Lieutenant Jessica Paris's Boston Police low-profile Ford pull into a parking space about fifty yards behind him. Jack smiled back at her. He waited for her to catch up to him as he looked upriver, going over his calculations again. He pictured the bodies of Seng Li and Rodney Riviera tumbling slowly along the river bottom. He looked to the group of converted garages, still almost half a mile upriver... and at first he didn't notice the ascending roar of the vehicle's engine.

Jack looked to his left and saw the powder blue soccer-mom van accelerating towards him in the snow. The front-wheel drive van had gotten up to about 40 MPH and was fast approaching from about twenty feet away. Kelly could see the eyes of Marcus Grace bugging out as he attempted to open his car door, possibly to fall out in the snow, sending the van straight into Kelly. Jack thought he could jump out of the way but began to realize he would not have time. He thought about reaching for his gun but there wasn't time for that either. Jack had run out of time. Then he heard the bang from Jessica's .38-caliber revolver and saw the bullet hit Marcus in the side of his neck.

As Marcus slumped over the wheel, the van kept speeding towards Jack, hitting him squarely. Kelly was knocked out cold as his face made a spider-web pattern in the broken windshield. He and the van, with Marcus in it, went through the old fence and partly flew and partly rolled down the five-foot embankment, plunging into the Charles River. Jack's life flashed before his mind's eye on a fast-forward reel… it played at the speed of a bullet.

The cuff of Jack's pant leg was caught in the front bumper as the van sank. The big vehicle rolled quickly down the riverbank and underwater to a depth of about twenty feet below the river's surface. Jack came to, bent down and freed his pants cuff while the van moved downward another few inches, just enough to put the right front wheel of the car on top of Jack's right foot. Jack struggled, but he was pinned. He wished he was dreaming, but he wasn't. Jack looked up at Marcus in the front seat of the van; Marcus had blood pouring out of his neck and he could no longer hold his breath as the water rose above his head. Marcus Grace swallowed water. The blood stopped pumping out of his neck, the light went out of his eyes, and he stared straight ahead.

Chapter 65

Bump in the Night

Moose had walked out of the garage/apartment to Beacon, up to Mass. Ave., and returned down Back Street, staying close to the brick walls of the townhouses and garages. In the darkness he walked up behind the battered red 1990 Nissan 240 SX. As The Musician sat looking straight ahead at the garage, Moose tried to pull open the driver's side door but it was locked. Moose took a big black poly-carbon nightstick from inside his fringed leather jacket and smashed the window. He reamed out the broken glass with the baton, reached in and pulled the thin bass player out through the window. He stood Willie Crawford up and punched him twice in the face with his right hand. Then Moose took the black nightstick and hit The Musician hard across the top of his head. Willie crumpled in Moose's arms.

When he woke up The Musician was lying on the floor in front of the couch near the bar in Tom Peters's garage/ apartment. He had silver duct tape around his ankles and wrists. Amanda was sitting on the couch with her ankles and wrists taped.

"We were just about to have a vodka on the rocks, isn't that right, Amanda? Would you like one? Ah… I didn't get your name?" Peters said to The Musician as he chopped a lime into slices with a meat cleaver at the bar. He walked across the wooden floor with two martini glasses and put one of them into Amanda's constricted hands.

"Oh, c'mon, now," Tom said. "We know you've been following us and that you work for the detective. What's your name? What shall we call you? Let's be civil about this."

"The Musician," Willie said, wincing from the pain of nightstick.

"'The Musician,'" Tom echoed as he stood over Willie. "Not a professional sleuth, I take it? Someone, perhaps, that works occasionally for Jack Kelly? Somebody, I bet, who gets paid peanut money? And here you are, risking your life. Is it worth it, Mr. Musician?"

"Well… no. Not when you put it that way. In fact, Kelly can go fuck himself for all I care. He just told me to follow you, he didn't tell me what for. As far as I'm concerned, you're cool, man, you're OK. I've got no problem with you. Kelly tells me nothing, so I won't tell him nothing. Now, if you could see your way to untying me, I'll just walk away and go spend some time with my six young children." The Musician was working it hard as he looked over at Moose; he smiled and said, "Four little girls and two boys. And I should get home in time to put them to bed if you don't mind."

The Musician looked back at Tom Peters. Tom seemed amused and asked The Musician if he'd like that drink as he leaned over and handed him the martini. Willie rolled into a sitting position and reached up and took the drink. Tom walked back behind the bar and put a CD into a player; a DJ Paul Oakenfold disc started pumping out its rave dance mix. Tom took the meat cleaver and sharpened it on a flat stone. He admired it lovingly as he continued to sharpen the cleaver to razor-blade thinness. He took a few minutes to wipe it down very carefully. Then he dumped some crack cocaine rocks on the bar and crushed them with the side of the heavy cleaver. He methodically began to chop the rocks into a fine powder. At times he moved in time to the hypnotic house dance music. At other times he seemed totally consumed and focused on the task at hand. He slapped the meat cleaver down on the bar, took the metal tube from his belt's buckle, snorted a line into each nostril, and shouted, "That's what I'm talkin' about!"

The Musician stole a glance over at Amanda. She looked scared. They both knew Tom was an insane drug addict who seemed to be working himself up. And they both knew that they were of no further use to Tom Peters.

"Can I ask you a question?" The Musician asked, sipping the martini.

"You just did," Peters said. A few seconds went by and he added, "Go ahead. What?"

"Where did they get that cow that the MIT students put up on the Great Dome's roof?"

"Hilltop Steak House, on Route 1 in Saugus," Tom answered matter-of-factly.

"How about the fire engine up on the roof?"

"It was a police car with a cop inside and an 'I brake for donuts' sticker on the back," Moose said, smiling.

"There was a fire engine up there at one time too, Moose," Tom informed him. "There was a house with a mailbox and a welcome mat out front, all up on the roof for a while. They were made of preassembled cardboard and went up piece by piece. Also, there was a phone booth up there and it had a real working phone line."

"Cool…," The Musician said as he looked over at Moose with his slick black pompadour hairstyle, long sideburns, fringed leather coat, jeans with the cuffs turned up, and blue suede shoes. Willie added, "So, what's with the Elvis look?"

"What Elvis look?" Moose asked dubiously.

"How about that dorm room set up out on the ice of the Charles River and the sailboat in the swimming pool?" Amanda asked quickly.

"It's amazing what hacks you can accomplish with fifty fraternity brothers in a short span of time," Tom said.

"How about the beanie with the propeller on the giant Dome or the big smiley face on Building 10…," Amanda started to say when Tom drained the contents of his martini glass and screamed very loudly.

"Enough! Shut the fuck up!" Peters said and threw his glass at Amanda, striking her and cutting her cheek. A small stream of blood started down the side of her face.

"You two! Are standing in my way! Well, you're not standing now…. And that fucking detective, Kelly!" Peters roared as The Musician took a drink.

"I thought we were going to 'be civil about this'?" The Musician requested and took another sip, draining the martini.

Tom Peters took a step towards The Musician and kicked at his head. The Musician moved back, dodging each kick; he was able to deflect some of them but was soon knocked out by a solid kick to the cheekbone, falling back on the floor.

Peters put on a Beck CD.

Chapter 66

From the Bottom of the River

After the van crashed into the river Lieutenant Jessica Paris was frantic. She had just shot a man and watched as the van he was driving hit her lover and knocked him into the dark waters of the Charles River with a huge splash. But now the river had swallowed up the van and Jack was nowhere to be seen. The air had escaped from the van and the stream of bubbles had diminished on the surface and now the river was quiet and dark. Kelly had not risen for over three minutes. The ordinarily unflustered Lieutenant Paris was near panic as the seconds ticked by. Almost by unconscious reflex she had pulled out her radio and called in for a rescue unit, the patrol supervisor, her commanding officer at Homicide, and two ambulances. But now as the snowstorm ended, Jesse stood in the water at the river's edge. She stared at the small bubbles rising to the surface in the quiet river as the distant wailing sirens drew closer. She stared at the river and screamed Jack's name.

Jack was pinned to the cold river bottom by the van. He couldn't pull his foot out from under the front tire. The struggle caused him to use the air in his lungs at a much faster than normal rate. He had pulled the Swiss Army knife from out of his pocket and pulled out the biggest blade. Jack jammed the knife into the side of the tire and pulled the blade downward with all his strength, creating a four-inch slit. He put his mouth on the slit and pushed his thumb in the crevice as hard as he could, and some of the compressed air from the tire shot out and into his mouth.

Kelly repeated this maneuver a half-a-dozen times until his heart stopped racing wildly and he could regulate his breathing. But it was no good. He was sucking in small amounts of water with the air and coughing with every other breath he took.

Kelly took his knife blade and located the tires valve stem. He was going to push down the pressurized spring in the valve's core to free some air, but in his desperation he simply cut off the entire valve stem and the compressed air shot out. Jack was able to get more air and less water.

Minutes went by as Jack's eyes scanned the area desperately. He looked up to the river's surface for help but the murky river water was nearly impenetrable in the night. The tire's air pressure was lessening as Jack tugged at his foot but it remained lodged under the wheel. His hand began to scrape and dig at the firm muck below his foot. Progress was slow and Kelly felt like he was getting weaker and could lose consciousness. He had to stop to get air from the tire every few seconds. After a minute of digging, he was able to wiggle his foot free. As he pulled his foot away, the van rolled downward another three or four feet onto the bottom of the river.

Kelly rose to the surface with the very last fragment of air left in his exhausted lungs. The sound of a dozen sirens and the cold night air hit Jack like a slap in the face. Cops were walking and running in every direction as he swallowed more water. He saw Jesse standing in the river up to her waist with her jacket and gun off. She was shivering and staring straight ahead.

When she saw Jack she jumped into the river, swam the few feet out to him, and pulled him back toward the riverbank. Jessica struggled as she got him up onto the muddy shore. She held him in her arms. Some of the cops standing above them clapped their hands as medical personnel scrambled down the embankment.

Jack didn't want to move. He liked it right where he was, even though the air felt colder than the water. He was glad to be alive.

Kelly knew the EMS workers would not leave them alone until he signed out as "a refusal." He struggled to his feet with Jessica's help. They staggered up to the Esplanade. Jack pulled off his wet jacket. Little by little he got his wind back as the paramedics gave Jessica and Jack blankets, took his blood pressure, and cleaned a one-inch cut on his forehead. Kelly soon grew strong enough to tell the medics he would be walking away on his own with Lieutenant Paris's help. He had no need for hospitalization. They seemed disappointed but they released Kelly from their care after he signed a waiver. Lieutenant Paris had convinced them Jack would be safe under her care.

Of course Sergeant Donavan was the shift supervisor, and he wanted a few words with Kelly. Jessica and Jack were draped in blankets but were wearing wet clothes, so the three walked back to Lieutenant Paris's Ford and Donavan got in back. Jessica started the engine and turned the heat on full blast. From Lieutenant Paris's car they could see the tow truck setting up to pull the van out of the water, with the emergency personnel standing by.

The flashing blue lights of the cop cars and the strobe effect from the red lights of the fire and rescue vehicles made Jack feel light-headed. When the tow truck arrived to add its flashing yellow lights, Jack was daydreaming about when he was a boy waiting for Christmas morning.

"How do you want to handle this, Lieutenant?" Donavan asked.

"You know the protocol. You take my gun. It's an 'officer involved' shooting. I want to go by the book on this, Donavan. It's a righteous shoot so let's not screw it up. The guy had been following Kelly and he attempted to kill Kelly. And I shot him."

"Sounds clean to me, Jesse. I'm advisin' ya ta save tha rest for I.A. and yor bosses. Do you wahnt a union rep?"

"No," Jessica said emphatically, and added, "I didn't want to pull my gun. I didn't want to shoot anybody. I've never shot anybody before... well, not since Vietnam."

Both Donavan and Jack stared at Jessica until she confessed, "I didn't shoot anybody in Vietnam. In fact I was never in Vietnam. I wasn't born yet."

"You know what I just realized? If Internal Affairs is I.A. and Artificial Intelligence is A.I., then would I.A. be Intelligence Artificial?" Jack said with an odd glint in his eye, smiling at Jessica and Sergeant Donavan.

"I tink ya both suffrin' from Post-Traumatic Stress Disordah. Lieutenant, you bettah get this sorry son-of-a-bitch home and intah bed. Have ya been drinkin' much, Kelly? You know, Kelly, some days yur dah dahg and some days yur dah hydrant. Yahr soakin' wet so I tink I knows which one yahr today. I tink that knock on ya head has got ya all discombobulated. Do ya knows what day it is, Jack?"

"Ah…" Kelly couldn't quite come up with the answer.

"I'll give you a hint. You're missing Monday Night Football."

"Ah…"

"I'm going to get you home, Honey. Jeez, you really are whacked, aren't you?" Jessica put her arm on Kelly's shoulder and rubbed it, saying, "You took quite a shot to the head, Honey."

"Tahk about getting' hit wid a ton o' bricks!" Donavan said, "Dhat was a ton of moovin' metal dat knahcked ya inta dah drink, Kelly."

"Curses… I was five seconds from a clean get-away," Jack lamented.

"And how is it that you didn't surface for well over five minutes? I… I thought you were dead. What were you doing down there?" Jessica asked in amazement.

Kelly had a headache. He took a strong sniff of the car's warm air through both of his nostrils before he answered. He remembered being under water and pinned down by the van. He looked at Jessica, then at Donavan, and back at Jessica, and said, "I think I lost consciousness when I got hit by the van. I remember going into the cold water, like waking up from a dream, just to find I'm in a real-life nightmare. I remember I got pulled down into the river with the van. When I tried to get free and go up… the van rolled onto my foot and pinned me down on the river bottom. I couldn't move! I looked up at the van driver, I think it was the same driver who has been following me, and he was bleeding from his neck. I saw him swallow water and die. *I* didn't want to die so I pulled my Boy Scout model Swiss

Army knife with its catalogue of ten separate functioning appendages out of my pocket. I cut off the air valve stem and liberated some compressed air." Jack held the Swiss Army knife up high.

"Oh, boy," Donavan said, shaking his head from side to side and looking at Lieutenant Paris. "I'll guess ya should be makin' a report at headquahters in the morn, Kelly. And show up this time, would ya please? But I'm tinkin'… due to yahr acute medical condition or lack thereof, or whatever, you should remain in the care of Lieutenant Paris. I think we know how ta get in touch wid ya… Isn't that right, Lieutenant Paris?"

"Oh, yes, Sergeant Donavan. I'll keep him under wraps and we'll straighten this out tomorrow, when all the facts are in," Jessica said as she took her gun and holster off of her belt and handed it to the old sergeant.

Jack asked Donavan if he wanted Jack's gun, too.

"Of course not, you son-of-an-Irishman! You didn't shoot anybody, did you? Although that wouldn't be anything out of the ordinary, Kelly, would it? Did you shoot anybody today?"

"Not yet."

"Well, you've still got time."

"I'm just playing with you, Moses," Kelly said and pulled his Colt Combat Commander modified double-action .45 from his shoulder holster and pulled the magazine out and watched as some water trickled out of the firearm and onto the car's carpet.

"I've got to get this home and cleaned," Jack said, shoving the bullet-filled magazine back into the gun's butt and holstering the weapon. Donavan got out of the car and walked over to where the tow truck had pulled the light blue van up onto the Esplanade. Jessica and Jack watched as water poured out of the van onto the street. Donavan stepped over to the driver's side and opened the jammed door and along with more river water from the Charles, the body of Marcus Grace fell out of the van and dropped three feet onto the ground with a thud.

Chapter 67

Wet Dreams

"I've got more guns at home," Jessica said to Jack.

Jack knew that Jessica might be emotionally crushed by the fact that the man she shot in the neck was dead. Marcus had just fallen out of the van onto the ground in front of her, and Jack knew she was putting on a brave front. Jack knew that Jessica was just trying to be macho and move ahead. After all, she had a case to work. *They* had a case to work. And a dead Marcus was just collateral damage. She didn't have time to be "crushed." She didn't have time to be a girl. She had to be a cop first. Jack understood this.

"What have you got for guns at home?" he asked her, playing along.

"Got a .44-caliber Bulldog with Uncle Mike grips and a built-in laser sight. It's bigger and better than the gun I just handed over to Donavan."

"That's my girl!" Jack said, sliding over a little and leaning in to her. She put her hand on his leg and leaned in and kissed him.

"Jesse, I hope you don't think I'm crazy but I want to follow the river upstream, just a little. Less than a mile."

"Sure, Jack. But you're still wet and my apartment is only six blocks from here. We can check Back Street first thing in the morning," she said, and then did a double-take and looked at Jack, saying, "You mean now?"

Kelly sat there looking at her, and she realized he was serious. She protested loudly, "Absolutely not! No! Not tonight. We've gotten in enough trouble for one night."

"I can walk," Kelly said, getting out of the car. With the blanket still draped over his shoulders, he walked over to the body by the van. He stood with Donavan and several other cops under the bright lights of the tow truck, looking down at the cold corpse.

Jessica couldn't believe him. At times, and there were many, he could infuriate her with his bold and stupid independence. This was one of those times. But Jesse knew Kelly was now officially obsessed. He would be fanatically single-minded now. He would put everything, including her if he had to, aside while he obsessed on this case. He would imagine himself the killer. He would think depraved. He would bring himself down to a much lower level. He would get inside the sick, perverted mind of the killer and begin to live on the dark side. Just as he had been immersed in the river, so he would immerse himself in the case until it was solved. Jessica knew that just as Kelly wore that blanket, so would he wrap the case around him. He would continue working until he was totally exhausted and drained of every bit of mental and physical energy. Jessica knew the pattern well. And she knew it was a part of what made Jack Kelly the best investigator Paris had ever known.

There were a lot of emotions rolling around inside of Jessica Paris. She drove her car around the scene, lowered the window, and said with a firm but pleasant tone, "Let's go, Kelly. I'll drive you," and muttered under her breath, "Son-of-a-bitch."

Kelly stared down at the corpse and bent down close to the dead body of the man who had tried to kill him. He wanted to check Marcus's pockets but Kelly looked up and saw a young BPD officer he recognized as Patrolman Hodge watching him like a hawk.

"Let's check his pockets, Hodge," Kelly said with a nod.

Hodge bent down and was reaching into Marcus's coat pocket when the booming voice of Sergeant Donavan sent a shock wave through Kelly and Hodge.

"What paht of 'Don't let anybody touch that fahkin' body' don't ya understand, Hodge? Not until the medical examinah and BPD Crime Scene Response Unit arrive!" Sergeant Donavan yelled from the other side of the tow truck.

Hodge stood up like a rocket but Jack was still crouched down by the body.

"Are you going to read the criminal his Miranda rights, Hodge?" Donavan said, nodding to the body on the pavement.

"I'm not falling for that one again, Sergeant," the young officer responded.

Kelly was staring at the left hand of Marcus Grace. He was staring at a gold ring. On a finger was a Massachusetts Institute of Technology graduate's ring with a beaver, the school mascot, engraved on it. It was the Brass Rat. And

Kelly was willing to bet that Marcus was not an MIT graduate.

Kelly walked over to Jessica's unmarked cruiser and got in.

"Brass Rat," Jack said and sneezed loudly.

"Excuse me?" Jessica said.

"Marcus has an MIT alumni ring on his finger and I don't think he graduated from the school. It may be a souvenir from the murder of Seng Li or Michael Rich. We'll have to check and see if there are any numbers or ways to identify the rings. Let's slowly cruise up Back Street; I think the bodies were dumped from a location just before the Mass. Ave. Bridge."

As the Taurus maneuvered slowly up the empty alleyway between Beacon Street and the Charles River, Jack sneezed again and pulled his little notebook out of his pants pocket to write himself a note as a reminder to see if it was possible to "ID the ring," but the notebook was still dripping and soaked all the way through. He tossed it up onto the dashboard.

Jack asked Jessica to slow it down a couple of times. He was trying to envision where the body could have been dumped from, in the area just ahead. He looked into the dark waters of the Charles for an answer.

The snowstorm had ended as the clouds lifted and the temperature dropped. The night was black as Jack noticed the Christmas lights in some of the apartment windows. The row of Back Street garages stood against a backdrop of four-, five-, and six-story red brick apartment buildings.

"Let's take a vacation next Christmas, Jesse. Let's go somewhere that's hot. The Caribbean, maybe? We'll rent a sailboat and cruise the islands drinking rum and snorkeling with the tropical fish. We'll sail to a different harbor every other day, maybe I could rent a windsurfer, or we could rent jet skis… or we could go out on a fishing party boat…"

"Just name the dates, Jack. I'm there," the pretty young detective replied.

As their car got within a few blocks of Mass. Ave., Jack said, "I don't know what I'm looking for, exactly. I think they dumped the body out into the river right around here. Goddamn it! From a car, I was thinking, but there's a high and heavy wrought iron fence all along the river. Ah… what do I know? I just had to take a look. Let's go take a hot shower and get your .44. I'll make you some of my outrageous eggs and famous spicy potatoes."

Jesse smiled as they rolled up Back Street almost to Mass. Ave., when Jessica saw a small red car with a smashed-out window. The patrol cop in her took over as she turned on her cruiser's police radio and selected the channel for the Back Bay's district police station and keyed the mike. She called for a patrol unit to check on the possible burglary of a motor vehicle. When Jack said it looked like The Musician's wife's red Nissan, she added that she'd be out of the car checking.

As she walked around the red car, Jessica answered her cell phone and after a series of responses shut the phone, putting it in her jacket pocket. "Trooper Archambeault heard, and he says 'be careful.' He says an advanced background check on Tom Peters reveals he was not only a victim of child abuse but he is a suspect in the disappearance, molestation, and murder of a half dozen young Baltimore area schoolboys."

"Ah! He likes sex with boys and likes to kill them. Is he bisexual?"

"I think he's a try-sexual. He'll try anything. And Archie says either Tom or his twin brother, who went out the window at MIT, was driving the car his parents were killed in. Archie has put a 'stop and hold for questioning' on Tom Peters. He wants to get a warrant and to know where Peters is. I told him your Musician is tailing him but may be missing; is that about right, Jack?"

"Yeah…," Jack groaned.

Lieutenant Paris and Jack took a look at the red Nissan 240 SX with a smashed-out window. Kelly made a positive identification of The Musician's wife's car by recognizing the bumper sticker on the rear of the trunk with the words printed on it: "Out of My Mind; Back in Five Minutes."

Jack took his cell phone out of his pants pocket and opened it up. Several drops of water fell onto the pavement so he closed it and put it back into his pocket. He borrowed Jessica's cell and called The Musician's house. His wife Cathy answered and told Jack that Willie had been at the Intermedia recording studio on Newbury Street, "then he came home about two hours ago and took the keys to her car and ran out the door." Jack thanked her and asked her to have The Musician call him at Jessica's number as soon as she heard from him. He didn't mention her vandalized red car, her missing husband, or the attempt on Jack's life.

Jack dialed Cooper's cell phone and he answered. Jack could hear what sounded like a party in the background.

"Where's Peters now?" Jack asked him.

"Ah… I don't know," Cooper stammered. "I didn't want to bother you, Jack. I needed a few hours. I got The Musician to cover for me. I'm going back to meet him in a half an hour."

"Meet him where?"

"I told him I'd call his cell when I was done at around nine. And I'm almost through shooting these models for a big agency."

"Cooper, I'm on Back Street. In the area I think the bodies were dumped into the river, and I've got The Musician's wife's car here with a busted-out driver's side window! Can you shed any light on this?" Kelly asked, holding back a little anger at the fact that his simple surveillance operation was being mismanaged by his operatives.

"No... He said he was going to use his wife's car because they may have recognized his van.'

"And him," Jack said as he walked around the car again, adding, "I pulled him off of this because he got burnt. He was made! He wasn't supposed to... aw..., forget it."

"Jesus Christ. I feel bad now. So, where is he?"

"I don't know. I'll call you later," Jack said. He was about to call The Musician's cell phone when Jesse caught his eye and Jack closed her cell.

Jessica had begun to follow a set of tracks in the snow as Kelly followed her back down Back Street. She lost the tracks but then picked them up again on the other side of the street by the garages.

"Do you see how it looks like one set of footprints and then two lines on top of them? That could be someone dragging an unconscious person."

"That's my girl!" Jack whispered.

Chapter 68

Waiting to Die

Moose had made himself a peanut butter and jelly sandwich so fully packed that the jelly was oozing out of the sides, sliding through his fingers, and landing on the floor. He sat on the couch and took a huge bite, chewed it a few times, and swallowed. He stuffed the remaining half into his mouth and took a little longer to chew. He washed it down with beer. Tom was using the meat cleaver to crush and chop cocaine rocks into powder.

Tom was getting very high from the booze and white powder. He danced around the apartment as he listened to an old Clash CD. He waved his arms and strutted with the beat. He bent his knees and bobbed his head.

The Musician looked at Amanda and his eyes widened as he felt the vibration of his cell phone. She looked down at his taped-up wrists and she watched as The Musician was still able to dip one hand into the front pocket of his jeans. She could see him opening the phone inside his pocket and caught a glimpse of the cell phone's light shining within. The Musician's cell phone accessed the open line.

"Want to hear my Joke-of-the-Day?" The Musician asked Tom and Moose loudly, in an attempt to humanize himself to them and to let the person on the other end of the open line know he was there.

"Only if it's dirty," Tom said and continued bopping around the room.

"A cowboy was riding his horse through the countryside one day and he met an Indian riding his horse with a dog and a sheep. The cowboy said, 'Howdy. Nice dog you got there; can I ask him a few questions?' The Indian said, 'Dog no talk!' but the cowboy asked, 'Hey dog, is everything good?' 'Pretty good,' the dog says and the Indian is shocked! 'Is this Indian your owner? How does he treat you?' And the dog answers, 'He's good to me, he feeds me good and lets me run around and play.' The Indian is stunned as the cowboy asked if he could talk to the Indian's horse. 'Horse no talk,' the Indian replied. The cowboy said, 'Hey horse. You doin' good, too?' The horse says, 'I get plenty of grain and water and the Indian rides me regularly. He puts me in the shade when it's hot and brushes me every other day. I can't complain.' The Indian is amazed. Then the cowboy said, 'Can I ask your sheep a few questions?' and the Indian screamed, 'Sheep is liar!'"

"That wasn't bad, Musician," Tom said as Moose chuckled.

"It's *The* Musician," Willie corrected Tom.

Tom kicked The Musician full in the ribs. He collapsed into the fetal position. Tom kicked him twice more and then threw a table lamp down on him, the cord ripping out of its socket and the bulb bursting on the floor.

"Listen, *The* fucking Musician! I got a fuckin' joke for *you*. Well, it's a story. I met a little cowboy buck-a-roo at a small-town carnival one night. He was a little fresh-faced Irish boy, probably just like you were. So we got to talking, this little boy and I... Well, to make a long story short, I decide to take this boy into the woods... you know. He was attractive in an innocent way. Scruffy, but plump. Well, I'm walking him into the woods and he says, 'Mister, I'm scared to go into these woods.' I looked at the little boy and said, 'Hey, I'm scared too. But I've got to come out alone!'"

The Musician groaned and Amanda looked sick. Even Moose was staring at his boss. And then Tom added, "You know what, *The* Musician? That's a true story."

"You've created a crawl space under the all-time low," The Musician said.

Even though Amanda's ankles and wrists were duct-taped, she stood up and hopped the three feet from the couch to where Tom stood in the middle of the floor over Willie. She screamed and tried to head-butt Tom. Amanda got a piece of him, landing the top of her head squarely on Tom's chin. Tom pushed her down on the floor next to The Musician. As he walked back to the bar, Tom realized he had a half-inch gash in his chin that was trickling a thin stream of blood down his neck and into his shirt. The Musician and Amanda were lying on the floor face to face. The Musician whispered, "Nice shot," as Amanda smiled at him.

"Aren't you my fucking bodyguard, Moose?" Tom said quietly and very controlled as he fixed himself another drink.

"Yeah. Sorry, Boss," the big black man said.

Tom put a Velvet Revolver CD in the player. He crushed up a big cocaine rock with the meat cleaver and continued the ritual of chopping lines. He knew he had to do something with Amanda and The Musician and he knew what that something was. He knew it was time to kill.

Tom thought about how he would do it. He would take care of it just like he had with the last three that had interfered with his acquisition of the Prototype. He had methodically stolen and patented every system involved with the Prototype Project. Every system but one. Michael Rich had the design for the ultimate control. Michael had developed a system to control all systems. And Tom Peters was taking steps to get control of the patent. All he had to do now was eliminate the threats. After these two… it would just be Kelly. The last stop. The end of the line and he would be home free.

Tom sucked the chilled vodka through his teeth and snorted another line of the rock cocaine. He looked down on the wood floor of the garage apartment and visualized pulling the .357 magnum revolver out of his belt and capping the two restrained victims. He always did it himself. He didn't demand that Moose be the one to pull the trigger. So many cowards hide behind others. But not Tom Peters. He always shot them himself.

Amanda looked into the eyes of The Musician. Even through her fear, Amanda wondered who this handsome man lying on the floor was.

She took a chance and whispered, "Don't think I'm crazy, but don't you feel like we were meant to meet… maybe we're soulmates?"

"No, I feel like we're cell mates," The Musician whispered back wondering if Amanda was feeling the

Stockholm syndrome, adding quietly but urgently, "He's gonna kill us!"

Both of them realized Peters was the serial killer that had taken the lives of Michael Rich, Seng Li, and Rodney Riviera. Both of them realized they would be killed sooner or later. Probably more sooner than later.

Chapter 69

A Sinking Feeling

As Jessica and Jack followed the trail in the fresh snow along a row of converted garages down Back Street, Jack punched in The Musician's cell number and sent it. Jack heard the ring tones and the line open.

"It's The Musician!" Jack said to Jessica.

"Where are you, Willie? Willie? I mean... The Musician...?" Kelly said, still hearing no response. He was about to close his cell phone when some instinct told him to keep the line open. He turned the volume up as he listened intently.

Jack could hear The Musician's voice. He seemed to be narrating some story about a cowboy and an Indian... Kelly listened as hard as he could. He heard The Musician shout, "Sheep is liar!" and then could hear other voices and a struggle.

"He's on the other end of this line," Kelly said, holding up his cell phone. "But I think he's in trouble."

Kelly put the phone back up to his ear as the two continued tracking the drag marks in the snow. As they headed towards a group of garages along the Charles River, Kelly idly watched a black-and-yellow Checker taxicab pull up in front of the entrance to an apartment building one block down the street. As the cab blew its horn, Jack noticed the tiny delay in hearing the horn from the cab and hearing it through the cell phone's open line. In a flash Kelly realized that the open line was most likely originating from one of the garages near the cab.

"I think we're heading for one of those converted garages up ahead, Jesse. The trail we're following will lead us there, I think.'

They continued on down Back Street to a group of garages; the trail in the snow ended at the front door of one. Parked next to the converted garage/apartment was the black Mercedes stretch limousine in which Peters had left the funeral home.

As Jessica followed the trail up to within six feet of the front door of Tom Peters's garage, Kelly walked across Back Street to the hole in the fence. Jack climbed down the riverbank and looked under the pilings beneath the garages. He tried to listen as intently as he could to the open cell phone line coming from The Musician's cell phone but the signal was fading.

In the garage above, The Musician moved his stiff and sore body. The cell phone in his pocket beeped once. Tom Peters was changing the CD and heard the beep. He inserted the "Best of No Doubt" CD and walked over to where The Musician and Amanda lay on the floor.

"What was that? I heard a little electronic toot, didn't I?" Tom said, standing over the two. Peters instructed his big bodyguard to search Amanda and The Musician but when Moose bent down over Amanda with a broad smile on his face, Amanda said, "Don't you touch me!"

"Don't worry, little dark princess, the darker the berry, the sweeter the juice," Moose said, trying to be charming.

"I mean, you are of dubious character and nefarious nature, sir!" Amanda clarified.

"I was never convicted of those charges," the big man said.

Peters told Moose to start with The Musician. In just a few seconds Moose retrieved the cell phone from Willie's pocket and handed it, still open, to his boss.

Tom listened for a minute, slammed the cell phone shut, and screamed "I can hear him. It's that fucking Kelly!" Peters dropped the cell phone onto the floor and stomped it over and over until it was just tiny pieces. He walked to the window and peered out from between the blinds. He saw Lieutenant Jessica Paris walking around his limousine. "And his cop bitch!" he said, waving Moose over to the window.

Amanda and The Musician looked at each other and began to yell and scream but Moose immediately took several giant steps over to them, withdrawing his black nightstick from his jacket and standing over them menacingly. The Musician looked at Amanda and shouted again anyway. Moose dealt him a vicious head blow with the black nightstick, which knocked Willie out cold. Amanda silently stared up the imposing man standing over her with the nightstick in his hand.

"Let's get rid of that loudmouthed motherfucker right now! We can't shoot him with the cop right outside," Tom said as he moved a small rug and opened the trapdoor in the garage floor. They pulled The Musician to the square hole, pushed him through, and heard the splash. Amanda screamed.

Moose slapped her and asked, "Shouldn't we weight him down, Boss?"

"Fuck him. He'll swallow water and sink within ten feet," Tom said, closing the door in the floor, replacing the rug, and returning to see if the lieutenant was still outside. She was.

"What about her?" Moose said, looking down at a horrified Amanda.

Under the garage, The Musician hit the cold dark river water and Kelly waded in up to his waist and pulled him to the riverbank. The Musician coughed and spit up water as he struggled to regain consciousness. Jack cut away the duct tape from Willie's wrists and ankles.

"He's got Amanda," The Musician stammered as his senses returned and he sat upright on the riverbank. "Peters and his driver, Moose. She's taped up. Where are we?" he asked as he looked around.

"If you can walk, I'd like to get you to an ambulance; you've got a bump the size of a peach on your forehead. Lieutenant Paris is up on the street," Jack said as picked up the blanket he had been using and draped it over The Musician's shoulders, helping Willie to his feet.

"I saw Peters's chrome revolver and Moose has a sawed-off shotgun and a nightstick inside his jacket."

Just then they heard another splash and saw Amanda resurface and float over to where they could wade into the river and pull her into the riverbank. She had been hit hard and was unconscious. The men put her on her side and water flowed out of her mouth and onto the riverbank.

"If they've dropped their hostages into the river they should be easy to surround and hold. They've got nothing to bargain with. Jeez, Jesse doesn't have a gun and she's still up there in front of the garage. Let me go tell her to call in the cavalry. Can you stay here with Amanda? We'll get a rescue unit on the way, too!"

As he pounded Amanda's back, The Musician said, "Be careful!" and Kelly scrambled up the riverbank. But it was too late. Peters and Moose had simply opened their door and pulled an unarmed Jessica Paris into the garage.

Jessica was sitting on the couch with her wrists duct-taped, thinking about how many times she had carried a gun and never needed it. And now when she needed one...

"Where's The Musician?" Jessica asked, looking from Tom to Moose.

"He went down cellar," Moose said laughingly and then nervously looked at his boss for appoval.

Chapter 70

Eye to Eye

In the darkness Jack couldn't see Jessica on Back Street or along the Esplanade that runs by the Boston side of the Charles River. He returned to the last place he had seen her, the garage where the footprints and drag marks had stopped. Kelly couldn't find Jessica and he headed down Back Street towards her cruiser to see if she had walked back to her car. She wasn't there. Jack began walking towards the garages when the patrol car took the corner at Mass. Ave. and Back Street and pulled over by the red Nissan.

When Kelly got closer to the two uniformed cops, one of them recognized him.

"Hi, Jack. Is Lieutenant Paris nearby? She called in this vehicle as suspicious. What's the story?" the older of the two patrolmen said.

"She's just come up missing. She doesn't have a firearm. I've got her cell phone here. We were tracking a suspect in the MIT murders to this location. She followed tracks in the snow to possibly one of the garages over there on the other side of Back Street. I think she may be a hostage with an armed and barricaded suspect. There are two hostage victims that were assaulted and thrown into the river under Back Street. They are on the riverbank under the street. They need medical assistance. Have the medics come in from the Hatch Shell. Both with possible head trauma and one female near drowned. Get the shift super, give SWAT a heads-up, notify the FBI and staties, and let's establish a perimeter. The suspect is Tom Peters. He's white, about twenty-six, five feet, ten inches, long greasy hair pushed back. And he's with an African American looks like a giant black Elvis."

The two patrolmen were shocked and stood motionless for a few seconds, running a quick evaluation on Jack Kelly. Then the older one keyed his shoulder mike and said, "821? Twenty-Five-Fifty to 821?" He looked at Jack and said, "She's not answering."

"She's probably a hostage. Now get on the horn and get some units down here!" Kelly shouted and walked back down to the hole in the fence. He looked back as he climbed down the embankment and heard the older patrolman calling for a supervisor and requesting several more units for scene containment.

"What have you got over there?" Sergeant Donavan's voice could be heard blasting out over the cruiser radio.

"Ah... that PI, Sergeant.... Kelly? He's making statements that there are two hostages and the... ah... an MIT suspect here on Back Street. Lieutenant Paris is... ah... nowhere to be found," the patrolman said, not convinced himself.

Sergeant Donavan's voice boomed out over the police radio, "Dispatch! I want two ambulances to Twenty-Five-

Fifty's location, notify the on-call Special Agent in Charge at the FBI Boston, and call Major Houston of State Police SWAT at home, then Trooper Archambeault. I will be establishing a command post as soon as I get on-scene, ETA two minutes."

Jack was back with The Musician and Amanda on the bank of the river. Amanda had come around and the both of them had the blanket wrapped around them. Jack gave Willie Jessica's cell phone and instructed him to call his wife and tell her that he was OK. As the sirens seemed to be converging from every direction, Jack told the two wet victims to go up to the street and walk towards the Hatch Shell.

Kelly began to walk and climb on the substructure under Back Street and over toward the underside of the garage. He climbed on some girders below the street and made his way to the trapdoor and listened for voices from the garage above. Kelly gave the trapdoor a push and he felt it move slightly. Jessica felt the trapdoor under her feet move.

As the sirens became louder, Tom put another cigarette between his lips and peered out of the window. Up the street several more patrol cars were arriving.

"You're not going to light that, I hope," Jessica said from the couch.

"Shut the fuck up, cop bitch!" he said and flicked the lighter in his hand. As he put the flame to the tip and inhaled, Jessica provoked him again.

"I guess it doesn't matter. You'll be dead before the night is over."

"Shut the fuck up!" Peters yelled, coughing and pulling the stainless steel .357 magnum revolver from his waistband.

"I've got a better gun than that." Jesse said as Tom pointed his gun.

"Boss! You can't," Moose said, referring to the loud bang the revolver would make as he watched more police cars turning onto Back Street. Both ends of the street were now blocked by police personnel.

Jessica's portable police radio crackled from the center of the coffee table as Sergeant Donavan arrived and established an on-scene command post on the Mass. Ave. Bridge at the end of Back Street. Moose, Jessica, and Tom looked at the radio as Sergeant Donavan requested that someone bring Jack Kelly to him. No one seemed to know the whereabouts of the private detective.

Peters put the gun back into his waistband and exhaled loudly. He walked over to the entertainment center and put on the Beatles "Love" CD. He turned the volume down a little as George Harrison sang, "While My Guitar Gently Weeps." Tom walked to the bar and poured the rest of the liquid into his martini glass. He pulled a vial from his jacket pocket and dumped half of the contents out onto the bar. He crushed and chopped the tiny rocks into fine lines of powder with the stainless steel cleaver.

"What are we gonna do, Boss? Leave her here? Let's break out! Want me to get the limo started?" Moose said as he peered out at the police moving around the outer fringes of the neighborhood. The streets had been plowed and the street lights were on as Moose looked at the colorful Christmas lights in some of the apartment windows.

"Well... we ain't going to give up, Moose, baby! I think we'll go down swinging. Yeah, let's break out of here. They won't shoot at us as long as we've got Little Miss Sunshine, here. Let's tape her up a little better and get her ready to travel," Tom said and snorted two lines of the white powder.

The two men stood Lieutenant Paris up on her feet and wrapped several extra turns tightly around her wrists with duct tape.

"How about her legs, Boss?"

"She's got to walk, Moose. But we should tape up that loud bitch's mouth," Tom said and pulled out several feet of tape from the roll. Jessica started to yell for help but Tom back-handed her across the face and the men taped over her mouth, pulling the duct tape tightly all the way around her head several times. Jessica's muffled voice protested intensely as Tom took out the silver-plated revolver and put the barrel to the back of Jessica's head.

"Tape it, Moose!" Tom demanded and the big man looked at him blankly.

"Tape my hand and Mr. Clean, just as it is, to her fuckin' head!" Tom shouted and Moose began taping Tom's hand with the gun pointed at the back of Jessica's head. "Just don't tape the hammer or the cylinder or the trigger, but make it strong enough so that she can't pull away. Where she goes, the gun in my hand goes. Hear that, Honey? I have any problems with you and I'll pull the fucking trigger. Any police sharpshooter takes me out and I'll be taking you out with me. I get shot, you get shot. Got that, bitch?"

Jessica struggled but it did no good as big Moose taped the barrel of the gun to the back of Jessica's head, then ran a few turns around the top of Jessica's head until it was mostly covered in silver wrap. Then Moose meticulously taped the gun to Tom's hand with his finger on the gun's trigger.

"She looks like a mummy. Or an alien. Or an alien mummy. Hey… any chance we could get out through that trapdoor, Boss?" Moose asked, picking up the sawed-off shotgun from behind the couch.

"No. There's no stairs. I don't think so. There are just a couple of girders and pilings. The river is about ten feet down."

"Yeah, I think I could hardly fit through," the big man said as he moved Jessica over a few feet and bent down. As he pulled open the square trapdoor in the floor, its hinges screeched. Moose looked down into the dark river. And Jack Kelly looked up at him.

Before Moose could move away or pull away the shotgun, Jack had reached up with one hand and grabbed the gun's barrel and gave it as strong a pull as he could. Moose released his grip on the gun. Jack took it away and flipped it up so the barrel was now pointing upward. Moose instinctively reached into his jacket for the nightstick but Kelly wasn't waiting to see what kind of weapon Moose had. Jack pulled the trigger on the shotgun, blasting a baseball-sized hole in Moose's chest. Blood splattered and dripped down on Jack as Moose pushed the nightstick back into his jacket. The color drained from the big man's face and his head went down through the hole. The enormous body followed, tumbling downward and hitting the water with a huge splash. Moose surfaced and as he choked on blood and water he yelled, "I can't swim," as the Charles River took him downstream.

"Never bring a nightstick to a gunfight," Kelly said, turning his attention to the trapdoor above.

Jack peered up through the hole in the floor and saw Tom standing behind Jessica. She was taped at the wrists, her mouth was covered, and duct tape ran all around her head, leaving only a slit for her eyes. She was wide-eyed and staring at Jack as Tom took a step to the side, exposing the revolver in his right hand, steadfastly duct-taped to the back of Jesse's head. Jack stared back, motionless.

McCartney's "Blackbird" ended and George Harrison sang "Taxman" as Jack realized that Tom couldn't shoot him. But he realized he couldn't shoot Tom, either. He pulled himself up slowly onto the hardwood floor of the converted apartment, saying, "Easy now, Tom. Hey, you're quite creative with that duct tape. You are an artist... But gee, I hope that gun isn't loaded."

"I'll pull the fuckin' trigger, Kelly. Stay where you are!"

Jessica was helpless as the demented serial killer held her in his executioner's grip. Kelly was scared to death that he was about to lose the love of his life. He didn't want to contemplate losing the beautiful girl that loved him as he was, with all his faults. Jack knew he didn't have a prayer, but he had to try something. He dropped the shotgun through the trapdoor and into the water. He reverted to his training as a hostage negotiator and said, "OK... OK... Take it easy. You're holding all the cards now. I'll do whatever you want. Whatever I can do, I will do. I know when I'm outclassed. Let's just do the right thing here. We can all walk away from this..."

"Maybe I don't want to walk away unless I take your little princess with me. I don't want to hurt her. But Mr.

Clean does. Why the fuck couldn't you mind your own business, Kelly? Why don't you take the fucking day off? Crawl back down that fucking hole in the floor and maybe your girlfriend and I will leave together, that's all. But you fucking just shot my driver and dumped him in the river and I don't like to drive. There was a… a bad accident when I was a kid… I was learning to drive… So maybe you'll have to drive us, now."

"That's not good, Tom. And there are a hundred cops out there that aren't going to let us drive away. But we can walk away from this without dying, Tom. It's not as bad as it looks," Jack pleaded.

"Not as bad as it looks? What are you, fucking crazy? Not as bad as it looks for you, dickhead. Securing the Prototype Project was almost in the bag. Now I've spent so much time chasing you around that I haven't sent in the copyright and patent paperwork. It was the perfect plan until you came along! How did you get on to me? Did Rodney Riviera figure it out for you? No offense, Kelly, but you don't seem too bright."

"No, I'm not very bright, but I can see the writing on the wall, Tom. Actually, it was Michael. His cell phone message from the College Escort Service said he had a date the night he went missing and his computer in his frat house room was open to your College Escort Service web page. Michael was dead, but still on the Internet."

"Ah, Michael… Now I've killed half a dozen people trying to secure the Prototype Project, starting with my own brother. Yeah! I drew a mathematical formula for falling bodies on the blackboard and threw him out a fucking thirteen-story window when he threatened to incorporate the Prototype Project into a nonprofit. It would have been a free technology program for the world. 'Free for the world!' my dear brother said. Fuck that. We're talking billions here. It will mean power and fame beyond your grandest imagination. And I will kill anyone who gets in my way!"

Jessica mumbled loudly and shook her head from side to side. Finally Tom reached over with his free hand and pulled the tape down below her upper lip, just far enough that she could be heard.

"Hey, Tom," Jessica said in a smooth and calm voice, "we could pin this whole thing on Moose."

The three stood in silence, contemplating the interesting idea Lieutenant Paris was selling, but Tom wouldn't be buying. After a long pause he simply said, "No."

Jessica began shouting and turning her body so that Jack had a clear shot, "Shoot him! Shoot the sick bastard, Kelly! Go ahead and shoot him!"

Kelly slowly pulled his double-action modified .45-caliber Colt Combat Commander from his shoulder holster and pointed it at Tom. Peters and Kelly looked at each other eye to eye.

Jessica continued to plead, "Go ahead, Jack. I'll take my chances! Empty the gun into this sick bastard, he wants to die."

"What happened to the 'We can walk out of here' speech?" Tom asked Kelly in a calm voice as all three looked at the gun in Kelly's hand. Water dripped from the butt of the gun. Jack wondered if it would still fire after being submerged in the Charles.

Chapter 71

100 Pounds of Dead Cop

Ten minutes after the discharge of the shotgun was heard, the SWAT team sharpshooters took up rooftop positions. Other members of the tactical team circulated around the perimeter in silence; their earphones mikes didn't betray their positions. Most of the sirens had ceased wailing. Every cop within a six-mile radius was at the scene in Boston's Back Bay. The whir of three helicopters, two of them from local TV stations, one of them from the Mass. State Police Air Wing, could be heard overhead.

Amanda and The Musician stood with Sergeant Donavan at the command post truck parked on the Mass. Ave. Bridge looking down over Back Street and the garages. *Boston Herald* reporter Gordon Little approached Donavan.

"Who let this reportah into my taped-off command post? Hodge! Are yah turnin' my incident command post into a clustahfuck?"

"Just tell me what you've got here, Moses... I mean… Sergeant Donavan. If it bleeds, it leads. What's going on?" the reporter pleaded with his pen and notebook in hand.

"Well… it's a bunch of computah geeks gone wild, Gordy. Don't write that down, for Christ's sake! These computah students crack up undah the pressure. It happens all the time."

"Does it have anything to do with MIT? Is it the serial killer?"

"I told yah, it's just somebody frustrated with a goddamn computah, is all. Now don't write that down, Little! Jesus! Call the station house. We're havin' trouble wid dah new computah system thar, too. The guys keep visitin' the wrong web spots or whatever… they go to 'youngpussy. com' and 'teensluts.com' and 'lonelywives.com.'"

"Wow," was the only thing the reporter could manage saying.

"Yes, and we ah more than a bit worried that one guy keeps goin' tah bigdicks.com!" Donavan yelled.

A cop in uniform a few feet away lowered his binocular and said, "I told you I was looking for a detective website."

"You were probably looking for a big dick, Hodge!" the Sergeant yelled back and added quietly to the reporter, "Thinks he's a big deal since he made 'Officer of the Month.'"

The reporter broke his pencil in half and walked away.

Amanda and The Musician had told Donavan and the State Police Special Operations Commander the layout of the garage as well as the weapons they had seen there. Donavan wanted two questions answered. What was the gunshot and where was Jack Kelly? Those questions were answered when the tactical team recovered the badly wounded Moose from the river. He was giving a statement to a detective from the DA's office as he lay handcuffed to a gurney between the command post and a waiting ambulance. His voice was hoarse and he was wheezing audibly with each breath he exhaled. But he was wasting no time in pointing the finger at his boss.

"Tom Peters is your man. He's got that lady cop tied up with a gun to her head. And Kelly is in there now. Kelly shot me and I want to press charges against him."

"Fat chance," Donavan said.

"I tell you, Sarge... Tom Peters is your man. He killed those students. I saw him do it. He used me. I didn't know what he was doing. This ring belonged to the Asian kid," Moose said, with blood gurgling in his throat and pointing to the gold MIT Brass Rat ring on his finger. Sergeant Donavan removed the ring from Moose's huge finger and handed it to the DA's investigator. Moose spit some blood on the pavement and continued, "That honky-tonk motherfucker. Tom Peters... He's a racist son-of-a-bitch. I hope he rots in hell. I just hope you can get that female police officer out of there before that sick fuck kills her."

"OK, now," Sergeant Donavan said to the medical attendants, "let's get the Black Elvis ahn his miserable way befoah the bullshit gets too fahckin' high I cahn't see ovah it. You're under arrest at least as an accessrie to mahrdah-one, big man."

"Hey, my father was a cop. He died in the line of duty," Moose said.

"I'm shar, if he *was* a police officah, he's real proud lookin' dahn at ya sorry ass now," Donavan said, wondering if Moose was going to make it.

"He was, really. West Roxbury. He gave me the nightstick I always carry. It's right here in my jacket," Moose said, wheezing and gesturing with his cuffed hands. Donavan reached over insde of the large man's jacket and pulled out a two-foot-long black police-issue poly-carbon Maadnock nightstick and shouted, "Who searched dis man? Who the fuck searched this man? Hodge!"

Chapter 72

Chop, Chop

"If you shoot her, you'll be dragging around 100 pounds of dead cop," Jack said as Tom Peters pulled Jessica with him over to the window and peered out.

"What are you going to do then? You can't drag a dead cop too far. She can be quite heavy. Take my word for it. She can be... dead weight."

Tom could see dozens of police cars about 500 yards away in almost every direction. There were cruisers on the street, on the bridge, on Storrow Drive, on the Esplanade, and the Harbor Police had three inflatables cruising the river. And he saw the helicopters overhead, one of them shining a bright spotlight down on the garage.

Kelly lowered his gun. He wasn't sure it would work, anyway. He thought about tackling Peters but he was afraid Tom's gun would discharge into the back of Jessica's head. He felt powerless.

A tear gas canister broke through the window and rolled across the floor. Gas sprayed out and began clouding the room.

Tom was near panic but Jack kicked the canister into the river through the open trapdoor. The three started to cough but the air soon began clearing from the draft created by the broken window and the open trapdoor.

The silhouette of Tom and Jessica looked surreal to Jack as he peered through the hazy smoke. He felt like he was in a dream as he stared at Jesse with silver tape wrapped all around her head. The wide silver duct tape made her look like she was morphing into a robot.

"Hey Jesse, let's see you dance like a robot now!" Jack shouted under the loud whir of the helicopters and boat engines.

Jesse and Tom looked at Jack through the haze. The gun was pointed directly into the back of her head from Tom's right hand. Jack could hardly breathe. The Beatles' CD was still playing and John Lennon began "Within You, Without You," singing, "Turn off your mind, relax and float downstream… it is not dying… it is not dying…"

Jack had to do something or the SWAT team would.

"I can't breathe!" Jessica gasped.

"Why don't you let me cut that duck tape off, Tom? You don't need to be tied to 100 pounds of dead cop, do you?" Jack said as he moved over and put his back to the bar.

"Stay the fuck back, Kelly! You'd kill me if you had the chance, just like I'd kill you!"

"That's what I'm saying, Tom. Let me cut her free and you can have me. Cut her loose," Jack pleaded as his left hand felt around on the top of the bar for the meat cleaver he had seen there.

"Tom! I've got a tiny jackknife in my pocket. And I can cut that tape away. Seriously, I'm not going to jump you as long as you have the gun," Jack said, tossing his .45 over the bar and showing Peters the tiny knife blade from his pocket.

Tom looked a little confused as Kelly took a slow step towards him. Someone outside started shouting semi-inaudible words through a megaphone: *"armed and barricaded... police officer hostage... release in thirty seconds..."* There was more breaking glass as another canister was tossed through the window into the room. This one was a percussion grenade; it hissed for a second, then a stunning flash was seen and it detonated with a thunderous boom.

Jack's training kicked in and he stepped through the smoke. He could barely see or hear. He held his breath and moved toward the sound of Jesse coughing. He recognized the silhouette of Tom's arm taped to Jessica's head. If ever Jack had prayed for a miracle, it was now.

Jack swung the meat cleaver down with all his might. He stood high up on his toes and followed through, bringing all his weight down with him. The sharp meat cleaver came down on Tom's arm just above the elbow, severing it cleanly... And the .357 magnum did not discharge.

Kelly pulled Jessica back with him, back to the bar. Jesse and Jack stood there, holding onto the bar for support, and they looked at each other. Jessica had her head covered with silver duct tape with a gun and Tom's hand, wrist, and arm to the elbow hanging off the back of her head.

"Thank God I'm alive; it's a miracle," Jessica said and added, "Thank you, Jack Kelly."

Jack turned back to see Tom standing by the front door.

Tom seemed to be in shock as he was just realizing his hand was gone. He pushed his arm forward, over and over, saying, "Click, click." He laughed nervously and then cried out in pain. He turned to Jack Kelly.

"Help me, Jack. Call the ambulance! Call this thing off, now, please. I'm done! You got me, Jack. Just take care of me now. Call them in. Please, Jack. The ambulance… Please!"

Kelly and Jessica just stood there, watching the blood squirt from Tom's right arm. Peters put his left hand around his arm just above the wound and he squeezed his fingers as hard as he could but the blood continued to squirt.

"Help me! Call an ambulance!" Tom screamed.

"I'll think about it,' Jack said as he just stood there, motionless.

After a moment Tom screamed again, "What are you doing?"

"I'm thinking about it," Jack said.

Kelly slowly pulled his cell phone out of his pocket and opened it. The cell phone dripped water out onto the floor.

"Oops," Kelly said and put it back into his pocket.

Kelly put the meat cleaver on the bar and took out his Swiss Army knife and began cutting the duct tape away from Jessica's wrists. When her hands were free, he handed her the cleaver, saying, "If he moves the wrong way, cut off his other hand.

"I've got a better idea, Tom," Jack said and he picked up the roll of duct tape from the bar and walked towards Tom. The Beatles CD played on as Peters was weakening from blood loss. Kelly wrapped the tape around Tom's right arm five times as tight as he possibly could, and the blood stopped squirting.

"'All You Need is Love,'" Jack said. Then Kelly took the jackknife out of his pocket and quickly taped it to the end of the bloody stump that was Tom's right arm. As another tear gas canister broke through a rear window of the garage, Kelly turned Tom towards the front door, unlocked it, pulled it open, put his foot on Tom's backside, pushed Tom out onto the street, and shut the door, shouting, "Leap into the future, NOW!"

As Jack walked back to Jessica, he heard a voice shouting through the bullhorn, "Drop the weapon! Drop the weapon! Do it now! Drop the weapon!"

Kelly walked Jessica over to the trapdoor, Jessica threw the cleaver over the couch and she dropped down into the cold river water. Jack heard the voice through the bullhorn shout again, "Drop the weapon! Stop where you are! Stop or we'll shoot!" and a long series of shots rang out. The water felt chilly but safe as Jack dropped down into the river as stray bullets ripped through the walls of the smoky garage.

The multiple bullets entered Tom Peters from different angles, hitting bone and passing through flesh, exiting out Tom's side and back. Blood splattered in the snow in many different directions. Several of the sharpshooter's bullets found their mark, causing pieces of skull to shatter and splinter. Kelly didn't see Tom's bullet-riddled body fall back against the garage wall and shake like he was having a seizure as the forty-one projectiles passed through him. The dead killer's blood soaked corpse fell into the pure white snow.

Aftermath

Nice Hat

"Can't yah fight fair, Jack Kelly?" Donavan said as the four medics crowded around Jessica and Jack, adding, "You had to find a guy with one arm to mix it up with… And you, Lieutenant Paris, why'd you let me take your gun when you were going to be with Jack Kelly? I let you go unarmed into trouble with a capital K. And between you and me, Lieutenant, you ought to do something about your appearance."

The medical personnel kept working but Jack, Donavan, Trooper Archambeault, The Musician, and Amanda all looked at Jessica with amazement as she stood there, soaking wet with a blanket around her, her makeup running. The medics were painstakingly cutting away the duct tape from her hair. The barrel of the loaded stainless steel revolver was still attached to the back of her head, along with Tom's hand and arm to the blood dripping elbow.

"Nice hat," Jack said.

Amanda and at least one medic groaned as Jessica took a step forward and kicked Jack in the leg. The four hostages looked like a tribe of lost early American Indians standing with blankets around them in the red and blue ambulance lights.

When the medical personnel had removed the gun with its attached hand from the back of Jessica's head, they put it on a gurney. A doctor and nurse stepped in with a satchel of medical implements and a cooler with lots of ice. The doctor carefully separated the flesh from the steel gun and packed the hand and arm in ice inside the cooler. Sergeant Donavan took charge of the gun and the doctor and nurse left quickly with the arm and hand.

"What are they going to do with that hand?" The Musician asked.

"Maybe them goddamn eggheads ova ta MIT are regeneratin' and clonin' and mixin' flesh with metal like the Bionic Woman," Donavan said, as the ambulance carrying Tom Peters's hand went over the Mass. Ave. Bridge towards MIT, rather than heading towards the morgue or hospitals.

The possibility that Tom Peters would be regenerated or cloned from the hand would have seemed ridiculous to Jack a month ago, but now, Jack wasn't so sure.

"So young Archie, where was yah when Kelly an' Paris was attemptin' to arrest the MIT Serial Killah?" Donavan asked, knowing that Archambeault would have treasured being there.

"When did *you* figure out Peters was the serial killer, Donavan?" Trooper Archambeault asked, getting more than a little irritated with Donavan's condescending remarks.

"Ray Charles could have seen that, Archie," the old cop quipped.

"Yeah, yeah... Congratufuckinglations, Kelly. And I've got to *hand* it to you, Lieutenant Paris...," Archie said, snickering. "But while Kelly was wreaking havoc..."

"See, you do wreak havoc, Jack," Jessica quipped as Archambeault continued.

"While you *two* were causing this clusterfuck over here I was executing an arrest and search warrant at the College Escort Service across the river, Sergeant; I had a *legal* arrest warrant for Peters that would hold up in court because it was built on solid investigative techniques and forensic evidence."

"Excellent work, really," Jack said, letting the trooper off the hook quickly, adding, "We're all on the same team that closed in on this sick bastard, and we all did good."

"But Jack saved our beloved Commonwealth's taxpayers a ton ah money fahr the trial and pahrmanent incahceration of a sick murdrah," Donavan said, handing Kelly the sergeant's personal cell phone.

When Jack answered it, Mr. Rich commended him for his efforts and invited him to dinner the following night to deliver the detective's final report. Jack told Rich that his son Michael owned the patents on some very important technology that could be worth millions of dollars. Rich stated that any money would be divided between the Rich family, charity, and the school Michael loved so much, MIT.

Archie told the group that although he was unable to execute the arrest warrant on Tom Peters, he was able to take the sister, Victoria Peters, into custody and conduct a search. Besides seizing a quantity of cocaine, meth, and assorted pills, Archambeault was clever enough to find the discs and flash drive containing stolen information, and other evidence of Peters's attempts to patent and copyright Michael Rich's software and inventions. This would provide evidence of motive for murder as well as a charge of receiving stolen property.

Apparently Victoria was watching the events unfold regarding her armed and barricaded brother, live on Boston TV news stations when Trooper Archambeault and a team of five detectives and four uniformed troopers arrived. The television coverage of her brother's violent death was so graphic that after being placed in handcuffs Victoria Peters seemed to lose all control. She began loudly talking to her dead twin brothers and her dead parents. She will be remanded to Bridgewater State Hospital for psychiatric evaluation.

"Ah… they'll prahbably bail her out on PR… By dah way, Jack, I pulled the Brass Rat off of dah fingah of the big black Elvis impersonatah, and another off dah fingah of Marcus Grace, the van driver. If we can link the rings to one of the dead boys, it's mahr evidence. And Jack, that was some hole yah put in his chest. The EMTs don't tink he'll make it," Donavan said.

"And also by the way, Jack Kelly," Jessica said. "At what point did you decide to take a chance with a Boston Police lieutenant's life by hacking off that bastard's hand?"

Now everyone looked to Jack for his answer.

"Ah…," Jack stammered and looked over at The Musician. "Ah…Willie. How about the Joke-of-the-Day?"

"OK," The Musician said and began, "A burglar broke into an apartment one night and he shined his flashlight around, looking for money and jewelry. He took some cash money off the dresser and he heard an extraordinary voice echo in the dark. It said, 'Jesus is watching you.' The thief was so startled he shut off his flashlight and froze in the dark. After a while he started moving around again, turned on his light, and picked up some jewelry from the other dresser and was putting it into his pocket when he heard the same voice say, 'Jesus is watching you!' The thief was scared and shaking. He turned his light around the room and he saw a large colorful parrot sitting on a perch in the corner. The burglar asked, 'Did you say that?' and the parrot said, 'Yes. Jesus is watching you.' The burglar asked the parrot his name and the parrot said, 'God.' The burglar laughed and said, 'What kind of people would name their parrot God?' And the bird said, 'The same kind of people that would name their Doberman Pincher, Jesus.'"

Jack laughed for the first time that night and looked out over the foggy river and let the air out of his lungs. He finally felt safe, warm, and sleepy enough to leave and go over to Jessica's apartment with her. He signaled Jesse with a nod that he wanted to leave, but as they turned from the group, the shadow of Moose's huge frame stood before them, silhouetted in the light from the ambulance's high beams. Jack was somewhat blinded but he could clearly see Victoria standing behind Moose.

Amanda screamed. Donavan struggled with his revolver in its holster and fell over the hood of a cruiser. Archie and The Musician sought cover behind the police mobile command center. Jack and Jessica were riveted to the street as Moose held an automatic shotgun and Victoria an AK 47. Each gun had a flashlight attached and the lights' beams found Jack Kelly. Jack looked into the shotgun's big barrel and then into the light.

The silence was deafening until Victoria screamed, "Kill them all!"

A police siren wailed and as the first shots reverberated in Jack Kelly's ears, he sat up in Jessica's bed. Sweat ran down his forehead and neck. His mouth was dry as he took a deep breath and looked over at Jesse. She was sleeping soundly and looked so beautiful. Jack thought she must have been made in Heaven and he knew he was in love. He took a sip of water from a plastic bottle and sat up with his back against the headboard.

Jack Kelly told himself he was the modern Zen detective and technology had catapulted the Zen detective into the future. Technology had allowed him to make incredible advancements in his investigations. Nowadays with electronic gear he could hear people talking when he is not there. He could see people when he is not there. He could see people in the dark. He could see where blood had been. He could trace a person's DNA code to microscopic trace evidence. He could imagine a world where robots do all the mundane work and Jack Kelly, AKA, Mr. Big, calls all the shots. He is future Zen. And as he approaches 2010, he is oneness. He is absolute. He is absolute oneness.

Kelly turned on the TV and watched ESPN Classic. It was the Harvard vs. MIT football game. A nude student streaked across the football field with "MIT" written all over his naked body. Jack fell asleep again and began dreaming.

In his dream God was an old man with snowy-white long hair and a beard. He was the ESPN TV announcer at the MIT-Harvard game. He looked out from the TV at

Jack and smiled. Jack looked back and returned the smile. "You did pretty good after all, Jack. You got the bad guy and solved the case with some closure for Mr. and Mrs. Rich. They'll end up donating a lot of money to charity and one of my favorite institutions, that wonderful beacon of knowledge and invention, the Massachusetts Institute of Technology. You worked it out, after all. You really had me worried, but you're a pretty good investigator," God said, smiling at Kelly, and continued, whispering, "Yes, you're a good guy, Jack. And don't worry; I know I scared you a bit, but my bark is worse than my bite. I knew you'd come through. I think you're a great guy."

Jack was surprised at the praise from the god of all gods and he felt really warm and happy. Jack Kelly settled comfortably down into the bed, looked up at God's smiling face sleepily, and said, "Really? Is your bark really worse than your bite?"

God's smile disappeared and his face turned sour quickly. God looked down menacingly as lightning flashed behind him. Jack cowered, wide-eyed, as God's many voices began to growl and thundered in unison... and the Lord screamed, "NOOOO...! Don't push it, Jack Kelly!"

About the Author

Johnny Barnes has been writing true crime reports for 11 years as a paralegal and private investigator in and around Boston and another 18 years as a detective and full time police officer. He has been a SWAT team member and an FBI trained hostage negotiator.

Born in New Bedford, Mass, Johnny spent many years in the Boston area. He attended Marlborough Academy, Southeastern Massachusetts University, Berklee School of Music, and the Harvard University Extension School.

For many years Johnny moonlighted as a record producer, nightclub manager, working musician, and songwriter. He periodically releases CD's of guitar driven originals or classic blues arrangements.

Johnny sails his boat out of Buzzard's Bay and likes to spend most of his summers anchored off the Elizabeth Islands fishing, reading and listening to jazz and blues.

Printed in the United States
202949BV00002B/58-201/P